Matteo Bandello, John Payne

The Novels of Matteo Bandello, Bishop of Agen

Volume Five

Matteo Bandello, John Payne

The Novels of Matteo Bandello, Bishop of Agen
Volume Five

ISBN/EAN: 9783337067700

Printed in Europe, USA, Canada, Australia, Japan

Cover: Foto ©Andreas Hilbeck / pixelio.de

More available books at **www.hansebooks.com**

The Novels of Matteo Bandello Bishop of Agen now first done into English Prose and Verse by John Payne

Author of The Masque of Shadows Intaglios
Songs of Life and Death Lautrec New
Poems etc. and Translator of The Poems
of Master Francis Villon of Paris
The Book of the Thousand Nights
and One Night Tales from the
Arabic The Decameron of
Giovanni Boccacci
(Il Boccaccio) and
Alaeddin etc.
V o l u m e
F i v e

LONDON: MDCCCXC: PRINTED FOR THE VILLON
SOCIETY BY PRIVATE SUBSCRIPTION AND FOR
PRIVATE CIRCULATION ONLY.

CONTENTS OF VOLUME V.

Part the Second.

(continued).

Part the Third.

Part the Second

(continued).

Bandello

to the magnificent Messer Girolamo Ongaro, merchant of Lucca.

There use oftentimes to happen cases so extraordinary that, whenas they are related, they seem rather fables than histories, and yet they have e'en happened and are true; whence methinketh must have arisen the current saying that truth, which hath a face of falsehood, should not be told. But, let folk say what they will, I am of the contrary opinion and meseemeth that whoso taketh pleasure in recording the various chances which are whiles seen to betide should not, if aught be told him by a person worthy of credit, forbear to write it, albeit it may appear a fable, for that, according to the Aristotelian rule, whenassoever the case is possible, it should be admitted. Wherefore I, who have, at the request of one who might have commanded me,[1] set myself to write all those cases which seem to me worthy of remembrance and from which pleasure and profit may be derived, stint not to set my pen awork, albeit the things which chance to be told appear hard to be believed; and accordingly I purpose presently to record a story which will seem very strange to whoso readeth it. Madam Costanza Rangona e Fregosa, my patroness, was at Bassens,

---

[1] *i.e.* his patroness, Signora Ippolita Bentivoglia.

whereas she hath now abidden a great while, attracted by
the amenity of the air, and thither this last July past came
Madam Marie of Navarre, who useth oftentimes to resort
thither for her diversions and who, it being one day spoken
of various matters, related to our mistress and to all us
others of the company how a gentleman unwittingly took
to wife one who was both his daughter and his sister, the
which seemed unto all a most appalling and extraordinary
chance.[1] I committed the story to writing, according as it
was related of the said Madam Marie, and have entitled it in
your name, so that I having a little agone sent one of my
novels to Signor Marco Antonio Giglio, who is so much our
friend, you also may have one thereof. Fare you well.

The Five-and-Thirtieth Story.

A GENTLEMAN OF NAVARRE UNKNOWINGLY ESPOUSETH ONE WHO WAS AT ONCE HIS SISTER AND HIS DAUGHTER.[2]

[1] This story was afterwards written by her sister-in-law, Marguerite
of Angoulême, of whose Heptameron it forms part, being the 10th
Novel of the 3rd Day.

[2] I omit this story, as it is practically but an abstract of the
Heptameron novel on the same subject.

Bandello

to the most magnificent and accomplished Messer Filippo Baldo of Milan.

The proverb is daily seen to be most true which saith that men meet whiles, but mountains never, and this should serve for an admonition to those who carry their brains above their bonnets[1] and reck not to do unseemly things and oftentimes to affront their fellow, saying, "I go my way and he goeth his; we shall see each other no more." Certes, a false and ill-considered opinion, as experience testifieth, for that oftentimes that which befalleth not in one nor in two years cometh of a sudden to pass at a given moment; and this holdeth good of our virtuous dealings as well as of the ill. Who had ever conceived, sweetest Baldo mine, that you and I should, after so many years, find ourselves at one and the same time in Aquitaine in the County of Agen and on the banks of the Garonne? It is two-and-twenty years, belike rather more than less, since we foregathered at Ferrara at the nuptials of Signor Gian Paolo Sforza, brother of Francesco Sforza, second of the name Duke of Milan, and of the Lady Violante Bentivoglia his consort, and there we abode some days together in the utmost pleasure; nay, you must needs remember what goodly sports were holden and how

---

[1] i.e. who are feather-brained.

blithely all those days passed in mirth and merry-making. The nuptials ended, one went hither and another thither, as useth oftentimes to happen. You, no great while after, doing penance for others' default, went wandering through Italy and Germany, Spain and Africa, blown and buffeted of the stormy winds of contrary fortune, and now you have traversed a great part of the realm of France, on your way from Flanders to Spain, whither you have for the third time been brought back by the hope of making an end of your many peregrinations and perils and hardships and of compassing for yourself, by the favour of the famous Archduke of Austria, King of Bohemia, a happy issue from your long and fashious travails. I on like wise, (albeit I began long before yourself to feel the keen envenomed fangs of sorry and contrary fortune, having seen my father's house burned by factious men and the modest substance left me by my ancestors confiscated by the fisc,) have, since I last saw you, gone long time wandering, far more aggrieved to see myself enforced to abandon the studies whereto I was bred from a boy than to have lost my patrimony. On this wise I travailed many and many a year and still found myself in the utmost perils, till, at the last, thanks to the never-enough bepraised knight of the order of His Most Christian Majesty, the noble Signor Cesare Fregoso of ever-sorrowful and honoured memory, and to his illustrious and incomparable consort, Madam Costanza Rangona, I have made an end of my long and bitter exile and of my many and various troubles and live here to myself and the muses, these eight years past, in peace and quiet, having exchanged my native streams, the Schirmia [1] and

---

[1] Apparently a local name for the Scrivia.

the Po, which mingle their waters well-nigh alongside my native place,[1] for the Garonne and once fortunate Lombardy for Aquitaine. Now, whenas I least hoped, nay, despaired of ever more seeing you, behold, you come hither unlooked for, on your way from Flanders. How gladly you were seen of Madam Fregosa, my mistress, and how blithely she received you, you yourself are the best judge and know far better than I to tell it; certes, she welcomed you as joyfully as if a brother of hers were come hither. Of myself I speak not, whose joy at your sight recalled the pleasure which I felt in my manifold contentments of the happy times bygone. It pleased you celebrate with us the festivities of the Nativity of our Saviour Jesus Christ, you having arrived here four days theretofore, and Saint John's Day[2] past, you would fain have departed and gone hence to Toulouse and through Languedoc to Perpignan and over the Pyrenean mountains; but it behoved you abide, for that Madam suffered it not, it being so long since we have seen you and enjoyed your sweetest company, which never suffereth whoso converseth with you to grow weary, so goodly and so eloquent is your speech and such merry and trenchant sayings you have in hand; more by token you tell the pleasantest stories in the world and with such a grace that all present hearken to you with the utmost intentness. Madam, then, willed you sojourn with us till the colds of December and of January should abate and the rigour of the weather be somewhat attempered, and you, being unable reasonably to deny her that pleasure,

---

[1] Bandello was born at Castelnuovo in Piedmont, near the confluence of the Scrivia and the Po.

[2] *i.e.* Dec. 27.

abode here with us. Amongst many other goodly things
which you related to us, you one day, in the presence
of her ladyship and of her gentlemen and gentlewomen,
told a story that much pleased us all ; wherefore, being
urged to write it by one who might command me, I
have committed it to writing and that certes entirely, in
as far as pertaineth to the facts; but, if I have not
availed to render the clear and chastened eloquence
of your polished style, be it my excuse in your eyes
that it is not given to every one to make the journey
to Corinth.[1] Algates, such as it is, meseemeth right that
it should be yours who narrated it ; and so I give and
dedicate it to you in testimony of our old and mutual
goodwill, beseeching our Lord God to keep and preserve
you.

𝕮𝖍𝖊 𝕾𝖎𝖝-𝖆𝖓𝖉-𝕮𝖍𝖎𝖗𝖙𝖎𝖊𝖙𝖍 𝕾𝖙𝖔𝖗𝖞.

THE LOVES OF DON JUAN DE MENDOZA AND OF THE DUCHESS OF SAVOY, WITH THE VARIOUS AND MEMORABLE CHANCES WHICH ENSUED THEREOF.

I thought not, most affable and illustrious lady, to have
come from Flanders into Aquitaine to tell stories ; I came
hither indeed to do you reverence, having these many years
desired an occasion of seeing you again, for the devotion
which I have still vowed to you since I knew you at Ferrara,
where I related the story of Queen Anne,[2] then no great

---

[1] *Non cuivis contingit adire Corinthum.*
[2] See ante, Vol. II. pp. 256-82.

while befallen. However, since you will e'en have me tell somewhat, I will (being ever ready to obey you in this and in all it may please you command me) relate to you a marvellous history, which was told me by a Spanish cavalier, during my sometime sojourn in Spain, and from which we may learn how great is the might of love, whenas it kindleth its fires in a noble heart. You must know, then, that there was in Spain aforetime a cruel enmity and a bloody feud between two most noble families, to wit, those of Mendoza and Toledo, both exceeding rich and puissant in lands and vassals. They had battled again and again with loss of many men slain on either side ; but the strife and dissension still went waxing and hate cankering in their hearts, there was no means found to reconcile them ; wherefore it befell that, Don Juan de Mendoza, a very wealthy youth and exceeding doughty of his person, being head of his faction, both parties took the field with numerous armies. Don Juan's sister, who had been the wife of a Spanish nobleman and becoming a widow, had taken refuge with her brother, learning this ill news, besought God to make peace between the two factions and to put an end to so many and such sore ills. But, hearing that it was determined to try the fortune of war and loving her brother even as her life, she made a vow that, an he came off safe and sound and gained the day, she would go pilgrim to Rome afoot to visit the church of the blessed Apostle Peter.

The battle was waged with exceeding great slaughter of those of Toledo and Don Juan abode master of the field, with little loss on his side. Isabella, for such was the widow's name, thereupon discovered her vow to her brother, who, albeit he was loath to have his sister go so long a voyage afoot, yet gave her leave and would have her make the journey by easy stages, with a sufficient escort and every commodity that might be. The Lady Isabella accordingly departed Spain and crossing the Pyrenean mountains, made her way through France and over the Alps to Turin. Now the wife of the then Duke of Savoy was a sister of the King of England and had the name of being the fairest lady in all Europe. Her, accordingly, the Spanish pilgrimess desired to see, so she might know the truth of the report which was bruited abroad of her exceeding beauty ; wherein fortune favoured her, inasmuch as, at her coming to Turin, she found many carts and waggons in act to enter the city, the which usurped and blocked the way of ingress and egress unto whoso was a-horseback, and the duchess herself, who was come forth in a very goodly coach to go a-pleasuring without the city, for that it was in summer time and after supper, was constrained to halt within the gates till the waggons should have entered. The pilgrimess, being afoot, entered without difficulty, she and her company, and being certified that she who waited in the coach was the renowned duchess, she posted herself overagainst the lady, who was at the coach-door ; then she fell to viewing the fair duchess intently and fixedly and considering her every feature with a judicious eye and herseeming she was in effect the fairest and lovesomest lady she had ever seen, she judged that fame had fallen short of the truth and that such beauty and grace as she saw in her might rather be admired than described ; wherefore, ravished out of herself, she said aloud in the Spanish tongue, "O Lord God, this is e'en the fairest and gracefullest lady that can be seen. What children would she not bear, an my brother should couple with her ! Certes, angels would be born of them." (Now Don Juan was one of the handsomest cavaliers of his time.)

The duchess, who was well versed in the Spanish tongue, which she had learned whilst she was in England, called

one of her lackeys and bade him observe where yonder
Spanish pilgrimess lodged and bring her to the castle, as
soon as she returned from her diversion ; the which was
diligently executed. What while she went a-pleasuring
along the banks of the Po, she could turn her mind to no
otherwhat than the words of the pilgrimess and made a
thousand conjectures thereanent, but could nowise hit upon
the truth. Then, returning to the castle, she found the
pilgrimess awaiting her with her company and taking her
apart, asked her of what province she was in Spain, what
was her lineage and whither she went ; whereupon she made
discreet answer of all and discovered to the duchess the
occasion of her pilgrimage. The duchess, learning the
lady's quality, excused herself to her for not having done
her more honour, forasmuch as she knew not who she
was, and therewith they abode awhile upon ceremonies.[1]
Ultimately, the duchess came to the point and would fain
know the meaning of the words aforesaid, which had been
spoken of the pilgrimess, when she saw her in the coach ;
whereupon the Lady Isabella, without hesitation, said to
her, "My lady duchess, Don Juan Mendoza, my brother,
is one of the handsomest youths of his day, by that which
every one who seeth him saith of him ; for that I would
not on mine own judgment believe his goodliness to be
such as I tell you, did not public report and the universal
accord of all who know him confirm it. Of his valiance
and of the other parts which pertain unto a notable cavalier,
it beseemeth me not to speak, I being his sister ; but an
you spoke thereof with his very enemies, you would hear
all say that he is a valiant and accomplished gentleman.

The duchess was already somewhat enkindled with love of

---

[1] *i.e.* spent some time in exchanging compliments.

the gentleman, through the words she had heard in the
coach, and was beyond measure desirous of seeing him ; and
now, hearing him thus confidently commended of his sister,
she opened wide her breast to the amorous flames and
embraced them with so whole a heart that she became all
afire nor could turn her mind to otherwhat than how she
might see Don Juan ; nay, so deeply was she absorbed in
these thoughts that she oftentimes abode as if beside herself
and unknowing how of her own motion to find any remedy
for her sufferings and her desire to see the gentleman
redoubling as hope failed, she determined to discover her
case to a very trusty chamber-woman of hers, called Giulia,
who was very fair and beyond measure quick-witted and so
pleasant and agreeable that she was the loveling of the
whole court. To her, then, she imparted the secret of her
love and besought her of aid and counsel. Giulia, hearing
the mind of her lady, whom she loved far more than her
life, was moved to exceeding compassion of her and studied,
as best she knew, to comfort her, promising her to bestir
herself to such purpose that she would find means to compass
that emprise. Her confidant's consolations and her lavish
promises in some measure assuaged the duchess's sufferance ;
but Giulia, after pondering and repondering her case and
debating a thousand devices in herself, concluded that,
without the aid of some sage and well-advised man, it was
well-nigh impossible to heal her mistress of her heart's
malady. Now you know it to be the general usance in
courts for the courtiers to converse and gallant it with the
ladies there ; and accordingly the duchess's then physician,
a citizen of Milan, called Master Francesco Appiano, (great-
grandfather to our most affable friend of the same name, who
was physician to Francesco Sforza, second of that name
Duke of Milan,) paid his court to Giulia. The latter had

thitherto made little account of the physician's love, albeit
she showed him a good countenance; but now, knowing
him for a man of good breeding, quick-witted and engaging
and apt to the achievement of whatsoever emprise, she
bethought herself that there was none more to her purpose
than he and imparted this her conclusion to the duchess,
who approved it and charged her go about to allure him
with sidelong glances and feed him with blithe and amorous
looks; which the sagacious and quick-witted damsel
diligently put in execution. The physician, being in good
earnest enamoured of her, was all rejoiced and accounted
himself most fortunate, looking for a happy issue of his
loves; and she, whenas herseemed she had sufficiently
inflamed him, said to him, one evening, in accordance with
her mistress's injunctions, " The duchess is somewhat
indisposed of her person and would have you come to her
chamber to-morrow, ere she be risen, when you shall hear
from her the particulars of her ailment and see the sign [1] and
make such provision as the case requireth."

Master Francesco promised to do her bidding and accordingly, the morning come, he repaired to the castle and
entering the antechamber, waited to be admitted. The
duchess and Giulia had already taken order together of
that which was to be said to the physician, who in truth
believed the lady to be indisposed and ailing of her person,
as indeed she was, but of no malady which might be
medicined by Galen, Hippocrates or Avicenna. Accordingly, as soon as she heard he was come, she caused admit
him into her chamber and dismissed all her women, save
Giulia only; then, turning to the physician, " If, master
Francesco," quoth she, "you are that debonair and well-

<hr />

[1] *Il segno*, i.e. her water. An identical idiom occurs in Arabic.

advised person which I am fain to believe you are, I am
assured that I shall find in you two things of whatsoever
I may discover to you; the one, that you will keep my
counsel with inviolable fidelity and the other that, being
moved to compassion of my sufferance, you will find means
to heal me, for that I account you a physician no less
sufficient unto the infirmities of the mind than unto those
of the body. You know very well what it is for a young
and delicately nurtured woman to find herself married to
a man stricken in years, who (to bespeak you frankly)
availeth little or nothing in the service of the ladies; yet
withal there hath never entered my head any thought other
than virtuous nor any wish to do aught which might mislike
my lord duke. But, now, since a few days agone, I feel
myself so sore enkindled with desire to see a man on whom
I have never set eyes that, except I satisfy this longing, I
am well assured that it will be impossible for me to maintain
myself on life, albeit I have used my every endeavour and
have studied by a thousand means and devices to banish
this fancy from my head; but all in vain, for that, the more
I labour, I say, not to quench, but even to cool this raging
desire, the fiercelier doth it blaze and waxeth momently
hotter. Wherefore, seeing that this manifestly bringeth me
unto death, an I provide not therefor with some remedy, I
have resolved to do everything so I may not die, seeing
I would e'en have it be the last thing I should do to give
myself up to death." With this she told him that which
she had heard the pilgrimess say of her brother and how
she was resolved to do everything to see that famous cavalier
and prayed him again and again to find some fitting means to
bring her to that her desire, promising him mountains and
marvels and ultimately pledging him her faith to give him
Giulia to his wife.

The physician, who loved Giulia as his life and desired no otherwhat than to have her to wife, no sooner heard that note sounded than he freely promised the duchess to set his wits awork to find a device behoving unto such an emprise ; but, the better to consider the importance of the case and to provide against discovery of the practice, he asked two days' time to ponder and reponder various means and having already in mind some inkling of a device which misliked him not, he exhorted her to abide abed and give out that she was somewhat indisposed, whilst, the better to colour his design, he prescribed her certain electuaries and other remedies. With this he took leave and withdrawing to his house, whetted his wits and fell to debating various schemes in himself, straining every nerve and every thought for the achievement of the emprise, and after he had pondered divers devices and cudgelled his brains to the utmost, it occurred to his mind that there could be no surer or better way than to go to Saint James of [Compostella in] Galicia, under cover of a vow made to visit the holy relics of that Apostle in person and afoot. Accordingly, having stablished himself in this conceit, the astute Appiano returned to the duchess and in his Giulia's presence discovered to her that which he had devised, counselling her, so she should have an honourable and legitimate occasion for such a vow, feign herself very sick and cause it ultimately appear that she had been healed by a miracle of Saint James. The thing pleased the duchess and the ingenious leach taught her a fine method of cozening the ladies of the chamber, so they should all believe that they had plainly seen the holy Apostle appear to her. The duchess accordingly proceeded to feign herself all squeamish and queasy and to show distaste for whatsoever meat was offered her, complaining sore of her stomach, more by token that, by means of certain suffumigations with cummin and other devices of Appiano's contrivance, she was become very pale. Other physicians were called in to attend her, who were aghast to see her so pale and hearing Appiano's account of the case (and for that matter he chanted them a litany of his own fashion concerning the malady and the various symptoms which had befallen the duchess) they committed themselves to him, as better acquainted with the patient's nature ; whereupon he, seeing the thing go as he hoped, conferred with them of the remedies which he purposed to use and which were of all judged excellent. But, the duchess feigning herself daily worse and feeding not, save in secret and on certain nourishing meats provided by Appiano, it was noised about Turin that she went in danger of death, and this the other physicians confirmed, forasmuch as Appiano, with Giulia's aid, so falsified her water that it showed signs of death.

Now there was a suffragan of the Archbishop of Turin, a bishop (as it is used to say of the bishops of places in partibus infidelium) of poortith and nothing holding,[1] a very simple man and a holy. To him the duchess resolved to confess herself and accordingly she made him a confession of Ser Ciappelletto's fashion,[2] giving him to understand that she felt herself certainly dying and failing little by little and beseeching him make orison for her. The credulous old man comforted her amain with good words, bidding her commend herself to God and trust in His mercy, and eke on the morrow let make a general procession of all the clergy of the city for the restoration of the duchess to health. Meanwhile, Appiano had with his own hand made a goodly

---

[1] Episcopus povertatis nihilque tenens, i.e. without a benefice.
[2] See my " Decameron of Boccaccio," Day I. Story 1.

image of Saint James of Galicia, as he useth to be depictured, curiously fashioned of pasteboard and wrought with very fair colours, for that, beside being a very learned doctor, he was skilled in a thousand goodly arts. This image he laid in a chest, wherein he placed also sundry pieces of linen soaked in spirits of wine or burning-water [1] (for so is it named of many) and gave the chest to Giulia, who let straightway carry it, as a thing of her own and full of her gear, into the castle and set it behind the duchess's bed. Now the latter had in that her feigned infirmity chosen two simple old women to sleep anights in her chamber and Giulia also slept there. Toward midnight, then, on the day of the procession, Giulia, seeing that the old women, who had been long on the watch, were over-come with drowsiness and slept fast, softly opened the chest and taking out the image, fixed it, with the duchess's help, to the wall behind the bed ; then, drawing back the curtains, she set light to the pieces of soaked linen, having first placed them near the image, which was so contrived that, by the pulling of a string, it raised its right arm, as if in the act of benediction. This done, she raised her voice and began to cry out so loudly that the old women awoke, whilst she abode kneeling between the wall and the bed and pulled the string, crying out, "A miracle! A miracle!" The duchess, arising from bed, threw herself on her knees before the figure, beseeching the saint to heal her and vowing to go visit his holy relics afoot ; and this vow she repeated again and again. The good old women, seeing the image give its benediction to the duchess and the pieces of linen which burned before it and made a brave show of fire of many goodly colours, firmly believed it to be Saint James

[1] *Acqua ardente.*

the Great, brother of Saint John Evangelist, and devoutly fell on their knees, weeping for piety. They heard the duchess repeat her vow several times till she, seeing the flame of the soaked linen on the wane, bade them go fetch the physician to the chamber, for that he had retired to sleep in a room not far distant in the castle; then, what while they were absent on this errand, she and Giulia took the figure and laid it hastily back in the coffer.

The two old women made such an outcry that they not only awoke Appiano, but, crying, "A miracle! A miracle!" drew all in the castle thither; nay, the Duke himself arose at the clamour and repaired with many others to the chamber of the duchess, who was by this dressed and showed herself as blithe and content as can be said. When she saw the duke, she came to do him reverence and said to him, all sprightly and joyful, "My lord, I feel myself the happiest woman in the world, since it hath pleased our Lord God, on the intercession of His glorious Apostle, Saint James of Galicia, to restore me to health." Thereupon she recounted to him the fine miracle that had betided and the two old women and Giulia declared to have plainly seen the Apostle; whilst Appiano, in whom the duke had great faith, avouched that, when he entered the chamber, he saw a great light about the saint and that he suddenly disappeared in the twinkling of an eye, well-nigh at the moment of the duke's entrance. It were over-longsome to tell the various things which were said; suffice it to say that the duchess besought the duke to consent to the vow which she had made and he accordingly confirmed it. On the morrow the report of the miracle was bruited abroad and it was discoursed of no otherwhat. The suffragan came to the castle and diligently examined the duchess, the physician, the two old women and Giulia, and all of one accord testified to having seen the Holy Apostle in act to bless the lady. And as there be many men and women who think it shame not to have seen that which others see, especially in matters of sanctity and miracles, there were sundry courtiers of both sexes who declared that they had, on entering the chamber, seen the saint and the splendour about him. Accordingly, that same morning the suffragan let chant the offices of the said Apostle, whereto all the people flocked, and amiddleward the mass, the good bishop made a short preachment and recounted the goodly miracle and the healing of their duchess by the grace of God, relating all as if he had seen it; whilst the whole court and city were in the utmost joy and there were tiltings holden and runnings at the ring [in honour of the lady's recoverance].

Meanwhile the Lady Isabella Mendoza, having accomplished her pilgrimage, retraced her steps and came with her company to Turin, where, according to promise, she went to do her homage to the duchess, who awaited her with great eagerness and received her with the utmost cordiality, making much of her and lodging her in the castle. Then, taking her opportunity, she told the duke how a Spanish gentlewoman was come thither from Rome, with a worshipful company, on her way homeward, and that, an it pleased him, she was resolved to go with her to give accomplishment to her vow. The duke, thinking no ill, consented to her going and honourably furnishing her with monies and companions, (among which latter the duchess would e'en have the most debonair Appiano and Giulia,) despatched her on her way in peace. The two noble pilgrimesses made a brave show, with so worshipful a company of men and women, all afoot and clad in the palmer's habit, and were followed, to boot, by sundry carriages, bearing beds and other commodities. Accordingly they fared on their journey and crossing the snow-clad Alps, traversed Provence and came to the Pyrenean mountains, whereover they crossed into Spain by the County of Roussillon,[1] still journeying by short and easy stages. Now who should offer to recount all the discoursements, which the duchess (who had straitly charged the Lady Isabella and all in her company not to discover to any who she was) held with Appiano and Giulia in the course of that journey, would have overmuch to do. Suffice it to say, she declared that that long and toilsome pilgrimage was nowise grievous to her, nay, that she felt herself hourly lustier and that, the farther they fared, the more she felt herself enkindled and the more did her eagerness redouble to see the so much bepraised and desired Don Juan. There might well be sung of her the goodly verse of our enamoured Petrarch, "A lively love that waxeth in afflictions."[2]

When they drew near the city where Don Juan commonly dwelt, the Lady Isabella said to the duchess, "Mistress mine, we are but two short days' journey from one of my lord brother's cities; wherefore, with your leave, I will fare forward to make ready lodging for you and your company and will, an it please you, tell my brother that a Lombard lady, who hath hospitably entertained me in her house, cometh to lodge with me, without anywise discovering to him who you are." Accordingly she fared on in advance, but could not forbear to tell her brother how she who came was the King's sister of England and wife to the Duke of Savoy, acquainting him with that which had passed

[1] Now the French department des Pyrénées Orientales, but then a Spanish province.
[2] Trionfo d'Amore, Cap. III. l. 37.

between them [1] and the vow [which she had made] to visit
Saint James his shrine, together with her desire not to be
known. Don Juan exhorted his sister to honour the noble
pilgrimess as most she might and like a shrewd and quick-
witted man as he was, began to suspect that this pilgrimage
might be of anothergates fashion than his sister thought,
but said no word of this. The Lady Isabella, having given
prompt order unto that which behoved, turned back to
meet the duchess, whilst Don Juan, whenas himseemed time,
mounted to horse with many of his gentlemen, giving out
that he had a mind to go course a brace of hares, and faring
across country by many ways, struck the road by which the
fair pilgrimess came. The duchess, [seeing him come,]
enquired what folk these were and Isabella answered her,
saying, "Madam, this is my brother Don Juan, who goeth
hunting for his diversion. That is he whom you see on
yonder jennet white as ermine, with the white plume in his
bonnet." The duchess who, without having seen him, had
fallen in love with him on the mere report of his beauty,
seeing him far handsomer and sprightlier than she had
imagined to herself, was so overcome with his grace and
goodliness and so ardently enkindled that, all ravished forth
of herself and transformed into the cavalier, she could scarce
move her feet, but abode intent upon his sight, herseeming
she had never in her life tasted such delight as she felt in
contemplating him ; nay, she had gladly halted there, the
better to view him at her leisure. Don Juan, dismounting,
came courteously to kiss her hands, as those of a gentlewoman who had made much of his sister in Italy, and

----

[1] Bandello, "the discourse which she had made to her in the
coach" (*il ragionamento che ella le fece in carretta*), forgetting, with
his usual carelessness, the particulars of the earlier part of the story.

bade her welcome, thanking her and proffering himself to her service in whatsoever he might and could. Himseemed she was the fairest and gracefullest woman he had ever seen, and what little while they talked together, their eyes chanced to meet, the which (an it were possible) added fuel to the duchess's fire, and the cavalier abode so sore inflamed with the radiance of those twin starry orbs of hers that he incontinent felt himself their prisoner and there was no part in him but was all afire with love for the lovely pilgrimess. But neither of them dared discover their poignant flames, nay, both studied to conceal them as most they might ; the which caused them languish miserably, for that the more the fire of love is kept hidden, so much the more it burneth and consumeth the lover.

The duchess abode three days to rest herself in Don Juan's house, where she was honoured and regaled to the utmost, and seeking with the sight of the beloved object to abate the fierceness of the flames which consumed her, she made it hourly greater. On like wise was it with the cavalier, who, the more he contemplated the lady's lovesome beauties and commended them in himself, the more he drank in the amorous venom with his eyes, so that, inflamed beyond measure, he knew not what to do. On the fourth day, whatever might have been the cause thereof, the duchess, arising betimes, took leave of the Lady Isabella and departing with her company, set out towards Compostella. Don Juan, learning her sudden departure, abode sore chagrined, unable to conceive what could have moved her to depart on that wise; then, letting saddle the horses, he went oft at a gallop with certain of his men in the duchess's track and speedily overtook the lady, who fared afoot. When he came up with her, he dismounted and making her due obeisance, said to her, "Madam, I know not what reason

hath made you depart thus unexpectedly and it irketh me
sore that I have not been able to render you the honours
and kindnesses which you of your courtesy did to my sister
and if, by mischance, there have been aught other than
seemly done to you or to any of your folk, I will, an you
will deign to acquaint me withal, make you just amends
therefor." The duchess thanked him and answered that
she had had of him and his nothing but honour and courtesy;
wherefore she avowed herself beholden to him and declared
that, if she had departed without saying a word to him, it
had been for no otherwhat than not to awaken him. This
discourse being toward, the cavalier fared on with her afoot
and the opportunity offering, so he might be heard of none,
he said to her, "Mistress mine, it irketh me sore that it hath
not pleased you be honoured in my house according to your
degree, for that, you being a king's sister and a duke's wife,
I shall still abide infinitely chagrined for not having entreated
you as you deserve and as was behoving upon me; nay, an
it be ever known that you have lodged in my house and that
I made so little account of so exalted a lady, the world will
hold me a cavalier of little worth, and whereas I am nowise
at fault, I shall yet abide blamed of all. At the least, lady
mine, vouchsafe me the favour of entertaining you, on your
return, as a lady of royal blood and one who meriteth it.
Indeed, an you do me so much grace, I shall hold myself
eternally obliged to you." Thereupon ensued words galore,
the duchess complaining of the Lady Isabella for that she
had betrayed her; but, ultimately, each being beyond
measure enamoured of the other, they knew not so well to
conceal their passion but that needs must their ardent and
lively flames give out sparks and discover themselves;
wherefore, after they had avowed their loves each to other,
finding that they burned with a mutual ardour, they abode

of accord that she, whenas she had visited the relics of the
saint, should keep the novenary there (according to the
fashion of all pilgrims, who for nine successive days use
certain ceremonies in Saint James's church,) and should
thereafter come to abide some days with him. With this
conclusion they took leave of one another and the duchess
continued her journey to Compostella, whilst the cavalier
returned home, rejoicing.

But now let us leave these lovers time to think upon
their loves and speak awhile of the Duke of Savoy;
who, himseeming, after many days, he had done very
ill to let the King's sister of England and his own consort go thus privately [1] on so long a journey, bethought
himself better and desirous of amending the default committed, convoked his councillors and propounded the case
to them. They all declared that it behoved to remedy
the oversight as quickliest might be and for better despatch it was judged expedient that the duke himself
should go thither by sea; wherefore, letting equip certain
ships which he had hard by at Nice, he embarked
with an honourable train of many cavaliers and gentlemen and sailing for Galicia with a fair wind, passed the
straits of Gibraltar and arriving [at Compostella] on the
last day of the novenary, found the duchess in act to
make an end of all the ceremonies of her vow. Great
was the joy of all the company, when they saw their
lord; but the duchess abode mighty disconsolate, seeing
the way estopped against her loves. On like wise, Appiano
and Giulia, being cognizant of their mistress's thoughts,
were sore concerned therefor; nevertheless, dissembling

---

[1] *Privatamente*, i.e. as a private person and without the state
befitting her rank.

their ill-content, they all three feigned themselves rejoiced. The duke acquainted his wife with the occasion of his coming and on the ensuing day, having visited and paid his devotions to the holy relics, he took ship with the duchess and all his company. Then, being minded to visit his brother-in-law, he let cast off the moorings and hoisting sail, steered for England, where he arrived, after a prosperous voyage, and was joyfully received by the king and entertained with many diversions.

The duchess, albeit she feigned herself blithe, was nevertheless sore cast down at heart and vented her chagrin to Appiano and Giulia whenassoever she had commodity thereof, bitterly bemoaning her ill luck, herseeming overhard to brook that, in the very blossom-tide of her loves, whenas the desired fruit was on the point of being born thereof, after so many toils and travails of mind and body, the flower should be despoiled and scattered and herself bereaved of all hope of harvest. Her confidants comforted her as best they might, telling her that Don Juan could not fail of coming to seek her at Turin ; but she was beyond consolation, so deeply had melancholy penetrated into her heart. Algates, not to give suspicion of aught to her husband or to the king her brother, she feigned herself outwardly blithe, dissembling her sufferance as most she might. They abode some days in England, whilst the king left nothing undone to pleasure and honour his sister and brother-in-law. The duke, wearied with his long sea-travel, would not go home by the way he came, but determined to pass over to Calais and to return to his duchy by way of France, and the king, ere he departed, gave his sister a very fine diamond, worth more than an hundred thousand ducats. The duke and duchess, accordingly, departing England, sailed to Calais and there making provision of horses, sent back the ships and journeyed to Paris, where they were blithely received and honoured by the Most Christian King, more by token that the Duke of Savoy was the latter's captain-general. Thence they passed into Savoy,[1] where they abode some days and presently fared over the Alps to Turin. The duchess was beyond measure woeful and her grief waxed the more that she might not openly vent it nor dared discover it to any save Appiano and Giulia.

But how deem you it fared with Don Juan meanwhile, who was no less ardently enamoured of the duchess than she of him? He awaited her in vain five or six days after the appointed time, numbering not only the days, but the hours, and not seeing her return, he marvelled exceeding sore and misdoubted him some extraordinary accident had befallen her; wherefore he despatched a trusty man of his into Galicia to learn what was come of her. The messenger accordingly repaired to Compostella and understanding from the people of the place that the pilgrimess, who had visited the shrine of the Apostle, was the Duchess of Savoy and that the duke had come thither and carried her off with him by sea, returned and duly related the whole to Don Juan, who, hearing this news, misdoubted him the thing had been appointed and ordained beforehand and that the lady had certainly cozened him; nevertheless, he suffered sore and inexpressible pain and still himseemed his flames waxed hotter and hotter and the desire of seeing the duchess redoubled on him momently; and so the hapless lover, burning and freezing, hoping and despairing in one breath and loving more than ever, led a very sorry life.

---

[1] *i.e.* the province proper of that name, as distinguished from Piedmont.

What while he languished on this wise and the duchess no less than he, it chanced that the Germans, levying a powerful army, invaded France and burned and laid waste whereassoever they came. The Duke of Savoy, as the king's captain-general, being advertised of this betimes, took horse with all his men at arms for the defence of the country; but, ere he departed Turin, he left one of his kinsmen, the Count of Pancalieri, his lieutenant-general, subject to consultation with the duchess. The count proceeded to govern the affairs of the duchy as best he knew, conferring of everything with the duchess, according as the duke had commanded, so that he was still about her; wherefore, conversing assiduously with her and seeing her very fair, he from a governor of the state became a contemplator and lover of her charms and fell so sore enamoured of her that he could find no repose. He had never had wife nor children, but entertained for his son a nephew of his, the son of one of his brothers who was Seignior of Racconigi, which said youth abode at the duchess's court and might be some fifteen or sixteen years old, when he first came thither; since when he had served more than two years and was very handsome and well-bred. The count his uncle, who savoured somewhat of the simpleton, carried away by greedy amorous appetite and flattering himself that there was no woman, how great and fair soever she was, but must have it in gree to be loved of him, made bold to require the duchess of love and tell her how he burned for her. The duchess, who had set her thoughts otherwhere nor would have deigned to show him the point of one of her shoes, bade him with a stern air never dare to bespeak her more of such folly; but the poor man, being overmuch goaded of the amorous fires, renewed his importunities, beseeching her more instantly than before to be pleased to have compassion on him. At this she was beyond measure incensed and rebuked him severely for his exceeding temerity, saying, "Count, I pardoned you the first offence, and although you deserve it not, I pardon you this your second fond and foolhardy presumption ; but look you return no more thereto nor ever make bold to bespeak me again of such wickedness ; else will I play you a trick that will not please you. Apply yourself to do the office committed to you by my lord consort and fall not again into such an error, as you hold your life dear."

The count saw the duchess's chaste and inexpugnable mind and judged that he wearied himself in vain ; but, misdoubting him she should give the duke to know of that his folly, he determined to be beforehand with her and ruin her. Accordingly, he in a trice changed his fervent love into cruel hatred and bethinking himself of a device that should answer his purpose, doubted not to be able to cause her die ignominiously ; wherefore, showing himself in words and deeds estranged from that his love, he addressed himself to the execution of his office of governance. Meanwhile, he began to entreat the nephew aforesaid more familiarly than of his wont ; nay, he showed him well-nigh a comrade's privacy, bespeaking him of no otherwhat than matters amorous, and amongst other things he said to him one day that there was no pleasure in the world equal to the exceeding delight felt by a youth enamoured of a fair and great lady, especially when the love proved to be reciprocal. Having by this talk allured the youth, he no great while after said to him privily, "Nephew mine, to me dear as my proper son, take good heed to that which I shall presently say to thee, for that, an thou be discreet and ensue my counsels, I promise thee thou shalt have the best time man ever had of this country." The lad, who

looked upon his uncle as a father, answered him that he was
ready to obey him and do whatsoever he should deign to
command him ; whereupon the villainous count said to him,
"I have observed, dearest my son, that the duchess willeth
thee great weal [1] and loveth thee beyond measure ; nay,
I see plainly that she goeth wasting as wax before the fire
and desireth no otherwhat than to come to close quarters
with thee ; but she doth as do women in general, who,
albeit they desire a thing, will e'en for the most part be
entreated and are well pleased that men should beguile
them, so it may appear they are brought either by craft
or by force to yield themselves to their lovers ; and when
they love a youth and perceive in the long run that he is
not quickwitted and bold, they are despited thereat and turn
their love elsewhither. I speak to thee, nephew mine, of
experience ; wherefore hearken to me and do that which
I tell thee. I will have thee this evening watch thine
opportunity to hide thyself under the duchess's bed and
there abide till seven of the night,[2] when she will be buried
in the first sleep and her women will all be asleep. Then
do thou arise quietly and coming up to the bed, lay thy
hand on her breast and tell her softly who thou art. I
know what I tell thee and bespeak thee not at hazard.
Marry, as soon as she knoweth thee, she will cause thee
enter the bed with her and thou wilt enjoy that noble lady
at thy pleasure. I for my part should account myself blessed,

---

[1] *Ti vuol un gran bene.* For numerous examples of this common
idiomatic expression in the sense of "loving," see my "Decameron
of Boccaccio," passim.

[2] We are not told the month in which this part of the story happens
and can therefore only guess at the equivalent of this hour according
to the clock. The season was probably winter, when "seven of the
night" would be 11 or 12 p.m.

were I in thy place." The simple youth believed his
uncle, thinking belike that he bespoke him by the duchess's
commandment ; and who indeed had not given credence
to an own uncle, hearing him speak with such assurance?
The lad, then, did according to the malignant counsel
of the base and traitorous count and taking his opportunity,
hid himself under the bed, in which the duchess couched
herself towards five of the night.

The wicked and disloyal count, so that his treason
might not be discovered, awaited not the hour which he
had appointed his nephew, but, as soon as it had struck
six,[1] took sundry of the guard of the castle and three
councillors (for that all obeyed him as their lord's lieutenant and he might enter and leave the castle whenassoever he would) and repaired, without possessing any of
that which he purposed to do, to the duchess's chamber,
where, knocking loudly and the door being opened to him,
he entered in, rapier in hand, with many lights and those
of the guard armed. The affrighted duchess marvelled
greatly at this act and knew not what to say, when the
villainous count let drag out his own nephew from under
the bed and (so he might not discover how his uncle
had caused him hide himself there) ere the poor wretch
could say a word, he stabbed him in the breast with
his rapier, saying, "Traitor, thou art dead," and pierced
him through and through. The wretched youth fell to
the ground, dead, and the felon and traitorous count,
turning to the councillors, said to them, "Sirs, these
many days past have I perceived the dishonest passion
of this malapert kestrel of a nephew of mine, who hath
died an over-goodly death, for that he deserved to be

----

[1] *i.e.* of the night; probably 10 or 11 p.m.

burned alive or torn asunder by horses. On the duchess I care not to lay hands, but you know it is the law in Piedmont and Savoy that every woman taken in adultery shall be burned, except within a year and a day she find a champion to fight for her. I will write to the king her brother and to the duke, telling them the case as it hath befallen, and meanwhile, the lady shall abide here in her chamber, under good guard, with her damsels."

The councillors and others abode aghast at so horrid a spectacle and the duchess called God and the saints to witness of her innocence and that the wretched youth had not hidden himself under the bed with her consent; but it availed her nothing. The disconsolate lady abode, then, imprisoned in her chamber and the ill-starred youth was that same morning buried without funeral pomp. The count hugged himself over the success of his plot, drunken as he was with hate, and wrote to the king of England and to the duke by a messenger, post-haste, possessing them of that which had passed and causing the councillors write letters to the same effect. Now the duchess was beyond measure beloved of all the people, for that she never sought to harm any, but helped all as most she might; wherefore all were infinitely grieved at her misfortune ; and for that those of the guard used great discretion in letting the physician go and come and paid no heed to him, she made shift by his means to have all her monies and jewels and great store of [ornaments of] wroughten gold conveyed away little by little ; all which he laid up in his own house. The king and the duke, having the letters, abode sore chagrined at such unseemly news and it gave exceeding credit to the perfidious count's story that he had slain his own nephew, it being known how much he loved him and how he had chosen him to his heir. The duke wrote back to his governor and council that the ancient usance of the country should be observed; wherefore there was set up, without Turin, in the plain between the city and the bridge over the Po, upon a lofty column of marble, which had long before been set up there for the like purposes, the Count of Pancalieri's impeachment in writing against the duchess, who, hearing the final ordinance come from the duke, was woeful beyond expression, more by token that she knew herself innocent of the sin laid to her charge. Accordingly, she set all her affairs in order and clothing herself in sad-coloured garments, led a very grievous life. She had, as hath been said, sent away the best of her gear to the house of her physician Appiano, keeping only, I know not for what reason, the precious diamond which the king her brother had given her in England. All the women who were used to serve her had been taken from her by the rascally governor; algates, Giulia contrived to have his leave to keep her mistress company by day.

Meanwhile Don Juan de Mendoza, who abode infinitely chagrined against the duchess and was fain to believe that she had made mock of him, was overtaken with another sore affliction, for that he was like to lose his dominion and his life at the hands of the seigniors of the aforesaid house of Toledo, who, as I told you, had suffered a sore defeat and awaited but an occasion of rendering him the like and (if possible) of slaying him. The King of Spain, for all he saw the grievous disorders which ensued in his kingdom through these two puissant factions, nevertheless concerned not himself overmuch to put an end to their contentions; nay, it seemed as he would fain have them ruin each other, so he might after have them obedient to himself. Accord-

ingly, the matter went on such wise that, both parties taking
the field with numerous and powerful armies, they came to
blows in a pitched battle, wherein Don Juan, albeit he
approved himself at once a stout and strenuous soldier and
a valiant and provident captain, was routed and saved
himself with great difficulty in a city, which was very strong
and well garrisoned and furnished with a year's victual.
There he was beleaguered by his enemies, with scant hope
of succour, so that the two lovers were reduced to a very
ill pass.

But who shall avail to tell the tears which Giulia shed
well-nigh every day, visiting the duchess? The latter
endured her afflictions with a steadfast mind and whereas
she should have been comforted, she exhorted Giulia to
suffer all in peace and not to afflict herself. Then, after
a while, they concluded that it could not be other than well
done that Appiano should go post haste to Spain, to seek
aid of Don Juan and certify him that the duchess was falsely
accused. The lady accordingly gave him a letter of credence
under her own hand to Don Juan, and Appiano, posting it
with the utmost diligence, came near the beleaguered city,
where he learned how the case stood and abode sore concerned, himseeming it was impossible that Don Juan should
go to succour the duchess. Nevertheless, like a loving and
diligent servant as he was and one who infinitely desired
to procure aid for his mistress, he determined not to depart
without having speech of Don Juan. Now it chanced that
there befell a great skirmish between those without and
those within, and the good physician, getting himself, I
know not how, a buckler, threw himself valiantly into the
skirmish, sword in hand, and pushed so far forward that he
was made prisoner by those of the city and said to them,
"Carry me straight to my lord Don Juan, for that I have

things of the utmost import to impart to him." He was accordingly brought before Don Juan, who knew him immediately for one of those whom he had seen with the duchess and received him graciously ; then, drawing him aside, he asked him what news he had of his mistress. Appiano replied that he brought very ill news, inasmuch as she was in sore peril of being ignominiously burned, an succour were not given her, and beginning from the beginning, recounted to him the chagrin she had suffered when the duke arrived in Galicia with the ships, seeing herself estopped from keeping her promise to him. Moreover, he told him that all her hopes of deliverance were in him and certified him that she was nowise guilty of that whereof she was accused ; wherefore he most instantly besought and conjured him not to fail her in that her urgent need, using every persuasive art he knew or might, so he should be moved to pity of the unhappy lady and apply himself to deliver her. Don Juan condoled amain with Appiano anent the calamity which had befallen the duchess, and it was the more grievous to him that he was presently besieged of his enemies nor might anywise abandon the city. The physician, who saw that he spoke sooth, knew not what to say and ultimately, seeing that he wearied himself there in vain, determined to lose no more time, but to return to Turin. Don Juan let make a good sally, under cover of which he brought him forth of the city and had him escorted by certain of his men to a place of safety. Thence Appiano made his way back to Turin and gave the duchess to know, by means of Giulia, the strait in which he had found Don Juan and the discourse which had passed between them. The lady, hearing this ill news, despaired of succour and knew not what to do or to say nor whither to recur for aid.

However, some days after Appiano's departure, Don Juan,

bethinking him of the duchess's calamity and calling to mind the love he bore her, judged that he had erred sore in not having straightway run to deliver her and set, not only his dominions, but his life, ay, and a thousand lives, had he so many, upon the hazard for her sake. Wherefore, unable to console himself for this his default, he determined, come thereof what would, to make such best provision as he might for his affairs in Spain and passing incontinent over into Italy, to use his every endeavour for the hapless lady's deliverance. Having made this steadfast resolve, he reviewed the affairs of the city and found it excellently well furnished with all necessaries and apt to hold out eight or nine months longer, whilst he knew the garrison and inhabitants to be most faithful. Accordingly, he assembled the chief men of the city and the captains of the troops and declared himself resolved to depart in quest of succours for the raising of the siege, adding that, an he returned not within such a time (and he appointed them a day certain), they must provide for their own affairs; but that they should, without fail, see him with a great succour before the term assigned; and withal he made one of his kinsmen, a very valiant cavalier, his lieutenant. Then, letting give the enemy a sharp alert, he mounted a fiery and spirited jennet and making his way out of the city, without being seen of the besiegers, set out alone towards France. There he bought him a good courser and arms [1] and took a serving-man; then, unknown of any one, even of his own servant, he crossed the Alps and made his way to Turin.

Now, as hath been said, the physician had already arrived there, and albeit the duchess had lost hope of Don Juan's succour, nevertheless, bethinking herself of that which

---

[1] *i.e.* armour fit for the lists.

she had done for love of him, she could not bring herself
to believe him so ungrateful but that he would come fight
for her against the disloyal Count of Pancalieri, and in this
expectation she abode awhile ; but presently, seeing that
there came neither letter nor message from him, she conceived such despite in her mind that her fervent love was
changed to bitter hatred and recalling that which she had
done for him, she entered into exceeding great choler and
said in herself, "Wretch that I am ! How blind and fond
and senseless I was to look for fidelity in a disloyal man !"
With this the disconsolate lady, overcome with the keenness
of her sufferance, berailed Don Juan with all the ill that
can be said of a most ungrateful and perfidious man and
on this wise she in some measure vented her bitter dolour.
Giulia, who could not believe but the King of England would
send a champion to his sister's aid, went twice or thrice
a day to the place of the lists to see if any champion appeared ; but the English king, believing that his sister had
in very deed been taken in adultery, was sore despited
against her and declared that she deserved to be burned.

Meanwhile Don Juan, arriving at Turin by night, took
up his lodging in the suburbs at the house of an innkeeper,
a man of worth, and entering into discourse with him,
learned that the duke was in the field against the Germans
and the duchess in prison, whose affliction, said the host,
was exceeding grievous unto all, for that the whole land
loved her marvellously. He heard also that there was in
the city a venerable Spanish friar in the utmost repute with
the ducal council and with all the folk and enquired the
name of the church where he dwelt. Then, next morning,
leaving the hostelry, he made his way to the church in
question and knocking at the parsonage-door, was admitted
by the friar in person, to whom quoth Don Juan in Spanish,

"Father mine, God pleasure you, I am a Spaniard, come into these parts for my affairs, and being a stranger here and understanding you to be a countryman, I am come to lodge with you. I want nothing but lodging; for the rest this my servant shall provide whatsoever is needful." The good father willingly accepted him and brought him into his house; and what while his serving-man went abroad to buy victual, Don Juan enquired of the friar from what part of Spain he was. He freely told it him and Don Juan, finding him to be of his own vassals and of that same city which was beleaguered, straitly questioned him of many things, till he certified himself beyond doubt that he was of his own faction; whereupon he discovered himself to him, telling him who he was. The friar, hearing this and considering him better, knew him, for that he had been but a little while in those parts,[1] and would fain have cast himself at his feet, after the fashion of the Spaniards, who worship their princes as Gods upon earth; but Don Juan suffered it not. Then, telling him why he came thither thus privily, he said to him, "Father, you know that I am a knight and am therefore bound to defend, over all others, ladies who are unjustly entreated. Now I have it on very good authority, that this lady hath been most wrongfully oppressed with false accusation; but the better to certify myself thereof, I would fain speak with her and learn the truth, under colour of confession. You shall clothe me as a friar and seek leave of whoso holdeth her in custody to visit her and exhort her to suffer death with patience, in atonement of her sins; and when we are there, do you leave the rest to me."

The simple father, who was not the quickest-witted nor most learned man of those parts, suffered himself to be persuaded by the cavalier's arguments and having first

---

[1] *i.e.* Savoy.

clothed the latter in a friar's habit and tonsured him, repaired to the governor and said to him, "My lord, the time of the death of the unfortunate duchess draweth nigh; wherefore I have been moved to compassion of her soul and would fain bespeak her of things spiritual, according as our Lord God shall inspire me, so that, if she be for her sins to lose her bodily life, she may at the least save her soul alive; and I trust God will vouchsafe me such favour that I may dispose her to die patiently." The governor, malignant and wicked as he was, answered, nevertheless, (to show the people he was concerned for the lady's fate,) that he was content and sent to the castellan, bidding him suffer the friar and his comrade enter the prison-chamber and speak with the duchess. Accordingly, they both entered, all believing, inasmuch as the term of her death drew nigh, that the governor had sent them to hear the poor lady's last confession. The chamber was large, but the windows were closed on such wise that little or no light was visible there, and Don Juan, who spoke the Italian tongue excellent well, said, "The peace of our Saviour be with you, madam." The duchess, who sat in a corner, all disconsolate, replied, "Who are you that bespeak me of peace, me who am bereft of all peace and all good and shortly expect a most ignominious death, against all right and without having anywise merited it?" Don Juan, following the sound of the voice, drew near to her and said, "Madam, I am a poor friar, who, arriving at this city, have learned your grievous misfortune and moved to pity of so horrible a case, am come to visit you and comfort you." Therewith he said many things to her and that on such goodly wise that the duchess resolved to confess herself to him and accordingly, as one past hope of life, proceeded to make an entire and general confession, whereby Don Juan lightly understood her to be altogether innocent. (Now in her confession she told him how her journey to Compostella had been feigned and how she had undertaken it solely to go see a most disloyal and ungrateful Spanish cavalier.) Don Juan strenuously exhorted her to forgive all the injuries she had ever suffered and she replied that she heartily forgave them all, as she would have God forgive her, but that she knew not how she might ever forgive that ungrateful cavalier, whom she had loved more than her life. Don Juan was inwardly rejoiced at these words and still exhorted her to forgive all who had wronged her, the which in the end she promised to do. Now she had, as we have seen, kept that most precious diamond; her gold and pearls and other jewels and what not else of hers, which Appiano and Giulia had, she purposed should remain to them, they having pledged her their faith to marry each other. Accordingly, having no otherwhat whereof to give alms, she said to the friar, "Father mine, of all my substance there is left me but this diamond, which the king my brother gave me and which, according to that which skilful jewellers have sundry whiles told me, is worth more than an hundred thousand ducats. I give it to you; you can sell it to the King of France, who much delighteth in such jewels, and with the price which you shall receive therefor let say masses and other offices for my soul, portion poor damsels and give alms without stint to Christ's poor and to pious houses. For yourself and your occasions keep such part as most pleaseth you and pray God for my soul." Then, after many other things said, the good friars commended the duchess to God and returned home, leaving her full of hope, but why she could not have told.

Meanwhile Don Juan, having given much monies to the friar, caused his serving-man set his arms in order, whereas it behoved, and array his courser for battle; then, on the eve of the last day of the term of a year and a day, he departed Turin late at night and turning back, betook himself to the hostelry where he had lodged before. On the morrow, at break of day, he mounted to horse, armed like a St. George, and repaired to the city-gate, where, calling one of those who abode on guard, he said to him, "Friend, go bid the Count of Pancalieri make ready to maintain the false accusation which he hath made against Madam the Duchess of Turin, for that there is a knight come who declareth himself her champion and will make him unsay that which he hath said in her dishonour." The watchman did his errand, whilst the cavalier, going up to the pillar whereon the impeachment was written, rested his lance against it and there abode awaiting the coming of the accuser. The news of this champion spread straightway throughout the city; whereupon Giulia ran thither and accosting the cavalier, asked him, the better to certify herself, an he came to defend her lady the duchess. He knew her for his mistress's trusty chamber-woman and urbanely replied to her that he was come for the duchess's deliverance and hoped that day with God's aid to make her innocence manifest. Giulia knew him not and returned to the city, like one frantic, crying out that God had sent an angel to defend her lady. The Count of Pancalieri played the punctilious and would not descend into the lists till he knew who he was that declared himself the duchess's champion; whilst all the city was in an uproar, every one desiring the lady's deliverance. It was replied to him by the councillors that the accuser was by the ancient statutes of the duchy bounden to fight whoso should present himself

as champion of the accused with such arms as were borne
of the latter, and that in the presence of the accused person,
who should be brought to the lists, under good guard.
The perfidious count had no more stomach for battle than
a coney, knowing as he did that he fought for a falsehood ;
nevertheless, seeing that needs must he fight, he plucked
up heart and arming himself, repaired to the lists, whither
the trembling duchess had already been conducted, accompanied by many. When she saw her defender, she fell
on her knees and with heart uplifted to God, devoutly
besought the Divine pity to vouchsafe her champion the
victory and not permit malice and falsehood to overmaster
innocence.

The two combatants fetched a compass and encountering
with couched lances, broke them lustily ; then, taking sword
in hand, they fell to dealing one another swashing blows ;
but they had not been long engaged ere Don Juan gave the
count so grievous a blow on the right arm and made him
so wide a wound in the wrist that he let fall his sword ;
whereupon the cavalier in a trice dealt him a parlous thrust
in the vizor of his helmet and put out one of his eyes. The
count was like to swoon for the pain of his half-lopped hand
and his lost eye, and letting fall the reins, was haled from
his horse to the ground by the valiant cavalier, who straightway dismounted and pulling off his adversary's helmet,
presented the point of his sword at his throat and said to
him with a stern and fierce aspect, "Traitor, needs must
thou declare, here in the presence of the duchess, of the
councillors and of all the people, who it was discovered to
thee that thy nephew was hidden under the duchess's bed."
The count, seeing himself nigh unto death, heaved a heavy
sigh and said, "God forfend that, since my body is perished,
I should lose my soul also ! " And accordingly he recounted

all the treason which he had plotted and how and why he had induced his poor nephew to do that folly. The populace cried out, "Slay, slay the traitor;" but Don Juan, mounting to horse again, said in a loud voice, "My sword imbrueth not itself in the blood of a slain man." Meanwhile, happy he who might draw near the duchess and certify her with words and gestures of the joy which all felt at seeing her delivered. Others of the people fell furiously upon the count, who was already well-nigh dead, and tearing off his arms, dragged him about the lists, so that he died forthright.

What while this was toward, Don Juan, making a sign to his serving-man, crossed the bridge over the Po and made off, rejoicing in his victory, to Cheri and thence by Asti to Genoa, where he took ship and passed over into Spain. The duchess was surrounded by such a crowd of her people of Turin and all were so busy about her that none noted the departure of her deliverer; whereat, whenas she became aware thereof, she was sore chagrined, but might find none who could tell in what direction the valiant knight had gone. Meanwhile, Don Juan arrived in Spain and understanding that his city still held out stoutly, pledged the duchess's diamond and also certain other jewels which he had with him to divers Genoese merchants for certain monies, with which and other monies he got from certain princes his friends, he levied some thousands of picked soldiers and having despatched spies to his folk of the city to advertise them of his purpose, fell in upon the besiegers' camp at unawares by night; whereupon those within sallied valiantly forth, so that the besiegers, being taken in front and in rear, abode discomfited and the most part of them were slain. Don Juan, having thus delivered the city, followed up his fair fortune and in a few days not only recovered his dominions, but occupied divers castlewicks of his enemies and made himself so puissant that he became in great credit with the king.

In those same days befell the [great] battle between the Germans and the French, wherein, after long fighting, the latter had the worse, and their captain-general, who was, as hath been said, the Duke of Savoy, was slain.[1] The King of England had by this gotten news of his sister's deliverance, whereat he professed himself infinitely rejoiced, not so much for her liberation as that she had been found innocent, and gave her joy thereof by one of his gentlemen, whom he despatched to her for that purpose. Then, hearing of the duke's death, he sent an honourable company to fetch her and bring her to England, purposing to remarry her; and against he should find her a sortable match, he gave her in governance a daughter of his from sixteen to seventeen years of age, whom he was in treaty to marry to the eldest son of the King of Spain. Moreover, understanding the manner of his sister's deliverance and finding that she knew not who her champion was, he promised her, if ever she came to know him, to reward him as he deserved. Now she desired nothing more in the world than to find her said champion, so she might honour and reward him as far as lay in her power, whilst, on the other hand, she was bent on using her every endeavour to have Don Juan assassinated, accounting him the most ungrateful man was ever born.

The treaty of marriage between the King's daughter of England and the prince of Spain being concluded, the

---

[1] The battle of Pavia (1525) is apparently meant; but no Duke of Savoy died there, and it is indeed difficult to make out what Duke of Savoy is referred to by Bandello, as all the princes of that house were on the Imperial side until a much later period.

latter's father chose out a number of the first gentlemen of his realm and making Don Juan their chief, despatched them to England with a patent of proxy to espouse the English princess in his son's name. The king, understanding the coming of so noble a company, received them very honourably; but the duchess, seeing Don Juan, was sore chagrined and would not be present, when he came to do his obeisance to the princess, but withdrew to another chamber, all full of despite and saying in herself, "How can these Spaniards be so presumptuous? Here is this traitor, who knoweth how heinously he hath offended against me, and yet he presumeth to come before me; but I shall never be content till I see him dead at my feet." The king, who knew nothing of that which had passed between his sister and Don Juan, sent to bid her receive and make much of the Spanish cavalier who came to espouse his daughter; whereupon she very unwillingly came forth the chamber and repaired, all disordered in countenance, to the saloon. Don Juan came up to her and offered respectfully to kiss her hand; but she suffered it not and drawing away her hand, fell to speaking with another Spaniard. That same evening, at the banquet, Don Juan was seated by the side of the duchess, who, seeing a great diamond on his finger and knowing it for that which she had given to the friar in prison, was curious to know how it had come to his hands and spoke thereof with Appiano, who had, together with Giulia, accompanied her into England. The physician, no great while after, entered into discourse with the cavalier and asked him whence he had gotten that rich ring; whereto he answered him, smiling, that he would gladly tell it to the duchess and at the same time impart to her things which would please her. The lady, hearing this reply, was mighty loath to speak with him; however, overcome with desire to learn how he had gotten the ring, she unwillingly consented thereto; whereupon Don Juan made her a brief discourse of the slight which himthought had been done him by her failure to return to him from Compostella and the manner in which he was beleaguered, whenas Appiano came in quest of him, and how he had repented him of not having forthright come to deliver her, as in effect he confessed himself bounden to do; after which he told her how he had come to Turin and made acquaintance with the Spanish friar and how it was he who said such and such things to her in prison and had of her the precious ring and gave her so many tokens of that which he said that she plainly knew him to be her deliverer; whereupon, laying aside all despite and feeling the quenched fire rekindle in her, she could scarce contain herself from casting her arms about his neck and kissing him a thousand times. Then, seeking speech of the king, she gave him to know how Don Juan had been her deliverer and said to him, "My lord, you promised to remarry me and to reward my deliverer; and what husband can I have, who is more deserving of me than this faithful and valiant cavalier?" The king readily assented thereto and much commending his sister's mind, let marry them, to the great satisfaction of both parties; whilst the new bride would have her trusty Giulia wed with Appiano. This added new gladness to the general rejoicing and a few days after, they all, together with the princess and a worshipful company of English gentlemen, sailed blithely into Spain, where the nuptials of the prince and princess were celebrated with the utmost pomp. Don Juan presently repaired with his bride to his estates, where he held open court many days, and they lived long together in peace and happiness, leaving children and grandchildren after them.

Bandello

to His Most Serene Highness Maximilian Archduke of Austria and King of Bohemia.

These many days, most august king, hath the renown of your glory and excellence, not content with the limits of Europe, gone flying about the other two parts of the world,[1] and waxing hourly more and more, possesseth whomsoever it reacheth with the desire to feed his eyes upon your royal presence, even as his ears are still filled with the report of your many and eminent virtues. But since your most devoted and affectionate servant Messer Filippo Baldo, gentleman of Milan, hath again and again expounded and supremely commended to me your many admirable gifts and graces and your inborn urbanity and courtesy, which never suffereth any to depart from you unsatisfied, I have still beyond measure desired an occasion to expatiate at mine ease upon the divine nature which shineth so brightly in you and the many precious and goodly parts wherein you abound; nay, I flattered myself that my vein, which hath of itself been still trivial, mean and insipid, might e'en wax great, copious, lofty and rich by dint of recounting the grandeur and majesty of those

---

[1] *i.e.* Asia and Africa, America being as yet held to be a part of Asia.

admirable things which you accomplish to such perfection
in this your lovesome flower of youth. Nor shall I ever
repent me of this my desire, the which must needs proceed
from a generous soul, albeit the effect oftentimes ensueth
not equal to the wish ; for that, as saith one of the Latin
poets, in great things to have willed is much ; and so it
is with me,[1] for that, whenas I took pen in hand to write,
I very lightly perceived that this was none of my emprise ;
wherefore such doubt of myself overcame me and so great
and thick a darkness obscured and blinded the feeble lights
of my understanding that I see not where to stablish
my feet, and meseemeth well-nigh as if these scant letters
of mine (if ever any I have learned from boyhood through
all my years) were vain and of little avail. Verily, the
sentiment of veneration implanted in our souls troubleth
and altogether dismayeth me, for that meseemeth I have
drawn overnear to the sublimity of your royal estate,
whereof the true praise were rather to admire in silence
than to presume to speak thereof on rude and clownish
wise. And in effect it behoveth humbly to revere and
honour kings of supreme excellence, such as we know you
to be, even as Gods ; nor might he escape the reproach of
sacrilege who should presume to name your name without
a preface of honour. Behold, I see spread out before mine
eyes the pomp of all those lofty deeds and achievements
which have in every age been most marvellous and are
now surpassed by you on such wise that, had they not
been seen of us, there were none to believe them. Let
the lives of many heroes of old time be passed in review
and their egregious deeds examined with diligence, and
we shall see what action of theirs may be, not to say,

---

[1] i.e. the effect correspondeth not to the wish.

preferred before yours, but hardly evened therewith. Marry, the resounding trumpet of fame proclaimeth with loud and clear and volant voice how, well-nigh in your first boyhood, adorned with various tongues, you propounded, in the Imperial Germanic Diet, in the name of your uncle Charles, Fifth of the name Cæsar Augustus, the affairs of greatest moment which were there to be examined and treated, and that in the purest German idiom and in the chastest and most elegant Latin and with such grace and majesty and such pure and flowery eloquence that all the hearers were filled with extreme amazement and abode still intent upon your every word. Again, it hath already been published in every place and confirmed by most credible witnesses how in the Saxon war you bore yourself, not as a tyro and a stripling, but as a very doughty soldier and a veteran and as a prudent and practised captain. All, great and little, who were present at that most parlous conflict [which ended the war aforesaid] proclaim with one voice that you, with bloody flashing blade in hand, gave manifest signal unto all the army, as well Imperial as hostile, for the slaughter and destruction which you, with your unconquered right hand, so valiantly wreaked upon the foe. Wherefore the emperor, a judicious appraiser of each man's merit, moved by your intrinsic worth and by your warlike valour, approved in that act of arms, dubbed you Knight of Saint George in the sight of all that unconquered host, the which is the true title of honour, when deservedly bestowed upon gilded knights. But what shall I say of the lively seed which your incomparable breeding hath implanted in the hearts of all Germany and which hath struck root into the deepest deep thereof and of that general and steadfast opinion which all the world hath conceived of your many rare gifts? Nay, who, good God, could see you, could

bespeak you, could hear you discourse, could consider
your well-ordered actions, your modesty, your urbanity,
your goodness, your mansuetude, without fire or simulation,
all pure, candid, native and proper to yourself, and note
how moderately you govern the peoples subjected to you,
how just and clement you are, and how in your every
action, whether grave or pleasant, you show yourself worthy
of all praise, without becoming your slave, bounden with
the lovesome and adamantine chains of your infinite courtesy
and of the many other precious qualities which continually
bud and wax in you anew? Certes, methinketh, no one.
But I suffer myself be carried away by the splendour of
your virtues to say that whereof Cicero or Demosthenes,
those clear-shining lights of Greek and Roman eloquence,
did they yet live, would doubtless confess that the most
learned and eloquent tongue, seeking to say that which
behoveth, would abide mute. Be it pardoned me, then,
of the clemency which showeth in you as a ruby in gold,
if, presuming to discourse of your sublime and royal
excellence, I attain not to the level of the truth. Nay, who
might suffice to speak of things divine? Who can express
the greatness of the splendour of the sun and show how he
shineth? Serenest king, whoso can avail to number and
show forth unto others the sands of the sea and the stars
of the sky, whenas it is most serene, may haply suffice to
discover to the folk how great is the dignity and worth
of your singular graces and rare virtues. Since, then, I
suffice not to make manifest to the world the height and
excellence of the gifts bestowed on you by God and nature,
I will content myself with notifying unto whoso is not
more than blind that the sublimity of your graces and
virtues overpasseth the power of human wit to expound ;
wherefore it behoveth that all bow down before you and

adore you, as a thing divine and beyond all belief rare and most admirable. Now, so that these my few uncultured words may not appear empty before your sacred tribunal, meseemeth not unmeet to send you therewith a brief anecdote of a most generous action, whereby Maximilian Cæsar (whose honoured name you bear and who was your paternal forefather), dealing magnificently and with infinite courtesy, exemplified unto the world how ever laudable is urbanity and courtesy in great personages and how well [in particular] it becometh exalted princes. But among the thousand memorable actions of the said Maximilian Cæsar, this was peradventure the least of those pertaining unto his moral dealings, according to that which is related by the trumpeter of your honours, the aforesaid Messer Filippo Baldo, who, whereassoever he findeth himself, is never weary of proclaiming them. Vouchsafe, then, most invincible king, to accept this little gift which I send you, having for the nonce nothing by me worthy of your exalted rank. In this I do as did a poor man, who, seeing many great gifts brought unto Artaxerxes and having no otherwhat to give, ran to the neighbouring river and filling both his hands with water, blithely presented it to the king. The magnanimous monarch took it with a blithe countenance, having regard to the giver's intent and not to the meanness of the gift. So poor folk, who cannot honour our Lord God with incense and Sabæan odours, adorn His sacrosanct and venerable altars with festoons and green leaves.[1] May He prosper all your thoughts ; and so, humbly commending myself unto your good graces, I with all reverence kiss your royal hands.

[1] Bandello, "Con feste e verdi fronti," *quære* "Con *festoni* e verdi *frondi*" ?

THE MEMORABLE DEALING OF MAXIMILIAN CÆSAR WITH A POOR COUNTRYMAN WHOM HE ENCOUNTERED WHILST HUNTING IN ALMAINE.

Many things, most lovesome ladies and you, courteous youths, have to-day been said and told, all indeed goodly and agreeable ; wherefrom we may take example for our lives, availing ourselves of others' actions. But, since you will have me also discourse and tell you somewhat or useful or delectable, I, being on my way from Germany to Spain, will imitate the merchants, who, returning from Syria, bring back of the things of that country, and will show you somewhat of German wares. You must know, then, that men, through being unknown or ill-clad, fall whiles into parlous predicaments and oftentimes into cases ridiculous, as happened to Philopœmen the Megalopolitan, general of the Achaians and a man most eminent in the military art. He was to go sup at Megara at the house of a friend of his, and albeit he was used to carry many folk with him, he chose for the nonce to enter Megara all alone, betaking himself to his friend's lodging, where great preparation was toward. The master of the house was abroad and his wife was busied in preparing the banquet. She, seeing Philopœmen and knowing him not, took him for one of the general's servants and said to him, "Thou comest in good season ;

take this hatchet and split me yonder logs;" whereupon Philopœmen, without saying a word, put off his cloak and fell to work. Presently, in came the master of the house, who, seeing the general engaged in splitting wood, was all amazed and said, "Marry, Philopœmen, what dost thou?" To which he answered blithely, "What else thinkest thou, but that I pay the penalty of the meanness of my dress?" Well-nigh on like wise was Maximilian Cæsar entreated, who, as is known, marvellously delighted in the chase, an exercise much extolled by Xenophon, who held that the Grecian soldiers became robust and doughty of their persons by the assiduous practice of hunting; and Pliny the Younger infinitely commended Trajan for that he exercised himself in the chase.

Maximilian Cæsar, then, being one day a-hunting with his men in that part of the Tyrol which bordereth upon Bavaria, suffered himself to be carried away in pursuit of a stag and chased it a good while; but, whether it was that he was better mounted than the others or that the courtiers followed him not with diligence, he outwent them all and fared on so far into the forest that he could no longer hear the horns of his followers nor might he have been heard of them, had he winded his own. Meanwhile, the stag gained upon him till he lost sight of it nor could see any trace nor track whereby he might follow it; and so, wandering in those thick woods, he came at the last to a very wide and open champaign. Here he found a poor man, who had laden his horse with faggots which he had cut in the wood, but the load had by mishap fallen to the ground and the good man was toiling ruefully to reload it. Maximilian saw that he laboured in vain and that he would have great difficulty in reloading the beast without aid; and after he had stood awhile looking upon him, he accosted him and asked him where he was and if there was a village near at hand. The good man, who had never belike seen the emperor, turned to him and nowise recognizing him, told him what he knew of the place ; then, with a piteous gesture, he said to him, "Sir, you would do me a great courtesy to aid me a little, so I may avail to make this fallen load fast on my horse's back and go about my business." The emperor, who was naturally the finest gentleman in the world and born to complease all nor ever vex any, hearing the countryman's piteous and urgent appeal and seeing that he toiled without avail, answered him not a word, but dismounting forth-right, made his horse fast by the reins to the branch of a tree. Now he was tall and well-proportioned of his person and of a truly imperial aspect, whose native good-ness and more than Cæsarean liberality all the writers who speak of him and all who have conversed with him supremely commend, for that he never closed his hand against whoso had recourse to him ; but, whenas he went a-hunting, he donned certain mean habiliments of hodden gray homespun, and albeit he was a very handsome prince, this his hunting dress nowise added grace to him. The countryman took him for some huntsman of those parts, who had happened there by chance, and seeing him dismount and prepare to lend him aid, said to him, all rejoiced, "Sir, hold fast here, set your shoulders under the pack, give me yonder rope, slacken it a little, lift yonder faggot, push it forward, do this and do that," ordering him neither more nor less than as he had been one of his peers. The good emperor did all that the countryman bade him and aided him with a cheerful countenance, so that whoso saw him, not knowing him, had deemed him the other's fellow or serving-man, so punctually did he obey him.

Meanwhile, the courtiers and other gentlemen, who had followed the emperor to the chase and had gone a pretty while seeking him, began to arrive by fours and fives and seeing him thus engaged, dismounted all, full of the utmost wonderment, and did him reverence, bonnet in hand; but he signed to them not to stir nor would have a man of them lay hand to the burden. The countryman, seeing all who came up reverently incline themselves to Maximilian, bethought himself that this must be the emperor, of whom he had oftentimes heard that he was a great lover of the chase; wherefore, falling on his knees before him, he craved him pardon for his overweening. The emperor bade the good man arise and asked him who he was; whereupon he told him, in a trembling voice, that he was a poor countryman, with a wife and children, and that, by the sale of the faggots which he made and what his wife earned at spinning and washing clothes, they gained their living, but that they had no otherwhat in the world than that rouncey. "With God be it!" said Maximilian. "Wait a little;" and doffing his bonnet, threw into it what monies he had about him. Then, going, one by one, to all who were there with him, he would e'en have each give the poor man an alms; after which he gave him all the monies he had collected and said to him, "Do thou come visit me to-morrow at such a hostelry and look thou fail not." He then mounted to horse and departed with his people; whilst the countryman returned to his hut, rejoicing, and told his wife all. On the morrow, mindful of the emperor's injunction, he presented himself before Maximilian, who, after bespeaking him with many gracious words, let count out to him a great sum of Rhenish florins and assigned him divers privileges and exemptions,[1] confirming them in due form to himself and his successors. Wherefore the good man was able honourably to marry two daughters whom he had, and with the rest of the monies he bought certain lands which yielded him and his family a livelihood, so that it behoved him no longer go miserably toiling.

Goodly, indeed, was this compassionate courtesy and liberality of Maximilian and an apt example unto all the great, although imitated of few. In lighting down from his horse and aiding the needy countryman with a cheerful favour, he displayed an inexpressible urbanity and deserving of all praise, and in uplifting him with monies and privileges from his toilsome life, he discovered his truly imperial mind. To make an end of my little story, it is actions such as these that endear princes to their subjects, whenas they see them urbane and liberal, succouring these and those with a lavish hand and still rewarding the deserving; even as, on the contrary, tyrannical and wicked dealings render the said princes odious to their peoples, their wretched subjects seeing themselves all day long, without any manner of need, oppressed with the most grievous extortions. Moreover, whenas need betideth for the defence and conservation of the State, the prince who hath justly governed his subjects hath not to fear lest they should rebel against him and abandon him, seeking a new lord, but still findeth them steadfast and disposed to put all their means at his service ; nay, he plainly perceiveth that they are nowise chary of venturing their very lives for his preservation ; wherefore it may with truth be concluded that one of the best and surest fortresses that a well-instructed prince can have is the love and goodwill of his people.

---

[1] *i.e.* from taxation.

Bandello

to the right illustrious and reverend seignior
Signor Ettore Fregoso.

We passed the late carnival-time at Bassens on such wise
as consorted with the gravity and gentilesse of madam your
loving and honoured mother, taking such innocent pleasures
and lawful diversions as the season and the place afforded
us.   There were with us sundry Italian gentlemen, whose
converse gave us blithe and joyous disport, they being never
at a loss for pleasant and merry discourse; so that there
were many very goodly stories told, which were written
down by me, according as they were related.   Amongst
others, Filippo Baldo, who is more abounding in stories
and anecdotes than is a lush and seasonable Spring in various
flowers and new herbage, told us a story of a lion, which
seemed a marvellous thing unto all, especially to certain
dames and damsels of the neighbourhood who chanced to
be in company with us.   And it being debated whence it
might proceed that a lion should suffer a lap-dog be taken
from his clutches by a young girl, many things were recounted of the nature of lions, all in truth notable and
marvellous.   It seemed a strange thing that the lion, who
is the king of fourfooted beasts, should so greatly fear the
crowing of the cock and should flee from so small and

unarmed a bird, even as doth the simple lamb from the
ravening wolf; and especially, according to Albertus Magnus,
will he be overwhelmed with terror and unable to brook the
aspect of the cock, if it be white. Moreover, he cannot
endure the noise of cart-wheels and greatly abhorreth fire;
so that he will never draw near whoso beareth fire in hand;
and yet he is a very fierce and strong animal, but, for all
his fierceness, he is the most generous of known beasts;
nay, it seemeth cunning Nature hath given him understanding and an inclination to hearken and apprehend the
prayers of those who prostrate themselves before him and
crave him mercy, as Pliny telleth of the Captive of Getulia,[1]
who in the woods with soft and humble prayers appeased
the fury of many lions. Indeed, he alone among wild beasts
useth clemency with suppliants and above all those deal most
generously who have long tawny manes on the neck and
over the shoulders, the which is only the case with those
who are engendered of lions and lionesses: for that, if a
leopard getteth a lioness with young, the lion born thereof
will never have hair upon his neck or shoulders. These
mixtures of various sorts of animals betide for the most part
in Africa, for that continent is not over-abundant in water;
wherefore various kinds of beasts assemble to drink where
there is water and there, urged by heat of lust, they
couple together and engender strange and monstrous births.
Hence the common saying among the Greeks, "Africa still
bringeth some new thing;" the which Aristotle usurped in
his treatise of the generation of animals and Anaxillas on

---

[1] "Captivam certè Gætuliæ reducem audivi multorum in silvis
impetum a se mitigatum alloquio, ausam dicere se feminam profugam
infirmam, supplicem animalis omnium generosissimi ceterisque im-
peritantis, indignam ejus gloriâ prædam."—C. Plin. Sec. Hist. Nat.
Lib. viii. 19.

like wise alludeth thereto in the fourth book of Athenæus.[1] It was also related that, when lions wax old and their natural powers fail them for age, so that they are unable to hunt and procure them their livelihood of the flesh of other animals, they greatly desire to feed upon human flesh ; wherefore Pliny writeth that such multitudes of old lions have bytimes gathered themselves together that they have laid siege to cities and that the Africans, to raise the siege, have gotten them one or two lions and hanged them upon the public gallows, whence it ensued that the other lions, for fear of such a punishment, gave over the siege.[2] Ultimately, it was told that, if the lion chance to be roused to anger against a man and a woman, he will vent his fury upon the male and will wreak blood-revenge upon him, rather than upon the female, and that he never harmeth little children, except extreme rage of hunger, he finding nothing whereon to feed, urge and goad him ; nay, unenforced of hunger, he doth hurt unto no one. In fine, he was most marvellously commended for the generosity, the clemency and the gratitude which (as many writers testify) he useth towards those who do him kindness, and it was therefore, after many things said, concluded that the lion had forborne to harm the girl, as well of his natural inclination to clemency and generosity as also for that his nature moveth him to have more com-

[1] *i.e.* of "the Deipnosophists" of that author, in which Anaxillas is one of the interlocutors.

[2] "Polybius Æmiliani comes in senectam hominem appeti ab iis refert, quoniam ad persequendas feras vires non superant; tunc obsidere Africæ urbes : eâque de causâ crucifixos vidisse se cum Scipione, quia ceteri metu poenæ similis absterrerentur eadem noxâ."—C. Plin. Sec. Hist. Nat. Lib. viii. 18. Cf. the terrible scene of the crucified lions in Salammbo.

passion upon the female sex, as the weaker, than upon the
male. Now, if nature teacheth so fierce and strong a beast
to be generous and clement, how should it be with a man
capable of reason ? Marry, this same virtue of clemency
is in truth ever laudable and commendable, the which is
none other than a temperance of the mind in abstaining
from vengeance, or, let us say, a mildness and mansuetude
on the part of the superior in determining the pains and
chastisements to be awarded unto delinquents. Nor must
you deem withal that severity[1] is anywise contrary thereto,
for that there can be no discord nor contrariety between
virtues. Contrary indeed unto clemency is the vice of
cruelty, the which is a bestial atrocity of the mind in desiring
the chastisement of errors in excess of that which natural
reason dictateth and making the penalty infinitely overpass
the sin ; a thing in sooth which savoureth more of the beast
than of the man. Wherefore, for that anger oftentimes
usurpeth our mind on such wise that no curb may be put
thereon and so blindeth it that it suffereth it not to discern
the truth, it useth to be said that an angry man should never
chastise a delinquent, what while anger predominateth in
him and inflameth him, inasmuch as he might not then avail
to hold the needful mean between the more and the less.
This have I chosen to say, Signor Ettore mine, so that in
all your actions you may strive to be mild, clement and
benign and to acquire the habit of this holy virtue, which
rendereth us like unto our Saviour, who biddeth us " Learn
of Me, for I am meek and lowly,"[2] the which is no otherwhat than to be clement and pitiful. And if it well beseem
every one to use clemency towards delinquents, methinketh

---

[1] *Severità*, i.e. strict justice.
[2] Matt. xi. 29.

it best beseemeth the clergy, especially those who are reared
and bred to become prelates and to have the governance of
many. Of the number of these latter are you, who, in a
little while hence, by your lady mother's diligence and with
the aid of your own merit, applying as you do, to good
letters, cannot, as you know, fail of this honourable bishoprick of Agen,[1] which is presently in keeping for you. Be
careful, then, to form a good habit in all the moral virtues
and especially in this so belauded quality of clemency, so
it may not after be lightly done away from you, and be
assured that it is a far lesser evil to sin in the matter of
overmuch mansuetude, pity and clemency than to be an
over-rigorous observer of justice, the which oftentimes
maketh us fall into cruelty, a vice altogether displeasing
unto mankind and to our Saviour, who is not only alien
therefrom, but hath (as daily experience teacheth us) for
His especial nature to be pitiful and to pardon those who
sin, so but they be heartily penitent. Woe unto us, indeed,
if in God, albeit He is justice itself, mercy overabounded not!
The which should be a lesson unto every one, and especially
unto those who have the charge of governance. It is, then,
a most praiseworthy thing to be clement unto whoso falleth
into any error and humbly craveth pardon ; wherefore I am
fain to believe that those two lines engraven in marble in
Campidoglio were set there to none other end than to
admonish magistrates to use clemency. They were in Latin

---

[1] Bandello was, in 1550, appointed to the bishoprick in question, as
" warming-pan " for Ettore Fregoso, his pupil and a son of his patron
Cesare Fregoso, on the understanding that Ettore, who had been
brought up for the church, should receive half the revenue of the
see. Ettore, however, appears to have predeceased Bandello, as we
find the latter succeeded (circa 1561) by Giano Fregoso, another son
of Cesare.

and their meaning in our mother-tongue is as follows: "Thou who art angry, remember that the wrath of the noble lion scorneth to wreak cruelty upon whoso is prostrate before him." Now let us see that which was told us of the lion in a brief, but truly admirable story. Fare you well and be mindful of me.

The Eight-and-Thirtieth Story.

THE CLEMENCY OF A LION TOWARDS A GIRL, WHO TOOK A DOG OUT OF HIS CLAWS, WITHOUT SUFFERING ANY MANNER OF HURT.

Alexander Farnese, Cardinal of Holy Church and nephew of Pope Paul III., who is lately passed to the other life, sent a few years agone to give Ferdinand, King of the Romans (amongst many rare things) sundry lions and tigers, which were graciously accepted by him and passed through Germany, to the amazement of the inhabitants, such beasts being unknown in that country. King Ferdinand, after he had kept them some days at his court and sated the country-folk with the sight of them, bethought himself to send them into Bohemia and without giving over-much delay to his intent, bade carry them thither. As they fared on their way, all the people flocked to see the unaccustomed sight, for that all new things commonly beget admiration and are gladly seen of all, be they goodly or foul; wherefore the conductors were well-nigh perforce constrained to halt in every place through which they passed, all taking the greatest pleasure in viewing these wild beasts which they had never before seen ; and so they came at last to Bohemia and halted in a city, where all the folk crowded to see the unwonted animals. Now there was in that city a gentlewoman, who had herself reared one of those little lapdogs you wot of, very handsome and agreeable, the which was beyond measure dear to her and she well-nigh always carried it in her arms. It chanced that a waiting-damsel of hers, hearing the report of the strange beasts and seeing all flock to look upon them, ran thither in company of others, with the little dog in her arms ; which her mistress seeing, she began to chide her and bade her leave the dog at home and woe to her if harm befell it ; but the girl, impatient to see the beasts, went off with the dog in her arms. When she came where there was a lion, whether it was that she was full of wonderment and in a manner beside herself or whatever was the cause thereof, the dog slipped from her arms and ran into the clutches of the lion, which took it and held it, but did it no manner of harm. The girl was like to die for dolour and dismay, remembering her of her mistress's threats (who, as she knew, loved the dog over all) and fearing to be cruelly beaten of her ; wherefore, without tarrying to take thought and made fearless by desperation, she went boldly up to the lion, to the stupefaction of all who saw her, and took the lapdog out of his claws, whilst he made no more motion to attack her than as he were a silly sheep ; the which gave all much cause for talk and there were many who attributed it to the girl's virginity and the lion's natural clemency. It sufficeth me to tell the thing as it was ; I leave it to you to enquire into the cause of this his mansuetude.

Bandello

to his nephew the magnificent Messer Gian Michele Bandello.

Women in general are used, when taken at unawares, to have answers ready, according to the circumstance, and to provide, on the spur of the moment, whatsoever the case requireth; and this being vouchsafed them of nature, it may not be doubted but that those will be the most quick-witted and provident who have had most experience of the world. And what women have to do with a greater diversity of brains than the courtezans of the court of Rome? Thither still flock all the goodliest and loftiest wits of the world, Rome being the common fatherland of all; there flourish good letters of all kinds, as well Latin and Greek as Italian; there be excellent jurisconsults, consummate philosophers, both natural and moral; there are wonder-goodly painters to be seen and sculptors who hew out live faces in marble and founders who cast what they will in metal. Brief, not to recount the arts, one by one, they are all in perfection there, so that whoso would fain make himself proficient in any manner of accomplishment goeth to learn at Rome. And for that (as saith the ingenious Sulmonese [1]) it happeneth often enough that one

---

[1] *i.e.* Ovid, who was born at Sulmo (*hod.* Sulmona) in the Abruzzi.

same soil produceth the rose and the nettle, so also at
Rome there are men good and ill. But, to leave the rest,
I will speak of the women of pleasure, who, to give some
little colour of decency to their trade, have usurped to
themselves this title of courtezans.[1] They are all in general
greedier of money than flies of honey and if there fall some
new-fledged youth into their clutches, who is not more
than [commonly] quick-witted and wary, I warrant you
they shave him to the quick, without a razor, and make
a skeleton of him. Now, it being devised, in a worshipful
company of many gentlemen at Milan, of certain courtezans
and their fashions, Captain Gian Battista Olivo, a very merry
and affable man, related a circumstance betided at Rome,
the which I, having committed it to writing, according as
it was told of him, am minded shall be yours; and so I
send and give it unto you, all that is mine being yours.
Fare you well.

[1] *Cortigiane*, lit. "she-courtiers."

ISABELLA DA LUNA, A SPANISH COURTEZAN, TURNETH THE TABLES UPON ONE WHO THOUGHT TO FLOUT HER.

Whoso should offer to make a catalogue of the things which courtezans do, whereassoever they are to be found, would methinketh have overmuch to do ; nay, whenas he thought to have finished, there would still remain as much again to say. But let us come to some particular act and relate somewhat of these barberesses' tricks. Amongst others at Rome there is one called Isabella da Luna, a Spaniard, who hath explored half the world. She went to La Goletta and to Tunis,[1] to succour the needy soldiers, lest they should die of hunger ;[2] moreover, she for a time followed the Emperor's court all through Almaine and Flanders and divers other places, never wearying of lending out her horse on hire, so but she were required thereof. Ultimately, she returned to Rome, where she is holden by those who know her for the quickest-witted and wiliest wench was ever there. She is of the utmost entertainment in a company of men of whatsoever degree ; for that she knoweth to accommodate herself unto all and to give each his own. She is

---

[1] *i.e.* she followed the army of the Emperor Charles V. as a courtezan, on his expedition against Tunis in 1535.

[2] The "hunger" here referred to is of course the "concupiscible appetite."

very sprightly, affable and quick-witted and exceeding
ready at repartee. She speaketh Italian passing well and
if she be attacked, you must not think that she is
abashed or that she is at a loss for words to requite
whoso girdeth at her; for that she hath a biting tongue
and hath regard unto no one's quality, but with her
stinging speech layeth about her at random; more by
token that she is so boldfaced and presumptuous that
she engageth to make all she will blush, without herself
changing colour.

Now there are presently in Rome certain of our Mantuan
gentlemen, very accomplished and gallant, and amongst them
Messer Roberto Strozzi and Messer Lelio and Messer Ippolito Capilupi, brothers. Messer Roberto abideth in Rome
for his diversion and Messer Ippolito is entertained there
for the affairs of our most illustrious and reverend Cardinal
of Mantua. They all three lodge in one house, but each
liveth apart at his own charge. Withal they mostwhiles
eat in company, each bearing his share, and so they
lead a blithe and joyous life. With them there are oftentimes divers others to be found, for that they are merry
companions and there is still playing and singing toward
in their lodging and discourse of letters, as well Latin
as vernacular, and of other matters of art, so that they
never suffer the time to hang heavy upon their hands.
Amongst those who commerced very familiarly with these
gentlemen and oftentimes ate with them was one Rocco
Biancalana, who passed for the agent of a very illustrious
and reverend cardinal and who, having been long in
Rome and being a merry man and no less sharp-spoken
than Isabella, was all day long at war with her in words.
On this same Isabella, who was also frequently to be
found with the gentlemen aforesaid, Messer Roberto was,

as the saying is, a little "gone"[1] and saw her full
fain ; but between her and Rocco there was a perpetual
war and they contended together which should be the
more evil-spoken, the more venomous and the more presumptuous, so that they were still at daggers drawn.
Wherein these gentlemen, seeing the promptness of repartee
of both and the outrageous revilements which they cast
one at other, took marvellous pleasure, and often, the
more to enkindle them to berate each other, egged them
on, as folk do dogs. In short, between Luna and Lana
there was a bitter enmity, Rocco being unable to brook
that so notorious and shameless a whore, who had gotten
more buffs in her life than there be flowers in the spring,
should consort with those gallant spirits, and he very
often chid Messer Roberto thereof.

Now the illustrious and reverend cardinal, who entertained Rocco at Rome, having belike to treat of affairs
of very great moment, despatched thither one Messer
Antonio Romeo, a man of exceeding capacity and apt to
treat the most difficult and intricate affairs, how embroiled
soever they might be ; nay, in effect, he had been a complete
man, but for a blot which altogether marred him, for that
he was out of measure niggard and miserly. When he came
to Rome, Rocco lost somewhat of his standing, for that
he abode subject to Romeo and undertook but so much
as was enjoined him of the latter and no more, so that
it seemed he was rather Romeo's agent than the cardinal's,
and abode in one house with him, and that not as a companion, but well-nigh as a servant. There was nought irked
Rocco more than Romeo's miserliness, the which was so

[1] *Guasto*, i.e. enamoured. It is curious that the old Italian idiom
should so exactly correspond to our modern slang expression.

fashious to him that he would, at the first opportunity, have (as it is used to say) left his cardinal in the lurch and engaged with others, though they had been private people and of no condition; for that he savoured amain of the parasite and would still have had the table full. In this his miscontentment, he was often to be found at dinner and supper with the aforesaid gentlemen and there vented his spleen, missaying of Messer Antonio's extreme avarice ; nor did he reck of Isabella's presence. He would say, to wit, that the bread was bought so stale that it might neither be chewed nor cut with a knife, that it was mouldy and that Messer Antonio very often let 'bake it anew, alleging that it dried up the rheum ; that he watered the wine, ere it came to table, with such a lavish hand that whoso had a thousand wounds in the head might have drunken thereof; that there was no other flesh-meat seen on the table than beef, the which had furnished three or four soups, ere it was set on ; that there was a knuckle [of ham] which had been more than twenty times at table, without being touched by any, for that it was a bare bone without meat, and that it sprang on the board of itself,[1] so soon as the table was set. Moreover, he declared that the cheese was all mite-eaten and marred and that the fruit was bought unripe and came five and six times to table ; and all this he said without any reserve nor recked if he were heard of all.

It chanced one day that ill words passed between him and Isabella and they came to such a pitch that Rocco said to her that, but for his respect for Messer Roberto, he would have told her things would make her blush. "And what canst thou say to me," quoth Isabella, "save

---

[1] Meaning apparently that it was alive with maggots.

that I am a whore? That is known already, nor shall I
blush for that." Rocco, heated with choler, engaged to
pay a sumptuous and magnificent supper, wherein, beside
other meats, there should be two brace of pheasants, so but
she would suffer him tell, in her presence, all the infamies
he knew of her; whereupon they agreed for the following
Thursday. Meantime, though he already knew ribaldries
galore of her fashion, Rocco learned from many who knew
her great store of other things, whereof, so they should not
escape his memory, he wrote a long memorial on three
sheets of paper. He was a fine writer and had written
down everything in the goodliest order. The appointed
evening come, Messer Antonio Romeo, who had heard of
the thing and chanced to be somewhat indisposed of his
person, betook himself to the Mantuan gentlemen's lodging,
to divert himself with the dispute which should ensue.
They were all with Isabella in a saloon about the fire, and
Rocco, clapping his hand to his memorial, said to her,
"Brazen-faced strumpet that thou art, for the nonce I will
make thee not only blush, but burst." At this she waxed
somewhat melancholy and said, "Is it possible, Rocco,
that thou wouldst have me dead? Let us sup in peace and
after supper thou shalt read thy bill of arraignment." "No,
no," replied Rocco; "I will have the supper seem to thee
bitterer than gall."

Isabella, seeing that he was e'en resolved to read ere they
supped, prayed the gentlemen do her the favour to let her
read at the least the first sheet of that which Rocco had
written, promising not to depart nor to tear or burn the
writing, but, having read the first sheet, to return it to him.
Her request seemed reasonable enough and all therefore
urged Rocco to complease her, which he did. When she
had the scroll in hand, she read eight or ten lines thereof to

herself and presently said, "Hearken, gentlemen, and you shall hear if there were ever in the world a more scurrilous tongue than this of Rocco's." Then, whenas she should have read the ill set down of herself, feigning not to know that Romeo was there, she punctually repeated all that Rocco had from time to time said in blame of the said Romeo, censuring with sharp words the latter's niggardliness. It seemed, indeed, as if she read that which she said from the scroll; and when she had said enough, she folded up the writing and said, "How deem you, gentlemen, of this scurril knave? Seemeth it not to you he deserveth a thousand gibbetings? I know not this Romeo, but I understand that he is a very well bred person and that he liveth very civilly in his house; yet this knave shameth not to missay of a man of worth and one in whose house he hath his living. Look, now, an he be a sorry rogue." Rocco was altogether taken aback and knew not what to say, but went off without taking leave, as also did Romeo, who knew all that had been said of his miserliness to be true; so that neither the one nor the other tasted of the supper prepared; wherefore it was said that Rocco had, as the saying is, made soup for the cats. Those who remained supped and laughed amain with Isabella for that she had so featly contrived to befool Rocco and save herself.

Bandello

to the most debonair seignior Signor Angelo
dal Bufalo.

We being, as you know, these days past at Casalmaggiore,
which castlewick the illustrious princess, the Lady Antonia
Bauzia, Marchioness of Gonzaga, hath boughten of the Most
Christian King with the monies of her dowry, she there held
the sumptuous nuptials of her most charming daughter, the
Lady Camilla Gonzaga, with the Marquess of La Tripalda,
of the honoured and royal family of the Castriots, who have
for many centuries ruled over Epirus. There were the
bride's three brothers, three truly magnanimous noblemen,
Signor Lodovico di Sabionetta, Signor Federico di Bozolo
and that exemplar of all goodness and lovingkindness,
Signor Pirro di Gazuolo, together with an honourable
company of many lords and gentlemen. And for that the
heat was excessive, we all, after dinner, betook ourselves
to a great ground-floor saloon, very cool for the season or,
at the least, much less warm than the other rooms, where
a very goodly discourse was entered upon of the liberality
and magnificence of certain great princes, and especially of
those who, having their arch-enemies in their power, have
not only forgiven them and granted them their lives, but
have replaced them in the realms and dominions they had
lost or lent them aid to recover them. From the ancients

they came to the moderns and Filippo Maria Visconti, third Duke of Milan, was supremely commended of all, for that, having Alfonso of Arragon and other kings, together with many princes, barons and gentlemen, under his hand as prisoners, he not only forbore to exact any ransom from them, but let honourably lodge each according to his degree and entertained them many days at sumptuous and Lucullian banquets, giving them all possible diversion by way of sports and festivals ; then he let them freely return home and helped Alfonso to recover the kingdom of Naples. No less was Lorenzo de' Medici, the father of Pope Leo X., who ruled the Florentine Commonwealth with such wisdom and glory and moderation, marvellously celebrated for that which he did with Ferdinand the Old of Arragon, King of Naples, who, having made a league with Pope Sixtus IV., to oust him from the governance of Florence, levied a great army, wherewith he attacked Tuscany and occupied many castles and strong places of that province, whilst Alfonso, Duke of Calabria, by practice and the aid of certain citizens, entered Siena with part of the army and proceeded to wage war upon the Florentines. Lorenzo, seeing himself abandoned of the Venetians and having no succour from Milan, by reason of the death of Duke Galeazzo Sforza and the discord which prevailed between the governors of the infant duke, resolved, after pondering many expedients for the salvation of his fatherland, to go himself in person (since his enemies declared they sought no otherwhat than that he, Lorenzo, should not govern,) to Naples to visit Ferdinand. Accordingly, having taken such order as himseemed best for the governance of Florence [during his absence,] he dropped down the Arno to Pisa and thence, taking a brigantine, sailed to Naples, where he arrived, after a prosperous voyage, and landing, repaired, without delay, to the castle.

He found King Ferdinand in hall with his barons and making him due obeisance, said to him, "August king, I am Lorenzo de' Medici, who am come to thy presence, as to a most just tribunal, and beseech thee to vouchsafe me a favourable audience." Ferdinand was filled with extreme amazement at the name of Lorenzo de' Medici and could not conceive how he should have dared to come to him thus unprovided and without safe conduct or other assurance in hand; nevertheless, moved by I know not what, he received him urbanely and withdrawing with him to a window, bade him say what he chose, for that he would hearken to him patiently. Now the great Lorenzo was not only versed in various kinds of knowledge, but was a fine speaker and very eloquent; and he accordingly propounded his case to the king on such wise and knew so featly to possess him of his arguments that, they having sundry times discussed the affairs of Italy and Lorenzo having debated of the humours of the various princes and peoples of the country and of that which was to be hoped from peace and feared from war, Ferdinand marvelled more than before at his magnanimity and subtlety of wit and at the gravity and soundness of his judgment and accounted him of the notablest men of Italy; wherefore he concluded in himself rather to let him go as a friend than to detain him as an enemy. Accordingly, he entertained him awhile about his person and studied to gain him to himself with all manner of kindness and every show of love, so that there ensued a perpetual accord between them for the common conservation of their estates; and thus Lorenzo, an he had departed Florence great, returned thither most great. On the other hand, even as Duke Filippo and Ferdinand had been commended, so on the contrary Louis XII. was censured for the little liberality which he used towards Lodovico Sforza, whom he let die in prison. At this discourse was present Messer Bartolommeo Bozzo, a Genoese, who, to the purpose of that which was in debate, related a goodly history betided in our time, the which, for that meseemed it was worthy of memory and little known among the Latins, I committed to writing. Then, bethinking me to whom I should give it, you straightway occurred to my mind, as one of the most courteous and liberal gentlemen whom I know at this present; and for that, of the long commerce we have had together, I know you for an enemy to ceremony, I will say no otherwhat to you. This story, then, I dedicate and consecrate to your name and so make a beginning of effectual acknowledgment for the many courtesies and kindnesses received from you.

The Fortieth Story.

MAHOMET, SEIGNIOR OF DUBDU IN AFRICA, OFFERETH TO TAKE A CITY FROM SAICH, KING OF FEZ, WHEREUPON THE LATTER BESIEGETH HIM IN DUBDU AND USETH EXCEEDING GREAT LIBERALITY WITH HIM.

Your talk, sirs, moveth me to tell you, to the purpose of the courteous dealings of the duke and the king, a story which befell in Africa, what time I trafficked in those parts. I have frequented all the African kingdoms and provinces for at the least twenty years and methinketh there are few cities but I have seen them and noted many of their customs; and amongst other things, I have found by experience a very great courtesy and loyalty in the African merchants.

Moreover, the commerce with the gentlemen of the country is very sure, inasmuch as they are for the most part worthy and well-bred folk and live very civilly and dress elegantly after their fashion. Indeed, I must confess to you that I have in many parts of Africa found far more lovingkindness and charity than (and it shameth me to say it) among Christians. The natives observe the Mahometan law far better than we Christians our own and are for the most part great almsgivers and loyal performers of all contracts made with them. This that I say I say of the most part, for that even amongst these there be found rogues and over-reachers, especially among the Arabs, who are scattered all over the country. Now, to come to that which I purpose to tell you, you must know that, not far from the great kingdom of Fez, is an ancient city called by the Arabs Dubdu, seated upon a high hill and abounding in very cool fountains, which run through the place for the use and commodity of the inhabitants. Of this city sundry gentlemen of the family of the Beni Guertaggien[1] have long been and are yet seigniors. When the house of Marino,[2] which lost the kingdom of Fez, was well-nigh destroyed, the Arabs made every endeavour to occupy Dubdu; but Musé Ibnù Cammù,[3] who was the seignior thereof, defended himself so stoutly that he constrained them to make certain conventions with him and to offer no farther molestation to the city nor to his other places. He, dying, left the seigniory of Dubdu to a son of his called Acmed,[4] very like

---

[1] *Benou Khurlejan?*

[2] *i.e.* the sovereigns of Morocco of the *Benou Merin* house, whose founder, Yacoub ibn Abdulhecc, in A.H. 678 expelled the Almohades from that country and established the third Berber or Merinide dynasty.

[3] *i.e.* Mousa ben Camin.   [4] *i.e.* Ahmed.

unto his father in fashions and valiance, who kept his domains in profound peace till his death. Acmed having no son, there succeeded him in the dominion a cousin of his named Mahomet, a youth of high spirit and doughty of his person, who excelled in the military art and conquered many cities and castles at the foot of Mount Atlas towards the meridian on the confines of Numidia. Moreover, he adorned Dubdu with many fine edifices and reduced it to more civility,[1] showing such great courtesy and hospitality to strangers and to those who passed therethrough, honouring all according to their merit and entertaining innumerable folk at his charge, that the report of his courtesies spread through all those parts. I myself once came thither in company of certain gentlemen of Fez and was lodged with my friends in his palace, where we were as honourably entreated as can be told, and the prince, understanding that I was a Christian and a Genoese, spoke with me awhile of the affairs of Italy and of our way of living, still using such urbanity towards all that it was a marvellous thing to see, and to myself in particular he made many offers of service.

Now, for that men are oftentimes unable to see or know their weal and wax blind in prosperity, and eke for that there is no greater plague in princes' courts than flattery, Mahomet took it into his head to occupy Teza, a city some five miles from Mount Atlas, belonging to the King of Fez. This conceit he imparted to sundry of his officers, who considering not the puissance and vast dominion of the King of Fez, with whom Mahomet was nowise to be evened, encouraged him with their vain

---

[1] _La ridusse a più civiltà_; i.e. brought it to a higher state of civilization.

adulations to attempt the emprise, and for that a great
corn-market is every week holden at Teza, whither flock
much people, especially mountaineers, they persuaded him
to attend this market in a mountaineer's habit and fall
upon the town-captain of the place with folk whom he
should carry with him, avouching to him that thus they
would without doubt take the city; for that a great part
of the inhabitants, hearing his name and seeing him
present, would rise up in his favour. However, the plot
came to the ears of Saich,[1] of the house of Quattas,[2]
King of Fez and father of the present king, who, understanding the peril that menaced Teza, let straightway
garrison the place and assembling a great army, went to
fall upon Mahomet, who, though taken by surprise, very
stoutly sustained the assault. As I have already told you,
Dubdu is seated upon a hill and is very strong by
position; wherefore the king's folk were once and again
repelled with great slaughter by the besieged. But
Saich reinforced his camp with many crossbowmen and
arquebusiers and did much hurt to the city, being resolved
not to desist from the emprise till he had made himself
master of the place and taken Mahomet prisoner. There
befell frequent skirmishes and in general those of the
city had the worst of it; which Mahomet seeing and
better considering his affairs, perceived that he had committed a great error in seeking to wage war upon the
King of Fez, with whom he might nowise be evened;
wherefore he pondered and repondered a thousand expedients to rid himself of the war and abide on good
terms with Saich and himseeming he could find none
which should avail him, he abode mighty disconsolate.

1 *i.e.* Saïc.   2 Khettas?

Ultimately, after long consideration, he bethought himself of a means whereby he hoped to find a way to his salvation, to wit, that he should put himself into Saich's hands and essay the latter's courtesy and mercy. Accordingly he wrote him a letter with his own hand and knowing that he knew him not, clad himself in a messenger's habit and betook himself, as an envoy from the Seignior of Dubdu, to the enemy's camp. Being admitted to the king's presence, he made him due obeisance and presented him with his letter, the which was credential.[1] The king, taking the letter, gave it to one of his secretaries and bade him read it, which being done in the presence of all there, the king turned to Mahomet, thinking him a messenger, and said to him, "Harkye, how deemest thou of thy master, who is waxen so arrogant that he hath dared to offer to make war upon me?" "Verily, O king," answered Mahomet, "meseemeth my master was a great fool to seek to molest thee, whom he should still entertain to his friend; but the devil hath power to beguile the great as well as the little and hath done away my master's wits and enforced him commit this monstrous folly." "Perdie," rejoined the king, "an I may win to have him in my hands (as without doubt I shall have him, for that he may not escape me,) I will give him such a chastisement that he shall abide a warning unto all not to take arms against their neighbours without just cause. I warrant thee I will let tear the flesh piecemeal from his bones and will keep him alive as long as I may, for his greater torment." Quoth Mahomet, "But an he came to thy feet and prostrating himself before thee, craved thee pardon of his follies and besought thee to have pity upon

---

[1] *La quale era credenziale*; i.e. was merely a letter certifying that the bearer was authorized to treat in the writer's name.

him, how wouldst thou entreat him?" Whereupon said the
king, "I swear by this my head that, an he showed himself
on this wise conscious of his mad error, I would not only
pardon him his offence against myself, but would, to boot,
make alliance with him, confirming him in his estate and
giving him two of my daughters in marriage to two sons
whom I understand he hath, with such a dowry as sorted
with my rank; but I cannot persuade myself that he will
ever consent to humble himself; so prideful and headstrong
is he!" Mahomet, hearing this, tarried not to answer, but
said, "All this will he do, so but thou certify him, in the
presence of the chief of thy court, that thou wilt keep thy
word with him." "Methinketh," rejoined the king, "that
these four may suffice him to witnesses who are here amongst
the rest, to wit my chief secretary, my captain-general of
cavalry, my father-in-law and the chief judge and high
priest of Fez." With this, Mahomet cast himself at the
king's feet and said, in a tearful voice, "King, behold, I
myself am the sinner and have recourse unto thy clemency."
The king raised him up with apt and courteous words
and lovingly embraced him; then, letting fetch his two
daughters, whilst Mahomet did the like with his sons, the
nuptials were celebrated with the utmost pomp. Thence-
forward Saich still had Mahomet to friend and kinsman,
as on like wise nowadays doth his son, who hath succeeded
his father in the kingship of Fez.

Bandello

to the most illustrious and accomplished lady the Lady Margherita Pia e Sanseverina.

The noble Signor Alessandro Bentivoglio and his consort
the Lady Ippolita Sforza, still to be mentioned with a
prefacement of honour, being this past August at their
country-seat near the Adda, were invited to go to Borghetto
on St. Bartholomew's Day, the titular festival of the place,[1]
which pertaineth to the Rò[2] family, an ancient and noble
house in Milan. There they were entertained with great
honour and passed the festival-day and the morrow in
pleasance and delight in company of many other gentlefolk.
On the second day, after dinner, the heat being very great,
for that the south wind blew, the company took refuge in a
great saloon of the palace there, which was very cool and
overlooked a vast and delightsome garden, with harbours
and trellises of such length that they had sufficed for the
exercising of whatsoever good horse. Here some talked
and some played at tables or chess, whilst othersome smote
upon instruments of music or sang; brief, each did what
most liked him, to while away the tedious midday season.

[1] Borghetto [di San Bartolommeo] is a small town of Lombardy,
situate between Pavia and Lodi.
[2] Sic; but *quære* rather *Rho*, which is the name of a celebrated
Milanese family?

As for the Lady Ippolita, she called the debonair and
well-conceited poet and doctor Messer Niccolo Amanio [1]
together with Messer Girolamo Cittadino and Messer
Tommaso Castellano her secretary, and would have me
make a fourth with these three most affable and learned
men; then, having in hand the divine poet Virgil and
reading many lines in the sixth book of the Eneid, she
fell to propounding very pregnant and ingenious questions
upon that which she read; after which, many and goodly
things having been said by herself and by the others, she
prayed Messer Niccolo Amanio to help with some story
blithely to while away the time which remained of the
hot season. Amanio excused himself amain; nevertheless,
seeing that Signora Ippolita accepted none of his excuses,
he told us the story of Antiochus and Stratonice, the which
I wrote down and bethought myself (it being so long since
I wrote you aught,) to send to you and put forth under
your name. I know that you, of your favour, gladly read
my toys; and so on like wise doth your accomplished
sister-in-law Signora Graziosa Pia; wherefore, when you
shall have read it, you will do me a pleasure by letting
the said Signora Graziosa see it. Fare you well, both
of you.

[1] See ante, Vol. I. p. 10, note.

The One-and-Fortieth Story.

SELEUCUS, KING OF ASIA,[1] GIVETH HIS WIFE TO HIS SON, WHO WAS ENAMOURED OF HER AND WHOSE PASSION HAD BEEN DISCOVERED BY A SKILLED PHYSICIAN WITH AN INGENIOUS DEVICE.

Albeit I had thought to-day to do anything rather than this of story-telling in such worshipful company, yet, to obey her who commandeth me, I will do as doth a gentleman, unto whom there cometh at eventide some dear friend to sup with him and who, knowing there is no flesh to be found at the shambles nor game for sale in the market-places, entertaineth his friend as best he may with the household poultry and salted meat. Marry, meknoweth not for the nonce where to provide me with a story, an I recur not to those which are daily in every one's hand; wherefore I purpose to tell one, of which our most accomplished Petrarch maketh mention in his Triumph of Love.[2] Wherefore do you deign to pardon me and hold

---

[1] Seleucus (Nikanor), the founder of the dynasty of the Seleucidæ, was one of the four generals of Alexander the Great between whom his empire was, after his death, divided. Syria fell to his share and he afterwards by conquest and other means became King of the greater part of Asia Minor.

[2] Cap. II. ll. 94–129.

me excused an I tell you no new thing, inasmuch as I put
before you that which I find in my hand. Accordingly,
not to keep you in suspense, you must know that Seleucus,
King of Babylonia,[1] a man who had laboured gloriously
in many battles and who was most fortunate among the
successors of Alexander the Great, had by a wife of his
a son, whom, in memory of his own father, he called
Antiochus. His wife died, but the lad grew up and gave
great promise of becoming a valiant youth and worthy of
such a father. When he was four-and-twenty years old,
it befell that his father Seleucus became enamoured of a
very fair damsel of high descent, by name Stratonice, and
taking her to wife, made her queen and had of her a son.
Antiochus, seeing his mother-in-law (who, over and above
her sovereign beauty, was exceeding sprightly and engaging)
every day, became, without showing any sign thereof, so
sore inflamed for her and fell so beyond all belief in love
with her that never was lover so enkindled for a woman.
Himseeming he did against natural right and reason in
wantonly loving his father's wife, he dared not discover
himself to friend or fellow; nay, he was ashamed of himself, far more of others; but, the more secretly he thought
of her, the more he became inflamed and went pining
and languishing from day to day; wherefore, feeling
himself gone so far that he could no more turn back,
he resolved to essay an he might by means of long and
toilsome travel avail to give some truce to his sufferings.
His father had many kingdoms and innumerable provinces
under his dominion; wherefore, alleging certain excuses of
his fashion, he got Seleucus his leave to go some months'
journey thereabout for his diversion; but no sooner had he

---

[1] See ante, p. 82, note.

left home than he found himself in sorry case, inasmuch as, being deprived of the sight of his fair Stratonice, him-seemed he was deprived of life. Nevertheless, intent, an it were possible, upon overcoming his obstinate passion, he abode some days abroad, during which time, burning as he did in secret and having none with whom to vent himself, he led a very sorry and disconsolate life. In the end, overcome by his sufferance, he returned to his father's court, where he daily saw her who was his only joy and his whole delight.

Knowing how his father loved and tendered his wife, he said many times in himself, "Am I Antiochus, son of Seleucus? Am I he whom his father so loveth, so mag-nificently honoureth and prizeth and esteemeth over all his realms? Woe's me, if I am he, where is the love and reverence which I owe him? Is this a son's duty towards a father? Wretch that I am, where have I set my mind, my hope and my love? Am I so blind and so senseless as not to feel that it behoveth me hold my fair stepmother in the stead of a very mother; and if it be so, (as indeed I know it is,) whom then do I love? What do I desire? What do I seek? What do I hope? Whither do I suffer myself be thus fondly carried away by blind and deceitful love and fallacious hope? See I not that these my desires, these my disorderly appetites and unbridled wishes savour of the dishonest? Marry, I do indeed see it and know that that which I go seeking is not seemly; nay, it is most dishonourable. And what blame should I not receive therefor, were this my unlawful love made public? Should I not rather choose death than ever anywise think to despoil my father of the wife whom he so loveth? I will, then, leave this shameful love and turning my mind elsewhither, act the part of a good and loving son towards my father."

Accordingly he resolved altogether to abandon that his
emprise; but scarce had he formed this design when the
thought of the lady's charms suddenly presented itself to
his mind and he felt himself wax anew so inflamed that,
repenting him of that which he had resolved, he craved a
thousand pardons of Love for having thought to abandon
so generous an emprise; wherefore, going back upon his
first reasoning, "How?" quoth he in himself. "Because
she is my father's wife, am I not to love her? Am I not
to follow after her, because she is my step-mother? Alack,
how fond is my thought! The laws which Love prescribeth
unto his followers are not like human laws and written;
nay, his laws override those both human and divine. When
he commandeth it, brother loveth sister, daughter father,
one brother another's wife and oftentimes stepmother
stepson; and an it be lawful unto others, why should it be
forbidden unto me? If unto my father, who is much more
advanced in years than I, it was not forbidden in his
old age to fall in love with this woman, why should
I, who am young and altogether subject to the flames
of love, be blamed for loving her? And if no otherwhat
be blameworthy in me than that I love one who chanceth
to be my father's wife, be fortune impeached, which hath
given her to my father rather than to another; for that
I love her and should love her, whosesoever she were,
since, sooth to say, such is her beauty and so gracious
and engaging her fashions and manners that she deserveth
to be revered, honoured and adored of all the world. Needs
must I, then, follow her and leave all else to serve her."

Thus the wretched lover, passing from one thought to
another nor abiding long in any and making mock of
himself, changed a thousand times an hour. Ultimately,
after long debate, giving place to reason, he concluded that

he could do no more unseemly thing than to love Stratonice; wherefore, unable to leave loving and resolved rather to die than ensue or discover unto others so unnatural a passion, he wasted away little by little, like snow in the sun, and losing sleep and appetite, sank into such weakness that for excess of chagrin he fell grievously sick and was constrained to take to his bed. His father, who loved him tenderly, was infinitely concerned at this and summoning Erasistratus, who was a most eminent physician and in exceeding great esteem with all, instantly besought him to take such diligent care of his son as behoved unto the gravity of his case. Erasistratus accordingly came and finding the young man's body sound in every part nor perceiving any ill sign in his urine or other symptom whereby he might be judged infirm of his person, concluded, after much debate, that his ailment was a disease or passion of the mind and such that he might lightly die thereof. This conclusion he imparted to Seleucus, who, loving Antiochus, as well because he was his child (for that children indeed are still loveable and bear with them a very great bond of affection) as also because of his singular virtues and qualities, was so aggrieved for this his infirmity and abode in such melancholy that greater might not be conceived. Now the prince was of his nature well bred and agreeable, valiant and doughty and comely of his person as any of his time, the which rendered him lovesome unto all.

His father was momently in his chamber and the queen on like wise visited him oftentimes and served him with her own hand, whenas he ate; whereof I know not, being no physician, an it profited him aught or whether belike it did him not more harm than good. Methinketh, indeed, he saw her full fain and would have had her

never depart his bed, setting as he did all his weal,
all his hope, all his peace and all his delight in her.
But after, he seeing so often before his eyes those charms
which he so much desired to enjoy, hearing her speak
for whom he pined and being fed and tended by her
hand whom he loved more than the apple of his eye
and to whom he had never dared proffer a prayer, meseemeth I may with reason believe that his dole overpassed
every other dole and that he languished without cease
therefor ; nay, who can doubt but that he, feeling himself
bytimes touched of those her daintiest hands and seeing
her sit beside him and whiles sigh for pity of him and
bid him with softest speech be comforted and tell her an
he would have aught, for that she would do all for the
love of him,—who can doubt, I say, but that he was racked
with a thousand conflicting thoughts and now hoped, now
despaired, yet still concluded rather to die than to discover
his ardent passion ? And if it be grievous unto all young
men, how mean and humble soever of condition they may
be, to leave life in their youth, what must we think of
Antiochus, who, being young and the son of so rich and
puissant a king and expecting, an he survived, to be heir
unto all after his father's death, elected voluntarily to die
for lesser ill.[1] Marry, methinketh indeed his dole was
infinite. Antiochus, then, torn with love, with hope,
with desire, with filial reverence and affection and a
thousand other conflicting sentiments, was like a ship
on the high seas, buffeted of contrary winds, and went
wasting little by little.

Erasistratus, seeing his body whole and free, but his mind
grievously sick and his soul altogether overcome with

[1] *Per minor male*, i.e. holding death a lesser ill than life.

passions, concluded in the end, after long debate in himself
over that extraordinary case, that the young man burned
for love and excessive desire and that this was the sole
cause of his malady and bethought himself that rage, hate,
despite, melancholy and other passions may lightly be both
simulated and dissembled by sage and prudent men, but
that love, an it be kept hidden, still harmeth more than
when made manifest; wherefore, albeit he could never learn
from Antiochus that he loved, nevertheless, having gotten
this conceit into his head, he determined, the better to
resolve himself, to abide still near him and with the utmost
diligence to observe all his actions, noting above all the
changes of his pulse and the circumstances under which it
varied. Accordingly, he seated himself by the prince's bed
and taking the latter's wrist, set his finger whereas the pulse
useth to make itself felt. At this moment, as chance would
have it, Queen Stratonice entered the chamber, whom
whenas the sick lover saw, his pulse, which abode depressed
and languid, awoke of a sudden and began to quicken and
gather strength with the mutation of the blood, as feeling
the feeble flame [of life] burn higher and stronger. Erasistratus felt this quickening of the pulse and to see how long
it should last, stirred not for the queen's coming, but still
kept his finger upon the prince's wrist. What while she
abode in the chamber, the pulse still beat quick and high,
but with her departure it returned to its wonted feebleness.
It was not long ere the queen returned and no sooner was
she seen of Antiochus than his pulse rose up anew and throb-
bing without cease, abode very strong; but, she presently
departing again, its vigour departed with her. The skilled
physician,[1] seeing such a change and that it befell but for

---

[1] *Il fisico gentile*, Petrarch's own phrase, *l.c.*

the queen's presence, thought to have found the cause of
Antiochus his infirmity, but chose to wait till the ensuing
day, that he might have greater certitude thereof, and
accordingly on the morrow he seated himself anew by the
prince's side and took his wrist in his hand. Many
entered the chamber, but the youth's pulse rose not; the
king came to see his son, nor therefor did it beat a whit
higher. But presently, behold, in came the queen and
immediately up leapt the pulse and awakening, clapped into
a lusty motion, as who should say, "Here is she who
consumeth me; here is my life and my death." Whereupon Erasistratus held it for certain that Antiochus was
ardently enamoured of his fair stepmother, but dared not
for shamefastness divulge his passion [to her] nor impart
it to others.

Being thus stablished in his opinion, he bethought himself, ere he should say aught thereof, what course it behoved
him hold in making it known to the king; and after he
had debated many things in himself, knowing that Seleucus
loved his wife without end and also that Antiochus was
dear to him as his very life, he thus bespoke him, saying,
"Seleucus, thy son is most grievously sick, and what is
(meseemeth) worse, I judge his malady to be incurable."
At this the woeful father began to make piteous lamentation,
weeping bitterly and bemoaning himself of fortune; and the
physician added, "I would have thee, my lord, understand
the cause of his ailment. Know, then, that the malady
which bereaveth thee of thy son is love and love of such
a woman that he, being unable to have her, will doubtless
die." "Woe's me!" cried the king, still weeping sore.
"And what is this woman whom I, who am King of Asia,
may not avail, by dint of prayers, monies or whatsoever
other means, to render compliant with my son's wishes?

Do but tell me her name, inasmuch as for his recoverance
I am ready to venture all I possess, even to my whole
kingdom, an it may not be done otherwise. Marry, an
he die, what reck I of the kingdom?" "Harkye, king,"
replied Erasistratus, "thine Antiochus is passionately enamoured of my wife; but, himseeming this his love is
unseemly, he hath never dared divulge it and chooseth
for shame rather to die than discover himself; but I, by
most manifest tokens, have certified myself thereof."

When Seleucus heard these words, "Then," quoth he,
"thou, a man with whom few can compare for goodness,
who art most straitly knit with me in love and goodwill
and bearest the name of being the very harbour of
prudence, wilt thou not save my son, a young man in
the flower of youth, who is most worthy of life and
unto whom the empery of all Asia is of right reserved?
Thou, Erasistratus, wilt thou not succour the son of
Seleucus, thy friend and king, who hasteneth to his death,
loving and keeping silence, and who, as thou seest, is
of such modesty and honesty that, even in this his last
extreme, he chooseth rather to die than anywise to
affront thee by speaking? This his silence, this his discretion, this reverence that he showeth thee, should move
thee to have compassion on him. Think, Erasistratus mine,
that, if he love ardently, he is enforced to love; for
that undoubtedly, an he might, he would do everything
not to love and do it more than willingly. But who
shall prescribe laws to Love? Love, as thou knowest,
not only enforceth men, but commandeth the immortal
Gods; and whenas he willeth, human wit availeth little
against him. Wherefore who knoweth not how much my
Antiochus meriteth compassion? For that, being enforced,
he might not do otherwise. But his silence is indeed a

most manifest sign of rare and shining virtue. Do thou, then, dispose thyself to succour him, for I warn thee that, an thou love not Antiochus his life, Seleucus himself will be hated of thee ; nay, he may not be injured but I myself shall on like wise be offended."

The sagacious physician, seeing his device succeed to his thought and hearing Seleucus thus urgently beseech him for the salvation of his son, bespoke him thus, yet better to spy out the king's mind and will, saying, "It is a common saying, my lord, that those who are whole can give excellent counsel to the sick. Thou dost nought but talk and wouldst have me give my dear-beloved wife to another and bereave myself of her whom I love most fervently and lacking whom, I should lack mine own self, for that, an thou take her from me, thou takest from me my life. Now I know not, my lord, if Antiochus thy son were enamoured of thy Stratonice, whether thou wouldst be so lavish to him of her as it seemeth thou wouldst have me be of mine own wife." Whereupon "Would the immortal Gods," cried Seleucus forthright, "he were enamoured of my dearest Stratonice ! For I swear to thee, by the reverence which I bear to the ever-honoured memory of my father Antiochus and of my grandfather Seleucus and by all our sacred deities, that I would straightway freely give this my wife, passing dear as she is to me, to my son, so all the world might know what is the due office of a good and loving father towards such a son as my supremely loved Antiochus, who, an my judgment err not, is most worthy of every aid. Alack, doth not this his great virtue, which he showeth in hiding so masterful a sufferance as is a vehement affect of love, deserve that every one should afford him succour? Deserveth it not that all the world should have pity upon him? Certes, he were the cruellest, the most inhuman and the most barbarous of enemies who should fail to have compassion of such continence as this that my dear son useth."

He said many other words, plainly showing that he would gladly have given, not only his wife, but his life for his son's salvation; wherefore the physician, himseeming it was time to discover the secret, took the king apart and bespoke him on this wise, saying, "My lord, thy son's recoverance is not in my hand, but abideth in thine own and in that of Stratonice thy wife, whom, as I have certified myself by sure signs, he most ardently loveth. Thou knowest now that which remaineth to thee to do, an his life be dear to thee." Then, acquainting him with the means he had taken to assure himself of the prince's case, he left him all rejoiced. There abode only one doubt in the king's mind, to wit, how he should prevail with his son to take Stratonice to wife and with her to accept Antiochus to husband; but he lightly enough persuaded the one and the other of all. As if, indeed, Stratonice made not a good exchange in taking a young man and leaving an old! Then, after he had accorded his wife with his son, he assembled his army, which was very great, and thus bespoke his soldiers, saying, "Comrades mine, who since the death of the great Alexander have gloriously shared with me a thousand emprises, meseemeth just that you be eke participants in that which I now purpose to do. You know that I have under my empery two-and-seventy provinces and that, being an old man, I can ill attend to so great a care; wherefore, dear my comrades, I intend to deliver both you from fatigue and myself from irksomeness. For myself I will only the kingdom from the sea to the Euphrates, and of all the rest I give the seigniory unto

my son Antiochus, upon whom I have presently bestowed
my Stratonice in marriage. That which hath pleased me
should also please you." Then, recounting his son's love
and sickness and the discreet aid of the skilful physician,
he let marry Stratonice to Antiochus, in the presence of
the whole army, and crowning the twain Kings of Asia,
let celebrate the nuptials so much desired of Antiochus
with exceeding great pomp. The army, hearing and seeing
these things, supremely commended the father's tenderness
over his son and Antiochus long abode with his beloved
wife in the utmost peace and happiness. This was not he
who warred with the Romans anent the affairs of Egypt,
as our divine poet seemeth to say in the Triumph of Love;[1]
he waged war only with the Galatians, who had passed over
from Europe into Asia and whom he overcame and expelled.
Of him and of Stratonice there was another Antiochus
born, who begat Seleucus, the father of Antiochus the
Great. This latter it was who had the great war with
the Romans and not his great-grandfather Antiochus, who
espoused his stepmother; as may be very plainly seen
of whoso diligently peruseth the ancient histories; and that
which the divine poet saith must be understood on this
wise, that, as we are all called sons of Adam, so this
Antiochus was son by direct succession to our Antiochus,
whose story I have presently told you. And now, to make

---

[1] " Ed egli, al suon del ragionar latino . . . .
" Disse, ' Io Seleuco son e questo è Antioco
" Mio figlio, _che gran guerra ebbe con voi.'_ "
(_i.e._ with the Romans, for one of whom Seleucus takes his inter-
locutor Petrarch, the latter having accosted him in Latin). Trionfo
d'Amore, Cap. II. ll. 108-10. There can be no doubt that Petrarch
made the mistake of confounding Antiochus I. with Antiochus III.
or Great.

an end, I say that, in giving his wife to his son, Seleucua did a most admirable deed and one worthy of eternal remembrance, for which he deserveth to be more commended than for all the victories he gained over his enemies, inasmuch as there is no greater victory in the world than to overcome our own selves and our passions, nor must it be doubted but that Seleucus overcame his appetites and himself in depriving himself of his dearest wife.

Bandello

to the most magnificent and excellent doctor of laws Messer Benedetto Tonso.

I came, this last spring, by commandment of Madam Isabella da Este, Marchioness of Mantua, to Lodi, to speak with the most illustrious and excellent Signor Francesco Sforza, Duke of Milan ; to the end that, by means of the said duke, the Marquess Federico of Mantua might release Messer Leonello Marchese, whom he had, on the requisition of the Lady Isabella Boschetta, imprisoned in the Citadel of Ostiglia.[1] The duke, knowing how much favour and authority you have with the marquess, by reason of your many rare and singular gifts, willed you come to Mantua and with your wit and address diligently pursue the said liberation in his name.   Accordingly we set out in company for Mantua and passed through Gazuolo, where the most magnificent Signor Pirro Gonzaga most courteously received us and entertained us for a day's space with all those marks of lovingkindness which it is his usance to show his friends. As we supped in the citadel, where we were lodged, the discourse turned, I know not how, upon Queen Giovanna the Second of Naples, sister to King Ladislas [of Hungary], who, in her day, recking little of feminine repute and honour, celebrated more nuptials by far and took more men

---

[1] A town near Mantua.

to lie with her than did Alatiel, daughter of Bemincdab,[1] Soldan of Babylon, according as Boccaccio recounteth in his most delightsome novels; and it being alleged for an extraordinary thing that certain ladies (and especially those of august and royal estate) should have made so little account of their honour, the adulteries of Giovanna the First, also Queen of Naples, of Bonne de Savoie, Duchess of Milan, and of many other great princesses were related. Now there was present Messer Gifredo da San Digiero,[2] a French man-at-arms, who had sojourned long in Italy, having come thither with Charles the Eighth, King of France, whenas he expelled the Arragonese from the kingdom of Naples; and he, after hearkening a good while in silence to that which was said, related a story to the purpose of the discourse ; the which pleasing all, I noted it roughly down, ere we departed Gazuolo, and having since written it out at large, I have dedicated it unto your name. May it please you, then, read and accept it, as you use to do with all my things and as indeed I am assured you will of your favour do, so it may remain unto those who come after us for a testimony of our friendship and so to boot they may abide without wonderment, whenas they hear bytimes that some lady hath been fain to make proof of other embracements than those of her husband. Fare you well.

[1] Bandello cannot even quote correctly from his beloved Boccaccio, whom he might be supposed, on the witness of his own writings, to know by heart. He writes "Alathiel" and "Memidedab" (*more Hebraico*) instead of "Alatiel" and "Bemincdab;" but the former mistake is interesting from a philological point, as settling the vexed question of the pronunciation of the name "Alatiel" and proving that the *t* is hard, instead of soft, as apud La Fontaine, who writes it "Alaciel."

[2] Godefroid de Saint Dizier ?

The Two-and-Fortieth Story.

THE MOST UNHAPPY LOVES OF TWO ROYAL LADIES AND TWO YOUNG CAVALIERS, WHO WERE MISERABLY DONE TO DEATH.

Meseemeth, sirs, you are all full of wonderment that these queens and dames of high degree, of whom you have spoken, should have opened their breasts to the flames of love, as if indeed they were not of flesh and blood, as are women of mean condition, and alike subject to carnal appetite. Certes, if you consider well, you will see that your admiration meriteth not the title of wonderment;[1] inasmuch as the more delicately a woman is nurtured, the more she feedeth upon noble and precious viands and the more she giveth herself up to sloth, to wantonness and to luxury, sleeping soft and passing the livelong day in songs, music and dances, devising without cease of things amorous and hearkening willingly unto whoso speaketh thereof, the lightlier is she netted in the toils of love, [nay, far more so] than those whose estate is mean and whom it behoveth take thought to the governance of the house and how, in the straitness of the goods of fortune, they may live honourably and bring their children to honour in the world. Marry, an you bereave women of ease and leisure, Love's shafts are launched at them in vain; for that, being quenched,

[1] Sic (*che l'ammirazione vostra non meriti titolo di meraviglia*); but the meaning appears to be "the subject of your admiration or that at which you marvel meriteth not a little of wonderment."

they have no power to kindle any flame in them;
whereas, on the contrary, great and delicate ladies,
nurtured in wantonness and sloth, incontinent take fire
and are limed in the snare. It is true that ladies of
condition have one curb, to wit, that, being in the eyes
of the general, their sin is plainer and more manifest
than that of women of mean estate; but this curb is
very lightly undone and broken of them, they flattering
themselves that none seeth their errors or that none will
dare rebuke or publish them; wherein they abide marvellously mistaken, the sin wrought being still fouler and
more enormous in itself, the higher and greater the sinner's
estate. And to this purpose I mind me to have read in our
Chronicles of France of two great ladies of royal estate,
who, breaking the curb of honour, precipitated themselves
into the abyss of death, as you shall presently hear.

You must know then, that Philip the Fair, King of France
had (amongst other children) three sons, who were all kings,
one after another; but none of the three had male issue,
so that the crown came after them into the hands of
Philip of Valois, whose lineage yet reigneth nowadays.
These sons of Philip the Fair were very unhappy in
their wives, for that two were proved adulteresses and
punished and the third was accused, but, the adultery
not being proved, she was acquitted. The first of the
three was Louis, King of Navarre, surnamed the Contentious,[1] who had to wife Margaret, daughter of Robert
of Burgundy. The second, called Philip the Tall, was
married to Joan, daughter of Otho, Count of Burgundy,
and Matilda of Artois, and was made Count of Poitiers
and Toulouse. The third, Charles by name, called also

---

[1] Le Hutin.

the Fair, was Count of La Marche and Angoulême and
to him was given to wife Blanche, also daughter of the
aforesaid Otho. Their father Philip had waged a fierce
and dour war with Edward, King of England, son of
Henry III., and against Guy, Count of Flanders, with
whom he came sundry whiles to close quarters, fighting
pitched battles, wherein there died men galore on both
sides, the Flemings having withal the worst of it for the
most part. The war lasted what while Philip lived, who,
dying, left it for an inheritance to Louis his firstborn
and all his other sons.

What while, then, the father was afield with his three
sons, warring at once against the English and the Flemings,
who were leagued together for the destruction of France,
it befell that Queen Margaret of Navarre and Blanche,
wife of Charles, being one day together and lamenting
the absence of their husbands, who were with the army,
avouched themselves persuaded that these latter abode nowise with their hands in their girdles, but gave themselves
a good time and took their pleasure with every woman
who came to their hands ; and after they had once and
again devised together of this, the Queen of Navarre, who
was somewhat bolder than her sister-in-law, said, "Madam
sister-in-law and sister, we do nought all day long but say
words, whilst our husbands do deeds. I know well what
is told me of those who come from the army ; marry, I
warrant you, if indeed they be in arms, they apply themselves to solace and diversion and fail not for women,
with whom they lead a merry life ; nor do they anywise
remember them of us who are here ; nay, when they
have some handsome wench or other, they say that we are
nothing worth compared with these that they enjoy ; but
I know well what, to my mind, they deserve. Now, I

know not how it seemeth to you thereof; but, were you
of my mind, I warrant me we would do on such wise
that, for whatsoever the ass giveth against the wall, he
should receive the like. They reck not of us and we
should render them a loaf for their bannock and reck
yet less of that which they do. Marry, they do all that
liketh them, whether it irk us or no; and certes it were
but giving them their due if, since they spare the household gear, we should spend it with the aid of others. How
say you thereof, sister-in-law? Deem you we should in
our flower of youth be entreated on this wise?" Madam
Blanche, hearing the Queen of Navarre reason thus and
being herself desirous of trying a fall with a gentleman
whom she loved, said, "I'faith, madam, you say sooth,
and I myself have oftentimes bethought me thereof, but
see no means how we may so order our affairs that they
shall not be known, we having so many eyes about us;
and were they ever known and did any inkling thereof
reach our husbands, we should be burned." The queen,
seeing Madam Blanche's disposition and having forethought
what was to do and what course it behoved them take,
so the thing should not be discovered, imparted it to her
sister-in-law, who approved it, and so they determined to
make no delay in putting it into execution.

There were at court two young cavaliers, one of whom
was he who pleased Madam Blanche; he was called Gautier
D'Aulnay[1] and had a friend and kinsman, by name Philippe
D'Aulnay, with whom he constantly consorted, both very
well favoured and adorned with fair fashions and engaging
manners. The queen, hearing that Gautier, whom she
very well knew, pleased her sister-in-law, set her heart on

---

[1] Bandello, *Di Dannoi*.

his friend and herseemed these twain would serve their
purpose excellent well on such wise as she had in mind.
The two ladies, accordingly, having taken counsel together, began, whenassoever they saw the two gentlemen,
(and they saw them daily,) to greet them with favour and
show them a blithe countenance ; nor was it long ere the
two friends, who were no simpletons, became aware of
the ladies' love and showing themselves exceeding rejoiced
thereat, studied as most they might to do all that could
be agreeable to them. The Queen of Navarre had a very
trusty usher, to whom she imparted her mind and instructed
him in full of that which she would have him do. He,
desirous of satisfying his mistress and finding the two
cavaliers together, discovered to them the ladies' purpose
and gave them such tokens that they were certified of
the fact and accounting themselves the luckiest men in the
world, awaited that which their mistresses should command
them. Now, for that, whenas both parties are of one mind,
there betideth scant delay in bringing things to the desired
issue, the new and blithe lovers found themselves, by
means of the usher, in a chamber, where the two ladies,
without other company, awaited them, full of joy and infinite allegresse. Their greetings were gladsome and full
of tenderness, wherefrom they came to kisses and amorous
embracements and ultimately gave accomplishment to their
desires, to the exceeding great contentment of all parties,
wrestling for the fall again and again, with all such amorous
endearments and dulcet sports as use to be between lovers,
and it still falling to the ladies to abide undermost, they
gave themselves exceeding great pleasure a good while. The
ladies sought to make up for lost time, and in this the
young men, being robust and well-thewed and passionately
enamoured of them, failed them not.

These their happy loves they ensued some months'
time, foregathering whenassoever they conveniently might,
and things went on such wise that none perceived it nor
was any suspect aroused at court. The ladies' husbands
whiles returned home and abode eight or ten days, (during
which time the lovers were careful to make no sign or
gesture which might give an inkling of their case,) then
went off again to the camp. Presently, however, Fortune,
which still envieth folk's weal and useth not to suffer
any live long in happiness, but studieth ever to mingle
mischances and chagrins with men's felicity and mostwhiles poisoneth and embittereth a fair estate with its
venoms, caused it begin (I know not how) to be whispered
at court of the four lovers' privacy and there befell
some words thereof; wherefore, the rumour going from
one to another, many courtiers opened their eyes, who
had before taken no heed to the matter, and diligently
spying upon the acts and motions of the ladies and the
cavaliers, moved partly by jealousy for the honour of the
royal house and partly by malignant envy, perceived full
well how the case stood and secretly advised the ladies'
husbands of all that they had seen and heard. At this
sorry and shameful news the two brethren abode beyond
measure woeful and full of rage and despite against
their wives and the two cavaliers, seeing themselves to
have passed oversea without a boat and gotten the ignominious domain of Cornwall;[1] wherefore, having imparted
the whole to King Philip their father and agreed together
of what was to be done, they set a snare for the
adulterers on such wise that they were all four taken
in the act by the provost of the king's household on

[1] See ante, Vol. I. p. 189, note.

the first day of May, 1313, as they took their pleasure together at the Abbey of Maubuisson, near Pontoise, and with them the usher by whose means the two gallants enjoyed the two ladies.

Great was the clamour and greater yet the wonderment about the court and everywhere. The Queen of Navarre and her sister-in-law were by the king's commandment carried straight to Château Gaillard d'Andeli, where, for duresse and hard living and other unease that they suffered, they died in great misery and were meanly buried without any funeral houours. At the same time that the adultery of these two ladies was discovered, Joan of Burgundy, wife of Philip the Tall, was (that no part of the royal household might abide without reproach) impeached, in her turn, of adultery and imprisoned in the castle of Dourdan ; but, being found innocent, she was formally absolved by the Parliament of Paris and adjudged a virtuous and honourable lady. The two other adulterers, Gautier and Philippe d'Aulnay, were arraigned before the counsellors of the Parliament and having, without torture, confessed the adultery, were condemned to have their genitals publicly lopped and their bodies flayed from head to foot ; the which was straightway executed by the common hangman, to the exceeding torment of the two young men ; after which they were ignominiously haled to a gibbet and there hanged by the neck; whilst the usher, who had favoured the adulterers, was likewise hanged. Queen Margaret having died in prison, Louis the Contentious wedded to his second wife Clemenza, daughter of Carlo Martello, eldest son of Charles the Second, King of Sicily, whilst Charles the Fair on like wise, Blanche dying, married Marin, daughter of John of Luxemburg, son of the Emperor Henry.

Bandello

I had from your servant, what time I was at the house
of his worship the Prothonotary della Torre, your melodious
and learned hendecasyllabics, wherein you sing of the
beauty, amenity and goodly situation of the famous lake of
Garda, by writers called Benaco. On my return home, I
read them all, ere they passed from my hand, and albeit,
as the saying is, they were rather bolted by me than masti-
cated, nevertheless, they much pleased me; then, taking
them up more at leisure, I began to read them and savour
them, word by word, as best I might. Good God, what
satisfaction they gave me, how much they delighted me!
But whom would they not please, they being dulcet,
rounded, smooth and melodious? There is none who hath
viewed those parts and sailed the lake but, reading your
ingenious poem, will think himself a-pleasuring there,
engaged as well in fishing as in spreading nets, toils and
birdlime for the silly fowls. What, again, shall I say of
the divine and truly poetic epigram which you, being in the
village of Andes (now called Petiole), the native place of
our great poet Virgil, on the banks of the lake which
encompasseth and embraceth Mantua, so happily composed?
Wherefore have I not that your clear, dulcet and inex-
haustible Latin vein, which welleth up in you on such easy

and erudite wise, so I might sing of you as you deserve?
Happy you, who can at pleasure indite things of such excellence as shall, after your death, hold you illustrious and famous
as in life and assure you, what while the world endureth,
against the voracity of all-devouring Time ! An you write
in prose, there is seen in your compositions the spirit of
Cicero, father of Roman eloquence, so well do you imitate
and reproduce him ; but; if you express your admirable
conceits in song and rhythmic ordinance of verse, Phœbus
himself singeth with you and giveth you melodious numbers
nor ever abandoneth you. But I have entered upon the
deep sea of your shining praises and helmless, sailless and
oarless as I am, I were better come forth thereof than lose
myself therein. I thank you, then, and confess myself
infinitely beholden to you for the pleasure which I have had
in reading your poems, and having no otherwhat wherewithal to requite you and show myself grateful to you, I
send and give you a novel, written by me a few days agone,
the which was, no great while since, related in the goodly
and delightsome garden of Messer Tommaso Pagliaro and
his brethren by Messer Giovanni Meraviglia, who, as you
know, hath traversed great part of Italy and who writeth
all the wars of our time, separately and by annals.[1] And
so, not to hold you longer in suspense, I commend myself
to you. Fare you well.

---

[1] i.e. year by year, after the fashion of the Annals of Tacitus.

The Three-and-Fortieth Story.

NICCOLO OF SIENA, BEING SCORNED BY HIS MISTRESS, HANGETH HIMSELF IN DESPAIR.

The exceeding amaze and wonderment wherein I see you all, most noble youths, anent the death of yonder miserly old dotard, who, for that corn was come to a low price and that he had not sold it, when it was dearest, hanged himself in his granary, remembereth me of a case otherwhiles betided in the city of Siena, albeit it is in some measure different from that of the old man aforesaid, inasmuch as the latter for greed of money is gone to the abode of all the devils, whilst the death of the Siennese befell of ill-regulated love and overweening desire ; and this circumstance I am the fainer to tell you for that I know there are some of you (nay, belike all) who are tangled in the toils of love and may take warning by the sorry fate of a hapless lover. Not, indeed, that I blame a young man for opening his breast to the amorous flames ; nay, I commend him, for that whoso loveth not in his youth is still seen to do follies in his old age ; but I would have all, at what age soever they love, (for that old men also may love,) make shift to temper their unbridled appetites nor suffer themselves be carried away into the unseemly and shameful acts which are too often done. And whoso is uncareful from the beginning not to let himself be beguiled by his senses will find himself go daily from ill to worse and will in the end be so blinded that he will no more be master of his actions, but will, like a buffalo, suffer himself be led by the nose of his passions and carnal appetites. But, for that example moveth more than talk, I will come to the telling of my story, the which befell on this wise.

In the days when Pope Pius II. of the noble family of the Piccolomini, who was a native of Siena, held a general council of all the prelates and princes of Christendom for the making of the crusade against the infidels, there chanced to be in Siena a young man of ancient and honourable family, called Niccolo, who, being abundantly rich in the goods of fortune, lived in splendour and magnificence. Happening one day upon a very fair girl, the daughter of a poor man, a mason, who gained his living by his craft, he became beyond all belief enamoured of her and so deeply did the amorous flames penetrate into his heart that in a little he avouched himself no longer his own man, but altogether dependent upon the beloved damsel. By her habit and raiment he judged her to be poor; nevertheless, having spied out her dwelling-place and learning that she was very poor and maintained herself by spinning wool, he was sore chagrined and blamed Nature a thousandfold, for that it had caused her to be thus meanly born; nay, as if taking shame for having set himself to love her, he would fain, an he might, have withdrawn from such an emprise. But that hangman Love had dighted him on such wise that the poor youth could no longer dispose of himself at his will, but must needs in his own despite love her whom he had seen and still ensue her steps. Accordingly, knowing her father's lodging and passing through the street twice or thrice a day, he saw the girl spinning wool in company of divers other poor women, and the more he saw her, the more he felt himself

enkindled and the more did desire wax in him to see her ;
wherefore, feeling himself languish amain and unable to
win a glance from his mistress, he abode the woefullest
man in the world ; and amongst his other ills, this was
no little grievous to him, that he dared discover to no
one that his malady, himseeming he should but be sore
blamed for that, being noble and of the first families of
Siena, he set himself to love thus meanly; albeit, had he
had some trusty companion, to whom he might impart his
sufferings, he would doubtless have gotten some comfort
and might belike have been moved by his friend's faithful
counsel to withdraw from so irksome an emprise. He
oftentimes thought of carrying her off by force, but this
himseemed was no action worthy of a gentleman, more
by token that he misdoubted him she would be despited
thereat, the which would have been grievous to him over
all, inasmuch as he would liefer have died than vexed her ;
yet to abide thus and pine for passion seemed to him
overhard.

What while he travailed on this wise, without finding
any peace, and went daily from ill to worse, he fell in
with a good woman (one of those bawds who go everywhere, beads in hand, and still move their lips, as they
were apes,) who was versed in the art of debauching girls
and married women, and to her himseemed he might without shame discover himself. Accordingly, he sent for her
to his house and after many words, punctually discovered
to her his case, instantly beseeching her to have compassion on him and prevail with the damsel (for that he
had given her to understand who she was) to comply with
his wishes. The accursed beldam, having gotten some
monies of the lover, promised to use her utmost endeavour
to persuade the girl to do his pleasure ; wherewith he

abode full of hope and awaited her return with the utmost impatience. Accordingly, the knavish old woman went, one holiday, and finding the damsel seated all alone in a court where many families of poor folk lodged, gave her good day and seated herself by her. The girl, who knew her not, returned her salutation and bidding her welcome, asked her what she went seeking; to which the crafty old woman, who knew the girl's mother to have died many months before, replied, well-nigh weeping, "Daughter mine, I am nowise surprised if thou know me not, for that I have sojourned these three or four years past in the country at the village of Corsignano; but I was a great friend of thy mother of blessed memory, (whom God have in glory) and have many a time had thee in these arms, when thou wast a little lass; nay, God only can tell how much the death of thy mother, who was indeed a good soul, grieved me; wherefore, chancing to come to Siena on certain of my occasions, I was fain to come see thee, meseeming I saw thy mother, when she was a girl, as thou art now, God bless thee, dear my daughter. I thought by this to find thee married, for that thou art fairly grown and shouldest not waste thy time; but doubtless thy father's poverty hindereth him from marrying thee, as he should do. Now, tell me, wouldst thou fain be married?" "Ay, would I," replied the girl, "an it pleased my father, for that I would do nought without his leave." "Harkye, daughter," rejoined the old woman, "it often happeneth that fathers care not to part with their daughters, whenas they make a profit by them, as methinketh thy father doth by thee; and if thou wait till he marry thee, thou mayst chance to be old ere it betide thee to get a husband; wherefore thou wilt repent thee in vain of having let so long a time pass without enjoying thy youth. Nay, to tell thee the truth, this thy beauty should not be thus lost without fruit. An thou wilt hearken to me (and needs must thou believe me, for that I know what I say), thou wilt provide for thyself, for that whoso doth his own affairs soileth not his hands. I came not hither to bespeak thee without cause, inasmuch as I love thee and would fain see thee lead a merry life and give thyself a good time and do on such wise that thou mayst not still wear thy fingers to the bone with spinning. An thou wilt, I warrant me I will cause thee have such a dowry that thou mayst marry a man with whom thou wilt not need to be all day spinning; nay, thou shalt have wherewithal to entertain servants and not weary thyself for ever thus. And since we have entered upon this discourse, I will e'en tell thee how and set thy weal before thee; and after do thou as thou wilt. One of the first gentlemen of the city is so enamoured of thy charms that he can find no rest, and except he have thy favours, he is like to go mad therefor. An thou wilt vouchsafe to love him, as reason will have thee do, thou shalt have a thousand gold florins to dowry. How deemest thou? Is not this a dowry for a gentlewoman and a knight's daughter? Take thy fortune, whenas God sendeth it thee, and let not the occasion pass, which is such as seldom offereth." "And how cometh it," asked the girl, "that he, though I know not who he is, is willing to give me such a dowry?" "Marry," replied the procuress, "thou must e'en be somewhat of a simpleton and apprehendest not or feignest not to apprehend the thing as it is. I have already told thee that he is sore enamoured of thee and desireth thy love more than aught in the world, and thou shouldst account thyself very lucky to be beloved of such a gentleman; wherefore, daughter mine, do thou dispose thyself to give him thy love and we will order things on such wise that neither thy father nor any other shall ever know aught of it."

Now the damsel, though of very mean and humble birth, was nevertheless chaste and high-minded ; wherefore, when she heard the wicked old woman's conclusion and knavish proposition, she waxed all red in the face and full of honest despite, said to her, with a threatening voice, "Hold thy peace, good-for-nothing old bawd that thou art ! May fire come from heaven to consume thee and the like of thee ! I know not what hindereth me from tearing out thine eyes with these fingers. Begone, God give thee an ill year, devil's wife that thou art, and mayst thou break thy neck ! Comest thou to me with thy lewd talk? An thou ever return hither, by Christ His Cross, thou shalt not depart from me whole ! Nay, I tell thee again, never dare to come hither again, else thou shalt assuredly pay for this and that together." The wicked old woman went off without more ado, all flouted and chapfallen, and related that which had passed to the lover, who, thinking the girl had belike not cared to trust the old woman, determined, much as her harsh response misliked him, to use other means and accordingly essayed to corrupt her father through one of the latter's familiars; but the good man would hearken to nought and answered the ambassador that he had liefer strangle his daughter than suffer her become any man's whore. The young man, sore chagrined at his ill success, tried many other ways, but all in vain, inasmuch as the girl was firmer and more constant in her chaste purpose than is a hard and ancient rock of the sea against the dashing billows. Indeed she merited that Nature should have given her a generous origin and riches sorting with the nobility of her soul ; algates, she deserveth to be celebrated, for that her noble and chaste mind rendered her commendable.

The unhappy lover, seeing himself altogether scorned by the damsel and availing not, for all he took courage to bespeak her himself, to get other answer from her than that she reserved her maidenhead unto him who should be her husband and was resolved rather to die than do otherwise, abode the despairfullest man in the world. He strove for some days to forget her, but found it impossible to banish her from his mind, nay, himseemed his love waxed momently hotter; wherefore he lost sleep and appetite for excess of melancholy and showed as one bewitched. Then, urged by his fierce passion, which cruelly consumed him, he went one day whereas the girl span in company of divers other women and there, weeping bitterly, strove to bend her to his wishes; but he did but entreat a mountain to bow down, for that she told him he sowed the sand. The wretched youth, seeing her obduracy, said to her, "Alack, fair damsel, since thou wilt not vouchsafe to have pity on my extreme torments and upon the grievous pains which I suffer for thee without cease and since I cannot live without thee, what wilt thou have me do?" And she, being fain to rid herself of that annoy, answered him angrily, saying, "An you would do me a pleasure, go and come nevermore before mine eyes." Niccolo, having gotten this response, said, "Well, I will obey thee and will do on such wise that neither thou nor any other shall henceforth see me more;" and therewithal, going home, he entered a chamber, where (as was after seen) he hanged himself with a rope made fast to a nail and thus miserably made an end of his youth and of his ill-regulated love. Wherefore, young men, I exhort you to love temperately, lest there befall you that which befell the poor Siennese.

Part the Third.

Bandello

to the ingenious and affable reader Greeting.

The pains and labour, kindest reader mine, which
I have suffered, since I departed Italy and came to
abide upon the Garonne in the Agenois, in collecting
the novels written by me, have been seen of many,
who know that I have twice sent expressly into Italy
for the recoverance thereof, nor yet, for all the
diligence I have used, have I been able wholly to
recover them. However, the first and second parts
thereof having been given to the world, meseemeth
for good reasons it were ill to tarry longer in sending
the third after the first two, wherein if I was unable
to observe any ordinance, still less hath it been
given me to do so in this ; the which certes importeth
nothing, my novels being no matter of continuous
history, but a medley of divers adventures, variously
and in various times and places happened to various
persons and recounted without any kind of ordinance.

Now there may peradventure be some who would have had me be eloquent (or far more so than I have been) in writing these novels and will say that I have not imitated the good Tuscan writers. To these I will say (even as I mind me to have written elsewhere) that I am no Tuscan nor do I well understand the properties of that tongue ; nay, I confess myself a Lombard, anciently descended from those Ostrogoths, who, warring under Theodoric their king and having settled at Dertona,[1] founded my native place upon the Via Æmilia[2] in Cisapennine Liguria, not far from the mouth of the Schirmia,[3] where it dischargeth its waters, drawn from the sources of the Apennines and swollen by torrents, into the king of rivers. This colony they called Castelnuovo, the which is nowadays famous for the good breeding of its noble families and the numerousness[4] of its people. It were, then, no great wonder if I should whiles employ some trivial and little-used word that smacked somewhat of the Gothic.

[1] The ancient name of Tortona in Piedmont.
[2] The great Roman road terminating at Aquileia in the Gulf of Venice.
[3] i.e. Scrivia.
[4] Numerosità.

Were the Tuscan language native to me or had I
learned it, I had gladly used it, for that I know it
to be very chaste and goodly. Nevertheless, in so
far as meseemeth, the elegant and inimitable Messer
Francesco Petrarca, who was a Tuscan, is found to
have used not more than two or three purely Tuscan
words in his vernacular rhymes, all his poems being
a texture of words for the most part common to all
the peoples of Italy. Algates, an there be any who
incline to blame me, it irketh me that I have been
unable to satisfy all. And who, indeed, may avail
unto that? Since folk spared not to missay of the
great poet Homer, shall I, who am nought, look to
be spared? Since there were those who called Virgil
a man without understanding and of scant learning
and avouched Livy to be a babbler, over-wordy in
his histories and beyond measure negligent, since
Asinius Pollio, as Quintilian affirmeth, declared that
in the said Livy he had noted a savour of Patavinity,[1]
the Livian vein being withal miraculous, and since
it e'en appeared to Cicero that Demosthenes whiles
nodded and Horace judged the like of Homer, shall

---

[1] *i.e.* a smack of the Paduan dialect, Livy being a native of Padua.

I take it ill that some (haply with just reason) may reprehend and correct me? Certes, I shall be beholden to them, whenas they rebuke me with reason, for that, an I avail not to amend mine own compositions, they will at the least open the eyes of many, who will [consequently] keep themselves from falling into the like errors.   Do you now, ingenuous reader mine, who read these my toys, vouchsafe to take the whole in the spirit wherein I have written all my novels, the which was certes to none other end than to divert and to warn all sorts and conditions of men to leave unseemly things and to apply to live honestly, it being manifest that lewd and vicious dealings are for the most part punished, or soon or late, and abide with eternal infamy in men's remembrance; whereas things well done and virtuous still live in glory and are praised and celebrated.   Fare you well.

Bandello

to the most illustrious lady the Lady Ginevra Bentivoglia Marchioness of Finario.

An one should offer, illustrious lady mine, to state the reasons of the variousness of the effects of love and to demonstrate whence it ariseth that one man, loving, abideth blithe and another is still of ill cheer, this feareth nought and that is without cease full of apprehension, the one believeth everything and the other scarce crediteth that which he seeth with his own eyes,—it were, certes, stuff for seven Iliads and matter rather for speculative philosophers, investigating the causes of things in general, than for me who apply but for the nonce to write the various chances which betide in divers places, as well in love-matters as in whatsoever else, an emprise which your mother it was who with many arguments exhorted me to undertake. Now, it being discoursed the other day, in the presence of the accomplished Lady Margherita Pia e Sanseverina, of him who lately slew his mistress by night in the suburb of Porta Lodovica, Girolamo Bandello, my cousin, a man well read in Greek and Latin letters and an excellent physician, who was then in Milan, related a marvellous adventure, which filled all with the utmost wonderment. And certes it was a very extraordinary case ; wherefore, my cousin (forby that I was present when he told it) having twice or thrice repeated the whole to me, point by point, so I might relate it to others, meseemed it was worthy to be added to the number of my novels; and because it is of those whereof we have many a time devised (that which our friend [such an one] doth seeming to us over-strange), I have chosen to entitle it in your name, so it may securely abide in every one's hands. I am well assured, indeed, that there will be some to declare that they believe not the thing to be true. To these I say that it is no article of faith and that each may believe what he will thereof; algates, my cousin assured me that he had heard it for most true. But, be that as it may, you, mistress mine, will, methinketh, believe the thing to be true, knowing that here in Milan there have betided things no less [strange] than this, which were it expedient to write, this would not be accounted so marvellous. And indeed, when a thing is possible, I for my part would nowise stop to contend that it had not actually befallen; whence the philosophers have it as a rule that, whenassoever a possible case is propounded, it behoveth to accept it. But let us come to the novel, which may it please you lay up with such other your writings as you most prize and keep me in your good graces. And so may our Lord God vouchsafe you the accomplishment of your every desire. Fare you well.

The First Story.

PANDOLFO DEL NERO IS BURIED ALIVE WITH HIS MISTRESS AND BY AN EXTRAORDINARY CHANCE ESCAPETH FROM PERIL.

It is no great while since, on my way to Loretto to accomplish a vow of mine, I came to the city of Rimini, where finding the accomplished and debonair Messer Antonio Cappo, doctor of laws and gentleman of Mantua, a man of exceeding skill and judgment in Greek and Latin letters, established as governor for the Holy See, it behoved me go lodge with him. He entertained me two days and would e'en have me promise, for old friendship's sake, to sojourn with him five or six days on my return. During my sojourn there, I heard a story said to have befallen a little before, the which, for its strangeness and for the great peril which figureth therein, was, meseemed, worthy to be punctually holden in remembrance, and albeit I know the true names [of the personages], I think well, for apt reasons, to suppress them and avail myself of feigned names. There was, then, in Rimini a young man of noble birth and very rich, called Pandolfo del Nero, who loved a gentlewoman of the same city so passionately that he could not abide an hour without her sight. The lady, whose name was Francesca and who had not yet overpast her twentieth year, was the wife of a rich gentleman, more advanced in years than she would have had him; wherefore, being without cease importuned by Pandolfo with letters and messages and herseeming her husband often put her in appetite and after availed not to give her due food, such as is used to be eaten abed, she began to lend ear to him, nor was it long ere, the young man pleasing her amain, she found means, by the aid of a waiting-woman of hers, to foregather with him. Pandolfo, if before he loved, having once tasted his Francesca's sweet embracements, was all afire; and she also, having essayed the savoury viands with which he plied her, could not live without him and cursed the hour a thousand times which had married her to an old man. Accordingly, each loving other without stint, Pandolfo oftentimes put himself in danger of death to enjoy his mistress, who for her part lost no opportunity of foregathering with him and made no account of life, so but she might avail to be with her lover. On this wise, then, they abode some two years' space, enjoying each other whenassoever they might, and it seemed their love waxed ever hotter and greater.

At the end of this time, Francesca fell grievously sick and in a little while, being taken with a most irksome flux, worsened on such wise that the physicians declared she could not live long and would die of a sudden, speaking.[1] Her poor old husband, who loved her tenderly, left nothing undone to recover her and sent to Bologna for eminent physicians, sparing no expense; but all was in vain, for

---

[1] *E che in un subito, parlando, si morirebbe.* It is difficult to apprehend the exact meaning of this phrase; it might perhaps be rendered "and that she might, if she spoke overmuch, die of a sudden;" but in that case the text should run, *E che in un subito, troppo parlando, si poteva morire.* Besides, what follows does not bear out this sense.

that she grew daily worse and wasted away as snow in the sun. Pandolfo, hearing the mortal peril in which his mistress abode, was like to die of grief and knew not whither to turn, holding it for certain that, if she died, he would have life in hate; wherefore he found means, by the maid who was cognizant of their loves, to send to comfort her and beseech her for his sake take heart and apply to recover her health. His greetings and consolations were marvellously pleasing to the lady, who loved him more than her proper life, and herseemed eke it should not irk her so much to die, could she but have him to abide and talk with her. Moreover, feeling herself declining hourly, she fell into such a jealousy lest any other lady should enjoy him after her that this thought tormented her far more than death itself; wherefore she went devising how they might be brought to die in company and be buried together, and having long dwelt on this thought, she resolved, ere she died, to speak with Pandolfo, in the hope (in so far as can be conjectured) that there should ensue that which did in effect ensue.

She had in her chamber a coffer, big enough to hold a man, the which had been provided of set purpose for the concealment of her lover in case of surprise, and it had sundry whiles befallen that Pandolfo hid himself therein for four or five hours' space. Now this coffer, when the lid fell down, shut on such wise that it might not be opened without a key and had divers air-holes, and in it she kept her most precious things. Accordingly, after much inward debate, she sent to pray Pandolfo come visit her that same night; the which was supremely pleasing to the youth, who went thither at the appointed hour and being admitted by the maid, was presently brought into the lady's chamber. Francesca's husband, since she was fallen sick, had gone to lie below in a ground-floor room and was used whiles to send and come anights to see how his wife did and that she lacked nothing whereof she stood in need; wherefore she, desiring that night to speak with her lover at her leisure, made shift, ere Pandolfo should come, to feign herself a little better and said that she would have no other woman with her for that night but the maid; and so they two abode alone.

Pandolfo presently arriving, many tears were shed ere the lovers could say a word; and at the last, after they had kissed each other, weeping, a thousand times and had exchanged a thousand endearing words, as useth to betide in such cases, the lady, heaving a heavy sigh, said, "Pandolfo, dear my life and term of mine every desire, tell me the truth; wilt thou not be grieved for my death? Will it not irk thee that thou mayst no more return to thy Francesca?" "How?" replied the lover, weeping. "Doubtest thou belike, my soul and mine only treasure, of my love? Could I but ransom thy life with mine own, nay, with a thousand lives, an I had them, thou mayst be assured that I would venture them all for thy salvation. And if, which God forfend, it befall that thou perish of this malady, I know not indeed what I shall do with myself, for at the mere thought I feel myself like to die. But take courage and be of good heart, for thou art not yet come to such an extremity but there may be some remedy given to thine infirmity; thou art young and youth overpasseth the greatest perils of disease; prithee apply thee to be of good cheer." "Pandolfo," rejoined the lady, "my life is gone and what little is left me is so weak that nought may be more. I feel my vital spirits fail me from moment to moment and myself melt away like mist before the wind; God knoweth

it grieveth me not to die save for thee; for that the
thought of leaving thee here below without me and that
in time another woman shall possess thee causeth me
such anguish that to die meseemeth is no pain, compared with this. Could I but do on such wise that thou
shouldst die with me in one same moment, so that we,
having in life been united by love, might in death be
buried together in one same sepulchre! I should e'en
die content, might I but have that assurance." Pandolfo,
still weeping, bade her put off these thoughts, for that
she would recover and they would yet have time enough
to abide together and live blithely, and studied to comfort her as most he might.

What while the lovers accompanied this and other discourse with tears and sobs, the husband, who had been
told by the physicians that his wife was still failing, arose
(it being a little past midnight) and calling to the servants
for light, that he might go see how the sick lady did,
was heard by the maid, who straightway advertised the
lovers and went to meet her master, so she might hold
him in parley and give Pandolfo time to depart the house
by the accustomed way, she having left the door open,
whereof her mistress had aforetime let make keys like
unto those in the master's keeping. When the lovers
heard of the latter's coming, Pandolfo would have left the
chamber and gone away, as was his wont; but the lady,
who saw all ensue according to her design, prayed him
hide in the coffer, so that, when the husband should
be gone again, they might yet talk together. Pandolfo,
who was but too fain to talk with her, accordingly entered
the chest, which shut of itself, as soon as the lid was down,
and the husband came up, having first understood from
the maid that her mistress had slept very quietly. As

soon as he entered the chamber, he went to the bed and asked his wife how she felt herself; whereto she answered that, albeit she had rested somewhat, nevertheless herseemed she should live but little longer, for that she felt herself momently sinking. The husband comforted her and bade her be of good cheer, declaring it to be an excellent sign that she had rested quietly and studying with many words to hearten her as most he might.

Meanwhile the maid, thinking Pandolfo already gone, went softly to lock the house-door and after, coming whereas the wife and husband talked together, was bidden by the lady wait without the chamber; whereupon Madam Francesca thus bespoke her husband, saying, "Dear my husband, of me beloved without end, I am, as thou seest, come to the ultimate term of my life, a pass to which needs must each come soon or late, none being privileged of God to abide perpetually on life. These few years I have abidden with thee, thou hast still, meseemed, loved me fervently and hast without cease studied to complease me, inasmuch as all I sought of thee hath been freely granted me nor was ever aught denied me that I asked; and in this my last extremity, I am fain to believe that thou wilt do with me on like wise. Wherefore I am the more emboldened to seek a favour of thee and instantly to pray thee be pleased to grant it me and thereof I would have thee pledge me thy faith. How sayst thou?" "Dear my wife," replied the husband, "prithee put this thought of death out of thy head and take good heart, for that I trust thou wilt yet recover. Nevertheless, both now and always I pledge thee my faith that thou shalt never ask of me aught that is in my arbitrament but I will accomplish it in so far as my powers shall extend. Marry, ask freely all that thou thinkest may be performed of me; nay, thou shalt never ask in vain, seeing I would satisfy thee with my blood." "Then," rejoined she, "I pray thee that, after my death, (which will certes betide shortly,) thou let place yonder coffer in the sepulchre whereas I shall be entombed. Therein are my trinkets and certain toys of no value, which would scarce fetch half a score florins; it is locked and there needeth nought save to let carry it with me, whenas I shall be borne to the sepulchre. An thou do me this favour, the which will be but a small matter to thee and to me a cause of the utmost contentment, I shall die happy." The husband, who in very deed loved his wife supremely, swore to her to complease her in this and in everything else which was in his power, never thinking that there was aught of moment in the chest, but deeming she had laid up therein some raiment of hers and other women's toys, which belike she cared not to have seen.

But what shall we say of Pandolfo, who, shut as he was in the chest, had heard all that passed? How true is that which is commonly said, "Happy he who chanceth to be enamoured of a discreet lady and eke most hapless he who happeneth upon a foolish and harebrained woman!" The luckless lover abode between the hammer and the anvil, inasmuch as, if he held his peace, he saw himself buried alive, without hope of succour, and if he discovered himself, he was certain to be torn limbmeal, being of the contrary faction to that of the lady's husband, to say nothing of the added offence of having made him a burgess of Cuckoldshaven. He debated a thousand things in himself and unable to imagine a means of escape, he resolved, for lesser ill, since he found himself taken like a rat in a trap, to die patiently in that coffer. I, myself, sirs, have sundry whiles pondered this case and

have come to the conclusion that Francesca, having fallen
into that melancholy humour of seeking to have her lover
buried with her, bethought herself to cause him enter
the chest, herseeming that, if he said nought, he would
be buried with her and that, if he sought to make any
stir, he could not escape, inasmuch as her husband and
his folk would have slaughtered him without mercy. Thus,
whether the unhappy lover was smothered in the chest
or was slain of his enemies, she had her intent, herseeming she could die happy, so but Pandolfo abode not
after her on life. God keep all men from the hands of
such madwomen !

The lady, having gotten her husband's promise and
being certified that her lover would be buried with her,
resolved to abide no longer on life ; wherefore, straitening
in herself such scant and feeble vital spirits as were left
her, she held her breath as most she might and replying
not unto aught that her husband said to her, gave up
the ghost. Great was the husband's lamentation and after
he had bewept her sore, he ordained that the obsequies
should be celebrated on the ensuing day at eventide. As
soon as it was day, there came kinsfolk and friends,
both men and women, to condole with him for the loss
of his wife and to take order for the funeral, and he,
being resolved that what she had asked of him should
be done, imparted it to some of his kinsfolk, who were
all of opinion that he should open the chest, for that
peradventure he would find somewhat therein which it
were ill done to bury ; but he, being minded to keep
the faith he had pledged to his wife, would nowise consent to its being opened. Accordingly, the evening come,
the body was taken up and the chest borne after it, to
the exceeding wonderment of the whole city. When

Pandolfo felt himself taken up and heard chant *Requiem
æternam* over him, it need not be asked what he felt.
He was sundry whiles like to cry out and discover himself, notwithstanding his determination to die patiently;
but, knowing that he would assuredly be then and there
hewn in pieces by the kinsfolk of the husband and the
lady, who accompanied the body to the sepulchre, and
calling to mind the lady's love and bethinking him that
she had done this, overcome with excess of tenderness,
he finally resolved himself to die in silence, so he might
not in death defame her whom he had in life so loved.
In this mind he suffered himself be borne to the venerable church of San Cataldo, which is that of the Preaching
Friars, and what while the accustomed service for the
dead was in chanting over the body, the chest was set
down in a corner of the tomb, which was very large.
The lady's body was in due course laid therein; but,
because it was now dark night, the mouth of the tomb
was nowise luted with plaster, but the top-stone was
only laid thereon, it being purposed to dight it as usual
on the morrow.

Poor Pandolfo, who had never stirred since he was shut in
the chest, feeling himself entombed, sought to lay himself on
one side and groping with his hands, found divers things in
the chest, wrapped in linen, but cared not to enquire what
they were, applying to settle himself on such wise that he
might die with as little unease as possible. Now, as hath
been said, the chest had divers air-holes; but, albeit a little
air entered, for that the tomb was ill luted, he felt his breath
thicken and there was a sore stench from the dampness of
the sepulchre. However, God had more compassion upon
Pandolfo than he had had upon himself and provided for
his salvation on this wise. A nephew of the dead lady's

husband had understood from the maid how all her precious
things were in the chest which was to be buried with her;
wherefore, the funeral ended, he sought out two comrades
and discovered to them that which he purposed to do.
They declared themselves ready to accompany him and
so, a little before the friars arose for matins, they found
means to enter the convent and thence made their way
into the church, where, finding that the stone had not
been made fast over the mouth of the tomb, they easily
moved it from its place. Pandolfo, who was half suffocated, hearing this, forthright divined how the case stood
and was altogether heartened. Then, the stone removed,
the nephew and one of his comrades entered the tomb
and opened the chest with certain tools they had with
them.

No sooner did Pandolfo feel the lock broken than he
sprang up with great fury, shaking himself on terrible wise
and bellowing fearfully; whereupon the two young men
scrambled out of the tomb in a trice and fled, as fast as their
legs would carry them, after the third, who had abidden
without and who had already taken to his heels in dismay.
You may conceive how greatly Pandolfo, finding himself
at liberty, rejoiced in such rare luck. He came forth the
tomb and taking a flambeau of those which are kindled
whenas the priest upreareth the body of Christ, entered in
again, wishing to see his lady dead; then, looking what
was in the chest, he found all the lady's chains and
rings of gold, together with a good sum of monies. He
took the whole and shut the chest again; then, issuing
forth, he with a crowbar that was there turned back the
stone over the mouth of the tomb, as it was before, and
making his way out of the church and the convent by the
garden, betook himself to his own house, where he abode

many days without showing himself, himseeming he was still entombed. Now I am fain to believe that, if after this he fell in love with any woman, he was prudent enough to let himself be no more taken in such perils, the which indeed are not things to be over-often affronted; nay, all should beware of loving women who tender their own disorderly appetites dearer than their lovers' lives.

Bandello

There was never, mine honoured lord, a doubt amongst wise men that all the innumerable disorders which are daily seen to betide in the world arise from this, that men suffer themselves to be overcome and subjugated by their passions and inordinate appetites; whence, blinded by the profit and pleasure which they think to derive therefrom, they cast right and reason (which should be the rule of all our actions) behind their backs and commit themselves to the unbridled governance of their senses. Who knoweth not that love is a good and holy thing, without which the world could not keep itself afoot? But, an one suffer himself to be ensnared of lewd and false love and follow it with a slack rein, have we not seen such an one imbrue his hands in the blood of his rival and infected with the serpent-stings of venomous jealousy, lay violent hands upon the life of the hapless woman whom he loveth? Again, whoso letteth himself be overcome of anger oftentimes, carried away by the whirlwind of passion, seemeth to delight in shedding human blood and robbing others of repute and to glory in using unwonted cruelty. But, an I sought to enumerate all the passions which trouble our

souls and urge them to the doing of innumerable shameful
and blameworthy actions, thanks to ourselves, who will
not govern ourselves with reason, I should not make an
end thereof in many days, such and so many are they.
But I will e'en say one word of the monstrous disorders
which arise from gaming, whenas men, allured by the
pleasure which they take in hazarding their own and
others' substance, abandon themselves altogether to that
pernicious pursuit. We must, from the first, hold it for
sure and established that whosoever giveth himself to
gaming, whether with cards or with dice, is of necessity
infected with the greedy desire of gain, for that all who
delight overmuch, in gaming are by nature exceeding
covetous and albeit gamblers mostwhiles lose, nevertheless
so potent is the vain hope of gain that they still return
to gaming, thinking to recover that which they have lost.
Now I remember me that, I being at Mantua in discourse
with Signor Giovanni di Gonzaga and it being told him that
Signor Alessandro his son had gambled and lost five hundred
ducats, he incontinent said to me, "I am nowise concerned, Bandello mine, for the monies lost by my son,
but it irketh me for that, in seeking at any cost to recover
them, he will assuredly lose others galore. And thereof
ensueth another and no lesser evil. When a gambler hath
five or six times lost what monies he hath and his patrimony
sufficeth no more to keep him in play, the unhappy wretch,
unable and unwilling to live without gambling, affronteth
kinsfolk and friends and taketh up on loan such most
sum of monies as he may. But, losing and having no
means of requiting him whom he oweth and being still
set upon play, he doth of those monstrous misdeeds which
not only render him infamous and odious unto all, but
ultimately bring him to a most ignominious death; where-

fore wisely singeth our Mantuan Homer, whenas in the third book of his divine Æneids he saith, 'O execrable greed of gold, to what dost thou not enforce the breasts of mortals!'"[1] Now, it being discoursed of this matter in a goodly company at Pineruolo, on the occasion of a dispute befallen between two gambling soldiers, Captain Ghisi of Venice, a man doughty of his person, after many things said, according to the various opinions of the speakers, related a heinous case betided a little before at Venice, which filled all with marvel and amazement. I, being there present, wrote it down, meseeming the case might advantage many by diverting them from gambling, and now that I am making a choice of my novels for publication, this one coming to my hand, I straight determined that it should be read under your name, as well for the ancient familiarity which I had aforetime in Milan with your honoured father, Messer Gian Stefano Gloriero of worshipful memory, as also to certify you that I have been ever mindful of you, since that day when, at the convent of Le Grazie in Milan, in company of the erudite Messer Stefano Negro and of Messer Valtero Corbetta,[2] a man learned in one and the other tongue,[3] (nay, if I remember me aright, methinketh Messer Antonio Tilesio was also present,) we discoursed at length of Messer Celio Rodigino's Commentaries of Ancient Readings.[4] Nay, Messer Giulio Calestano, an unwearying proclaimer of your singular gifts, can certify you of the remembrance in which I hold you, he with whom I have so many a time devised

[1] *Quid non mortalia pectora cogis, Auri sacra fames !—Æn.* iii. 56-7.
[2] Walter Corbet?
[3] *i.e.* in Latin and Greek.
[4] *Dei commentari delle lezioni antiche di Messer Celio Rodigino.*

of you and of your most urbane and courteous nature and polished manners, recounting how prudently and with what unheard constancy you suffered the cruel and vehement blasts of contrary fortune, which long showed itself so hostile to you. Nor did you only suffer its adverse strokes and buffetings heroically, (as indeed do many,) but you availed so sagely to defend yourself with the shield of innocence against its envenomed darts that in the end you exhausted its every violence and altogether quenched its raging fury. Vouchsafe, then, to accept this my trifling gift with that serene countenance which you are used to show your friends; for what else can I give you, except it be some unpolished writing of mine own? Our Lord God prosper your every desire! Fare you well.

PIETRO, [SON] OF THE DRUGGIST OF THE GOLDEN APPLE AT VENICE, GAMETH AWAY HIS WHOLE SUBSTANCE AND LACKING MONIES TO PLAY WITHAL, MURDERETH A WIDOW WOMAN, HIS AUNT, TOGETHER WITH HER TWO CHILDREN AND A SERV-ING-WENCH ; THEN, BEING TAKEN BY THE OFFICERS OF THE LAW, HE EMPOISONETH HIMSELF AND JUSTICE IS DONE UPON HIS DEAD BODY.

Since, sirs, the quarrel and parlous affray, which hath befallen between our two soldiers, arose of no otherwhat than those pestilent dice (which are indeed the cause of so many monstrous ills, as also are the accursed cards,) and each of you hath said his say thereof, I will in my turn tell you that which presently occurreth to me to the purpose. And albeit it is said all day long that this sport [1] cometh from an ill quarter [2] and there be daily seen a thousand examples of its malignity, I have nevertheless bethought me to tell you a strange, piteous and cruel case which befell, no great while agone, at Venice, my beloved [3] native place. As you

[1] *i.e.* gaming.

[2] *Mala parte*, i.e. hell, as we say that "cards are the devil's picture-books."

[3] *Amabile* for *amata*. This use of the adjective for the past participle (and vice versâ) is, as I have before noted, of constant occurrence in the elder Italian writers.

must all know, there is no garden, how little soever it
be, so well and so assiduously tended, but that still, among
goodly and wholesome herbs, there spring ill and useless,
nay, whiles, harmful and pestilent weeds ; whence oftentimes, among beets and parsley, there sprouteth the deadly
hemlock. Let the diligent gardener weed as most he may,
dig, hoe and turn the soil over and over, still weeds will
grow there in plenty. It is, then, no matter for wonderment
if in a vast city, such as is my native place, Venice, so fair,
so rich, so populous and so puissant by land and by sea,
there be whiles found ruffians and caitiffs and reprobates,
who commit innumerable misdeeds. But, God be thanked,
they go not long without due chastisement, for that our
most sapient Senate, with its officials appointed to deal
with evildoers, hath its eyes on their hands on such wise
that in the end evildoers and criminals are most severely
punished. But to return to the subject of the foul deeds
and villainies which are daily done, I am convinced that
they mostwhiles proceed from gaming.

You must know, then, that, not many months agone,
there was in the said city of Venice one Pietro, the
youngest son of that druggist who hath for ensign a golden
apple ; which said Pietro was from his childhood given
to gaming and as he grew in age, the disorderly appetite of play waxed on him so terribly that he altogether
abandoned himself thereto, forsaking all else, and still
had a pair of dice in hand ; nay, the matter came to
such a pass that, whilst yet a lad, wrangling with a
fellow dice-player over a difference which arose between
them, he stabbed him in the breast with a poniard and
slew him. The murder discovered, Pietro took to flight
and being cited by justice and not appearing, he was
for his disobedience and contumacy outlawed as a homi-

cide. However, he abode no great while in exile, but presently, according to our laws, which we call capitulations,[1] he compounded for his offence and paying the capitation,[2] was purged of the outlawry and returned to Venice. Withal, he nowise desisted from gambling, nay, he still gamed away all he could get, so that, whereas he might lay his hand on the household gear, nought was safe, and eke in the druggist's shop there was often many a thing missing. His father, chagrined beyond measure at his son's love of play, bethought himself to give him a wife, so haply she might avail to divert him from gambling; but this was in vain, for that Pietro still followed his ordinary course. Wherefore, having innumerable times rebuked him thereof and had many ill words with him thereanent, seeing that it profited nothing to chide him or to complain of that his abominable vice, he determined to rid the house and himself of him. Accordingly, he (as is commonly said) emancipated him and assigning him his part of his patrimony, left him to his own devices, hoping that, it behoving him apply to the governance of his household and to provide for his wife's and his own occasions, he would leave gaming and become a new man. But it is a parlous thing to have become inured to an ill and inveterate usance, for that methinketh, by what I have heard tell thereof, a habit once contracted in a vicious usance cannot be left without the utmost difficulty and without unspeakable toil. Accordingly, Pietro went daily from ill to worse, gambling more than ever and selling now one piece, now another, of

[1] *Parti* for *Partiti*, capitulations or conventions.
[2] Lit. "He bought an outlaw's head" (*comprò un capo d'un bandito*).

the household stuff, to the perpetual chagrin and annoyance of his wife.

Now he had an aunt, his mother's sister, who, being left a widow, was well enough in case and had still some monies in hand. She loved Pietro amain and had often succoured him with monies, giving him now twenty, now thirty ducats; but, after awhile, understanding that he kept his wife in great unease and gambled away all he had at a truck-house,[1] she was vexed and resolved to give him no more monies. Accordingly, whenas next he had recourse to her, she chid him severely, rebuking him with sharp words, and finally told him that he must never hope to have another groat from her, except he changed his manner of living and usances. Nevertheless, ere he departed, he contrived to betalk her to such effect, promising her to gamble no more, that the good woman gave him half a score ducats; but no sooner had he them in hand than he gamed them all away and they went, like so many others, into Persia;[2] which when his aunt heard, she altogether determined in herself and gave him to understand that he must not expect another farthing from her. Pietro nevertheless went often to visit her, in the hope of getting somewhat from her, and still feigned a thousand occasions for the household; but he preached to deaf ears and sowed the sand; for that the aunt had gotten it fast in her head that she would give him no more monies, since he chose not to abstain from gambling, nay, was so inured thereto that he would have staked his part of the sun. He, seeing that he wearied himself in vain and knowing not what other

1 *Barrattaria*, an old name for a gaming-house.
2 *Persia*, quasi *Perdita*, loss, in modern vulgar parlance, "went to pot."

means to use to have money, was sore chagrined and knew
not whither to turn, himseeming that to live without
gambling was far worse than to be dead ; wherefore,
debating a thousand devices in himself and finding none
which might avail him to get wherewithal to play, he
abode sore disconsolate and knew not what to do.

See, now, gentlemen, what this pernicious vice of
gambling doth and whither it oftentimes bringeth its
followers and to what heinous and outrageous misdeeds
a man, be he good or ill, is carried away by greed of gain
and disorderly appetite, so he may avail to get monies
to keep himself in play.   Pietro, at the last, unable to
hit upon any device which was apt to put money in his
pocket and blinded by his disorderly desires and perverse
will, bethought him that it were well done, come what
would, to kill his aunt and rob her of all her monies and
trinkets of gold and silver ; nor did it suffice him to slay
her only, but he resolved to massacre all those of the house.
Having come to this heinous determination and himseeming
he might not of himself conveniently carry it into effect,
he discovered his purpose to one Giovan Nasone, a man
of very lewd life and a native of the village of Le Gam-
barare,[1] where there be many who, for every least price,
seem to glory in assassinating, despoiling and maiming men ;
for such is their repute.   Nasone needed no great persuasion,
more by token that Pietro promised to give him an hundred
gold ducats for the business.   Accordingly, having taken
order with his accomplice for that which they meant to
do, Pietro let make two great knives and sharpen them
till they were very razors ; one of them he gave to Nasone

---

[1] The little town of Gambara, some five miles distant from Venice,
is apparently meant.

and kept the other for himself. Now he was very familiar with his aunt's house, for that he oftentimes resorted thither; and albeit she would give him no more money, nevertheless he still went frequently to visit her and eat with her.

In those days there died the true father of our native country, the most serene prince Messer Andrea Gritto, a very wise doge, who was, in the course of the month of January,[1] succeeded by Messer Pietro Lando. Now our Venetian seigniors use to hold, in token of rejoicing for the accession of a new doge, great triumphs and festivities in the Place of St. Mark, whither all the city flocketh. Pietro knew that his aunt would not go thither, having asked her thereof and been answered by her in the negative, for that she was somewhat ailing of her person through a rheum which distilled from her head. Wherefore, no whit moved from his fell purpose, he determined not to lose so opportune an occasion, but to put his wicked design of murdering her in execution on the day of the festival, and appointed Giovan Nasone to be at the first hour of the night at her house in the Field[2] (as we use to say) of St. Maurice, a place of much resort in the main city, whilst he himself would await him in the house and would give him a certain signal when he should enter. Accordingly, towards four-and-twenty of the clock,[3] Pietro, taking his knife with him, went to visit his aunt, who was at home with a daughter of hers of twelve to thirteen and a little

---

[1] A.D. 1545.

[2] *Campo*, i.e. square.

[3] i.e. the last hour of the day, from 4 to 4.45 p.m. in January, according to sunset, from which Italian time is reckoned right through the twenty-four hours, so that one of the night would, in January, have been from 5 to 5.45 p.m.

son of some six years old and a maid; and there was also a cordwainer who frequented the house. Now, for that it had snowed hard all day, the maid went down to sweep away the snow before the door and with her went the cordwainer and there they abode awhile, talking, upon the fundament,[1] as it is there called. Pietro chose not to await Nasone, but, feigning an occasion of his own, went down and seeing that the maid still gossiped with the cordwainer, shut the door, so that she abode without. Then, returning forthright aloft, he at one blow cut the aunt's throat and passing into another chamber, where the girl plied her childish games with her little brother, he there on like wise, without the least humanity or compassion, (as he were an anthropophagist[2] or cannibal, rather than a man and a Venetian,) slew the little creatures, as they had been two lambs; after which, going down again, he opened the door and hid himself behind it, against the return of the maid, who, having made an end of sweeping, entered in and was forthright, without knowing who smote her, struck dead by Pietro with a great blow on the head. This done, he shut the door again and betook himself upstairs; where, knowing the money-box, he took the key from his luckless aunt's girdle and possessed himself, at his leisure, of what monies it contained, amounting to a thousand ducats, and all her jewels, together with divers silver ornaments, wherewith having filled the sleeves of his jerkin (which was what is called at Venice cubit-sleeved[3]) he went down and locking the door, made off. He found

---

[1] *Fondamento*, i.e. the quay or pavement of such streets as are actually paved, as distinguished from those in which the houses abut directly upon the canals.

[2] *Antropofago.*

[3] *A gomito*, i.e. with wide, hanging sleeves.

Nasone awaiting the signal, according to appointment, and saying to him, "Come, comrade, let us go, for I have despatched all," told him how he had dealt. And in so far he had fortune favourable, for that they met no one. Accordingly, by the light of the moon, he counted out to Nasone the hundred ducats he had promised him, instantly praying him keep the thing most secret and get him gone and not return to Venice for some months ; and so they went each his way.

Now the cordwainer, who was, as you have heard, in the widow's house, what time Pietro came thither, and who abode hard by, was used bytimes to do sundry small offices for the lady and was that evening to fetch her candles for the use of the household ; but, he having been to see the festivities which were toward at St. Mark, it was not till about three of the night[1] that he bought the candles and carried them to the house. He knocked twice or thrice very hard and hearing no answer, concluded that the lady had gone with Pietro, whom he had left in the house, to sup with their kinsfolk, it being the Venetian custom to sup very late in winter. On the morrow, after sunrise, he came back with the candles, but, getting no answer to his loud knocking, concluded that there was no one in the house and abode till the evening, not withal suspecting aught. Then, at one of the night,[2] he returned and knocked again ; but, none answering him aught, he went enquiring of the neighbours if they knew where the widow was and getting no news of her, betook himself to her nearest kinsfolk. She being found with none of them, great was the clamour and perturbation, none being able to conceive what was come of her and her children ; wherefore the cordwainer went,

[1] 7 to 7.45 p.m.   [2] 5 to 5.45 p.m.

with some of her kinsfolk (and amongst the rest the cruel
murderer Pietro himself, who ruffled it more than any), to
advertise the police of the case. The seigniors of the night[1]
(as they are called) forthright sent their sergeants, who broke
in the door and found the wretched maid weltering in her
blood, with her head cloven to the teeth; whereupon all,
aghast at so horrid a sight, went upstairs and found the
lady in one chamber near the hearth, and in another, the
two little ones dead in their blood, [a spectacle] that would
have moved to pity the fiercest and cruellest tigers of
Hyrcania. The seigniors, advised of that most heinous and
unnatural case, proceeded to make the strictest and most
diligent enquiry, so such wickedness should not go unpunished; whilst the dead woman's kinsfolk also bestirred
themselves amain for the discovery of the murderer, above
all Pietro, who made a greater show of grief than the rest,
feigning himself unable to put up with so cruel a calamity,
and threw himself on his aunt's body, crying and raving
and saying that nought he spared to find the evildoer.

Now, nothing coming to light, save that the cordwainer
declared to have left Pietro in the widow's house, when he
himself departed thence, and the latter confessing it, but
averring that he had departed immediately after him, Pietro
was, on this indication, attached by the captain of the
watch and told that he must present himself before the
seigniors of the night. He was nowhit dismayed, but,
with a show of great composure, embarked in a boat with
the captain and a cousin of his own, a sister's son of the
murdered aunt, to whom drawing near and bidding him
aloud be of good cheer, he secretly gave him a little book

---

[1] *i.e.* the night-marshals, the officials charged with the care of the
public safety during the night.

of tablets, wherein for remembrance one writeth what one
will with a latten style and wherein he had noted the number
of the monies, jewels and ornaments of silver which he had
stolen and likewise the hundred ducats given to Nasone,
and said to him softly, "Dear my cousin, prithee burn these
tablets and seek me out forthright Gian Nasone and bid him
begone without fail. Have no fear for me, for I shall know
how to defend myself. I trust to you; the thing is done
and there is no help for it." Pietro was carried off to prison
and his cousin went home, sore dismayed and perplexed and
unknowing what to do; however, after he had pondered the
case amain, he ultimately (whether moved by indignation at
so enormous and monstrous a crime or for fear of justice or
what not else) carried the tablets to the seigniors and told
them what Pietro had said to him. Nasone was straightway
taken and without awaiting torture, confessed the whole
thing exactly as it had ensued; what while the tablets were
shown to Pietro, who denied all that his cousin said and
being confronted with his accomplice, declared, with a
steadfast countenance, that he knew nothing of that whereof
he spoke; nor was it anywise possible, for all the evidence
they could produce nor for all the torments they could inflict
upon him, to make him confess aught; nay, he undauntedly
denied everything. Now he had, whilst talking with Nasone,
thrown his knife into a canal and on the latter's confession,
it was sent to fish it up. Moreover, Nasone knowing who
the cutler was that had made the knives, he was sent for
and deposed to having made them at Pietro's instance.
Pietro, however, denied all and declared, with an assured
countenance, as he had been most innocent, that the
villager and the cutler were drunkards, dotards and
besotted dreamers. Being asked how he came to have
his jerkin bloody in so many places, he replied that he had

bloodied himself in passing by a butcher's shop and belike
also on the body of his aunt, whereon he had cast himself.

The judges were in some doubt for Pietro's assured
answers; nevertheless, holding him, upon the evidence of
the tablets, which were proved to be in his handwriting,
and of the many other circumstances which had come to
light, for guilty, they condemned both him and Nasone to
be tanacled[1] and after quartered. The sentence pronounced,
the wretched Pietro's father and mother and brother went
to the prison, to see him and comfort him, and abode with
him a good while. Now his brother had spoken with him
on the foregoing day and had been besought of him to give
him some poison that should kill him immediately, so he
might not die that ignominious death in the sight of the
people, and had accordingly prepared a terrible and instan-
taneous poison; then, placing it in a little phial, he hid
the latter in a pantable and telling Pietro what he had done,
changed pantables with him, unobserved of any. Pietro
refusing to confess and declaring himself unjustly condemned, it was sent for Fra Bernardino Occhino of Siena,
who was presently preaching in Venice with marvellous
success and devoutness, but hath since apostatized and
turned a violent Lutheran. Accordingly, he came to the
prison the day before the sentence was to be executed and
proceeded to exhort Pietro to confession and penitence.
Now the latter had a little before swallowed the poison,
nor had the friar said fifty words to him when the drug,
which was exceeding violent of its nature, began to work
its effects, so that, Pietro's eyes rolling and his face swelling
on extraordinary wise, he became so horrible to look upon
that he resembled anything rather than a man. His eyes

---

[1] *Tanagliato*, i.e. tortured with red-hot pincers.

and nose ran and there issued from his mouth slaver of
various colours, fetid beyond measure ; whereat Fra
Bernardino was sore affrighted and rose up, fearing lest
the unhappy wretch thus disfeatured should tear the cowl
from his head. Then, the gaolers becoming aware of this
and advertising the seigniors, it was sent in haste for
physicians ; but all succour was in vain, the poison having
already usurped the heart and all the vitals. But see now
if Pietro had altogether given himself in prey to the arch-
fiend. Having done so frightful a wickedness and finding
himself without hope of escaping death, he might and should
at the least have saved his soul and not let it perish with
his body, by confessing and heartily repenting of his sins,
there being no sin so great but our Lord God pardoneth
it unto whoso turneth unto Him, confessing himself to the
priest. But the wretched man chose rather to die a sur-
passing villain than a repentant Christian. He altogether
refused to confess or to repent him of his many misdeeds ;
nay, in the very agony of death, the poison having usurped
the vital arteries, so that he could no more speak, he
scrupled not, at his last moments, (having already done
so many wrongs to God, his neighbour and himself) to
persist in evildoing ; for that, dumb as he was become, he
sought yet (speaking Lombard-fashion) to add iron to the
cruzet and studied to compass the death of one of his
keepers, whether for that he had belike done him some
displeasure or to free his brother from suspicion, striving
as most he might, with signs and gestures, (for that he was
unable to speak) to inculpate the warder aforesaid and
making signs that it was he had given him the poison ;
wherefore the poor wretch was taken and cruelly tortured,
but suffered the torments with constancy and confessed
nothing ; for what indeed should he confess, being innocent?

However, the brother's pantables being recognized and a little hole found in one of them, wherein the phial of poison had been hidden, the judges sent to cite him and finding he had departed Venice, concluded that it was he who had given Pietro the poison. Moreover, the lads of the druggery being taken and examined, one of them confessed that he had seen Pietro's brother prepare he knew not what poisonous matters, but to what end he knew not; wherefore the fugitive, being cited by the court and not appearing, was outlawed and the poor warder liberated. Meanwhile Pietro died and dead as he was, was embarked with Nasone aboard a barge and carried throughout all Venice, what while both were tanacled sore with red-hot pincers, albeit Pietro, being already dead, felt nothing; after which they were, as they deserved, hewn into four pieces and hanged on the gibbets in the Lagoons for food to the corbies and other birds of prey. Such, then, was the end of the wicked gambler Pietro, who had eke another very great default, in that, by what I hear of him, he was the foulest blasphemer and denier of God and the Saints in those parts; but it is no marvel that he should have blasphemed, that heinous vice being as proper and peculiar unto gamblers as heat to fire and light to the sun.

Bandello

to the illustrious Signor Manfredi Seignior of Correggio.

I am fain to believe that the story hath not escaped
your memory which Signor Tommaso Maino narrated last
year, what time you were a-pleasuring with divers other
lords and gentlemen in the most delightsome garden of
your fast friends, the noble Seigniors Attellani, the discourse
turning, I know not how, upon the barbarous cruelties
wreaked by that most impious and ferocious tyrant, Eccelino
da Romano, upon men and women of all ages in various
places. Some thereof were cited, and amongst others,
that which he wrought at Verona upon twelve thousand
young men of Padua, whom he had, during his occupation
of that city, chosen from the chief families of the place
and carried off with him as hostages ; how, to wit, understanding that Padua had revolted against him, he caused
the whole twelve thousand hapless youths to be piteously
slaughtered by his soldiers nor would, for all the prayers
or monies which might be proffered him, grant any of them
his life. From that grisly subject we passed to speaking
of the qualities that a good prince, who would fain eschew
the name of tyrant and make himself rather loved than
feared of his people, should study to have and exercise ;
for that the greatest strength and wealth that a prince,

of whatsoever estate and dominion he be, can hope to have, an he think to maintain himself against his enemies, must certainly be the love [of his subjects ;] since, when a people loveth its lord, he may rest assured that it will be faithful to him and will nowise lust after change of masters. Thereupon, the most debonair Signor Tommaso Maino told us his story, which seemed to us all who were there marvellous and worthy of remembrance, as well for showing the monstrous tyranny of an inhuman despot as also for making known that in every age and nation there are to be found among women some of great excellence and deserving to be still recalled with a prefacement of honour. You then turned to me and said, smiling, "Bandello, this will certes not show ill amongst thy novels." "Nay, indeed," replied I and promised to write it, as I did on my return home. Now, going collecting and putting together these my novels, according as they come to my hand, I have chosen to set your name in the forefront of this one, so it may be seen and read of all in witness of the friendship which is between us, I having no otherwhat to bequeath to the world that may testify to our mutual goodwill. Fare you well.

The Third Story.

A VERY GOODLY VENGEANCE WREAKED BY THE ELIANS UPON ARISTOTIMUS, A MOST CRUEL TYRANT, AND THE DEATH OF THE LATTER, TOGETHER WITH OTHER INCIDENTS.

The cruelty of that perfidious monster Eccelino hath brought me in mind of a story no less memorable than pitiful, which I read, the year after the battle of G[h]iara d'Adda,[1] in the house of that most learned and upright man Messer Giacomo Antiquario, to whom the most debonair Messer Aldo Manuzio,[2] who deserveth well of all tongues,[3] made gift of sundry books of Plutarch of Cheronæa, not yet rendered into the Roman tongue, albeit many thereof are presently to be read translated both into Latin and into the vernacular. In this Greek book, then, (I mean that wherein Plutarch speaketh of many illustrious and excellent ladies,) I read the story which I am about to recount to you. Aristotimus, a man of his nature savage and most inhuman, made himself, by the favour of King Antigonus, tyrant of his native place, Elis in the Peloponnesus, a region of Achaia now called the Morea, and making

---

[1] Or Aignadel, 14th May, 1509.
[2] Aldus the printer.
[3] Or "languages" (lingue).

ill use of his authority, like a tyrant as he was, daily
vexed and harassed the wretched townsfolk and all his
subjects with extraordinary oppressions; the which befell
not so much for that he was by nature cruel and ferocious
as that he had to counsellors barbarous and vicious men,
to whom he had committed all the administration of the
realm and the guard of his person; and amongst his innumerable crimes and iniquitous actions, one wrought by
him against Philodemus, which after cost him his kingdom
and his life, is especially memorable.

Philodemus had a daughter called Micca, who was, for
her exceeding beauty and her chaste and virtuous fashions,
holden of all the city in the utmost admiration. Of her
a certain Lucius, a soldier of the tyrant's body-guard,
was passionately enamoured, if, indeed, love his [appetite]
deserve to be named and not rather, as the issue showed,
a filthy, fell and bestial lust. He was very dear to
Aristotimus for the likeness of their evil usances and commanded these and those of whatsoever liked him; wherefore he sent one of the tyrant's satellites or sergeants to
bid Philodemus bring him his daughter without fail at
such an hour. Hearing so dire and unexpected a message,
the father and mother of the fair and hapless Micca,
constrained by tyrannical force and fatal necessity, exhorted
their daughter, after innumerable tears and piteous sighs,
unresistingly to suffer herself be carried to the despot's
favourite, since there was nothing for it but to obey.
However, the high-hearted damsel, who was naturally magnanimous and had been sagely nurtured with the best
instructions, being minded to die rather than let herself
be violated, cast herself at her father's feet and clasping
his knees, instantly besought and entreated him as most
effectually she might on no wise to suffer her be led to

so ignominious an office, but rather to slay her than allow her to be deflowered and losing her maidenhead, shamefully to abide on life, branded with eternal infamy. What while they were in this debate, Lucius, waxing impatient for the long delay and raging with drunken fury, betook himself to the virgin's house and finding her prostrate and weeping at her father's feet, with her head in his lap, commanded her, in an imperious voice and full of the most grievous menace, to arise forthright and follow him; which she refusing to do, he fell into a most masterful passion of choler and tearing her garments from her back, scourged her alabaster shoulders on such pitiless wise that the blood ran on every side and the virgin abode stricken with many deep and grievous wounds. Yet think not, sirs, that she was any whit stirred from her steadfast purpose; nay with such fortitude did she endure the inflicted stripes that she was nowise heard to utter any word of complaint nor bemoan herself with groans or otherwise; but her wretched father and mother, moved by parental pity at so cruel and woeful a sight, wept sore and seeing that neither prayers nor tears availed to deliver their daughter from the hands of that most barbarous monster, began in a loud voice to invoke and implore the aid and succour of the Immortal Gods and of their fellowmen, themseeming they were e'en unjustly vexed and afflicted; whereupon the arrogant and inhuman barbarian, frenzied with wine and fury, butchered the constant maid in her father's lap, slitting her ivory throat with a knife.

The perfidious and cruel tyrant, learning this unheard wickedness, not only refused to punish the miscreant for so horrid a misdeed, but showed him more favour than ever and entreated those citizens who blamed so dire a cruelty with a fierceness and barbarity beyond his wont;

nay, he let hew a great part of them piecemeal in the
market-place, as calves and oxen are butchered at the
shambles, and the rest he condemned to perpetual exile.
Of the banished folk, eight hundred fled into Ætolia, a
province near Epirus, which is now called Albania, and
thence most urgently besought Aristotimus that he would
suffer their wives and little ones to rejoin them in their
exile. But they preached to deaf ears and their prayers
were scattered to the winds; algates, (and you shall soon
hear why) a few days thereafterward, he sent a trumpeter
through all the city and let make public outcry that it should
be permitted the outlaws' wives to go seek their husbands
with their children and such gear as they could carry.
This proclamation was hearkened with the utmost satisfaction by the women whose husbands were exiled and
who, according to that which report avoucheth, were at
the least six hundred in number ; and to confirm them in
their hopes, the perfidious tyrant ordained that they should
all depart in company on a certain day. Meanwhile, the
rejoicing women made ready all that they thought to carry
with them, providing themselves with waggons and riding-
cattle, and the appointed day come, all betook themselves
to the gate assigned them, one [afoot] with her little children
in her hand and bearing certain of her goods on her head,
another a-horseback and yet others in chariots, with their
household stuff and little ones, according as they chanced
to be rich or poor. All being in readiness, the gate was
opened and they proceeded to issue forth ; but scarce were
the poor women without the place when up came the
sergeants and satellites of the tyrant and cried out to them
from afar to halt nor dare to fare farther ; then, bidding
them re-enter the city, they turned the waggons about by
main force and violently goading and lashing the oxen

and horses, harried and worried them on such wise,
suffering them go neither forward nor backward, that
many of the wretched women fell to the ground with their
little ones and abode miserably mangled by the wheels
and the hoofs of the cattle, all bruised and many killed.
And what was pitiful to see was that they could not help
one another and still less could they succour the tender
little children ; whilst, to make matters worse, those ribald
sergeants still smote and lashed them cruelly with staves
and whips, driving them towards the city and enforcing
them enter in. Some died of the crush and many abode
crippled; but of the children many more perished and
were maimed, and all who survived were thrown into
prison ; whilst the goods which they carried with them
all fell to the tyrant. This brutal and monstrous misdeed
was infinitely grievous and vexatious to the Elians ; wherefore the priestesses consecrated to Bacchus went in procession, invested with the sacerdotal robes and bearing in
their hands the sacred emblems of their God, to seek
Aristotimus, who was then walking in the market-place,
surrounded by his satellites. The sergeants, for reverence
of the religious ladies, gave them passage to the tyrant's
presence and he, seeing them clad on that wise and bearing
in hand the sacred Bacchic mysteries,[1] halted and hearkened
to them in silence ; but, when he knew that they came
to entreat him in favour of the imprisoned women, he was
straightway possessed with diabolical frenzy and harshly
and with horrid clamour rated his satellites for admitting
them to his presence. Then he bade drive them forth
the market-place with many lashes, regardless of their
sacred office, and amerced each one of them, for having

---

[1] Sic (*misteri*).

dared to intercede with him for the wretched prisoners, in two talents, the minor Attic talent, a money current in those times, being, as we learn from the writers of the day, equal to some five hundred crowns, a little more or less.

After so many and such enormous crimes committed by Aristotimus, Hellanicus, one of the chiefest and most considerable citizens of Elis, resolved, albeit he was wellnigh decrepit, to expose himself to every risk and essay an he might not avail to deliver his country from the fell tyranny of that most wicked despot. Of him, as well for the impotency of his age as that he had no sons, they being dead, the tyrant took no great heed, himseeming he was unapt to make a tumult in the city. Meanwhile, the Elians, who had (as I said awhile agone) taken refuge in Ætolia, agreed amongst themselves to try their fortune and do their utmost endeavour to recover their fatherland and slay Aristotimus; wherefore, mustering some squadrons of soldiers, they occupied a certain place near the city, where they might abide in security and attack their native place at their commodity and advantage, to drive the tyrant thence. No sooner were they encamped there than many citizens fled forth of Elis and joined themselves to the exiles; so that these latter grew speedily to a right army; whereat Aristotimus being grievously troubled and as it were foreboding him of his coming ruin, he went to the prison where the exiles' wives lay and for that he was by nature turbulent and ferocious, he concluded that he would gain his end with the said women by means of fear and menaces rather than with prayers and fair usage. Accordingly, entering where they were, he imperiously and fiercely bade them send messengers with letters to their husbands, who were

in arms without, praying them most instantly desist from
the begun war; "else," said he, "I certify you that,
an no effect ensue of that which I command you, I will
first tear all your children limb from limb in your presence
and after scourge you all on the cruellest wise and put
you to a dire and ignominious death." There was no
woman who uttered one least word in reply to so cruel
and tyrannical a declaration, and the perfidious tyrant,
seeing their silence, impatiently bade them answer what
they meant to do. But they, albeit they dared not proffer
a word of response, nevertheless by their silence, mutu-
ally looking one another in the face, showed plainly
enough that they made no account of his menaces and
were ready to die rather than give effect to his will
and commandment. Then Megisto, wife of Timoleon,—
a matron illustrious as well for her proper worth as for
her husband's nobility and chief amongst all those women,
who had not moved from her seat at the coming of the
tyrant nor deigned to do him honour, nay, had forbidden any to arise,—loosing her tongue and abiding
seated on the earth as she was, replied on this wise,
with a firm voice, to the tyrant's demand, saying, "If
there were in thee, Aristotimus, any least part of manly
prudence or of counsel, thou wouldst certes not have
bidden women write to their husbands and prescribe to
them what they should do, but wouldst have let us all
go to them, as to our lords and masters, and have used
modester words and better counsels than those wherewith
thou hast presently reviled and affronted us. Marry, an
thou find thyself bereft of all hope and flatter thyself by
our means to hoodwink our husbands, I certify thee
that thou art greatly mistaken, inasmuch as we will
nowise suffer ourselves to be duped by thee; and to

boot we would have thee to know that they[1] are not
nor will ever become such fools as to neglect and mis-
prise the welfare and freedom of their fatherland for the
sake of their wives and children. Nay, thou mayst be
assured that it will not cause them so much hurt to
lose us and their children, whom they cannot presently
have, as they will gain in contentment and advantage
an they avail to deliver their fellow-citizens and themselves from the yoke of thine arrogant and insupportable
tyranny." Then, as she ensued her free speech, the
villainous Aristotimus, enraged beyond measure and unable
longer to contain the fury with which he was like to
burst, bade bring her little son before him, as he would
then and there have butchered him ; and as his ministers
sought him, his mother, seeing him at play with the
other infants, (for that of his tender age he knew not
where he was,) called him by name, saying, "Come
hither, my son, so thou mayst lose thy life ere age bring
thee any sense or experience of the frightful tyranny
under which we live. It were far more grievous to me
to see thee serve against the nobility of thy blood than
to have thee torn limb from limb here before my feet."
At these words, steadfastly and undauntedly uttered by
Megisto, the furious tyrant drew his sword from the
sheath and made at her to slay her ; but a familiar of
his, called Chilo, interposed and hindered him with fair
words from committing so horrid and atrocious a misdeed. Now this Chilo was a feigned friend to the tyrant
and conversed with his other familiars ; but [at heart] he
hated him with an incredible hatred and was one of those
who had conspired against him under the headship of

---

[1] *i.e.* their husbands.

Hellanicus. He, then, seeing Aristotimus run so furiously
to wreak cruelty upon Megisto, cast his arms about him,
telling him that it was a mark of a base mind to imbrue
one's hands in female blood and that it behoved a man
of high degree on no account so to degenerate from the
nobility of his ancestors; whereupon Aristotimus, suffering
himself to be persuaded, with difficulty suppressed his
anger and leaving the women, went off elsewhither.

Not long after there befell a prodigy after this sort.
What while the tyrant's supper was making ready, he had
withdrawn to a chamber with his wife, and presently,
there came an eagle flying high over the palace, which
descended little by little and let drop a great stone, as
if of set purpose, on the roof of the aforesaid chamber,
then soared aloft with great noise and clamour and vanished
from the sight of those who stood watching it. Aristotimus, aroused and appalled by the noise and the outcries
of the spectators and learning what had betided, was sore
troubled in mind and sent to call his augur, so he might
resolve him what the presage signified. The augur bade
him be of good cheer, for that the portent betokened him
to be beloved of Jove, who would be favourable to him
in everything; but to such citizens as he had proved true
and faithful he discovered that there overhung the tyrant's
head the greatest peril he had ever suffered; whereupon
those who had conspired with Hellanicus declared that
there was no more reason for delay and resolved to slay
Aristotimus on the morrow. That night, as Hellanicus
slept, himseemed he saw his son, who said to him,
"Sleepest thou, father? I am thy son whom Aristotimus
hath slain. Knowest thou not that on the morrow thou
art to be captain and leader of the fatherland?" Heartened
by this vision, Hellanicus arose at daybreak and exhorted

his fellow-conspirators to execute without delay that which they had already ordained for the benefit of the fatherland. Now Aristotimus had certain news that Crater, tyrant of another city, was on the march with a great army to succour him against the revolted Elians and was already arrived at Olympia, a city between Mounts Ossa and Olympus. Accordingly, full of hope and confidence and thinking already to have defeated and taken the exiles, he made so bold as to come into the market-place, without his body-guard and attended but by Chilo and one or two others of his men, what time the conspirators were assembled there. Hellanicus, seeing so goodly an occasion of freeing his beloved fatherland by the death of the perfidious tyrant, tarried no longer to give the appointed signal to his accomplices; nay, the intrepid old man, turning to his companions and raising his hands and eyes to heaven, said in a clear and sonorous voice, "Why tarry ye, fellow-citizens, in the eyes of your city, to achieve that goodly and splendid emprise which you have so nobly undertaken?" At this speech, Chilo was the first to unsheathe his flashing sword and slay one of those who accompanied the tyrant, whilst Thrasybulus and Lampis set upon Aristotimus, who, fleeing from their onslaught, ran to the temple of the God Jupiter, where he was, as he deserved, despatched with a thousand strokes. The conspirators, having killed him, haled his body into the market-place, calling the people to liberty; whereupon all ran thither and there were few forewent the women, who flocked to the first call, giving the deliverers of the fatherland joy of so worshipworth a work, what while their glad voices made manifest token of their allegresse. Meanwhile, a great crowd ran with unspeakable clamour to the tyrant's palace and the latter's wife, hearing the vociferations of the populace and being certified of her husband's death, shut herself with her two daughters in a chamber, where, knowing how much they were hated of the Elians, she made a noose of a rope and hanged herself to a beam. The chamber-doors were cast down by many, who, no whit moved by the horrid spectacle of the hanged lady, took the two trembling daughters of the tyrant, who were very fair and in the flower of marriageable age, and haled them away, thinking first to ravish them and amply to sate their lust on them and after kill them. At this moment up came Megisto, accompanied by other matrons, and understanding what they thought to do, chid them severely, telling them that they, [who] wished to establish a civil[1] state, did things which the most dishonest tyrant would not have done. All yielded to the authority of the noble matron, who thought it excellent well done to deliver the two virgins from their hands and accordingly brought them into the chamber where their dead mother was; then, knowing all to be resolved that none of the tyrant's blood should abide alive, she turned to them and said, "All I can say to you is that I suffer you choose that manner of death which least misliketh you." Thereupon the elder damsel loosed her girdle and proceeded to make a noose thereof to hang herself withal, exhorting her younger sister the while to follow her example and beware lest she did aught base or unworthy of their degree. At these words, the younger laid hands upon the girdle which her sister was in act to knot and instantly besought her to let her die first; whereto, "Sister mine," answered the elder, "I could never deny thee aught, what while it was permitted us to live, and since it presently pleaseth thee that I abide

---

[1] *Civile*, or, in modern parlance, "civilized."

awhile after thee, so be it ; but I assure thee, dearest sister mine, that it will be far more grievous to me than death itself to see thee dead before me." So saying, she gave the girdle to her sister, counselling her have a care to set the knot near the nape of her neck, so she might be the quicklier and more easily suffocated. When she saw her sister dead, she undid the deathly girdle from her neck and modestly covered the dead maiden's body with her clothes ; then, turning to Megisto, she urgently prayed her be pleased to take order that her own and her sister's bodies should not be seen of any naked, and this said, she intrepidly strangled herself with the same noose and made an end of her life. Megisto presently let bury them both in one grave and I am fain to believe that none of the Elians was so inhuman and so inveterate against the cruel tyrant but he was somewhat moved to compassion by the noble bearing of these two young virgins and the greatness of their minds. Alack, with what far greater praise had these two sisters been celebrated, had they not been daughters of so wicked a father ; but the sins of the parents should nowise be suffered to obscure the good and virtuous actions of their descendants.

Bandello

to Messer Tommaso Castellano.

Messer Antonio Castellano, your uncle, is (as you know better than I) very prompt and ready in general converse and hath still some new quip in hand. Being banished from Bologna by Pope Julius II., for his devotion to the Bentivoglio faction, he abode long at Milan in the house of Signor Alessandro Bentivoglio, who had, after the loss of the Seigniory of Bologna,[1] retired to Milan, where the Lady Ippolita Sforza his consort had inherited castlewicks and estates from her father. And for that your uncle was a fine talker and had still some story or anecdote to the purpose of whatsoever was said, it befell that one day, the said Lady Ippolita being ailing of her person, Firenzuola,[2] a very famous Bolognese physician, who had been fetched

---

[1] Alessandro Bentivoglio, one of Bandello's patrons, was the son of Giovanni Bentivoglio, Seignior of Bologna, who, after nearly half a century's rule, was expelled from his dominion by Pope Julius II. in 1506. Five years after, Alessandro and his brother were reinstated by the French in the seigniory, but only held it till the next year, when, the French being compelled to retreat after the battle of Ravenna, the Papal authority was definitively re-established in Bologna.

[2] Apparently not the well-known contemporary poet and novelist of that name (Agnolo Firenzuola, 1493-1545), who was a churchman and an advocate.

to attend her, told a merry story of one Barbaccia, a Sicilian doctor, who had long lectured on civil law at Bologna, whereto Messer Antonio forthright added another, which made us laugh no less than the first. Firenzuola, then, told us that, Barbaccia having advised one of the Ghisilieri family anent a lawsuit he had with a nephew of his, his client sent him five-and-twenty ducats; but Barbaccia, finding seven or eight of them lighter than he could wish, sent them all back, saying that he wanted good money and not gold that lacked of the true weight. Ghisilieri, having the ducats again, put Barbaccia off from day to day, himseeming he should not, for four pages he had written, have shown such greed of monies, and would nowise give him another groat; whereof Barbaccia complaining, he answered him nothing save that he deserved an hundred lashes for sending back the ducats. Messer Antonio, as I have said, incontinent told another story, which I wrote down and meseemed it should be given to you, it being fruit grown in your uncle's garden. Accordingly, I send it to you, so it may be to you a pledge of friendship. Fare you well.

The Fourth Story.

DOM BARTOLOMMEO DA BIANORO RETURNETH A DOUBLOON RECEIVED BY WAY OF ALMS AND NOT GETTING IT AGAIN, PROCURETH HIMSELF TO BE SCOURGED.

If Barbaccia, gentlemen, complained of our fellow-towns-man, as our excellent Firenzuola hath presently told us, meseemeth he had some reason therefor, for that, he being a very famous jurist and one whose opinions were much esteemed, it may be supposed that he had laboured amain to turn over the many books in which the voluminous laws of Bologna are comprised and that he had taken great pains to find reasons to the purpose, as well for his own honour as for his client's advantage; nor would I venture to say that our friend Ghisilieri is to be commended for retaining the monies. Algates, I will aver and take my solemn oath that a gentlewoman of ours, called Mistress Giovanna dei Bianchi, deserveth great praise for having played an avaricious priest a merry turn, the which was on this wise. No great while agone, it being the season of Lent, whenas it behoveth all good and true Christians confess themselves to the priest, the said Mistress Giovanna went to confess herself at the church of San Petronio to a priest called Dom Bartolommeo da Bianoro, who passed for a very learned man and a godly liver, but was greedier after monies than cats after mice. Our gentlewoman diligently made her confession and having gotten her penance and absolution, gave the priest a double ducat of gold, of those which Signor Giovanni Bentivoglio let strike in the good [old] times. The priest took the doubloon blithely and betook himself to his chamber, where, as he had sold pepper and cinnamon,[1] he weighed the coin and finding that it lacked some two grains of the just weight, returned to the church, where he found the lady yet at her orisons. He had indeed discretion enough to await her rising; but, as soon as he saw her arisen, he came up to her in haste and said, "Madam, you gave me a double ducat, which is under weight. Prithee be pleased to change it; here it is." The lady, knowing the priest's greed by this act, took the money and said, "Sir, in good sooth I have no other monies with me for the nonce, for that I took this a'purpose, thinking it to be good, it having been given me by Messer Taddeo Bolognino, whom you know to be a gentleman of honour; but I will bring you another to-morrow." The priest believed her and abode in expectation of a better. However, she that same day went to San Domenico and there confessed herself anew to one of the friars, to whom she gave the doubloon, praying him have Gregorian masses chanted for her father's soul. The friar took it and calling the sacristan, showed him the alms and charged him let say the masses bespoken by the lady, then dropped the doubloon into the alms-box, as is the usance of officiating priests.

Next day, Mistress Giovanna went, according to her wont, to the preachment at San Petronio, and the sermon over, up came Sir Priest and said to her, with a certain air

---

[1] *i.e.* as if he were a grocer, taking money in the way of trade.

which savoured somewhat of the imperious, " Madam, have
you brought the money?" She, seeing that his presumption, answered him, saying, "Sir, to tell you the truth,
seeing you refused my gold, I went to confess myself to
another priest, who found it good and full weight." At
these words the scurvy priest abode dumbfounded and
knew not what to do or to say, himseeming the ceiling of
the church had fallen on his head; wherefore he betook
himself, without saying a word, to his chamber and dined
but ill that morning, swallowing more sighs than bread.
Then, unable to forgive himself for having lost so much
money by his over-greed, he called a clerk of his, a native
of Val di Lamone, who was young, but very shrewd and
quick-witted, and shutting the door, threw himself across
a bench, with his buttocks uncovered, and said to the lad,
"Naldello,"[1] for such was his name, "take that scourge
on the table yonder and give me five-and-twenty good lashes
on the backside." The clerk, seeing the Colosseum[2] of
Rome in the air, asked him what was to do; but he
answered nothing save, "Strike, strike, I tell thee, and
ask no further." The clerk, thereupon, hearing his master's
deliberate commandment, dealt him five-and-twenty good
stripes with a heavy hand, charcoal-measure[3] (as the saying
is), so that the Colosseum showed many bloody tokens.
The priest, having gotten his full measure, arose and said
ruefully, "Marvel not, my son, if I have willed thee scourge
me, for that I have committed an exceeding great error,
which deserved a much greater chastisement than that which
thou hast given me;" and told him how he had lost the

[1] Dim. of Rinaldo.
[2] *Culiseo*, the old spelling of the word *Coliseo*, here used by
Bandello for the sake of a play upon words with *culo*, arse.
[3] i.e. *good* measure, full-heaped and running over.

double ducat. When the lad heard the parson's folly, he turned to him with the foulest possible aspect and said, "Alack, what do I hear? Thirty thousand murrains take you! What have you done, man of little worth and sorrier far than I can say? You have, then, given back a doubloon for that it was not so heavy as your miserly greed would have it, you having gained it by making the sign of the cross over a woman's head! Pox take you! One would think you had sold her saffron.[1] By the body of what I will not presently name,[2] had I known this, I would have given you an hundred strokes with the buckle of the scourge. Go, go, you know not how to behave yourself." And so the poor priest got both stripes and mockery for his pains.

[1] *i.e.* one would think you had given merchantable value for the money, that you were so particular about its full weight.

[2] A common fashion of avoiding manifest swearing by the Divine attributes, etc. (*Corpo di Cristo*, etc.), which was forbidden by the Church, although little attention was commonly paid to the prohibition. Cf. the old English "Cock's-body," etc.

Bandello

to the most accomplished seignior Signor Cabaliere Antonio Fileremo.

The illustrious and accomplished lady, the Lady Ippolita
Sforza e Bentivoglia was drinking the waters of the Baths
of Aquario and chose (as you know) for her more commodity and pleasance to sojourn at her garden in the
borough of Porta Comense,[1] where she hath a very com-
modious house or palace. Thither all day long flocked the
chief men and ladies of the city and there was still after
dinner some goodly and ingenious discourse agate of various
matters, according to the condition and learning of the dis-
putants, and bytimes to the purpose of questions broached
by the said lady and others. It chanced one day that,
passing from one talk to another, the company fell to
commending the female sex and telling of divers illustrious
women, ancient and modern, who by their rare and goodly
gifts won themselves worship and high renown in the world ;
amongst whom, not to stay to make a calendar of all the
praiseworthy women of whom it was devised, Panthea was
especially lauded and admired. Certain of the ladies seeking to be more plainly certified who was this Panthea,
Signor Niccolo, Count of Arco, (a young man, over and

---

[1] A suburb of Milan.

above the nobility of his blood, his wealth and rare personal gifts, very lettered and a most dulcet and polished poet, as is seen by his elegies and other poems) briefly related her history, the which no little pleased all ; and for that the story is a rare and memorable one, meseemed well to write it down, according as the said count recounted it, and if not, indeed, with the same grace and elegance of diction, at the least point by point as it was told by him. When I had written it, I bethought me to whom I should give it and you straightway occurred to me ; wherefore I send it to you and dedicate it to your most noble name, as well because you were not (contrary to your accustomed usance) present there whenas it was told, as also because you are fain, of your favour, to read and praise my compositions, both in rhyme and in prose. Moreover, the other discoursements, which were holden of those days of things marvellous and scarce credible and in which you figured once and again as hearkener and narrator, have been collected by me in an especial book, but have not yet received the finishing touch. Vouchsafe, then, to accept this little gift with your wonted affability and courtesy and eke to impart it to your honoured kinsman, Messer Bartolommeo Simoneta, a man in Greek and Latin letters most learned among the noble and among the learned most noble ; and so I commend myself to you both with all my heart. Fare you well.

The Fifth Story.

STORY OF THE CONTINENCE OF CYRUS AND THE WIFELY LOVE OF PANTHEA.

We have entered upon a vast and goodly field of discourse in treating, in so worshipful a company and especially before the never enough commended Signora Ippolita and these other ladies, of the praises of their sex; and indeed many things have been said of women, ancient and modern, well worthy of historic record. Albeit by all laws, human and divine, the man is the head of the woman, it ensueth not withal that women are to be slighted and holden for slaves, their sex being apt unto every virtuous and excellent office behoving unto human life. The which, indeed, hath no need of proof, many illustrious women having already been enumerated by us, of whom some, such as the Amazons and others, have been miraculous in arms; some have made the Roman Empire tremble, as did the valiant Zenobia; some have been very rare and prudent in governing and administering kingdoms and provinces, some of most exalted wit in composing poems, some most gifted in oratory and in the defence of lawsuits and others very famous and singular in various exercises. And who doubteth but there are many nowadays who would do the like of that the ancients did, ay, and belike more, an they were not (thanks to the waste world) hindered by us men, who will have them suffice but for the needle and the distaff? But let us pray God that the wheel turn not, for, should it ever fall to their turn to govern us, (as they are presently holden of us under a most grievous yoke of servitude,) an they rendered us not bread for biscuit, I should say that they were void of understanding. Algates, for all we keep them low and clip their wings, so they may not avail to soar, we cannot withal do so much nor contrive so astutely but that they hoodwink us all day long and lead many of us by the nose, buffalo-fashion.

But I suffer myself be carried away by the just indignation which possesseth me to see so little account made of this most noble sex; wherefore, to come to the story of Panthea, I must tell you that she was an Assyrian damsel reputed in her day to have few peers and no superior for beauty in all Asia; and besides that she was exceeding fair, she was adorned with many virtues and above all she was a right shining mirror of true chastity and a paragon of conjugal love, as you shall hear in the course of my story. She had to husband one of the lords of the King of Assyria, by name Abradates, a man in exceeding great esteem with the king and employed by him in all state matters of import. It chanced that in those days Cyrus, King of Persia, resolved to take up arms against the King of Assyria and to that end made exceeding great provision of all that behoved unto the coming emprise; which being understood of the King of Assyria, he also proceeded to set himself in order, so he might not be taken unprovided of his enemies, and amongst his other provisions, he let fortify Babylon and furnish it with all manner of victual, on such sort that he rendered it inexpugnable. Cyrus, drawing near to the land of Assyria, was hindered from faring farther, for that the Cydnus,[1] a very deep stream, might not be passed without boats; whereupon he did this memorable feat that, one of the horses which he had consecrated to the Sun being drowned in the said river, he set all his host awork and in a little while divided it into an hundred and fourscore little rivulets,[2] which might all be crossed of a woman without risk. When he had passed over with all his host, he found the Assyrians drawn up to oppose him and defeating them in pitched battle, made them retire within the city. Abradates was engaged in this deed of arms and seeing the field lost and the army in disorder, would not abandon his king, but brought him safely into Babylon. Now it was the usance of these peoples to carry their wives and exceeding great riches with them in the field; wherefore Panthea abode a prisoner and was given in charge to Araspas, a Mede. Cyrus then laid siege to Babylon and pressed it hard. The king, finding himself beleaguered, sent Abradates ambassador to the king of the Bactrians for succour; but Cyrus in the meantime took Babylon by craft and practice and the king was slain in the mellay. Abradates, learning this, returned to Assyria, where he found that Cyrus went daily gaining head.

Meanwhile, Panthea was led under guard, with the other ladies, as a prisoner after the army, and the repute of

---

[1] This is a mistake; the river was of course the Gyndes, not the Cydnus, which is in Cilicia, the narrator being apparently misled by the similarity of the names and probably also having in his mind the story of Alexander's death by drowning in the latter river.

[2] The actual number of cuttings, by which the Gyndes was reduced to knee-depth, is stated by historians at 360, the number of the days of the ancient year.

her beauty was so blazed abroad everywhere that folk talked of no otherwhat. It chanced one day that Araspas, extolling her charms in the presence of Cyrus, declared that of a certainty there was no woman to be found in all Asia adorned with such beauty and merit as she. Now Cyrus applied to conquer the whole kingdom of Assyria and to subject it to the crown of Persia, and therefore, albeit he had sundry whiles heard Panthea's incredible charms commended of many, had not chosen to see her, lest he should be diverted from that his great emprise. Withal he had determined to take her to wife; wherefore, divers lords going one day to visit her and finding her sore disconsolate and melancholy (for that she still had her mind set on her husband and was more afflicted for his absence than for her own captivity), one of them, who was cognizant of the king's purpose, bespoke her on this wise, saying, "Panthea, put away all melancholy from thee; nay, be of good cheer and live merry; for that, if indeed thou hadst a husband young, rich and handsome, fortune hath presently appointed thee one yet handsomer, more puissant and a king. Live assured, then, that thou shalt shortly be our queen, for that Cyrus is resolved to take thee to wife." Think you she anywise rejoiced or was glad or uplifted or showed any sign of contentment? Nay, she forthwith melted into woeful tears and tore her garments from top to bottom, pitifully bemoaning herself and saying that never was woefuller woman than she in the world and that, an she must e'en lose the husband whom alone she loved and for whom alone she wished to live, none other should ever anywise enjoy her. "The Immortal Gods forbid," quoth she, "that another should possess me! From the first I pertained unto Abradates; his am I yet and will be eternally. Do you,

lords, certify King Cyrus that I will rather die than cease
to belong to Abradates and certes I will die his."

These words were repeated to Cyrus, whose breast they
so pierced that he sent to comfort her and proffered himself
to her every pleasure ; but she asked no otherwhat of him
than the restitution of her husband, the which he graciously
conceded her. Abradates accordingly came to rejoin his
wife and understanding from her the continence of Cyrus,
abode full of exceeding great wonderment and said to
Panthea, "Wife mine, of me more beloved than my very
life, what thinkest thou it behoveth me do to make satisfaction both for thee and for myself unto so great a king,
so I may not with reason be called ungrateful?" [Quoth
she,] "What canst thou do, husband mine, worthier of
thee and of me than to imitate so excellent and virtuous
a prince and (since contrary fortune hath deprived us of
our own king) to serve him who hath by his valour gotten
himself the kingdom?" Panthea, then, was cause that Cyrus
not only reinstalled Abradates [in his offices,] but kept him
about himself, reckoning him among his dearest, and
employed him in many emprises, wherein he, approving
himself a valiant soldier and a wise captain, gained Cyrus his
favour on such sort that he called him his friend and would
have him styled by all the king's friend. Nor withal would
Cyrus see Panthea, fearing belike lest her beauty should
lead him into lust, and Abradates still besought Jupiter to
vouchsafe him to be a worthy husband of Panthea and
a worthy friend of Cyrus. Thereafterward, Cyrus waging
war upon Tomyris, queen of the Massagetæ, Abradates
was slain, fighting valiantly, and his body was carried to
Panthea, who bewept him sore ; whereafter, choosing not
to abide subject to the dubious shafts of fortune, she took
a sharp knife and with it pierced her gullet through and

through ; then, falling prone upon her dead husband's breast, she mingled her blood with his and so made an end of her life, leaving behind her an eternal name for virtue. Now what shall we say, ladies mine, of the soul of this rare and incomparable lady? Certes, it deserved to be long preserved alive and not to be sundered from her body with so bloody an ending ; nay, if she be blameworthy in aught, it is in this alone that she grudged other women her virtuous company, which might unto many have been an example of well-doing ; for that in truth she should nowise have slain herself, but should have awaited a natural death.

Bandello

to the Reverend Doctor in Theology Fra Cristoforo Bandello Administrator of the Order of the Minor Brethren in the Province of Genoa.

If Pope Leo X. had, whenas first Martin Luther began to spread abroad the pestilent venom of his heresies, lent a favourable ear to the Master of the Sacred Palace, it had been an easy matter to quench those nascent flames, which have since waxed to such a height that, except God put hand thereto, they are more like to increase than to abate. And certes meknoweth not what spirit was this of Luther's, which so many admire, as if he were an acute dialectician, an ingenious philosopher and a profound theologian, he having in all his various idle devisings adduced no single plausible argument of his own invention, but having only tricked out anew the false opinions condemned and reproved by so many holy Councils-General and ultimately by that of Constance. The following he hath cometh from no other-what than that he and his followers open the way to a licentious and wanton way of living. In truth, he is to be blamed and there should be no audience given to his fables, which are all void of true foundation. Algates, I cannot deny that the lewd life of many churchmen is a cause of scandal to unstable minds, but it behoveth us not therefor fall away from [the faith of] our forefathers. Moreover, those indiscreet and ignorant friars [whom we wot of] should, when they are in the pulpit, take good heed lest they say aught to the people which may give rise to scandal and not (whereas they ought to incite their hearers to devoutness) provoke them to indecent laughter, the which [1] nowadays bringeth the things of the faith into little esteem. I am not presently concerned to speak of the follies which idiots oftentimes say in the pulpit, but will speak of those who follow indiscreetly after certain fables which bring preachments into derision, as it befell Fra Bartolommeo da Feltro in Pavia, according to that which I heard one day told of Fra Filippo da San Colombano, a Minor Brother of the Franciscan Order, who, being in company of certain gentlemen at their [2] place of the Garden in Milan, related the thing for their diversion, as it happened in the days when he was a student of the law at Pavia. And for that it is a thing to be noted, I have chosen to send and give it to you, so that, we being of one blood, you may eke be a sharer in my novels. Fare you well.

[1] *i.e.* the buffoonery of the preaching friars.
[2] *i.e.* the Franciscans'.

The Sixth Story.

FRA BERNARDINO DA FELTRO, SEEKING TO SET SAINT FRANCIS OVER ALL THE OTHER SAINTS, IS CONFOUNDED BY A STUDENT.

You must know, sirs, that, when I was yet a student and abode at Pavia to learn the civil law, Fra Bernardino da Feltro, a man of exceeding consideration in our order, preached a whole year long in the Cathedral Church of Pavia to as great a concourse as was ever seen in that city. He had preached the foregone year at Brescia, where he had let publicly burn in the market-place the false tresses which the women wore on their heads, to enhance their native beauty, and other like womanish vanities. Moreover, he let burn all such copies of Martial's Epigrams as were in the city and did many other things worthy of memory. Now, being in the pulpit at Pavia on the feast day of our Seraphic Father St. Francis, he entered, in the presence of a great concourse of people, upon discourse of the many virtues of that saint and having descanted thereon at large and recounted store of miracles by him wroughten in his life and after his death, he bestowed on him all those praises, excellences and dignities which behoved unto the sanctity of so glorious a father. And having, by most effectual arguments, authorities and ex-amples, proved that he was full of all the Christian graces and was altogether seraphic and afire with charity, he kindled into an exceeding fervour and said, "What seat, now, shall we assign thee in heaven, holiest father mine?

Where shall we set thee, O vessel full of every grace?
What place shall we find apt unto such sanctity?" Then,
beginning with the virgins, he ascended to the confessors,
the martyrs, the apostles, to Saint John Baptist and other
prophets and patriarchs, still avouching that St. Francis
merited a more honoured place than they; after which,
raising his voice, he went on to say, "O saint truly most
glorious, thou, whom thy most godly gifts and singular
merits and the conformity of thy life unto Christ exalt
and uplift over all the other saints, what place shall we
find sorting with such excellence? Tell me, my brethren,
where shall we set him ? Tell me, you, gentlemen students,
who are of exalted understanding, where shall we place
this most holy saint?" Whereupon Messer Paolo Taegio,
then a student of laws and nowadays a very famous doctor
in Milan, who was seated on a stool overagainst the pulpit,
being weary of the friar's useless and indiscreet babble
and belike misdoubting him he meant to put St. Francis
above or at the least on a level with the Holy Trinity,
rose to his feet and uplifting his settle with both hands,
said so loudly that he was heard of all the people, "Father
mine, for God's sake, give yourself no more pains to seek
a seat for St. Francis; here is my settle; put him thereon
and so he may sit down, for I am off." And so, departing,
he gave occasion unto all to arise also and depart the
church; wherefore it behoved the Feltrine[1] come down
from the pulpit, without finding a place for his saint,
and return, all crestfallen, to San Giacomo. And indeed
that which a man saith in the pulpit should be well considered, lest indiscreet preachments bring the word of God
into derision.

[1] Native of Feltro or Feltre.

Bandello

To the most illustrious the Lord Marquess Gian Lodovico Pallavicino.

As I went this September last past to Bargone, a castle-wick of your brother, Signor Manfredo, on some affairs which I had occasion to treat with the Lady Ginevra Bentivoglia, your sister-in-law, I found myself by chance at Corte Maggiore, unknowing where I was, and as I was about to ask a countryman of the name of the place, you at that moment came up, on your return from hunting, and would have me ride no farther. Nay, it sufficed you not to keep me that day with you in the citadel, but you entertained me there five whole days, lavishing on me such caresses as would have been enough, not only for the like of me, your old servant and familiar, but for whatsoever great gentleman. I will not presently offer to recount the various sports and diversions with which you entertained us, to the pleasure and satisfaction of all. Now, for that in princes' houses and courts there are still divers sorts and conditions of men and all cannot be alike sagacious and well advised, your [fool], whom some call Polito[1] and others

---

[1] Spruce, dapper.

Mosca,[1] (albeit meseemeth he should rather be called Ragno,[2] for that he hath long thin legs and goeth still a-tiptoe,) gave us much matter for laughter, for that, abhorring to see the least hair on his clothes and having somewhat still cast on him, he fell into such a choler and ruffled it with such fierceness and bravado that whoso knew him not had thought himself in the hands of raging Rodomont.[3] Nevertheless, for all his threats, he had not dared to strike a fly; nay, if whatsoever little child turned upon him, he had fled away like a wild coney. Messer Giacomo da San Secondo, (who, being a most excellent musician, kept us oftentimes merry with playing and singing,) being present and seeing Polito's chafe, told a story to the purpose of those who make it their whole study to keep themselves spruce and you then said to me that this would sort well with my other novels; wherefore, having written it, I have willed that it be yours and go about the world (an indeed it ever leave the house) with your name in its forefront, the which will, in the eyes of those who come after us, be a very manifest token of my devotion to you. Fare you well.

---

[1] Fly, a nickname frequently given to little dapper men, who take great pains to keep themselves spruce, a fly being constantly engaged in cleaning itself.

[2] Spider.

[3] The well-known character of Boiardo's *Orlando Innamorato*.

The Seventh Story.

TWO YOUNG MEN, CLAD ALL IN WHITE, ARE, BY WAY OF JEST, BEFOULED BY A THIRD.

The sight of yonder serving-man of yours, who showeth himself so curst and crabbed in speech and who cannot brook to see a least straw on his clothes, putteth me in mind of a chance which befell no great while agone in a city of Lombardy, and which since you pray me tell you, I will very gladly obey you. There were two young men of good birth enough, who savoured somewhat of the simpleton, for that the priest who baptized them put very little salt in their mouths. Being, then, (as it is used to say of such in Milan) natives of the parish of St. Simplician, they had, for the likeness of their humours, clapped up a great familiarity and still went in company and apparelled after one same fashion. Moreover, an they found themselves with other young men, they talked the greatest nonsense in the world and could not brook that other than they should speak; nay, oftentimes, they interrupted others' discourse without the least consideration, and if they chanced to have mean neighbours, they did nothing but vaunt and extol their own belongings, so that they were wearisome unto whosoever hearkened them and were ill-seen in [all] company. Now it chanced one summer-tide that they clad them in white taffety doublets and cassocks, with hosen of white linen and shoes and bonnets of white velvet, the latter being adorned with white plumes. In this accoutrement they appeared in public and went peacocking it at a foot-pace, casting their eyes askance in every direction to see if any viewed them, themseeming all must needs be talking of that their apparel. Moreover, when they came in company with others, they still fell a-prating thereof, out of all season, so that all shunned their converse as most they might, themseeming they had ever in their ears, "View me this galloon, how aptly it sitteth upon this doublet. See these feathers, how fine they are and how they stir with every least breath of air and keep the goodliest fluttering in the world. How deem you of these aglet-points and of this cunningly-wrought bonnet-jewel? Certes, all is of a piece for excellence, and I warrant you few, except ourselves, could so well have accorded the whole." With these and other like pratings they were irksome unto all.

Now there was a young man, very well bred, quick-witted and well-advised, to whom the fashious ways of these two Ganymedes were marvellously unpleasing and who went still casting about how he might give them a rap and rid the general ear of their fashery, and accordingly, having bethought himself of a device to that end, he took his measures and awaited an occasion of putting it in execution. It was, as I have already told you, the summer season; wherefore, having noted that the two white peacocks passed well-nigh every evening through the street where he dwelt, (for that therenigh abode two fair damsels, to whom they paid their court), he one day after supper posted himself at his door, to take the fresh air. He had not abidden long when up came the two amorists, flaunting it as usual, where-

upon he accosted them and taking them both by the hand,
said to them, " You are my prisoners and shall not go hence
without drinking a draught." The twain accepted his
invitation and entered the house ; where, the servants offering to rinse the beakers, " Nay," quoth the host, " let us
go down to the cellar to drink ; we shall be cooler there,"
and letting kindle a torch, for that the hour was late and
the cellar dark, carried them down thither. What while
the beakers were washing, the three young men fell to
walking about the cellar, which was very great and spacious.
Now there was a great vessel full of water, which the host
had let place there of set purpose and appointment ; and
for that it seemed of such bigness that a man might not raise
it, he said to his guests, " I have a man who hoisteth this
vessel on his shoulders and carrieth it aloft." One of the
Ganymedes, who thought himself mighty lusty, [put his
hand to the vessel and] being scarce able to move it, said,
" I do not believe that a man can carry such a weight."
" Ay can he," [replied the other] and so, disputing among
themselves, they wagered six brace of partridges. Thereupon they drank and presently in came one, whom the host
had bidden to that end and who, taking up the vessel,
set it on his back. The host, without saying aught,
made for the stair, followed by the serving-man with the
torch and by him who bore the vessel, whilst the two gallants
came after, laughing. The stair was steep and he who bore
the burden went very slowly, feigning himself over-laden.
When he came well-nigh to the stairhead, he affected to
stumble against somewhat and let the vessel dash against
the wall, so that the contents spurted out upon the two
minions and bedabbled them on rare wise, he being careful
withal to keep hold of the vessel, for that, had he let it
fall on them, it had done otherwhat than befoul their

clothes. Now the water that was therein was mingled with ink and mud, so that the gallants, who were before white as ermines, showed now like very pards, so bedappled were they with the splashings of the cask. The master of the house feigned to be sore incensed with him who bore the vessel and made a show of offering to beat him; but he took to his heels, whilst the two youths abode with the loss and the flout, it behoving them provide themselves with other clothes, for that those they wore were all marred.

Bandello

to the Reverend Father Fra Girolamo Ticione Preacher of the Order.[1]

The reverend father Fra Eustachio Piatesio of Bologna, a great doctor in theology and very eminent in the study of the humanities, was used, in recreation-time and whiles as he rode for his diversion, after lecturing upon theology or philosophy, to have still some pleasant story in hand, wherewith he blithely entertained his companions. He was a good and facetious talker, so that, whenassoever we went a-riding, he diverted us a good while with one of his novels. Now it remembereth me, once amongst other times, whenas we were all at Poggio Reale, without the city of Naples, with my uncle of pious memory, Messer Vincenzo Bandello, General of the whole order,—it remembereth me, I say, that, what while my said uncle walked to and fro with Messer Barnaba da Salerno, Inquisitor-General of the kingdom,[2] we others being all seated in those delightsome gardens, Piatesio related a merry story, which greatly pleased us all and which, on my return to Naples, I wrote down, meseeming it deserved to be consecrated to posterity. Now, since I am in act

---

[1] i.e. that of St. Dominick, to which Bandello himself belonged.
[2] Naples.

to collect my novels [for publication], I give you this, in fulfilment of that which I promised you aforetime, when we were a-pleasuring at the castle of your lord father. I know that it will be acceptable to you, my compositions being ever dear to you; and do you now in return let me see something of your own, whether Latin or Italian. Fare you well.

The Eighth Story.

THE SHREWD DEVICE OF AN EMINENT PREACHER TO CONFUTE AN OUTRAGEOUS LIE OF ANOTHER PREACHER.

We are come, most reverend fathers, to this delight-some place, to enjoy the fragrant and dulcet coolness of the air beside this limpid rill, where, seated as we are upon this velvet turf, dappled with so many kinds of colours, as well of the flowers that it produceth as also of those fallen from yonder orange, lemon and pomecitron trees and other odoriferous shrubs, methinketh it will be no other than well to entertain ourselves with some honest and pleasant discourse. And what while our most reverend general walketh with the inquisitor under yonder grateful shades, meseemeth we ought not to play the mute, lest sleep should lightly close our eyes; wherefore, since none of you hath a mind to talk, I will entertain you awhile with a merry story. You all know that our order, in the matter of the conception of the glorious queen of heaven, the immaculate Virgin Mary, ensueth the authority of Holy Writ and of the pious doctors of the Church, as the father-general hath most learnedly

collated[1] in his book of the Conception, whereas he proveth
our opinion to be orthodox with more than four hundred
authorities and many arguments, founded as well upon
Holy Writ as upon the writings of the pious Fathers ;·
but the friars of St. Francis (I mean of our day) are
of another way of thinking. Wherefore, whenas I was
a very young lad, a minor friar, who must have studied
history in Mother Goose's Tales[2] and Bucolics in the
kitchen upon a melon,[3] declared publicly, whilst preach-
at Faenza, that one of the popes, to determine that controversy,[4] appointed both orders to hold their chapters-
general at Rome and to bring thither their most
erudite brethren to argue the question before himself and all the cardinals, so an authoritative declaration
might be made on the matter. This great chronologist
said, then, that the Franciscans brought thither the
subtle doctor Scotto[5] and the Dominicans Fra Tommaso
d'Aquino,[6] in whose learning they much trusted ; and the
question being argued between these twain in the pope's
presence, Scotto advanced certain arguments, which Aquinas[7] might nowise avail to refute ; whereupon the pope
and the cardinals gave definitive judgment against the
preaching friars.[8] And upon this his fable the Minor
Brother said a thousand extravagances, like an ignoramus

[1] *Ricolto.*
[2] Lit. "The Chronicle of Follies" (*La Cronica delle Fole*).
[3] I need hardly remind the reader that the melon is with the
Italians a favourite emblem or symbol of stupidity and clownish
dulness.
[4] *i.e.* anent the Immaculate Conception.
[5] *i.e.* Duns Scotus.
[6] *i.e.* St. Thomas Aquinas.
[7] Lat. for native of Aquino.
[8] *i.e.* the Dominicans.

as he was. There was then preaching at our Convent of San Andrea in Faenza Fra Tommaso Donato, a patrician of Venice and a very learned, eloquent and popular preacher, who was for his learning and integrity of life made Patriarch of Venice and methinketh yet liveth. He, hearing what the sandalier[1] had preached on the Feast Day of the Conception, abode very dubious of that which was to do. He knew well enough that, when St. Thomas Aquinas died, Scotto was not yet born;[2] but himseemed unmeet to bring the chronicles into the pulpit and prove the Franciscan a liar on historical evidence, and withal it irked him that the Faentines[3] should abide with so lying a fable in their heads; wherefore he cast about for a means whereby he might confute so manifest a falsehood. After he had racked his brains awhile, he bethought him of a fable far subtler and more plausible than the Franciscan's lie and concluding that he could not do better than assail the latter with those same arms which he had brought into the field against St. Thomas, resolved to rout his adversary by means of an ingenious and pleasant (though false) invention. Accordingly he made shift to have the greater part of the townsfolk and populace of Faenza particularly invited for the ensuing Sunday, for that he was to say certain very marvellous and delectable things.

The day come, all Faenza flocked to the preachment and Fra Tommaso, mounting the pulpit, briefly expounded the

---

[1] *Zoccolante*, a name given to the Franciscans from the sandals or clogs (*zoccoli*) they wore, even as they were called "cordeliers" (*cordiglieri*) from their rope-girdles (*cordigli*).

[2] This is not quite correct. St. Thomas Aquinas died 7th March, 1274, whilst Scotus is supposed to have been born about 1265.

[3] *i.e.* inhabitants of Faenza.

Evangel for the day, then said, "Faentines mine the
Franciscan preaching father preached last Lady Day, as
many of you know, that Scotto confounded Saint Thomas
at Rome in argument anent the Conception and that the
Pope gave judgment in favour of his order ; which being
repeated to me, I saw that he was far and away mistaken
and that he had studied ill. Whereupon I proceeded to
turn over and read the true chronicles, wherein all the
disputations erst made anent whatsoever matter are recorded,
and turned and read to such purpose that I found where
Scotto disputed with Saint Thomas. I read the whole with
the utmost diligence, word for word, and found altogether
the contrary of that which the Franciscan preached to you ;
indeed I marvel amain how he can have dared to preach
so manifest a falsehood in this your magnificent city, and
so that you may know how this disputation was holden,
hearken to me and I will punctually tell you all. You
must know, then, that, the minor friars and the brethren
of our order being congregated in chapter-general at Rome
and Scotto and Thomas disputing, in the presence of the
Supreme Pontiff and the cardinals, Scotto, to the authority
of Holy Writ, the declarations of the Councils-General and
the arguments of so many notable and pious doctors, alleged
against him by St. Thomas, could answer nought that availed
and abode confounded. The pope would have had other
Minor Brethren come forward ; but, when Scotto sufficed
not to answer, who had dared to put himself forward?
Wherefore the Holy Father gave them to understand that,
at the first consistory he should hold, he meant to publish
a bull in favour of the Preaching Order. Some thirty of
the Franciscans, unable to brook this, conspired together
to assassinate the pope, who abode not under such guard
as is kept nowadays, and accordingly, entering the palace

one night by stealth, they made their way, unobserved, to
the papal chamber ; where, as they sought to open the door
with their counterfeit keys, they were heard by the chamber-
lains, who began to cry out, "Thieves ! Thieves ! To arms !
To arms !" Whilst the pope made his escape by the rear
issue and took refuge in the Castle.[1] There ran many to
the outcry, soldiers as well as others, so that the friars were
well-nigh all taken and confessing that they came thither
to assassinate the pope, were condemned to the gallows.
The pope was urgently supplicated not to put such a shame
upon so great an order ; wherefore, moved to pity, he
caused them all come before him and said to them, "I
grant you your lives, but will have you henceforth wear
a rope girded about you, so that, an you fall again into
a like misdeed, there may be no need to seek ropes to hang
you. Moreover, you shall no more touch monies, so you
may not again avail to debauch any withal, for mescemeth
impossible but you must have corrupted some of my household ; and to boot, you shall wear clogs or sandals of wood,
so you may be heard whenas you go about." For you
must know, Faentines mine, that their founder St. Francis
forbade them not in his rule to touch monies and still less
did he bid them wear clogs."

Now there were sundry minor brethren present at this
preachment, to whom Fra Tommaso turned and said,
smiling, "Fathers mine, you have heard my story ; go and
tell your preacher that, whenassoever he shall prove to me
that Scotto ever (I will not say disputed with, but) saw St.
Thomas, I bind myself to show him altogether the contrary
of that which he hath falsely preached." This said, he
pronounced the benediction and came down from the pulpit.

[1] Of St. Angelo.

By this sermon it was holden among men of judgment that
Fra Tommaso, albeit he had caustically rallied the Franciscan's ignorance, had withal entreated him according to
his desert and had very handsomely exposed the shallow-
ness and witlessness of this fellow, who had found in the
meat-pipkin that Scotto was of Aquinas his time, it being
withal certain that the former was not born till after the
death of Saint Thomas, whose works he did his utmost
to impugn ; but after him came Capreolo Tolosano,[1] who
most learnedly refuted his arguments ; whence arose the
proverbial saying, "Except he had scalded[2] Scotto, as
men do prunes, Capreolo had not leapt like a lively
agile kid."[3]

[1] Jean Capréole of Toulouse, a Dominican monk of the fifteenth
century, who wrote a defence of St. Thomas.
[2] Scottato.
[3] Capretto. A play, of course, upon the two names, Scotto and
Capreolo.

Bandello

to Signor Elia Sartirana.

A marvellous thing is the prick of shame, whenas it toucheth to the quick a person who feareth dishonour; nay, we oftentimes see men, who, falling into some shameful error, have been unable to brook the sight of other men and overcome with extreme chagrin, have for lesser ill elected death. And this much lightlier betideth with women, for that their sex is feebler than ours and that they commonly fear shame more than men. There were [the other day] many good men and true in the delightsome garden of Messer Ambrogio, a patrician of Milan and a man famous for letters and integrity of life, and we discoursed of a poor youth, who had lately hanged himself in Porta Orientale, I know not why. Thereupon our most learned Messer Antonio Tanzio told a story [of a case] befallen in the kingdom of Naples, the which I have written down and given to you, so you may know that I am mindful of you. Moreover, it having been told in your cousin Messer Ambrogio's goodliest garden, what time he was from home, be pleased to impart this novel to him, as well because he loveth me greatly as also because he is a man of good letters and a debonair as any I know in Milan; wherefore I know he will have pleasure in seeing it, not that there is aught therein of his goodly wit, but that it is of my writing. Fare you well.

The Ninth Story.

LEONZIO OF CASTRIGNANO LOVETH NEERA AND AFTER FORSAKETH HER; WHEREUPON SHE DROWNETH HERSELF IN A WELL.

There was, in the province of Otranto, at a hamlet called by the country-folk Castrignano,—no great while after the glorious victory by which Alfonso, Duke of Calabria, expelled the Turks, who had seized upon the city of Otranto, from the kingdom,[1]—a very fair and engaging damsel, but born of mean parents, whose name was Neera. Of her a rich and noble youth of those parts, overcome with her charms, became enamoured, and for that he was well provided with the goods of fortune and being fatherless, spent lavishly, he had the utmost commodity to bespeak her and possess her of his love; but she, being discreet and high-minded and knowing the youth, whose name was Leonzio, to be of the first families of the place and herself of mean birth and no match for him, gave no great heed to his letters and messages. Withal, Leonzio, who was all afire and would fain have come to love's conclusion, ceased not to essay her with letters and messages, daily beseeching her to have compassion on him and promising her to love her always and never to abandon

[1] Naples.

her. Herseemed, indeed, he was worthy to be loved; nevertheless, knowing him rich, she sore misdoubted her lest, whenas he should have had his will of her, he should abandon her and turn his love elsewhither, and accordingly she nowise returned him a favourable answer, but showed herself ever dourer and more inflexible. Her obduracy but inflamed the youth's passion and he resolved to compass his desire at whatsoever cost. Accordingly, seeking out a crafty old woman, he sent her to Neera, with whom she knew to say and do so much that she persuaded her to turn her mind to Leonzio and little by little to love him; and so, in course of time, he contrived, by means of the wily crone, to have speech of the damsel, who, for all she wished him well, would nowise yield herself to him, except he promised her, in the old woman's presence, to take her to wife. Indeed, she was ill advised, for that she should rather have caused him marry her and not have trusted to the mere pledge of her wily lover, who, to gain his intent, made her a thousand promises. But we daily see poor women without end (poor, I mean, in counsel and prudence) abide thus deceived, for that lovers promise lavishly, so but they may have that which they seek.

Now Leonzio, having many a time amorously lain with Neera and consorted so familiarly with her that they were holden throughout the hamlet for husband and wife, fell in love with another damsel and she pleasing him more than Neera, he began to neglect the latter; whereof she abode infinitely disconsolate, unknowing how she should do to regain her lover. He little by little forgot her altogether and unmindful of his promises, became so enamoured of the other damsel that he publicly espoused her and carried her home to his house; the which was a sore affront for Neera, it being known throughout the place that he had taken amorous pleasure of her. The poor damsel bewept her mischance amain, bewailing herself without end thereof, and abode at home many days, well-nigh distraught. Awhile thereafter, she chancing to be seated one holiday before the house in company of many women of the neighbourhood, as the usance is, and it being spoken of many things, it seemeth one of them gainsaid Neera of I know not what ; whereupon she, somewhat angered, answered her in a loud voice and one thing leading to another, they came to high words together. The other, who carried not a-crupper,[1] arose and setting her hands on her hips, said to Neera, with exceeding great choler, "Begone, begone to the stews, shameless strumpet that thou art ! Marry, Leonzio hath used thee as thou deservest. Thinkest thou the whole castlewick knoweth not thou hast been his doxy and art not ashamed to show thy face among honest women ? " At this speech, the hapless Neera, without answering a word, rose up from the company and casting herself headlong into a deep well which was there, was straightway drowned. The neighbours flocked to the noise and seeking to give her aid, after great toil, drew her forth of the well, dead.

---

[1] *Non portava di groppa*, i.e. was not long-suffering, was quick to take offence, to give as good as she got.

Bandello

to the reverend and learned father Fra Leandro
Alberto of Bologna Preacher of the Order.

Many a time, Leandro mine, whenas you were in Milan,
have we devised of the ignorance of certain folk who in
the public pulpits preach many things out of all reason,
and especially of those who seek with feigned miracles
to excite their hearers to devotion. Such men pretend
with their meagre figments to confirm the things prescribed by the Catholic Faith and sealed with the blood
and testimony of so many glorious martyrs and perceive
not that they study with a tiny taper to add light and
heat to the sun. And for that the Christian religion
hath no need of lies, being true and catholic, it was
by the last Lateran Council, begun under Julius II.
and ended under Leo X., expressly forbidden that any,
of what degree soever he were, should presume to preach
these chimerical inventions of false miracles; the which
in truth was most piously done. Now it is no great
while since it was discoursed of this matter in the garden
of Le Grazie,[1] where Fra Salvestro Prierio, Master of
the Sacred Palace,[2] was present, being come from Rome

[1] The well-known Dominican Convent (Nostra Dama delle
Grazie) at Milan, so frequently mentioned by our author.
[2] *i.e.* Intendant of the Vatican.

to Milan, as also was Messer Francesco Mantegazzo, a patrician of Milan and a man of the utmost consequence; and some said that the errors sown by Martin Luther had in great part arisen from the indiscreet superstition of many friars and the avaricious greed of certain of the clergy, as well as from the scant provision which had in the beginning been made therefor.[1] Each having said that which seemed to him most to the purpose, the worshipful Mantegazzo turned to the Master of the Sacred Palace and craving leave to speak, related a story on the subject, which made us all laugh. I was present at his discourse and meseemed the story was worthy of record; wherefore I wrote it down then and there and a Bolognese making a principal figure therein, I bethought me of yourself to whom it should justly be dedicated, you having been born at Bologna of a worshipful and ancient family and being engaged in writing the annals of the city from day to day, not to speak of many other works which you have in hand. This story, then, I send and give you in witness of our mutual good will. Fare you well.

[1] *i.e.* the scant precautions taken to prevent the spread of the new doctrines.

The Tenth Story.

A GOODLY DEVICE TO CONFUTE THE INDIS-CREET ZEAL OF CERTAIN IGNORANT FRIARS.

I mean, reverend father mine, to tell you a short story, to the purpose of that whereof it hath been spoken, so you may see what evil is done by those who, neglecting the Holy Evangel, preach cock-and-bull stories in the pulpit, whereas our Saviour bade His disciples, "Go and preach the Gospel to every creature." What time I was yet very young, a Minor Brother from the Marches [1] preached in the Cathedral of this our city of Milan to an incredible concourse of men and women of every sort and said whiles in the pulpit that Saint Francis had gotten of God a great privilege for all who wore the rope-girdle in life, to wit, that they went not to hell when they died, but passed, according to their sins, into purgatory, whither the said Saint descended once a year and let down his girdle, whereon all the souls which had worn it on life laid hold and were taken up of him into heaven; nay, so featly did he contrive to colour and adorn this fable that there was none but girt himself with the cord and I myself, not to be wiser than the rest, fell to wearing it. Towards the end of the Lenten season in which the Marchegan preached, the plague began to wax

[1] Of Ancona.

in the city and speedily made very great progress, so that between April and October the officers of health reported some two hundred and thirty thousand persons to have died in the city and suburbs. Thanks, however, to the stringent measures taken for the purification of the city, the pest was at last quelled; whereupon Fra Girolamo Albertuzzo of Bologna, surnamed Il Borsello, a man of fine presence, learned, eloquent and full of unction in his sermons, was sent by our superiors to preach the following Lent in the Cathedral. He understood, how I know not, that which the Marchegan had preached of the rope-girdle and marvelling sore at such an extravagance, determined to rid the Milanese of so fond a belief nor awaited otherwhat than an apt occasion. It chanced that, as he preached one Sunday after dinner on the occasion of certain jubilees[1] in behalf of the Great Spital, Duke Ludovico Sforza, then governor of his nephew, was present at the preachment, with all the court and nobility of Milan, so that the Cathedral (though you know how large and spacious it is) was altogether filled. Borsello, himseeming an excellent occasion offered for what he thought to do, after he had commended the said jubilees amain, turned to the duke and said to him, "This many a day, most excellent sir, have I had ill news to give your people of Milan, but have tarried till now, for that it irketh me to afflict any; algates, the thing being of the utmost importance and growing worse, the longer silence is kept thereof, I have determined to discharge me of my burthen in your presence." Herewith he proceeded to tell that which had been reported

---

[1] A jubilee is a church festival during which plenary indulgences are offered to all who do certain prescribed acts of devotion or charity, here presumably almsgiving to the hospital.

to him of the Marchegan and added, "Hearing, my lord, so
excellent a privilege of the rope-girdle, I had bethought me
to send to Rome and obtain the pope's brief and dispensation,
licensing me to wear that blessed girdle, albeit I am a
brother of Saint Dominick; but, one night, as I was at my
orisons, an angel appeared to me and said, 'Borsello, come
with me.' Accordingly I went with him not very far and
felt the whole frame of the earth tremble and shake with
a great noise; and presently, behold, I saw it open before
my feet, leaving a deep and wide gulf. I bent down, by
commandment of the angel, and looking therein, saw
purgatory open and the souls in purging in that penitential
fire; nor was it long ere I saw Saint Francis descend from
heaven with his rope-girdle in his hand. You know, my
lord, that in the past pestilence there died thousands of
persons, of whom the most part, for the Marchegan's
preachments, girded themselves with the rope; wherefore ·
Saint Francis found purgatory much fuller than of wont.
Accordingly he let down the girdle, to which so many souls
clung that, being unable to support the weight which dragged
him down and feeling his hand already afire, the blessed
father, not to fall headlong into that fiery torment and make
undeserved assay of such cruel pains, relaxed his hold and
let the girdle drop, souls and all, into the fire; where it
was forthright consumed by the devouring flames like a dry
straw. The angel, thereupon, charging me announce to my
credulous Ambrosians [1] the case as it had befallen and give
them to understand that Saint Francis his rope is no longer
extant, I have chosen, most excellent sir, to set forth the

[1] The term "Ambrosians" is generally applied to the Puritan sect
which followed the teachings of St. Ambrose, the reforming bishop of
Milan. Here it seems to mean the Milanese in general.

whole to the people in your presence, so that all may be undeceived and made aware of the error wherein they were involved." Thereupon the fluent and fertile Borsello proceeded to rebuke those foolish superstitions, nay,'rather harmful and noxious conceits, and said many goodly and useful things, manifesting unto all, with most evident arguments, that, to gain the kingdom of heaven, it sufficeth not to be white, brown, black, blue or whatsoever other colour, but it behoveth to do the will of the Father Eternal and have His grace, without which none can do aught good or deserving of life everlasting; nay, the ingenious and eloquent preacher spoke to such purpose and said such goodly things and so vehemently impressed his pious words upon the hearts of his hearers that well-nigh all, as well men as women, who wore the rope-girdle, put it off, acknowledging the error wherein they had been thitherto sunken; wherefore, the fruitful and wholesome sermon ended and the people having departed the church, more than seven thousand rope-girdles were found fallen on the floor; and to tell you the truth, I myself was one of those who ungirt themselves and cast their girdles on the ground, meseeming Fra Girolamo had opened our eyes to know the truth. Duke Lodovico and all his lords and gentlemen and indeed the most part of the listeners abode excellent well satisfied and it was deemed of the wise that Borsello had shown good judgment and had done prudently to make mock of the superstitious inventions of those who think to be saved by clothing themselves in such and such a colour or girding themselves with the rope-girdle or the leather surcingle, instead of doing works of charity and obeying the commandments of Christ.

Bandello

to Signor Giason Maino[1] Grand Monarch of the Laws.

There being nothing more certain unto man, what while he liveth in this world, than death nor more uncertain than the time and manner thereof, meseemeth a marvellous thing that this it is whereunto less thought is commonly taken than unto whatsoever else. I say not indeed that it behoveth us keep our thoughts continually fixed upon the bitterness of death, for that I would not so severely constrain any; but I am persuaded that it were of the utmost profit unto every one of whatsoever condition to bethink himself often that he is a man and consequently mortal. I would not, indeed, have us presently enter upon discourse of things sacred, citing the saying of Holy Writ, "Remember the end of thy life, which is death, and thou shalt not sin eternally;" and still less would I recall the admonition of the pious doctor who saith, "He lightly contemneth all things who bethinketh him that he must die;" nay, putting aside the health and profit of the soul, I will that we speak politickly[2] and consider of how much utility and profit it were unto whatsoever person to have often before

---

[1] Maino of Pesaro, one of the most celebrated jurisconsults of his time.

[2] *Politicamente*, i.e. from the point of view of worldly expediency.

his eyes the fear and horror of death, [bethinking himself]
that he cannot avail to know the time nor the place in
which he is to end his days nor by what manner of death
he is to pass into the other life and that belike, within the
hour, some strange chance (of the many and various which
are still in wait for us) may lightly befall to sunder his
vital thread and turn him from a man into a frightful corpse.
Oh, how profitable were such thought-taking unto all sorts
and conditions of men ! Think you, if the great and those
who so lightly, scorning all laws human and divine, harry
these and those, took thought unto death, that they would
commit so many errors and that they would not oftentimes
bridle their disorderly appetites? For that, even if a
man be of that reprobate sect which holdeth that there
is no difference between our soul and that of the beasts
without reason and that the end of the one and the other
is the same, he should nevertheless live politickly and leave
a good repute of himself. Moreover, if rogues and ruffians
and those who abide without cease in lewd and wicked
works were to remember them of the gallows, the axe,
the stake and the many other punishments which the laws
have ordained unto evil-doers, I am convinced that they
would not be so prompt and ready to engage in the many
abominations which they do all day long ; whence it would
ensue that human life were far more tranquil than it is
and the much bepraised (and of us never seen) age of gold
would return for these our times ; but, for that men consider
everything rather than their end and think to abide still
here below, there betide the many evils which we see every
day. It being reasoned the other day of this matter here
in Milan in the palace of the most illustrious and reverend
Signor Federico Sanseverino, Cardinal of Holy Church,
what time he let cut out of his bladder a stone of marvellous

bigness, a Navarrese his chamberlain, by name Enrico
Nieto, related the cruel death of a King of Navarre, which
meseemed was of a sort never before heard ; wherefore I
wrote it down forthright and added it to the number of
my novels.   Then, remembering me that, when I was late
in your museum[1] at Pavia (which is indeed the very oracle,
not only of Lombardy, but of all Europe), it being spoken
of this matter of dying, anent the sudden and untimely
death of our most excellent doctor, Messer Lancillotto
Galiagola—a young man who, had he lived, would certes
have deserved to be evened with the most eminent jurisconsults,—you said many things of the uses which attend
the thought that we must die, I have been fain to send
you [the story of] the frightful case of the said King of
Navarre, so it may abide with you for a pledge of the
reverence in which I hold you and of the obligation I bear
you for many kindnesses received from you.   Fare you well.

---

[1] *i.e.* library or study.

The Eleventh Story.

THE MISERABLE DEATH OF KING CHARLES OF NAVARRE FOR EXCESS OF LUST IN HIS OLD AGE.

You have seen, gentlemen, how many good things were wrought by the fear in which our most illustrious and reverend Cardinal went of death, what time he was about to let take out the stone which you have all seen and which tormented him cruelly night and day. For that, albeit he still liveth like a Catholic and a good Christian, nevertheless, being come to this pass and neither Messer Matteo of Rome nor Messer Romano of Casalmaggiore willing him for other than a dead man,[1] an they were to lay hands on him to rid him of the stone, he, unable longer to brook the cruel sufferings which made him die a thousand deaths an hour, submitted himself with a stout heart to the surgeon's knife, but first confessed himself and took the Eucharist and did so many almsdeeds to pious places and other good works that it was a marvellous thing; all which was caused by the fear of death, added to his natural benevolence. Now, had King Charles [the Second] of Navarre thought thus, he had lived more quietly and had escaped the ill end which befell him. I must tell

---

[1] *i.e.* refusing to be answerable for the result of the operation, refusing to operate upon him except as if he were already dead.

you, then, (as it remembereth me to have read in the
Chronicles of the Kings of Navarre) that in the year of
our Salvation 1385[1] died Charles, King of Navarre, who
was son-in-law unto King John of France, having to wife
Joan his daughter. This said King Charles was a man
of very ill fashions and very cruel and men might have
little faith in him, inasmuch as he rarely observed aught
that he promised. What while his father-in-law King John
lived and ere he was taken prisoner by Edward, Prince
of Wales, son of King Edward the Third of England,
he let assassinate the Constable of France and agreed with
the English to the prejudice of the French. Being after
taken by his said father-in-law, he broke prison, during
the king's captivity, and raising the Parisians against the
Dauphin Charles (after Charles V.), wrought many ills,
not only in the slaughter which befell in Paris by his means
of those loyal subjects who took the Dauphin's part, but
throughout all France, whereas he sacked and burned many
places and slew folk without end. He was also the cause
of many troubles under Kings Charles the Fifth and Sixth
and in his own realm of Navarre he wrought exceeding
cruelties and shameful spoliations, massacring men and
ravishing women, so that all willed him ill. He having
laid an impost of two hundred thousand florins on his
kingdom, threescore of the chief men of the realm came
to seek him at Pampeluna and besought him to abate the
tax; whereupon he forthright bade strike off the heads of
three of the principals and casting the others into prison,
within two or three days let behead them all in cold
blood. Now he was very old and indeed decrepit, but
so lustful and immersed in venereal pleasures and appetites

[1] 1387?

that he was never without a concubine, and he had then a very fair damsel of two-and-twenty years of age, of whom he was sore enamoured. Wherefore, that same day he let behead the ambassadors, being all afire with exceeding great choler, he, to solace himself, went to take his pleasure with his fair mistress and seeking to do more than pertained unto his age, felt himself wax very feeble. Thinking to recover his lost strength, he (according as he was used to do otherwhiles) let enwrap himself, like a liver in its caul, in two sheets steeped in spirits of wine, and abode, thus enwrapped, in a warm room, midmost three great copper vessels full of red-hot coals, what while certain of his servants blew up the fires with bellows. What while he thus bewarmed himself, a spark lit upon the sheets, the which caught fire forthright and the flames waxed on such wise that it was impossible to quench them, and so the wretched king, full of rage and fury and unable to extricate himself, was miserably burned to death and died like a brute beast. The chronicles, speaking of this his death, declare that it was an express judgment of God, to punish the execrable wickednesses of so vicious a prince ; but God alone knoweth the truth, unknown to us, for that the Divine judgments are an unfathomable abyss. True, indeed, it is that it is exceeding uneath to live ill and die well.

Bandello

to the illustrious Signor Pietro Fregoso, seignior of Novi.

None need ever lack of an excuse for writing unto whoso most pleaseth him, and so there hath presently befallen me an occasion of writing to you and sending you, not only this letter, but a merry novel, to boot. I went the other day from Milan to Mantua and on my passage through Bozzolo, Signor Federigo Gonzaga, seignior of the place, kept me there eight days, entertaining me of his courtesy as blithely as can be told with all seemly diversions, such as might be given to the like of me, and would nowise let me depart. Moreover, when my lord Pirro, his brother, knew that I was there, he came thither also and on my departure for Mantua, would have me go with him to his delightsome Gazuolo, where he entertained me some days in exceeding great pleasance. There I found Signor Sebastiano da Este, who was newly returned from Naples and who one day, we being in company in the citadel, told a merry chance befallen at the city of Reggio in Calabria, the which, having written it down, I now send and give unto you, in token of my devotion. Fare you well.

The Twelfth Story.

BIGOLINO, A CALABRESE, COZENETH HIS ● MASTER, THE BISHOP OF REGGIO, WITH CERTAIN FORGED WRITINGS.

I being minded to depart Naples and return hither, it behoved me betake myself to Reggio in Calabria, a very ancient city, from the seaboard whereof folk will have it that Sicily was sundered by an earthquake and from the mainland became an island, as it now is; so at the least is it recorded in the ancient chronicles and so is it there [1] affirmed of all. There was then at Reggio, in the service of the right reverend prelate, the bishop of the city, a Calabrese named Bigolino, the blithest and merriest man in those parts, who mimicked with his voice now the braying of the ass, now the whinnying of horses and now the cries of other animals, and there were few birds whose voice and song he counterfeited not; moreover, he let few weeks pass without playing some merry prank, so that he was very dear unto all the Regginese and there was still matter for talk of him. He had served various masters in various places and ultimately engaged with the said bishop, where, finding that he got nothing by his service, barring meat and drink and two suits of apparel a year, he resolved to play his master a trick

---

[1] _i.e._ at Reggio.

and imparted his device to a fellow serving-man of his. Accordingly, having bethought himself what he should do, he went one day to the stable and mounting a horse which the bishop had lately taken from the stud and which was vicious and restive, rode forth the city, as he was oftentimes used to do, to a place where there were certain diggings agate for the drainage of some fields which were often flooded. There he proceeded to drive the colt into the midst of the mire and soft soil thrown up by the labourers and digging his spurs into his flanks, caused him play the devil, so that both stuck fast in the mud and fell to the ground, at some distance from the diggers, who ran thither, crying, "Help! Help!" and found Bigolino all bemired and bleeding at the mouth and moving no more than as he were dead. They, thinking that the horse had trampled the poor wretch to death, pulled him out of the mire and laying him on a litter, carried him to the episcopal palace, to the general compassion of the Regginese, who all loved him for his merry ways; and still, as they went, he from time to time let a drop or two of blood issue from his mouth.

The bishop, who loved him greatly, hearing the case, was sore concerned and letting set him in a chamber, sent forthright for the leach; whilst Bigolino's accomplice, posting himself by his side, applied to tend him and whiles abiding alone with him, replenished him a sponge full of blood, which he had in his mouth, for the carrying out of the cheat. The physician, who was not the expertest man in the world, seeing the blood and looking the patient in the face (which he had made livid with certain fumigations, so that he showed like one dead,) concluded that the poor fellow had been all-to-trampled of the horse and that there was no whole bone in his body and declared him to be in danger of death. Presently, however, he began to open his eyes and breathe somewhat ; whereupon a priest was called to confess him, but could get no otherwhat from him than certain gestures which showed that he was ill at ease for his sins. Now the sow-gelder of a leach [1] had prescribed certain inunctions, which Bigolino's accomplice declared to have made, and night come, the latter proffered himself to watch the sick man. At nightfall, my lord bishop came to see Bigolino and bespoke him with the best and lovingest words in the world, for that in truth it irked him sore to lose his jester ; then, he offering to go away, the sick man made a gesture with his hands, as he would fain say somewhat ; whereupon the bishop drew lovingly near him, saying, "Bigolino mine, pluck up a good heart, for God will help thee. Wilt thou aught of me ? " The rogue signed Ay and his friend and accomplice still asked him what he would, for that my lord was ready to do all ; whereupon Bigolino made such and so many signs and gestures that his fellow said, " My lord, meseemeth the poor fellow would have his cassock ; what will he do ? Methinketh death followeth hard upon him." Accordingly, the cassock was fetched and Bigolino, having it in hand, signed to the bishop to take it and look in a certain part thereof which he showed him. The bishop took it and would have ripped it open at the place in question, but Bigolino signed to him as best he might to carry it away.

The prelate, curious to see what manner of thing this was, went off with the cassock to his chamber and there, being all alone, took a knife and opened the part to which the

---

[1] *Il medico Castraporci*, as we should say "a horse-doctor," a man only fit to dose cattle.

sick man had pointed. There he found a banker's bill, so well counterfeited that it seemed in very deed to have been made in the bank of the Spinelli at Naples, whereby the latter bound themselves to repay six hundred gold ducats to whoso should present the said bill to them, as it were Bigolino had laid up the monies in their bank. The bishop, seeing the script, never doubted but it was true and thought that Bigolino had deposited the monies what while he was at Naples, the date of the receipt tallying with his sojourn there, more by token he knew that many presents had been made him by the viceroy and his barons and that he had, to boot, gotten many ducats for his merry pranks and pleasantries; wherefore quoth he in himself, "Faith, Bigolino is not such a fool as he is accounted; he hath contrived to govern himself mighty well." Now the bishop was very rich, not only of the income of his bishoprick, but of many other revenues, but he was exceeding avaricious; wherefore he persuaded himself that Bigolino had given him the bill, so the monies should fall to him, and so he laid up the writing. Meanwhile, all being asleep, Bigolino, with his friend's aid, supped at his ease and after slept till past midnight, what while his accomplice found means to have a bason full of blood and poured it all out before his bed, after he had first all-to-bloodied his face. He then raised an outcry that the patient was at the point of death; whereupon the chaplain came and proceeded to commend his soul [to God], after the usance of prayers for the dying; and there came yet others, whilst Bigolino made such gestures and motions as are made of those in the last agony and ultimately abode as he were dead. All, seeing the prodigious quantity of blood, which they deemed the poor fellow had vomited, and the paleness of his face, held him

for dead and his accomplice, letting fetch water, declared
that he would himself wash him and would have no help ;
wherefore, being left alone with him, he washed his face
and wrapped him in a sheet, it being now hard upon
daybreak.

The bishop, hearing that Bigolino was dead, was concerned to have lost him, but rejoiced to have gained the
six hundred ducats. After a while, the accomplice came
and said to the bishop, "My lord, I have washed my
poor friend, who is all disfeatured by the horse's kicks,
and for that he is so marred that he seemeth no more
himself and eke stinketh already, being all perished inwardly, I have wrapped him in a sheet. It were well
that the funeral be holden betimes." Quoth the bishop,
"I will have honour done him, nay, all the priests and
friars of the city shall be bidden to his obsequies ; " then,
turning to one of his men, he ordered the whole on such
wise that it cost him more than thirty ducats. Now the
accomplice, so that none might go to lay hands upon
Bigolino, had sewn up in the sheet a piece of carrion,
which stank terribly. A little before dinner-time all the
people of the place came with the clergy to accompany
Bigolino to the sepulchre, all being sore grieved to have
lost him, and the body, being laid on the bier, was
borne in procession through the city and brought back
to the cathedral, where it was to be buried. The obsequies were celebrated with the utmost solemnity and the
bishop himself said the mass for the dead, none coming
near the catafalk [1] for the stench, whilst Bigolino was
like to burst for laughter, awaiting the end of the comedy.
The mass ended and the wonted offices chanted for the dead,

---

[1] *Catalitle.*

the gravediggers took the bier and carried it to the burial-place, where the stone was already removed from the sepulchre. One of the bearers perceived that the covering over Bigolino's face moved somewhat (for that he was tired of holding his breath and breathed as discreetliest he might) and said to the other, "Comrade, seest thou not this fellow is not yet dead? Look how the sheet stirreth for the breath." Whereupon the other gravedigger, who also saw how the sheet stirred from time to time, turned to his mate and answered, "Hold thy peace, fool that thou art, and say nothing, an it be e'en so. The expense is already incurred and the man hath smashed all his bones on such wise that he cannot live. Leave me do and cast him me down; take thou the feet and I will take the head. Smellest thou not how he stinketh? To it!"

Bigolino, hearing this, said in himself, "'Sblood, these curs would fain do in good earnest, whereas I will have it in sport; but they shall find themselves mistaken." Accordingly, what while one said to the other, "Take thou the feet and I will take the head," Bigolino, who was enshrouded on such wise that, by shaking himself, he abode free, said in a loud voice, "You shall not catch me yet awhile," and with a lusty toss of the sheet, leapt forth the bier, howling and making the frightfullest yells in the world; the which put all the folk to flight and the priests and friars also made off, letting the crosses fall to the ground. Bigolino, seeing every one pay with his heels [1] and hearing the terrified women scream for mercy, wrapped his sheet about him anew and taking in

---

[1] *Pagare di calcagni*, Italian form of our "take to his heels." The phrase is originally applied to a runaway debtor.

hand one of the fallen crosses, proceeded to imitate Dan Jackass his song[1] and to frolic it after the fugitives, so that those who first fled from the church and had now taken somewhat of heart perceived that this was one of Bigolino's pranks and all ended in laughter. My lord bishop was not so much rejoiced at the restoration of his buffoon to life as he was chagrined for the expense which he had incurred; wherefore, coming up to Bigolino, who was compassed about of many and was still wrapped in his sheet, he said to him, "Thou hast e'en served me a fine trick; go to, go to, I warrant thee it was a fine one, bedlam fool that thou art!" "Most reverend my lord," replied Bigolino, "pardon me, but you apprehend it not. I wished to send the light[2] before me, seeing I know not if, when I die in good earnest, there will be any to light a single candle for me, for that all cannot read bankers' bills." Then, falling into other merry traits of his fashion, "My lord," quoth he, "let us go dine, for I am like to drop of hunger." Moreover, he went about the city all that day with his sheet about him, making all who saw him laugh; and the bishop must needs abide the expense, knowing the bill to be counterfeit.

---

[1] Or "to play the part of Dan Jackass" (*Far il verso di Messer l'Asino*).

[2] *i.e.* the illumination commonly used at funerals, which is held by the Catholic church to enure to the health of the dead man's soul.

Bandello

Your most goodly madrigals, which you sent me by the hands of the Lord Count Ercole Roscone, made by you in praise of the marvellous and incredible beauty and of the other divine gifts of the never enough belauded princess, the Lady Giulia Gonzaga e Colonna, I have as gladly received as aught which could have come to my hands in these days and have read them again and again with inexpressible pleasure, as well because they are the birth of your sublime intellect, which I at once honour, revere and admire as one of the rarities of our age, for the singular gifts which, like flaming stars, shine in your every action, as also for that they are goodly, ingenuous, dulcet, elegant and terse and full of a sweet and pure native eloquence, without aught of affectation. Moreover, they have been no little dear to me for that they speak of that excellent lady, whose name nowadays soareth to such a height on the wings of clear-shining renown and approveth itself so famous throughout every clime that all the lofty wits of our age, who have wetted their lips some little in the Pegasean fount, study to celebrate her, not, indeed, to add any praise to her or to augment her true honours, the which cannot be augmented by others' writings, however learned and skilful, nor be abated by the blame of the malevolent, but for that their writings and poems may take worship and value from her ever-glorious name. I have, as you charged me by your letters, despatched the said madrigals to Fondi, by the hand of a trusty messenger of Signor Cesare Fieramosca, whom he sent of late to Capua to Signor Federico his brother, and the said Signor Cesare in my presence commanded his man that, when he came thither, he should straight-way present your letters and madrigals to the Lady Giulia, unto whom he also wrote a long letter under his own hand, commending you to her in that soldierly style of his. I am fain to believe, nay, I am firmly persuaded that, when the said Lady Giulia seeth your madrigals (nor can it be long ere the messenger reach Fondi), she will, like a most debonair and judicious lady as she is and is holden of all the world, read them with infinite pleasure and receive them with as much honour as aught that could be presented to her; nay, it is like she will prize and tender these your goodliest compositions more than those of whatsoever others celebrate her. The others, who write and sing of her all day long and strive to show her such as she is, are men, whose natural devoir it is to love, honour, reverence and celebrate all ladies, and especially those who deserve it, as doth she, who might afford ample matter [for discourse] unto all the writers of our times. But, sooth to say, men's praises of ladies are still open to some suspicion lest, for the overmuch love that is borne them[1] or to acquire their favour, the limits of truth be somewhat overpassed. But

---

[1] *i.e.* the ladies, the subjects of commendation.

if a judicious lady, such as yourself, praise another lady,
what suspicion can be conceived but that she saith the
naked and manifest truth? You, (be it permitted me so
to say, speaking the truth and that which all the world
seeth,) who were born fair and are most nobly and illus-
triously married and being, to boot, adorned with good
letters, do gracefully compose in the vulgar tongue and
set your rhymes to music, nay, these your songs, masterly
wrought, you sing and play, with swift and nimble hand
accompanying the sweetness of your voice,—you, I say,
being such as you are, praise the Lady Giulia. Marry,
this must needs be a sincere and true praise, wherein no
whit of suspect can be found by Momus[1] himself, it being
notorious that truth alone moveth you to sing thus of her.
Happy she, then, who hath found so noble a songstress
of her merits! Now, for that you bid me send you somewhat of my fashion, I must tell you that, during the
excessive heats which prevail in Milan in this season of
the dog-days, I have laid aside all my graver studies and
if I e'en read or write aught, it is some trifling matter,
wherein it behoveth me not rack my brains for arguments nor weary my feeble fancy, unapt unto great things.
Wherefore, remembering me of much pleasant and precious
discourse which we had this past April and May at your
castle of Deciana, at Ponzano in Monferrato and at your
other places, whereas it was oftentimes spoken of the
tricks which women play men, I bethought me of the
story which our learned Messer Giacinto Arpino told us,
seeking to show that men whiles render women bread
for biscuit; the which, meseeming it was very goodly and
such as might profit many, I have in this sultry season

[1] The God of raillery.

written down and dedicated to your name. Accordingly, I send it to you, so that, when you are tired of study, you may read it for your recreation. Oh truly happy this our age! For that, if the ancients had one Sappho, we moderns can vaunt ourselves of two, to wit, your learned, fluent and sprightly aunt, the Lady Camilla Scarampa, and yourself, her honoured niece, more by token that the ancient Sappho was not more learned than you twain and you twain are far honester and chaster than she. Fare you well.

The Thirteenth Story.

SIGNOR FILIBERTO DA VIRLE FALLETH ENAMOURED OF MADAM ZILIA DUCA, WHO FOR A KISS CAUSETH HIM ABIDE LONG MUTE; BUT HE AFTER SIGNALLY AVENGETH HIMSELF OF HER.

In Moncalieri, a castlewick not far from Turin, dwelt a widow called Madam Zilia Duca, whose husband had died a little before, leaving her a young woman of four-and-twenty and very fair, but crabbed and uncivil of her fashions, which smacked rather of the peasant than the townswoman; wherefore, being resolved not to marry again, she applied herself to lay by for a little only son she had of three to four years old. She lived at home, not like a gentlewoman of her degree, but like a poor woman, and did all the menial offices of the house, for saving's sake and to keep as few servants as possible. Moreover, she seldom let herself be seen and on holidays went betimes in the morning to the first mass at a little

church hard by her house and returned home forthright.
It is the general usance of the ladies of those parts to
kiss all strangers who come to their houses or by whom
they are visited and to converse familiarly with every one;
but she shunned all these practices and lived alone. It
chanced that Monsignor Filiberto da Virle, a gentleman of
the neighbourhood, who was a soldier and very valiant and
doughty of his person, came to Moncalieri and being about
to return to Virle, went to hear mass at Madam Zilia's
church; where he saw her and himseeming she was very
fair and engaging, he felt himself inwardly all afire with love
of her. Accordingly, he asked who she was and was
made acquainted with her fashions, but could not, for
all they misliked him, help loving her. He went that
day to Virle, where having set his affairs in order, he
resolved to return to Moncalieri, which was not far distant, and there abide as most he might and use his every
endeavour to gain the lady's love. Accordingly, alleging
certain excuses of his fashion, he hired a house at Moncalieri and there took up his abode, using every diligence
to see the lady often, but might scarce espy her on holidays,
and when he offered to speak with her and enter into
discourse, she with two words took leave of him and went
off home; whereat he abode sore disconsolate, but might
nowise desist from that his love. He found means to get
other ladies to bespeak her; he wrote to her and did
everything possible; but all was in vain, inasmuch as she
abode harder than a rock of the sea nor ever vouchsafed
him a fair answer; wherefore the wretched lover, finding
no solace for that his love nor availing to desist from the
emprise and having already lost sleep thereby and well-
nigh appetite, fell grievously sick, and the physicians, unknowing what ailed him, knew not what remedy to give

him, so that the poor youth ran with long steps unto death, unsuccoured of any.

What while he was abed, there came a man-at-arms to see him, who was a native of Spoleto and a great familiar of his, and to him Filiberto related all his love and the dire rigour of his obdurate and most cruel mistress, ending by telling him that, finding all his pains in vain, he was dying for excess of grief and chagrin. The Spoletine, hearing what ailed the sick man, whose great well-wisher he was, said to him, "Filiberto, leave me do and I will find thee means to speak with her at thine ease." "I want no other-what," replied the other; "for that, if I have this, my heart warranteth me I can prevail with her to have pity on me; but how shall I do, for that I have done my utmost endeavour in the matter, have sent her messages, with rich gifts and exceeding great promises, and have never been able to obtain aught?" Quoth the Spoletine, "Apply but to wax whole and leave the care of the rest to me." With this promise Messer Filiberto abode so content that he speedily felt himself marvellously recovered and in a few days left his bed. Now the Spoletines are, as you know, all great talkers and [it is mostly friars from that province that] go about all Italy, collecting Saint Anthony's pence; for that they are all-powerful in talk, audacious and ready-witted, are never at a loss for matter of discourse and are marvellously skilled in persuading folk of all they have a mind to make them believe. Moreover, most of those who go bubbling silly folk, paying them in monkey's money, and those who carry adders and asps and other snakes and go plying the like crafts and singing about the market-places, are Spoletines. Filiberto's friend was, then, of this race and belike in his time had found himself selling bean-powder for ointment against the itch in half a dozen market-places.

Accordingly, Messer Filiberto recovered, he forgot not the
promise he had made him, but clapped up with one of those
who go about the streets with a basket made fast to the
neck and hanging under the left arm, crying and selling
ribands, thimbles, bodkins, tapes, laces, chaplets and the
like women's toys, and made a bargain with him for his
clothes and basket ; then, donning the pedlar's habit, he
betook himself to the street where Madam Zilia lived and
began to pass to and fro before her house, crying out as
is usual.

The lady, hearing the cry and having occasion for some
lawn, called him in ; whereupon he, seeing his device in
a fair way of success, boldly entered the house and saluted
her with fair words, as he had been very familiar there.
She put her hand into his basket and turned over this thing
and that, whilst he, compleasing her of all, displayed
ribbons and lawn and what not else, till she, seeing certain
gauze for which she had occasion and which seemed to
her mighty fine, said, " Good man, how sell you this
gauze by the yard? An you give me good cheap thereof,
I will take as much as thirty yards of you." " Madam,"
replied the Spoletine, " an the gauze please you, take it
and seek not to know the price, for that it is already paid ;
nay, not the gauze only, but all I have here is yours without
price, so but you deign to take it." " Nay," said the lady,
" that will I not, for it is not honest ; though I thank you
for your proffers. Tell me but what you will have for the
gauze and I will satisfy you ; for it beseemeth not that you,
who gain your living by these toils, should lose thus whole-
sale thereat. Make me a fair price and I will give you your
monies." Quoth the other, " Marry, I do not lose, nay,
I profit amain, an there be aught here that liketh you, and
if you are as kindhearted as your face promiseth, you will

accept this gauze and such of these other things as please you to gift; for that one giveth them to you who would spend, not only his substance, but his life, to complease you." The lady, hearing this, waxed red as a vermeil rose, whenas in May at the appearing of the sun it beginneth to display its new leaves, and looking the Spoletine fixedly in the face, said to him, "You give me much cause for marvel with your talk; wherefore I would fain know who you are and to what end you say these things to me; methinketh you mistake me for some one else, for that I am not such as you belike conceive." He then, no whit abashed, told her with apt words (for that he came, as I have said, from Spoleto,) in what torment Messer Filiberto lived for love of her and how he was her faithful servant and there was no one in the world of whom she might dispose more than of him and his, more by token that he was rich and [of the family] of the Seigniors of Virle and a most gallant gentleman. Brief, he contrived to say so much and to persuade her to such purpose that she consented to her lover's coming privily to speak with her and assigned him time and place.

Messer Filiberto, learning this good news, held himself excellent well apaid of the Spoletine and went at the appointed hour to speak with Madam Zilia, whom he found awaiting him in a ground-floor room of her house, attended by a maid of hers. The room was very large and they might talk at their ease, without being overheard of the maid; wherefore he began, with the aptest words he knew, to set out to her his amorous torments and what he suffered for love of her, instantly beseeching her to consider his case and vouchsafe to have compassion of him and assuring her that he would eternally be her servant. But, for all he said, he could get no otherwhat from her than that she was a widow, whom it ill beseemed follow after such toys, that she was minded to apply herself to the governance of her son and that he would not lack of other ladies, fairer than herself. After much discourse, the poor lover, seeing that he laboured in vain and that she was not disposed to content him in aught and feeling himself like to die for exceeding chagrin, said to her piteously and with tears in his eyes, "Since, mistress mine, you deny me all hope of acceptance as your servant and it behoveth me, to my sore affliction, depart from you, nor belike shall I ever again have an occasion of conversing with you,—at the least, at this my last leavetaking, give me, in guerdon of the much love I have borne, bear and shall bear you what while I live, one sole kiss; which, when I came hither, I offered (according to the custom of our native land) to take of you, but you, against our laudable usance, denied it me, albeit you know it is no shame to kiss in the public street, whenas men meet ladies." The lady abode a little while in doubt and presently answered, "My lord Filiberto, I will e'en see if your love be as fervent as you pretend. You shall presently have of me the kiss which you seek, an you swear to do that which I shall ask you, so I may certify myself if you love me as much as you say."

The unwary lover swore to do everything in his power and bidding her command him whatsoever she would, abode awaiting her behest; whereupon she put her arms about his neck and kissing him on the mouth, said to him, "My lord Filiberto, I have given you the kiss you sought of me, in the expectation that you will do whatsoever I shall command you; wherefore I tell you that I will have you, in fulfilment of your pledge, from this time forth until three whole years shall have passed, speak not with any one in the world, man or woman, be it who it may, on

such wise that you shall abide mute three years long."
Filiberto, hearing this, abode all amazed; algates, albeit
himseemed this commandment was indiscreet, unreasonable
and most uneath to be strictly observed, he signed to her
with his hand that he would do all that which she bade
him and inclining himself before her, took leave of her
and returned to his lodging. There, bethinking him of his
case and revolving in his mind the hard oath he had taken,
he resolved, if he had lightly bounden himself by sworn
faith, to seek to maintain it with a steadfast heart and an
entire observance. Accordingly, feigning to have acciden-
tally lost the power of speech, he departed Moncalieri
and returning to Virle, lived there mute-fashion, making
himself understood by means of signs and writing. Great
was the compassion in which he was had of every one
and it seemed to all a marvellous thing that he should
without mishap or illness have lost his speech. Meanwhile
he took order for the governance of all his affairs, making a
cousin german of his his proxy; then, providing himself with
good riding-cattle and appointing how monies should be
sent him at certain times, he departed Piedmont and passed
over to Lyons in France. He was very goodly of his
person, well-made and gallant of aspect, so that, whereassoever he went and his mischance became known, all had
compassion of him.

Now in those days Charles VII., King of France, had
a most cruel war afoot with the English and still battled
with them, recovering by force of arms whatsoever they
had for many years before usurped upon his foregoers and
having ousted them from Gascony and other parts, applied
to make an end of wresting Normandy from them. Filiberto,
learning this, repaired to King Charles his court, which was
then in Normandy, and found there certain barons his

friends, by whom he was kindly received and who, understanding how he was by an unknown chance fallen dumb, had compassion of him. He made signs to them that he came to bear arms in the King's service, the which was very welcome to them, of their fore-knowledge of him for a man of an exceeding great spirit and very doughty of his person. It chanced that the assault was presently to be given to Rouen, a chief city of Normandy, in which emprise Messer Filiberto, having equipped himself with arms and horses, bore himself as valiantly as any other there and was sundry whiles seen of King Charles to approve himself a very stout and prudent soldier, so that, thanks to his prowess, the assault being renewed, Rouen was taken. The city gotten, the king let call Filiberto to him and would fain know who he was, so he might give him a sortable guerdon for his valour, and understanding that he was of the Seigniors of Virle in Piedmont and was a little before fallen dumb, on what wise was not known, appointed him a gentleman of his chamber, with the wonted entertainment, and let pay him two thousand franks then and there, exhorting him to serve as he had begun and promising to do everything to heal him; whereupon he with gestures humbly thanked the king for all his favours and raising his hand, made sign that he would not fail to serve faithfully.

It chanced one day that, at the passage of a certain bridge, there befell a great skirmish between the French and the enemy and the trumpets sounding to arms and the clamour still waxing among the soldiers, the king, to hearten his men, went thither. Now Talbot,[1] captain-general of the

---

[1] *Bandello* gives the name of the great English soldier as *Talabotto*.

English, was himself in person upon the bridge, at the head of his men, and had taken it well-nigh all. The king heartened his men and sent these and those to their succour, whenas there came up the doughty Messer Filiberto, armed and mounted upon a high-mettled courser, and spurring straight at Talbot, lance in rest, bore him and his horse to the earth. Then, taking in hand a strong and heavy mace, he drove among the English, striking lustily at these and those and never dealing a blow in vain, but overthrowing or slaying an Englishman at every stroke, so that the enemy was enforced to abandon the bridge and flee in disorder and Talbot himself, remounting to horse with the help of his men, was compelled to give ground.[1] This victory gave well-nigh all Normandy into King Charles his power, wherefore the good king, seeing what help Messer Filiberto had afforded him, very honourably praised him in the presence of all the lords of his court and gave him divers castlewicks, with the command of an hundred men-at-arms,[2] and largely increased his entertainment, daily making more of him. The war ended, the king let hold a solemn jousting at Rouen, wherein all the valiant and chief men of France took part, and of this Messer Filiberto carried off the honours.

The king, who loved Filiberto greatly and supremely desired to see him recover his speech, so he might be able to converse with him, let cry abroad through all his provinces that he had a gentleman, who was fallen dumb in a night, and that any who would heal him should incontinent

[1] Lit. "had dearth of ground" (*ebbe carestia di terreno*); we should perhaps read "was hard pressed in his flight."

[2] About equivalent to a modern brigade, a "lance" (as a man-at-arms and his company were technically called) comprising from ten to fifteen men of all ranks.

have ten thousand franks. The thing was published throughout all France and came eke into Italy; wherefore many, as well Italians as French, drawn by greed of monies, set themselves to the proof, but no effect ensued thereof and indeed the physicians' labour was thrown away, the pretended mute choosing not to speak. Wherefore the king, despited that no leach was found who might avail to cure him and seeing that innumerable folk came all day long, as well physicians of note as others who thought to recover him with their experiments,[1] and deeming them drawn rather by greed of gain than by knowledge or hope that they had of availing to heal him, let proclaim that whoso undertook the restoration of Messer Filiberto to speech should take such a term as himseemed was apt thereunto and should, if he cured him, have the ten thousand franks, together with other gifts which he would give him, but that, an he cured him not, he should lose his head, except he found means to pay ten thousand franks. This rigorous proclamation, getting wind, checked the concourse of physicians and yet there were some who, sustained by vain hope, feared not to expose themselves to so great a risk, so that some, availing not to heal him, were doomed to pay the ten thousand franks or lose their heads, and others were condemned to perpetual imprisonment.

Now the report of this thing had already reached Moncalieri [and it was known] how Messer Filiberto da Virle was in great favour with the King of France and grown very rich. Madam Zilia, hearing this and well knowing the cause of the gentleman's muteness, (two years [of the three] being by this passed), thought that he spoke not, less for reverence of the strait oath he had taken than for love

---

[1] *Isperimenti*, in modern parlance, "with their empirical remedies."

of herself and not to fail her of the promise made, and
concluding that he still loved her as fervently as when
he departed Moncalieri, she resolved to go to Paris,
where the king then lay, and by making Filiberto speak,
gain the ten thousand franks; for she doubted not but
that he, having become dumb at her instance, would speak,
whenas he saw her and was prayed of her to speak. Accordingly, having set her affairs in such order as herseemed
well and given out certain fables [of her fashion, to colour
her departure], she betook herself into France and came
presently to Paris, where, without making any delay about
the matter, she repaired to the commissaries, who had
charge of Messer Filiberto's healing, and said to them,
"Sirs, I am come to heal Messer Filiberto, having certain
secrets of great efficacy in such cases, by means whereof
I hope with God's help in fifteen days' time to cause him
speak excellent well; and if I make him not perfectly whole
within the appointed term, I submit to lose my head
therefor. But I require that none but myself abide in the
chamber with him during my tending of him, meseeming
unmeet that any learn the means which I purpose to
use for his recoverance; nay, I must abide with him
night and day, for that anights also at certain hours it
will behove me use my remedies." The commissaries,
hearing her speak with such assurance in so parlous a
case, where the most learned men of France and other
countries had failed, gave Messer Filiberto to understand
that there was a gentlewoman come from the land of
Piedmont, who offered herself to cure him. He let bring
her to his lodging and knew her as soon as he saw
her; wherefore, concluding that she had undertaken the
fatigues of that journey, not for love of him, but for
greed of the ten thousand franks, and calling to mind the

great harshness and cruelty which she had used with him and the torments he had suffered for her, he felt his fervent love, which was already grown cool, give place to the desire of just vengeance; wherefore he determined to take of her that pleasure which fortune threw in his way and pay her in such coin as she merited. Accordingly, they being left alone in the chamber, she bolted the door from within and said to him, "My lord, do you not know me? See you not that I am your dear Zilia, whom you professed to love so much aforetime?" He signed that he knew her well, but, touching his tongue with his finger, showed that he could not speak and shrugged his shoulders. The lady told him that she acquitted him of the oath and the promise made her and that she was come to Paris to do all he should command her; but he did nought but shrug his shoulders and touch his tongue with his finger.

Madam Zilia, seeing these his fashions, was sore chagrined and finding that no prayers of hers availed aught, proceeded to kiss him amorously and to caress him as most she knew, so that he, being young and having ardently loved the lady, who was in truth very fair, felt carnal appetite awaken in him and that astir which belike slept; wherefore he, without word said, took of her that pleasure which he had so eagerly desired and many times, during the fifteen · days' space, diverted himself amorously with her, but withal would nowise unknot his tongue, himseeming the kiss she had given him at Moncalieri merited not so long and grievous a penance. Wherefore whoso sought to recount the arguments with which the lady plied him, the urgent prayers she proffered him and the tears she shed to persuade him to speak would not make an end thereof in all this day. Then, the appointed term come and Filiberto still refusing to speak, she knew the greatness of her folly and presumption

and eke the cruelty she had used with her lover and gave
herself up for lost; inasmuch as, the fifteen days past,
it was bidden her pay the ten thousand franks or confess
herself, for that her head should be stricken off on the
morrow, and thereupon she was removed from the gentleman's chamber and carried to prison. Her dower sufficing
not unto the payment of the penalty, she resigned herself
to die; which Filiberto understanding and himseeming
he had sufficiently avenged himself of her, he went to seek
King Charles and making him due obeisance, proceeded,
to the marvellous joy of the king and his court, to speak
and telling him the whole history of his long silence, humbly
besought him to pardon all who were in prison and the
lady among the rest ; the which was granted him.

Madam Zilia being accordingly released from prison and
thinking to return to Piedmont, full of shame and confusion,
Messer Filiberto would have her and her company lodged
in his own hostelry and calling her apart, thus bespoke
her, saying, "Madam, you know how many months I did
you service at Moncalieri, for that in good sooth I loved
you most ardently. You know, moreover, that you for a
kiss charged me abide three years mute, and I swear to
you that, had you, then or after I went to Virle, absolved
me of the oath, I had eternally remained your servant ;
but your cruelty hath caused me go wandering some two
years' space, during which time (thanks to God and not
to you) it hath so well betided me that I am grown rich
and in high favour with my king. Now, meseeming I
have taken just vengeance of you, I mean to do you such
courtesy that, whereas I might have suffered your head
to be cut off, I will amply repay you the expense of the
journey you have made and eke of your return. Learn
for the future to govern yourself with prudence and illuse

gentlemen no more, for that (as the saying is) men meet and not mountains." So saying, he let give her monies in sufficiency and dismissed her. The king would have him take a wife and gave him a rich damsel with an inheritance of divers castlewicks; whereafter he sent to fetch his friend the Spoletine and entertained him about himself, giving him the means to live at his case. Messer Filiberto still lived in the king's good grace and after the death of Charles the Seventh, he abode in like favour with King Louis the Eleventh.

Bandello

to Signor Don Pietro Cardona Count of Collisano Admiral and Lord High Constable of the Kingdom of Sicily.

If I have tarried till now to send you the novel, or rather history, which Signor Lodovico Landreano, Provost of Vicobaldone, told you at Milan in the house of your brother-in-law, that most gallant and splendid cavalier, Signor Alfonso Visconti, be it my excuse in your eyes that, the very day whenas you so urbanely required me thereof, it was enjoined me of my superiors depart Milan on the morrow and betake myself to Monferrato on certain business of no small moment, and there, as you have seen, it behoved me sojourn three weeks' time. Now that, having happily despatched the affairs I had in treaty, I am returned, remembering me of your commandment, (for that I will have your prayers, nay, your least signs, still stand me in stead of behests) I have, putting aside all else, taken pen in hand and written down, as best I might, the novel aforesaid; the which I now send you with these presents and will have abide inscribed unto your name, that it may bear witness to those who come after us (if my writings endure so long alive) of your courteous goodwill unto me and of my observance towards you. Fare you well.

The Fourteenth Story.

ROSAMUND LETTETH ASSASSINATE HER HUSBAND AND AFTER, BLINDED BY DISORDERLY APPETITE, EMPOISONETH HERSELF AND HER SECOND HUSBAND.

The goodly and venerable ancient writing, compiled in authentic form,[1] which Signor Gian Lodovico di Corte-maggiore, Marquess of Pallavicino, hath let read here and which clearly establisheth the descent of his most noble house from the Longobards, (who not only founded the most worshipful families in Lombardy, such as our Vis-conti and Landriani, the Vicedomini, the Valvassori, the Cattanii and many others, in Tuscany the Marquesses Malaspini, in Frioul the Savorgnani and the Counts of Canossa, of whom was the glorious Countess Matilda,[2] most puissant both in Tuscany and Lombardy and in the Patrimony,[3] and likewise the house of Este, but sowed

---

[1] *i.e.* well-authenticated.

[2] The last Countess or Marchioness of Tuscany (ob. A.D. 1115), renowned for her devotion to the Papal See, which she defended by all means in her power against her kinsman, the Emperor Henry IV. of Germany. She was contemporary with Gregory VII. and it was at her castle of Canossa that Henry IV. made the celebrated act of submission to that pope which was so often referred to by Prince Bismarck and others in the course of the so-called Culturkampf.

[3] *i.e.* the States of the Church.

the seeds of their nobility in many families throughout
all Italy,) and the mention of their King Alboin move
me to relate to you his untimely death and the vengeance
which speedily ensued thereof. You must know, then,
that, after the expulsion of the Goths from Italy, Narses,[1]
a patrician and a man of exceeding renown, who had
laboured amain with hand and counsel to that end, ruled
the country with prudence and to the great satisfaction
of the people ; but, being flouted by Sophia, wife of the
Emperor Justin, with shameful menaces, he wrote to
Alboin, King of the Longobards, who then reigned over
Pannonia and with whom he had contracted a great
familiarity during the war with the Goths, and invited
him to come and make himself master of Italy. The
said Longobards, who came from Scandinavia, an island
of the Ocean,[2] had theretofore occupied the country
adjoining the Danube, on its abandonment by the Heruli
and the Thuringi, whenas Odoacer their king led them
into Italy and occupied Rome, and there they reigned
till their kingship came into the hands of the said Alboin,
a cruel and audacious prince, full of fierce and barbarous
usances and very expert in matters of war, who, passing
the Danube, for that Cunimund,[3] King of the Gepidæ, had
broken the conventions made between his father Turisund

---

[1] The celebrated general of the Emperor Justinian, who succeeded
Belisarius in the commandment of the imperial armies and expelling
the Goths from Italy, was appointed Exarch of the peninsula.
Bandello calls him " Narsete."

[2] Sic. The Longobards are generally supposed to have come from
the shores of the Baltic, somewhere between the Elbe and the
Oder, but some historians hold that they were originally natives of
Denmark.

[3] Bandello, " Comondo."

and the Longobards, encountered and overcame him in a pitched battle, in which few of the Gepidæ abode alive. Cunimund their king was among the slain and Alboin, taking up his severed head, let make a cup of his skull set in gold, wherein he drank at state banquets. Amongst the booty was Rosamund, the king's daughter, a damsel beautiful beyond belief, who, being seen of Alboin, was espoused of him to wife, Clodsuinda, his first wife, daughter of Clotaire, King of France, having died a little before. Being, as hath been said, invited by Narses into Italy, he resolved to go thither and calling the Saxons to his aid, departed Pannonia, of which the Longobards had taken possession two-and-forty years before, on the second day of April in the year of our redemption 568, leaving that country to the Huns, (wherefore Pannonia was after called Hungary,) on condition that, if the Longobards returned, they should have their fields again; then, passing the Alps, with all his people, men, women and children, he entered Italy by the province of Frioul. Now that wretched country was presently unprovided with arms and captains, for that Narses had retired to Naples, having been deprived of his commandment, and had been succeeded by Longinus, who was far inferior to him in the military art and in the governance of the people; wherefore Alboin in a trice made himself master of Frioul and assigned it for dukedom to Gisulf his nephew, unto whom he gave many noble Longobard families to people the country. He after subdued the whole country now called the Trevisan Marches, except Padua and Monfelice; Mantua he might not avail to take, but he conquered the state of Milan and all Liguria and made himself master of well-nigh all the rest, with the exception of Rome and Ravenna, where Longinus lay, and certain castles builded upon the sea-shore, so that there remained to the Greek Emperor but a part of the kingdom of Naples and some few other places.

The barbarian king was, as hath been said, very cruel and inordinately arrogant, presuming so much upon himself for the acquisition thus suddenly made of such a country that himseemed the dominion, not only of Italy, but of all Europe, could not fail him ; wherefore, leaving the care of the war, he gave himself up to pleasure and festivity. Accordingly, being one day at Verona, which much pleased him for its site, he ordained a magnificent banquet, whereto, by his commandment, were bidden the chief men and women of the Longobards, and applied to eat well and drink better, inviting this one and that to do the like, so that, for excess of wine, he became merrier than of wont, not to say drunken, and called for the cup made of the skull of Cunimund his father-in-law, which was straightway brought him. The barbarian let fill it with good wine and bade his cupbearer carry it to the queen, saying, "Harkye, take this cup and give it to Rosamund my wife and bid her drink and make merry with her father." Rosamund, who sat with the women at another table, overagainst her husband, hearing his speech (for that he had cried out loudly,) was inwardly sore incensed and hearkened his message with a heart full of rage and ill will against him. Nevertheless, taking the cup in hand, she set it to her mouth with disgust and despite and making a show of drinking, returned it to the esquire, concealing her chagrin as most she might. Now she could not brook that Alboin should, in presence of all the Longobard nobles, have not only reminded her of the death of her father, but, to slight her the more, willed her drink in the cup made of the latter's skull ; wherefore, unable to master her anger, she abode thenceforth so full of ill will against her husband that

herseemed she might not live nor have any content in this
world, except she signally avenged herself of so great an
affront, feeling his words still pierce her through and
through with lively dolour and gnaw at her heartstrings
without cease like a biting, fretting worm ; nay, overcome
with the fierceness of that incessant and tormenting passion
which gave her no whit of rest, she inwardly resolved to
procure her husband's death at all hazards and though it
should cost her her life. Accordingly, fixed in this her
purpose and doing no otherwhat all day long than rack her
brains and cast about how she might avail to avenge herself
of the king, she could find no device to her mind ; but,
what while she wavered between a thousand conflicting
thoughts, swerving withal no whit from her fell purpose,
chance threw in her way a means which seemed to her much
to the purpose and sure to effect her intent and do unto
Alboin that which he had done unto Cunimund.

There was amongst Alboin's courtiers a Longobard youth,
his foster-brother, called by some Helmichis [1] and by others
Almachild, who bore the king's helmet in battle and who,
for all he was young, was much esteemed, having still
approved himself a man of understanding and valour. Upon
him the queen wrought to such purpose that he consented
to slay Alboin his king, but, doubting his ableness to achieve
so great and parlous an emprise alone, he exhorted her to
persuade Peredeus, the strongest man of all the Longobards,
to bear him company in the matter. Peredeus, however,
refused to consent to such a crime and Rosamund, fearing
lest he should discover the plot and knowing that he oftentimes lay with her wardrobe-woman, persuaded the latter
to appoint him to lie with her that same night, when she

---

[1] Bandello, " Elmige."

herself would take her place by his side. The adultery consummated, Rosamund made herself known to the affrighted gallant and said to him, "Thou seest, Peredeus, that which thou hast done against Alboin's honour and what penalty thou hast incurred; wherefore needs must thou resolve thyself either to slay him or to be cruelly slain of him." Peredeus, perceiving the cheat which had been put on him and constrained by fear, promised that which he had before refused voluntarily to do; and so the queen, not content with assassinating her husband, must needs, ere she let put him to death, send him to Cornwall. Now Alboin was wont to lay himself on his bed at noontide to sleep; which he doing one day, Rosamund commanded that all should withdraw and that no noise should be made in the palace, inasmuch as the king was indisposed and would fain repose; then, adroitly removing all her husband's arms from the chamber, except his sword, which she made fast to the sheath, so he might not avail himself thereof, and left at his bedhead, the wicked woman admitted Helmichis and Peredeus armed. Alboin, awaking and perceiving the manifest peril in which he stood, clapped his hand to his sword, but, finding it secured on such wise that he might not unsheath it, took up a stool, wherewith he defended himself awhile; but what might he avail, unarmed as he was, against two armed and stalwart men, whereof one had not his match for strength? Thus Alboin, a man most warlike and of extraordinary audacity, was slain and he, who had been still most fortunate in battle against his enemies, died of a woman's treason. His body was buried under a stair of the palace at Verona and great was the mourning of the Longobards for his death. Helmichis, whom Rosamund had promised to make him king and take him to husband, seeing that, for the resistance of the

barons who were then in Verona, he might not avail to
occupy the throne and misdoubting him to be put to death
whenas the other princes came to choose them a king, abode
sore troubled ; wherefore, what while it was yet unknown
who were the king's murderers, Rosamund, Helmichis
and Peredeus, laying hands upon all the Longobard
treasures, took ship with Albisuinda, daughter of Alboin
and his first wife Clodsuinda, and sailed to Ravenna, where
Helmichis, who had meanwhile espoused Rosamund to
wife, was, with her and all his company, very honourably
received by Longinus and assigned a goodly lodging in
the city.

What while these things befell in Italy, Justin, Emperor
of Constantinople, died and was succeeded in the empery
by his adopted son Tiberius, who was then warring against
the Persians and who, had he had in Italy the prosperous
fortune which he had in the East, would have been a
most happy prince ; wherefore he might not apply to the
deliverance of Italy, which was well-nigh all occupied
by the Longobards. Longinus, seeing that Tiberius was
not for concerning himself with Italian affairs, thought to
make himself master of the peninsula and by means of
Rosamund, to win the most part of the Longobards, she
being loved and esteemed by many of them, more by
token that he knew her to have brought incalculable
treasures with her. Accordingly he with many words
imparted to her his purpose and persuaded her to such
effect that she promised to empoison Helmichis and take
himself to husband. Marry, here was a fine patch of a
woman for you ! It seemed not enough to her to sunder
the marriage bond and adulterously to abandon herself
to a simple esquire ; it sufficed her not to let assassinate
Alboin her husband by practice, to steal all the crown

treasures and carry off the king's daughter, but she must, to boot, for no fault of his, empoison her second husband, who deserved well of her and who had for her sake exposed himself to such a risk. But I am not presently concerned to do the satirist's office, more by token that I see the Lady Antonia Gonzaga, wife of the Signor Cavaliere, and the other ladies who are here look on me with an evil eye, and I would not on any account displease them, it being still my wont to honour the ladies and do their every pleasure. Rosamund, then, having prepared a cup of poisoned wine, took her opportunity one day, whenas Helmichis came forth of the bath, and entering the chamber with the cup in her hand, proffered it to him, saying, "Dear my husband, drink and recruit your languid body with this healthful beverage which I have prepared for you." Helmichis, being athirst, took the cup and drank off a great part of the wine, but, feeling his stomach overset and all his vitals racked with cruel pains, divined the treason and taking sword in hand, said to Rosamund, with a stern countenance, "Base and wicked woman (may fire fall from heaven to burn thee!), either do thou drink the rest of this wine, wherewith thou hast empoisoned me, or I will slay thee, as thou deservest, with this whinger." She, seeing her treason discovered and it behoving her die on one or other wise, forasmuch as there was none in the chamber to afford her aid, took the cup and swallowed the rest of the wine, and so in a little while they both died thereof. Longinus, having lost his hope of making himself king, took the treasures and sent them, together with Alboin's daughter, Albisuinda, to Tiberius at Constantinople; whither the historians allege that Peredeus was also carried, declaring that he one day slew a very great and fierce lion in the presence of the emperor and all the people. Tiberius, for fear of his strength, let put out his eyes; and thus none of Alboin's three murderers abode unpunished. Meanwhile, the Longobards, not to abide without a ruler, assembled at Pavia, which city they after made the seat of their monarchy, and elected to king one Clepho, a man very noble amongst them and of exceeding great renown in the art of war; but he also, after an eighteen months' reign, was foully murdered by a serving-man of his.

Bandello

to the reverend Messer Giacomo Antiquario Apostolical Prothonotary.

There were divers gentlemen with you, this past week,
at the venerable monastery of Our Lady of the Graces in
Milan, and you all went modestly disporting yourselves
under the long trellis of the garden.   There it was told
how once upon a time Fra Michele da Carcano (one of his
brethren having gotten a girl with child at Cremona and
the populace kindling into fury) mounted the pulpit and
made a goodly preachment ; then, ultimately, turning to
the people, "Cremonese mine," quoth he, "I have ever
accounted you men of sagacity and of perfect and sound
judgment, but I find myself much mistaken in my opinion.
What miracle or thing unwonted is this, that a man should
get a woman with child? See you not this betide all day
long and do you make such an outcry for the like thereof?
It were a miracle, indeed, and a thing to make a tumult
about if the girl had gotten the friar with child." And
with these toys he appeased the Cremonese.   To this
purpose there were many things said of the dissolute life of
many churchmen and of the little pains which are taken
to amend their lewd fashions, as well among the secular
clergy as among the regulars[1] or those at the least who

---

[1] *i.e.* monks (*regolari*, those subject to a monastic *rule*).

should be regulated.[1] Whereupon our well-bred and erudite Messer Gian Giacomo Ghillino most modestly entered into discourse of the matter and saying that it were well bytimes to do as did Tiberius, Emperor of Rome, with the priests of the Goddess Isis, related that which befell a Roman gentlewoman in those times; the which I wrote down according to his narration and make you a little gift thereof, having for the nonce no otherwhat to give you. And if it should belike appear to some that these toys sort not with the gravity of the philosophical studies wherein you are all day long engaged and yet less with the integrity of your most goodly life, it behoveth whoso is guided by reason to bethink him that it is whiles necessary to relax the rigour of one's life and to recreate oneself with things honest and pleasant, to be after stronger and brisker for the labours of the intelligence. Thus Socrates, the father of academical learning, after his continual disputations upon the most difficult and profound questions, after instructing and training the many eminent disciples who hearkened to his teachings, accounted it nothing unworthy of his most virtuous life to divert himself at home with his merry children and to share with them in those pleasures which are proper to childhood. Nay, the most bepraised Scipio Africanus the Elder disdained not, after his gravest ponderings over the governance of the states [committed to his charge], to go with his Achates, Lælius, a-pleasuring along the sea-shore and gathering small stones and sea-shells. Fare you well.

---

[1] Or "ruled" (*regolati*).

The Fifteenth Story.

PAULINA, A ROMAN LADY, IS UNDER COLOUR OF RELIGION COZENED BY HER LOVER; BY REASON WHEREOF THE WORSHIP OF ISIS IS DONE AWAY.

We have, gentlemen mine, embarked upon a vast and darkling sea [in treating] of the corrupt life of persons dedicated to the service of God, their lewd fashions standing more in need of amendment than of reprehension; wherefore it were behoving to put hand (as the saying is) to the dough and come to the reformation of their lives, they being those from whom we laymen should take example of godly living and not see the unseemly and perverse doings which we see all day long. I for my part, after [despatching] my domestic concerns and those of my friends, oftentimes find no other solace than to come hither and abide awhile with these venerable brethren and other like practising monks and friars, in whom there is nought but good usances to be seen, and to receive from them the best of counsel for the course of this our perilous life. And albeit there are others to be seen who bear the name of monks and whose life is altogether contrary to the profession they make, as many there be in this our city of Milan, we laymen must not withal be their imitators nor eke presume to judge of things sacred,[1] but eschew their ill customs and leave unto those to whom it pertaineth the care of chastening them and giving them due punishment. Do we but our duty and betide thereof what will. Algates, it is manifest that evil examples are the occasion of very great and parlous disorders; wherefore, as Messer Giacomo Antiquario here well knoweth, if Duke Lodovico Sforza had not lost the duchy, he had already taken order to seek to reform the whole clergy and every other sort of religious persons of this state, supplicating the pope to compel the bishops and heads of religious orders to see that all under their charge lived according to their rules; but his unfortunate expulsion and imprisonment hath put an end to that godly, necessary and praiseworthy work. Peradventure God will one day inform our Most Christian King with His grace, so that, according as he hath begun to reform the convent and brethren of Sant' Eustorgio, he may do the like with the rest; nay, calling to mind that which the Emperor Tiberius did with certain priests at Rome, methinketh it were haply not altogether amiss bytimes to do the like with one or two of our ill-living priests and friars, for it would serve to terrify the others, so that what they will not for love of virtue they should do for fear of punishment.

Now, to come to my story, you must know that, what time the Emperor Tiberius ruled Rome, there was a very wealthy Roman gentleman, called Saturninus, who took to wife a most noble damsel, left beyond measure rich by the inheritance of her parents, so that she brought her husband gold and silver and exceeding great estates and

---

[1] Lit. "to put our mouths in heaven" (*porre la bocca in cielo*), i.e. to talk of things beyond human (or at least beyond lay) competence.

was, to boot, accounted one of the fairest ladies to be found
in those days at Rome. But what made her most famous
and most estimable in all men's eyes was her true and
chastest honesty, unpliable unto whosoever it might be for
gold or silver or any other thing; and this her chastity
was the more marvellous and praiseworthy that the Roman
women, of whatsoever degree and quality, had already in
her day begun to give loose to their wanton appetites without
any regard for decency, committing adultery without fear
of reproach and behaving themselves as shamelessly as
public harlots; nay, so far had they suffered themselves
be carried away of their lusts that, had their forefathers
returned to life and seen the pomp of their raiment,
enhanced with such wealth of gold and precious stones
and orient pearls, and heard their speech, unbecoming
as it was unto virtuous dames and ladies, and considered
their wanton and unchaste manner of life, with their mere-
tricious talk and gestures, they would have been filled
at once with wonderment and despite and would have
avouched that this was not the dress, the fashions, the
usances, the manners, the temperate way of living and
the laudable converse which they had left for inheritance
to their daughters. Nor must you believe that the life
of the men was anywise less licentious than that of the
women. That Roman breeding, that ancestral virtue, that
antique valour, that temperate life and those goodly usances,
which had so gloriously gained and kept them the empery
of the world, were no more to be found; so that both
sexes were fallen into the filthiness of every abominable
vice; and those who lived after the true Roman fashion
and imitated the old and good customs were very rare,
the perfect Roman way of life going daily from ill to worse.
Among these rare persons, then, in whom the ancient virtue

was not yet extinct, might, without a doubt, be numbered
the most fair and virtuous Paulina, who, loving her husband
sincerely and applying herself to the household cares which
pertain unto women, was in no particular inferior to the
ancient Lucretia, to Cornelia, mother of the Gracchi, nor
to Brutus his Portia.

It chanced that a Roman youth of an equestrian family,
Mundus by name, seeing Paulina's beauty and discreet
manners, fell passionately in love with her and seeing her
often, became little by little so inflamed that, whenas he
saw her not, himseemed he was like to die for excess of
amorous sufferance. Now the equestrian order was midway
between the patricians and the plebeians and in this order
Mundus was one of the first for wealth and lived very
splendidly. Finding himself enamoured of Paulina and
feeling that life without her sight was worse than death,
he fell to following her whereassoever she went, whether
to the public games and spectacles or to the temples or
whatsoever other place, hoping with assiduous court and
gifts to gain her love and favour. But she recked no
whit of aught he did and made a show of not seeing him,
taking neither more nor less heed to him than to whatsoever
other she saw or who set himself to speak familiarly with
her; wherefore Mundus abode sore disconsolate, nothing
he might do profiting him aught. Algates, albeit he knew
her to be most austere and to have a heart of adamant and
full of coldest ice, which no flame of love could penetrate,
he resolved to essay her with letters and messages; wherefore he wrote her an amorous billet and sent it to her
by a cunning woman, who was skilled in such crafts. She,
finding Paulina at home awork with her maidens at her
woman's labours, entered into discourse with her, feigning
certain excuses of her fashion, and ultimately, after various

talk, discovered to her Mundus his love, studying to show
her how the wretched lover burned for her and assuring
her that he was not only most ready to do all she should
command him, but would make her mistress of himself
and all he had. Paulina suffered not the vile woman
to make an end of her discourse and would neither take
the letter she proffered her nor hear another word from
her, but, inflamed with just despite, drove her from her
with angry words, bidding her nevermore present herself
before her, as she tendered her life, for that, if she were
so foolhardy as to return thither, she would play her such
a trick that she should for ever remember her of Paulina,
and sent to Mundus, charging him nevermore presume to
send her or letters or messages, an he would not have ill
betide him thereof.

The procuress went off all crestfallen and returned,
trumpet in bag,[1] to Mundus, to whom she reported the
lady's reply and all that she had said and done, exhorting
him with many words to desist from that emprise, forasmuch
as she, having essayed, attacked and overcome innumerable
Roman matrons, had never found a woman of whatsoever
condition firmer or more averse from things wanton than
was Paulina and she must give her the credit of being the
chastest and most virtuous damsel was ever in Rome;
wherefore she judged all but labour wasted which should
be done to move her to love other than honourably.
Mundus, who was (as the saying is) sodden[2] with love
of Paulina and who knew no other delight or solace for
his sufferings than her sight, strove with many words to
persuade the bawd to return to her with fresh messages

[1] *Con le trombe in sacco*, Italian equivalent of our " With her tail
between her legs."
[2] *Cotto.*

and not so lightly suffer herself to be put off with one
repulse, telling her she should see the profit she should
have of him for her pains. The woman, who was an
adept at such emprises and who had in good sooth apprehended Paulina's mind to be altogether averse from such
traffickings, answered him, saying, "Mundus, I am well
assured that my pains would nowise be thrown away, in
so far as pertaineth unto thee, and that I should never
weary myself in vain to do thee service, inasmuch as I
know thee to be courteous and liberal and thou art so
abundantly endowed with the gifts of fortune that thou
mayst still give lavishly unto whoso doth thee pleasure ;
nay, I have already an earnest thereof in hand. But I
affirm (and indeed I am nowise mistaken) that I shall never
compass aught with this woman which may anywise profit
thee ; and indeed I should know what I say, for the long
experience I have of the trade. Wherefore do thou hearken
to my rede and put this fancy out of thy head. There
are other women in Rome as noble and as fair as this
Paulina ; and I know none other of whatsoever degree
whom I cannot with mine arts bring to do mine every
will. Do but look who is most to thy liking and trust
to me for the rest. But think not to prevail with me to
return to the attack with Paulina, for that I should nowise
advantage thee thereby, whilst mine own affairs would go
from ill to worse and it would belike prove the last of
mine emprises." With this she took leave of him, leaving
him so cast down and confounded that himseemed the
whole earth failed beneath his feet ; nay, so sore did he
take the thing to heart that he not only passed that day
and the ensuing night in tears and sighs, but persisted
sundry other days in his melancholy, weeping without stint
and refusing to be comforted, till, losing sleep and appetite

thereby, he was constrained for weakness to take to his bed. The physicians were called in to visit him, but, for all they could do, they might never hit upon the truth, inasmuch as he chose not to discover the cause of his ailment. However, finding his vital powers much cast down and prostrate, they applied with what means and remedies they knew to restore his lost forces ; but the more they strove to fortify the body, the more dejected became the mind and so the poor lover still grew worse.

Now Mundus had a serving-woman, a native of Alexandria of Egypt, whom he had otherwhiles bought for a slave and whom, finding himself well served by her, he had a little before set free, and she still abode in the house. She, loving her master over all and seeing him so grievously sick, was greatly concerned for him and sorrowed sore over his malady, tending him day and night as lovingly as if he were her son. She left him well-nigh never and seeing him still weep and sigh, studied, as best she might and knew, to comfort him with all care and solicitude, beseeching him be pleased to discover to her the cause of his infirmity and melancholy. Herseemed indeed her master's sickness arose from inward sufferance and chagrin and that the best remedy which might be given him was to cheer him ; but this was a difficult thing to do, except she knew the cause of his melancholy. Wherefore she stinted not to pray and beseech him, on every such wise as seemed to her most to the purpose, that he would deign to confide in her, as in his most faithful slave that she was, and discover to her his affliction, for that, in all which might be done of her, she would nowise fail to use her wit and her powers to succour and solace him. Of this she prayed and pressed him most instantly again and again, till, moved by her entreaties, the love-sick youth, who had still found her loyal, loving and faithful, resolved to impart to her his love and sufferance, albeit he looked for scant succour from her in such a case. Accordingly, beginning from the beginning, he with tearful and piteous voice discovered to her the whole story of his love for Paulina and assured her that, finding his mistress so froward and so disdainful, he was resolved to die, him-seeming it was a far lesser ill to suffer death than to abide alive, racked with such fierce and cruel torments and in disfavour with her he loved so dear; wherefore he prayed her discover that his love unto no one. The slave wench, hearing that Saturninus his wife was the cause of her lord's probable death, strove, as best she might, to comfort him and exhorted him to be of good heart and apply, setting all else aside, to recover his health, telling him that there was a remedy for all things, so but life were preserved, and adding that she would cast about to find some device, so he might compass his intent, and that she would not long tarry to bring him good news. Mundus avouched himself much comforted with this hope that she gave him and answered her that he would do all he might to amend, but that she must not fail of her promise to him.

The woman was, as hath been said, from Egypt and was very inward with certain Egyptian priests, who served the temple of the goddess Isis at Rome, it having been brought thither from the parts of Egypt. Now, when I consider the achievements of the ancient Romans and the glorious works wroughten by them, or ere their republic was usurped by the tyranny of Julius Cæsar, Perpetual Dictator, and the particular actions of many citizens, I abide full of marvel and admiration and cannot but adjudge them to have been most wise and prudent; but, when again I turn my thought to matters of religion and call to mind the multitude of Gods they worshipped and the

new deities which they daily brought from this and that
city and which were withal no otherwhat than pieces of
wood or stone wroughten in some effigy or another, I
abide aghast and know not what to say, meseeming, indeed,
they must have been scant of wit to believe that mortal
men and unchaste women could anywise acquire divinity.
True, we cannot but supremely commend the reverence
and observance of things sacred which distinguished the
Romans in general, as is clearly seen in their annals and
histories, where it will be found in many places that they
had far more fear of breaking the oaths taken by them
than of infringing their laws and the ordinances of the
senate; the which arose from none otherwhat than that
they accounted it a far graver thing to offend against the
Divine puissance than to affront men. Now how much
weight religion had with the Romans, at a time when
well-nigh all good usances were marred, you shall hear
out of hand, for that I care not presently to say aught
of the follies of their innumerable Gods, it behoving me
in the course of my story relate one [1] of no little moment.
To return, then, to Mundus his handmaid, she was familiar
with these Egyptian priests and especially with their chief;
wherefore she went to speak with him and acquainting him
with her lord's infirmity and the cause which had engendered it, most urgently prayed him consent to do that
which you shall presently hear; whereto the good priest,
moved by her prayers, and blinded by the gold she gave
him, yielded a ready assent.

Now the Romans in those days honoured the Goddess
Isis exceedingly and celebrated her mysteries with the
utmost solemnity and marvellous ceremonies, holding her

---

[1] i.e. a folly.

priests in great esteem; wherefore the chief of these latter
repaired one day to Paulina's house and with a great
show of sanctity and godliness in his venerable aspect and
lowly and modest carriage, sought speech of her. The
lady received the hypocritical priest with all reverence
and setting him a seat, seated herself beside him and
respectfully awaited that which it should please him say to
her. The holy father, then, with a sanctified countenance
and solemn parlance, proceeded to recite a long litany
of his fashion anent the divinity of the God Anubis, who
was holden in great veneration among the Egyptians,
and told her how the said God, knowing she much desired to have a son and being enamoured of her chastity
and many other virtues, for that she was one of the most
virtuous ladies of Rome, desired to be the father of her
child and to lie with her in the temple of the Goddess
Isis, whither he would come to join her, in the form
of a young man, for that, should he appear on godlike
wise, she might not avail to endure the splendour of his
divinity. It was an easy matter to delude the good and
simple matron, more by token that it was a firm belief
among the Romans that the Gods and Goddesses had
children amongst themselves and eke oftentimes coupled
with mortal men and women; a thing indeed full of
ignorant and sacrilegious folly to make the Gods whore-
mongers, adulterers and incestuous; but so it was. Nay,
they were firmly persuaded that their forefather Æneas
was the son of Venus and Anchises and that their founders
Romulus and Remus had been begotten of Mars and
suckled by a she-wolf. Again, it was reported that
Alexander the Great was the son of Jupiter Ammon and
a thousand other heroes were alleged to be of divine
origin. It was holden for certain that Scipio Africanus

the Elder had been begotten of a god, who had taken
the form of a serpent and gotten the said Scipio's mother
with child; and indeed the ancient books are full of
these fables; wherefore it was no great wonder if Paulina
lent the false priest an undoubting faith and told the
whole to her husband Saturninus, who, being certified of his
wife's virtue and sharing his countrymen's superstition
that the Gods got women with child, (a thing esteemed
by them laudable and honourable, for that they could
never have suspected such wickedness to be hidden under
colour of religion,) consented that she should go lie with
the God Anubis.

Accordingly, on the night appointed for the divine
nuptials, Mundus having beforehand, by the priest's contrivance, been hidden in the temple, Paulina came thither
and was couched by her women in a bed which was prepared in a corner of the temple. The lamps were then
all extinguished and the priest, going out with Paulina's
women, locked the gates of the temple behind him; whereupon Mundus, coming forth of his hiding-place, laid himself
beside Paulina and to approve himself no mortal gallant,
but divine, wrought exceeding great prowess of his person,
so that Paulina after avouched that the God Anubis had lain
with her on otherguess wise than her husband. Mundus,
then, amorously disported himself with Paulina all that
night and did his every pleasure of her. A little before
dawn he arose and leaving the bed, returned to his hiding-
place; and at sunrise Paulina's women came and the temple
being opened by the priest, accompanied her home, where
she told her husband how she had passed the night in the
arms of the God Anubis. A few days thereafter, Mundus
met Paulina and himseeming his pleasure was incomplete
except she knew the cheat, said to her, moved by youthful

levity, " Paulina, you would nowise complease me with your love; but the God Anubis hath done me such favour that I have taken amorous pleasure of you in his stead a whole night long;" and giving her divers tokens, related to her the thing as it had passed. Paulina was beyond measure chagrined at so shameful a cheat and with bitter tears discovered the treason to her husband, who, full of ill will as ever man was, went to the Emperor Tiberius and demanded justice of Mundus and the priests. The emperor, hearing such a wickedness, let extort the truth with torments and finding that many like adulteries had been wroughten in the temple by the priests' contrivance, let crucify them all, together with Mundus his slave-girl. The temple, a very sink of vices, was razed to the foundations and the statue of Isis cast into the Tiber. On Mundus more compassion was had; but he was nevertheless condemned to perpetual exile. Now, returning to that wherewith we began, if in our times religious persons were punished according to their demerits, we should have the things of the faith purer and holier and those who dedicate themselves to the worship of the Divinity would, leaving all other concerns, apply to serve God and pray Him for the peace and quiet of Christendom.

Bandello

to the most debonair Messer Domenico Campana
yclept Strascino.

Albeit the instinctive horror and fear of dead bodies and
of spirits, (especially in the night-time, whenas darkness and
silence make fear greater,) which is by nature implanted in
most men's hearts, is for well-constituted minds no small
argument of the immortality of our souls and of the existence
of another life to be desired of us, beyond this wherein we
presently live, nay, rather, run still with a slack rein unto
death,—I have not taken up my pen to enter upon these
questions, but to have an occasion of sending you this my
novel [of a case] which befell immediately after your
departure from Milan on your return to Rome. The story
was told in the presence of the affable and accomplished
Signora Chiara Pusterla, in whose house you were well seen
and made much of during your sojourn here in Milan; for
that in truth the said Signora Chiara, among the many and
rare qualities which make her admirable and singular, hath
this, that she entertaineth and welcometh strangers (and
especially men of parts) better than whatsoever lady here.
It was related by the most affable and valorous Messer
Girolamo Sereciato Guidone, of the troop of Signor Galeazzo

Sanseverino,[1] Grand Equerry of France; and since it treateth of spirits and of affrights befallen for fear thereof, I was led to begin by speaking of them, more by token that imagination is whiles seen to work the effect of reality, as happened in this case, and likewise for that there had then lately been a trick played upon the aforesaid lady's coachman with masks in guise of demons, which made the company laugh heartily and was the occasion of Messer Girolamo's relating this that I presently send you, so you may not say that I am unmindful of you. But indeed who could be so featherbrained that, having had your company, sweetest Strascino mine, he should forget your fashions? I, for my part, shall still, so long as I live, be mindful of you and of your delightsome entertainments. Now in this novel you will laugh at a rare cheat put by a lady upon her husband, under colour of spirits; and certes there are some women who hit upon extraordinary devices to send their husbands to Cornwall and cause them cross the sea without a boat; but, to come to the novel, I say no more to you. Fare you well.

---

[1] I render this passage exactly as it stands, i.e. *Messer Girolamo Screciato Guidone, della banda*, etc., but I suspect a mistake in punctuation and am inclined to believe that we should read *Messer Girolamo Screciato, guidone della banda*, i.e. "Messer Girolamo Screciato, cornet (or ensign) of the troop, etc."

The Sixteenth Story.

A RARE CHEAT PUT BY A LADY UPON HER HUSBAND, WITH MANY INCIDENTS BY WAY OF INCANTATIONS.

It is no wonder, noble lady mine, if the trick played upon your coachman have made the whole company laugh, seeing it seldom happeneth but we laugh whenas we see any one fall, so but he do himself no hurt, and on like wise, whenassoever a cheat is put upon any, it seemeth as if folk cannot keep themselves from laughing thereat. But I purpose not for the nonce to bespeak you of tricks of this fashion, played for the sheer sake of mirth and laughter; having in hand a story befallen no great while agone in this our city of Milan, which will show you what some women can do, an they have a mind to satisfy an appetite. There was, then, to keep you no longer await, a gentleman of great wealth and nobility and married to a very fair damsel of one of the first and most worshipful families of her native land sent by an Italian prince on an embassy to this city, so he should, as is the usance, lie lieger there about the duke. Understanding that he was to abide a good while abroad, he brought his fair wife to Milan and had to lodgment the palace hard by San Giovanni in Conca, anciently the court-house of Signor Bernabo Visconti, the which is, as you know, very spacious and ample for whatsoever great household. There established and provided

with all that behoved, he took up his abode with his wife,
who, being (as I have said) very fair and to boot very
agreeable and accomplished and skilled in playing and
singing, was daily visited and courted by all the nobility
of Milan, nor was there any man of parts or merit but
might be found there. She showed all a good countenance,
honouring each according to his degree and entertaining
now these, now those, to eat with her, and her husband,
who was liberal and magnanimous, took pleasure in seeing
his wife honoured on this wise. Meanwhile there was
sent by another prince to Milan another ambassador, who
was young and much given to the service of the ladies
nor left aught undone to win the love and favour of her
who pleased him, but spent and gave lavishly. Him we
will for the nonce call (not without cause) Vittore,[1] inasmuch
as I choose not for considerations of policy to give the proper
names of any of the persons who figure in this my story ;
wherefore we will name the other ambassador Ferrando
and the latter's wife Filippa. Vittore, then, resorting
familiarly to Ferrando's house, waxed very intimate there
and Filippa's converse pleasing him beyond compare, as
his did her, their intimacy grew to a most fervent love ;
wherefore, having daily and hourly commodity of privy
speech, they discovered their loves each to other and found
means bytimes amorously to disport themselves together ;
but, using their intercourse less than discreetly, they did
on such wise that not only their familiars, but all Milan,
became aware thereof. Ferrando, however, seemed, for
whatsoever cause, to perceive nought ; wherefore it was
the general belief (seeing he still showed himself sage and
wary in all his other actions and transacted his prince's

---

[1] i.e. victor.

business with great prudence) that his wife had bewitched
him with some sorcery or other. Be that as it may, Madam
Filippa, Vittore's converse pleasing her much more than
that of her husband, took it into her head to wish to lie
with him every night; the which, in so far as it concerned
the one and the other's servants, was easy, for that there
was no man in Vittore's house but knew his master to be
enamoured of Ferrando's wife and to enjoy her favours.
On like wise, Filippa's serving-men and women knew it
full well, but none dared broach a word thereof to Ferrando,
knowing that he, though in other things shrewd and well
advised, was in this purblind, for that he put overmuch
trust in his wife, as do well-nigh all husbands in many
cities of Italy.

It was the month of May, when the heat useth oftentimes
to wax on extraordinary wise, and indeed that year the air
was exceeding sultry, for that if the heat be great elsewhere,
in Milan at the like season it useth to be excessive; wherefore Madam Filippa proceeded to toss and turn about the
bed all night long, complaining of the great heat which
prevailed and saying that it suffered her neither sleep nor
rest. The husband, hearing his wife's complainings, said,
"I feel no such great heat as thou sayst thou feelest; but,
to ease thee, I will have my camp-bed[1] set on one side of
the chamber and leave thee to sleep alone." She, seeing
that her design began to succeed, answered, saying, "Be
it as you will." Now she knew her husband to be the
fearfullest man in the world and that he was like to die of
affright at every least noise he heard anights nor would ever
dare to go about the house without lights and except he
were well accompanied; nay, when it was spoken of the

---

[1] Or "travelling bed" (*letto di campo*).

dead or of spirits that had been seen in whatsoever place,
he for excess of fear abode two or three days ere he was his
own man again; wherefore, having debauched three of the
boldest serving-men of the house and certain of her waiting-
women and imparted her design to her lover, she took
measures to play her husband a rare trick. Vittore, learning
his mistress's design and himseeming it might lightly be
brought about that he should lie with her every night at his
ease, sent for a merry rogue, Gabbadio by name, whom he
had long known and who knew better than any man alive
to counterfeit the voices of birds and other animals, to his
house and (for that he was unknown in Milan) charged him
on no account imitate the cry of bird or beast [till he should
bid him]. Meanwhile Madam Filippa let counterfeit all the
keys which herseemed were necessary for her emprise and
gave them to Vittore; then, all being in readiness, the latter
one night clad himself and Gabbadio and four of his serving-
men on such wise that they seemed devils, with great horns
on their heads, full of wildfire, which gave out flame and
smoke at pleasure, and frightful masks on their faces, where-
through they from time to time belched out tongues of fire.
Thus horribly disguised, they entered Ferrando's house and
betaking them to the neighbourhood of the chamber where
he and his wife slept, made a very devils' racket in a saloon
and a gallery there, whilst Gabbadio counterfeited now the
ass, now the ox and now some bird or other, so that it
seemed as the animals themselves were actually present.
Ferrando's master of the household, a man stricken in years,
and others of the serving-men, hearing this, rushed forth,
but, seeing, as they thought, demons, withdrew in haste to
their chambers, shrieking aloud; while those whom the lady
debauched and who were cognizant of the trick, cried out,
saying, "Jesus! Ave Mary! These be very devils of

hell!" and repeating this twice or thrice, shut themselves up in their chambers. Ferrando, aroused by the clamour and hearing speak of "Jesus" and "devils," leapt forth his bed and ran to that of his wife, trembling like a leaf in the wind and crying out, "Alack, Filippa, hearest thou not that which I hear?" The lady, feigning herself fast asleep, suffered him give her two or three nudges ere she avouched herself awake; then, shaking herself, "Alack," quoth she fearfully, "who toucheth me? Who is there?" And made a show of offering to jump out of bed. Ferrando, embracing her, said, "O my soul, I am thy husband." Whereupon, "God pardon thee!" replied she, somewhat peevishly. "I was fast asleep. What would you?" "Woe's me," rejoined Ferrando, "hearest thou not the racket and the outcry that is toward? Certes, the house is full of demons. Hark, how they thump and howl in the saloon. Jesus, aid me!" and crossed himself a thousand times. The lady laughed and said, "Methinketh you dream. I hear nothing. This is one of your pranks, for that you cannot endure to let me sleep." The noise was in effect very great and there were certain appalling yells and howlings apt at that hour to affright the valiantest man alive. The lady, feigning to hear nothing, arose and went to a pallet bed in the chamber, where lay two of her women, who, by her commandment, made a show of sleeping. There was a light in the chamber; wherefore they, as they had been aroused by the lady, said to her, drowsywise, "What is your pleasure, madam?" Quoth she, smiling, "See you not yonder husband of mine, who saith he heareth exceeding great noises and is fled into my bed?" The damsels, making a show of shamefastness, as who should say that the master had come thither to divert himself, answered, saying, "Go, go, madam, and you shall be the bride."

Ferrando, seeing the women also declared that they heard nothing and hearing the while cries, yells and noises beyond measure, was like to go mad and the lady said to him, " Methinketh, husband mine, thou hast overdrunken thyself yesternight and that thy brains are gone woolgathering. It is a strange thing that none of us three heareth aught and that you hear marvels; I know not what to say. But, if you have the heart to go forth the chamber, I will go with you and we will see what manner devils are these and you will find that you take fireflies for lanterns." However, he would nowise suffer the door to be opened, albeit the two waiting-women also offered to go with their mistress; and this bourd lasted more than three hours, after which the maskers departed and went home.

The lady arose betimes, as also did Ferrando, who was all a-tremble for fear and scarce dared go about the house, more by token that he heard from his master of the household of the strange fashion and accoutrement of the demons. Moreover, those who were in concert with the lady told the most extravagant fables in the world and the most marvellous and stupendous things, still adding to that which they feigned to have seen. The report of the spirits soon got wind in Milan, for that Ferrando's servants could speak of nothing but the terrible noises and howlings which had been heard that night. After dinner, there being many lords and gentlemen in Ferrando's house and Vittore being also of the company, it was variously reasoned of the matter, themseeming a great marvel that all had seen and heard the spirits except the lady and her women, and one said one thing and one another, some opining that this might be for that those who thought to have seen and heard those wonders were unchrisom. The lady laughed at this, saying that all who thought to have seen and heard the marvels aforesaid had taken a card over one-and-thirty[1] aforenight and had over-drunken themselves; whilst Vittore declared that he believed not in such visions and that he had never in his life seen or heard aught. Others said that it was no wonder if there were somewhat heard in that palace, seeing men without number had been strangled and done to death there with the frightfullest torments in the time of Signor Bernabo Visconti, who was a most cruel prince, and so each said his say thereof; but nothing availed to allay the fear felt by Ferrando, who said to the lady, "Wife mine, we were best have four or five beds set in our chamber and let all thy women sleep there, whilst the master of the household and three of my serving-men sleep in two other beds for my assurance." Quoth the lady, "I will have no men other than thyself sleep where I have my bed, for in the first place this medley of men and women pleaseth me not (more by token that, if you others chance to hear any noise, though I understand not how it may be, you will not let me sleep,) and moreover, husband mine, I tell thee that, if these alarums are to continue, I will have thee do one of two things, to wit, thou must either leave coming to awaken me or set thy bed in another chamber." Therewith they agreed to await what should happen that next night, without making any change of beds. Algates, they sent to fetch Fra Vincenzo Spanzotto of the Observants of San Dominick from the convent of Le Grazie and caused him sprinkle all the house with holy water and bless it with psalms and orisons.

[1] A metaphor drawn from the game of trente-et-un, where the object is, by taking fresh cards, to make up one-and-thirty or as near as possible to that number, without exceeding it, in which latter case the dealer can claim the stake.

Vittore was present at all these ceremonies and night come, he made his way into the palace, masked as before, and sent two of his men up to the loft over the chamber where Ferrando and his wife lay. Now whoso sought to tell the noise and racket which befell that night aloft and alow would have overmuch to do. Ferrando, after he had endured awhile, overcome with fear, ran to his wife's bed, who with her women made a show of sleeping, and awaking her (as he thought), was like to go mad for that she heard not the battering and thumping which were toward overhead, as if the whole house should fall. Nay, she feigned herself angered and said, "Husband mine, needs must thou abide in one chamber anights and I in another, and we can be together by day; for I see clearly that, if my sleep is to be broken on this wise, I shall go mad or fall into some grievous sickness." The maskers kept up their frolics till hard upon daybreak; wherefore there was matter enough for talk on the morrow, no man in the house having had the courage to leave his chamber; nay, all were so affrighted that none dared shake himself. Ferrando let move his bed to a chamber at the end of a gallery and would have seven of his men sleep in the room with him, whilst his wife, seeing that her device had succeeded, advised her lover of all; whereupon he came that night to visit her, bravely apparelled, and brought with him his maskers, who made no noise near the lady's chamber, whereas she was engaged in repairing her past losses with Vittore, save that Gabbadio all night long counterfeited now the nightingale, now the woodlark, the goldfinch, the linnet and other birds of those which sing most melodiously; what while his fellows kept up the frightfullest din in the other parts of the house, and especially in the neighbourhood of Ferrando's chamber.

Herein lay the serving-men debauched by Filippa and
one of them, at the beginning of the uproar, seeing
their master arise and kneel down to say his orisons
before a crucifix, said to him, swaggeringly, "Master,
meseemeth it is a great disgrace for us and yourself that
you have no serving-man in the house who hath the heart
to go see what manner of thing be all these noises which
befall every night. Methinketh it were well that four or
five of us sally forth and see what these spirits can do."
And the master of the household, who was a good old
man and had a mind to look closelier into the matter, himseeming he had seen ill the first time, exhorted Ferrando
to suffer him go with them; but he would not hear of it.
However, they did and said so much that he at last
consented and accordingly they opened the door and
sallied forth, arms in hand. Scarce were they out when
the maskers, who never removed over-far from that part,
but still frolicked it thereabout, came at them, howling
and making the strangest gestures in the world; whereupon
those who had shown such eagerness to go forth ran back
to the chamber, feigning themselves like to die for fear,
and let themselves fall on the threshold (and this they did
of set purpose and appointment, as it had been enjoined
them,) what while up came the maskers, casting forth their
artificial fires and sending the flames even into the chamber,
and passed along, dragging divers iron chains after them,
which made such a clatter that it seemed the world was
about to come to an end. Those serving-men [who were
without] were haled within and the door shut, but not till
all in the chamber had seen the maskers pass, who seemed
indeed very devils of hell; wherefore Ferrando abode more
dead than alive and said his orisons, with more signs of
the cross than Spring hath flowers. With this the maskers

gave over their riot and there was nought to be heard save Gabbadio's song. But who shall tell the delight of Vittore and Filippa, who, meanwhile, to conjure away fear, thrust the devil in hell as most they might and laughed the timorous Ferrando to scorn.

The noises continued night after night and rose to such a pitch that Ferrando, remembering him not to have been christened in his childhood, procured himself to be baptized by the Archbishop's suffragan and took Vittore to his god-father, in the hope of hearing no more noises; but in vain, for that the maskers ceased not to do their office. The poor master of the household, who must needs play the dare-devil and go forth the chamber with those who were in the secret of the matter, had such a fright that he fell grievously sick and lost thereby not only his hair and beard, but his skin to boot, as do vipers; nay, he was like to die thereof. Meanwhile Vittore had a son by his wife and took Filippa to gossip, but stinted not withal to lie with her whenassoever he might, haply holding that for true which Tinguccio said to Meuccio, whenas he appeared to him in a dream.[1] Now, matters being at this pass and it being talked of no otherwhat in Milan than of the spirits heard in Ferrando's house, there was a certain gentleman, who, hearing this tale and knowing that there had never before been aught heard in that palace, misdoubted him of the truth of the case; wherefore he imparted his suspicions to another gentleman, his dearest friend, and they agreed to keep a watch on those parts of the house whereat themseemed folk might enter in. Accordingly, they one night plainly saw Vittore enter with his men, who were presently undisguised, for that

[1] See my " Decameron of Boccaccio," Vol. III. p. 30.

they masked themselves in the house, and awaiting their
coming out, fell upon them with swashing sword-strokes ;
nay, the thing went so far that Vittore received a brace
of wounds and one of his men left his masker's habit in
the hands of the assailants.   Gabbadio was also grievously
wounded and the affray ended without Vittore knowing
who had attacked him, nor was he recognized of the latter.
However, it getting wind on the morrow that the Lord
Ambassador was wounded, the gentlemen aforesaid became
aware of the case and kept it very secret.   On the other
hand, Vittore, understanding the loss of the masker's habit,
resolved to desist from that his emprise, unknowing against
whom it behoved him be on his guard and misdoubting
him of many; and Ferrando, good simple man, ascribed
the cessation of so grievous a tribulation to the prayers
which he had let offer up in the convents and nunneries
and by which the monks and nuns had gotten good
pittances.

Bandello

to the valorous and affable seignior Signor Vincenzo Goscia Patrician of Naples.

It remembereth me to have read otherwhiles, in certain
Latin writings of our divine poet Messer Francesco Petrarca,
that those who keep serving-men cannot do ill in letting scourge
pages with moderation, whenas they err childishly, what
while they overpass not fourteen or fifteen years of age,
for that stripes cause them amend and from good become
better, (wherefore saith the wise Solomon that whoso spareth
the rod hateth the child ;) but that serving-men should only
be beaten once and straightway paid their wage and sent
about their business nor taken again, especially in the
case of Moors or boughten slaves, for that they are of
very ill nature ; as was lately proved by the Moor of
Monsignor Negri, Abbot of San Simpliciano, who, having
received a buffet from his master, slit his weasand and
slew him that same night, albeit he had been with him
more than thirty years.   When the villainous Moor was
brought to the Broletto Vecchio [1] of Milan to be publicly
justified, he said, laughing, "Quarter me, wreak your worst
on me, for that, if I have received a buffet, I have signally
avenged myself thereof;" whence it may lightly be seen

---

[1] *i.e.* the old market-place.

how dangerous it is to hamper oneself with the like of such a brood of vipers. It being discoursed of this matter no great while agone in the house of the Lady Camilla Scarampa, it was said that the Genoese were well aware thereof, inasmuch as, if they have a slave who doth aught deserving of chastisement, they sell him or send him to Evizza, to carry salt, and thereupon our pleasant Messer Lione da Iseo related an extraordinary case betided in the island of Majorca, the which (to name it after the ancient fashion) is one of the Balearic Islands. This story I wrote down and knowing that you Neapolitan gentlemen marvellously delight in keeping slaves, I have bethought myself to send it to you and make you a gift thereof, assured that you will not look to the triflingness thereof, but to the goodness of my intent, you having aforetime had good proof how much I love you and on what wise I wrought with the most illustrious Signor Prospero, our common patron, in the matter committed to my charge by yourself and our debonair Messer Girolamo Gargano. You must know, also, that this story hath been written at length in Latin by the great Pontanus, but I need not withal scruple to give it you, such as Iseo told it. Fare you well.

A SLAVE, BEING BEATEN BY HIS MASTER, MURDERETH HIS MISTRESS AND HER CHILDREN AND AFTER CASTETH HIMSELF HEADLONG DOWN FROM A HIGH TOWER.

In the island of Majorca there was, no great while agone, according to that which certain Catalans affirm, a gentleman called Rinieri Ernizzano, who was very rich in lands, cattle and monies and who, taking a wife, begat on her three sons, born at as many births. He went one summer to his estate in the country, where he had a very goodly and spacious mansion and a rich farm, and there abode many days with all his household, diverting himself with the chase and other pleasures. The house stood on the sea-shore and he had builded there a tower on a rock which rose out of the sea and joined it to the house by a little drawbridge, so that, if corsairs should at any time come thither, he might take refuge there with his family. What while he abode there, it chanced one day that a Moorish slave of his did I know not what; whereupon Rinieri, incensed, dealt him so many buffets that for much less an ass had gone to Rome. The Moor took it to heart[1] nor could anywise brook to have been beaten like a boy

[1] Lit. tied it to his finger (*se la legò al dito*).

and resolving to avenge himself cruelly, awaited but an opportunity. Accordingly, Rinieri going one day a-hunting with many of his men, the treacherous Moor saw his mistress enter the tower with her children, of whom the eldest was not yet seven years old, on some occasion of hers; whereupon, himseeming the much-desired occasion was come to avenge himself, he took a rope and followed them; then, falling upon the gentlewoman, who took no heed of him, he suddenly bound her straitly with her hands behind her and making the rope fast to the foot of a great chest that stood there, raised the drawbridge which joined the tower to the house. The poor lady cried out for aid and menaced the slave with angry words, but he recked of nought; nay, the hangman, in her despite, took amorous pleasure of her as often as he had a mind thereto. The poor children, seeing their mother outraged on this wise and hearing her weep and cry aloud, wept also bitterly, and their weeping and the lady's shrieks were heard by those of the house; but, the villain having raised the drawbridge, none could give her aid. The Moor, having taken what pleasure he would of the lady, posted himself at a window and there, laughing and making divers antic gestures, he abode awaiting the coming of Rinieri, in quest of whom one of the household had gone a-horseback and told him all.

The poor gentleman came back, full of rage and despite against the disloyal Moor and thinking to lead him a dance that would not please him; wherefore, as soon as he saw him at the window, he proceeded to give him the foulest rating in the world and threatened to string him up by the neck. The Moor answered, grinning, "Signor Rinieri, what aileth you to cry thus? What empty vauntings are these? You can do me no manner of hurt, save in so far

as I will. Remember you of the buffets you so unhand-
somely gave me the other day and how you used me
worse than a packmule ; now is the time come to render
you the like. I have here your wife and children and
would you were here also, so I might give you to
know what it is to beat slaves ! But that which I cannot do to you, I will do to your lady and your children.
To begin, I have taken of your wife such pleasure as
seemed to me well and have planted the horns on
your head ; and for the rest I will do on such sort
that you shall ere long have both yourself and your life
in horror." Thus saying, he took the eldest boy and
cast him down from the window, so that he fell upon
the rocks and was all dashed in pieces. The father,
seeing such dire cruelty, fell down in a swoon and the
Moor waited till he came to himself ; when, fearing lest
the villain should hurl down the others, he began, weeping the while most bitterly, to seek to appease him with
fair words, promising not only to pardon him the wickedness he had done, but to set him free and give him a
thousand ducats, so but he would restore him his wife
and the other two boys safe and sound. The slave
feigned himself willing to consent to this and said to
him, "Harkye, you will gain nothing by these fallacious
words and promises ; but, if you tender these two boys,"
and he showed the two children at the window, "as
dear as you say, cut off your nose and I will restore
them to you ; else will I do with these as you saw me
do with the eldest." The unhappy father, never considering the faithlessness and wickedness of the perfidious
slave, who was not like to perform aught that he promised,
but having only in mind paternal love and before his eyes
the horrid spectacle of the dismembered boy and fearing

the like fate for the others, let fetch a razor and cut off his nose; but scarce had he done this when the barbarous villain, taking the two other boys by the feet, dashed their heads against the wall and launched them to the ground. At this sight the wretched gentleman, overcome with extreme anguish, went beside himself and shrieking piteously, would have moved stones to compassion; but the barbarian only laughed, himseeming he had done the finest thing in the world. With Ernizzano were a great number of people, drawn thither by the report of the slave's villainy and by the exceeding clamour which filled the air; but, had there been thousands of men, they could not without cannon have taken the tower, so but it were victualled.

What while the clamour was at its height, the cruel Moor took the lady, whose hands he had bound behind her, and setting her at the window, there left her awhile, what while she screamed and cried for mercy till she was well-nigh hoarse; then he slit her throat with a knife and let her fall from top to bottom of the tower; whereat great were the cries and infinite the tears of those below. Then, there being none other to cast down, the ruthless murderer said, " Rinieri, cry thy fill and weep as most thou mayst, for thou wilt do all in vain. Thinkest thou belike that this which I have done I have not beforehand well considered in myself and taken order so thou shouldst not avail to avenge thyself on me ? It irketh me only that thou wast not at these nuptials, so there were no relic left of thy house.[1] But live, for thou wilt still have my vengeance before thine eyes nor wilt ever purge thy nose without remembering thee of me, and thus wilt thou learn to thy

---

[1] Lit. "affairs," *casi*, but this seems a misprint for *casa*, house.

cost to beat poor slaves." This said, he betook himself to the window which looked toward the sea and cried out in a loud voice, saying, "I die content, having avenged myself of the buffets and beatings I have suffered." Therewith he threw himself headlong down upon the rocks and breaking his neck, was carried to the dwelling-place of all the devils, leaving the wretched Rinieri heir to eternal dolour. Wherefore methinketh men should not make use of slaves of this sort, for that they are seldom found faithful and are mostly full of all manner of filth and uncleanness and stink at all seasons like buck-goats; but all these things are nought compared with the inexorable ferocity which reigneth in them.

Bandello

to the illustrious and accomplished seignior Signor Cesare Tribulzio.

Albeit our age in many things is, if not superior, at the
least equal to the ancient and famous times of old, even
as you yourself and the learned Messer Girolamo Cittadino
have many a time avouched, devising with me in my
chamber and discoursing of matters of arms and modern
soldiership and of every sort of letters, in one thing it
may be said that it is far inferior (nor methinketh will
you and Cittadino gainsay me in this, for that the thing
is overplain and manifest,) and that is the dearth of good
writers,[1] wherein those ancient times were most copious.
In those days, if a man or woman did a deed that deserved
praise or said an argute word, it was straightway written
down ; nor did it suffice them simply to write the thing,
as it had been done or said ; nay, but with titles, with
epigrams, with statues and with [triumphal] arches they
honoured, lauded, celebrated and besang it. In our days,
on the contrary, not only do we neglect to exalt and
magnify praiseworthy actions and to commend goodly
and ingenious sayings, spoken to the purpose of the various

[1] *Scrittori*; but writers of history or annalists, who make it their
business to record what passes day by day, are evidently meant.

occasions which betide, but (what is much worse) there is
none to write them, thanks to the corrupt and ungracious
time and the many cruel and deadly wars which have so
many and many a year oppressed unhappy Italy, wherefore it may be truly said that the Muses, scared by the
horrid thunder of drums, trumpets and artillery, have fled
to the summit of Parnassus ; and yet we daily see most
goodly things betide, which are worthy of eternal remembrance. Now, our [friend] Signor Giovanni Castiglione
having made a dinner to many gentlemen and gentlewomen
and it being thereafter reasoned of various things, Signor
Guarnero, his brother, bade Messer Giovanni Antonio
Cusano, an excellent physician, cut short the various discoursements which were toward and entertain that fair
company with some goodly novel. Cusano, who, over
and above the nobility of his family, is a courteous and
very learned person, could not gainsay the request ; wherefore, silence being made, he related a circumstance befallen
at Milan ; the which, for that meseemed it was worthy
of memory, I have chosen to write and to give to you,
not, indeed, that I do not esteem your merit and your
illustrious qualities, excellent well known of me, worthy
of far greater things, but to give a godfather to this my
child, so it may under the protection of your name go
everywhere about in safety, especially if our judicious
Signor Renato Trivulzio, your honoured cousin, deign to
praise it. Fare you well.

The Eighteenth Story.

A GIRL, HER BROTHER BEING ATTACKED BY A CATCHPOLE, SLAYETH THE LATTER AND IS ACQUITTED OF JUSTICE.

Since, lovesomest ladies and you, courteous gentlemen, Signor Guarnero will have me entertain this most noble company by story-telling, I will very willingly do it, to the intent that, when those men, who have little of the man, blame the female sex and say that women are good for nought save the needle and the distaff and to abide in the kitchen and talk with the cats, whosoever is a true man and you all, ladies, may answer them as such fond and discourteous churls deserve, so that, as the saying is, like as the ass giveth against the wall, such he may receive. Nor must you think that I purpose presently to speak of Evander's mother Carmenta, of Penthesilea, of Camilla, of Sappho, of the famous Zenobia of Palmyra, of the ancient and valiant Amazons or of the many other women who have achieved renown in arms and letters and are celebrated by famous writers; marry, I mean not for the nonce to depart Europe. What say I, Europe? I will not depart fair Italy nor our fertile and rich native place, Milan, abounding in every good thing; nay, being here in Signor Giovanni's house at Porta Vercellina,[1] I will but have you pass over to the populous suburb of Porta Comense[1] and enter the garden

---

[1] Suburbs of Milan.

of the very virtuous and affable lady Signora Ippolita
Sforza e Bentivoglia. See now how short a journey I
will have you make. You must know, then, that, not
yet two months agone, a young man of mean condition,
but bred among soldiers and having himself served under
arms, a son of the gardener in charge of the said garden
and of the mansion thereto appertaining, went home
about dinner-time and being all a-chafe for certain words
which he had had with I know not whom in Milan, kept his
hand upon his sword, as swaggerers of his fashion mostly
use to do, and not taking overmuch heed to that which
he said or did, went ruffling it fantastically and saying
aloud, "Zounds, I will be even with him; ay, marry,
will I, by Christ His body! Nay, needs must I thrust
this sword," and with this he drew it half out of the
scabbard, "into the traitor's guts and pierce him through
and through till he fall dead at my feet!" And so,
still fuming and muttering between his teeth, he went
saying I know not what under his breath, with a most
angry aspect. Now he was amiddleward the way which
goeth straight to San Simpliciano and which you know
to be very wide and open. What while, then, he, with
these maggots in his head, said what I have told you,
one of the sergeants of the court, whom we call catch-
poles,[1] passed by him, on his way back to the city from
executing certain warrants in the suburb, and he also
had his lodging hard by the garden aforesaid. He, seeing
the angry youth's lowering aspect and hearing the big
words he said, took it into his head (he having other-
when had words with the gardener, the youth's father)
that he made these rodomontades in his proper dispraise

---

[1] *Sbirri.*

and shame; wherefore, having a mind to resolve himself of the youth's purpose, he said to him, "Giovan
Antonio," for such was the other's name, "I know not
an thou speak to me; but, seeing there is none other
presently near, I cannot think otherwise. An thou have
any crow to pluck with me, speak plainly, for that I
am man enough to answer thee on whatsoever wise thou
wilt." At this the young man halted and answered him,
saying, "Enough; I am not bounden nor am I minded
to render thee an account of my doings; I have only to tell
thee that this sword," and here he drew it halfway out, "I
mean without fail to plant in the paunch of a vile traitor;
ay will I, by Christ His body!" He said no more, but
made off homeward nor halted till he came to the palace,
which was not far distant.

The sergeant, hearing this answer, was persuaded that it
was himself whom he threatened; wherefore, determined to
certify himself thereof, he turned back and betaking himself
to the house of the young man, (who was about to dine,
there being none other in the house than a sister of his,
some twenty years old,) knocked at the door. Giovan
Antonio, coming to the window, asked what he wanted
and the other replied, "I would fain say two words to thee."
Whereupon the young man came down, with his sword by
his side, and opening the door, came out into the street.
The catchpole then very arrogantly told him that he would
fain know if he had said these words for him, and the
other bade him go about his business, saying that it was
no time to confess himself, that what he had said was well
said and that he would say it to him anew. Quoth the
sergeant, "Thou liest in thy throat;" whereupon the other
incontinent dealt him a lusty buffet and clapped his hand
to his sword. The catchpole did the like and so they strove

to wound each other. Many folk ran to the noise, amongst others a sister-in-law of the officer, a woman of thirty, who had the butt of a broken pike in her hand and laid on to the young man as most lustily she might, whilst he, thinking shame to strike a woman, occupied himself with the catchpole. However, his sister, hearing the noise, put her hand to a sword and running boldly out, snatched the pikestaff from the other woman's hand and gave her two or three great clouts withal, so that she was glad to take herself off, then said to Giovan Antonio, "Brother mine, leave me to deal with this vile catchpole; marry, I will punish him." The youth essayed again and again to drive his sister away from the medley, applying more to cause her depart than to beat his enemy; but she would not be persuaded, nay, she threw herself on the sergeant like a lioness and smote him on the head. The young man, seeing his adversary wounded, withdrew and would have had the damsel withdraw on like wise, but all in vain; she dealt him so many blows that she slew him; the which seemed to the bystanders, who had been drawn thither by the noise, a miraculous thing and seeing that which they saw with their proper eyes, they thought to dream. At this juncture up came one of the lieutenants of the captain of the watch, who, finding his officer dead and seeing the young man and his sister yet arms in hand, let seize the former to carry him to the court-house. But the damsel, who was all afire for the affray, as she were a blazing coal, seeing her brother carried off to prison, pressed up to the lieutenant and said to him boldly, "Sir, it was I with this sword slew yonder traitor, who would have murdered my brother, and if any deserve to be punished, it is I; but methinketh to defend oneself meriteth no punishment." The lieutenant, unable to conceive that a girl should have done that homicide and seeing that the youth himself said nothing, enquired no farther, but carried his prisoner to the court-house.

The thing was reported to the most courteous and worthy Signor Alessandro Bentivoglio, who, being fully possessed of the whole, found means to put the damsel (who was called Bianca) in safety, so she should not fall into the hands of the police. Then, the captain of the watch offering to proceed against Giovan Antonio, Signor Alessandro undertook his defence and many witnesses having been examined, it appeared that the young man was not to blame for the sergeant's death, nay, it was proved that he had been at great pains to divert his sister from the emprise ; so that he was acquitted and came out of prison. It was then attended to the acquittance of the damsel and it being proved that what she had done was all in her brother's defence, she also abode free. How say you now, fairest ladies? Deem you not this damsel deserveth to be praised ? Verily, if a man of her age had done a like office in aid of a friend or a kinsman, all men would extol him and exalt him even to the skies ; and because this lass is of low extraction and a woman, shall she have none to exalt, to praise and to celebrate her as she deserveth? Certes, if due praise behove to be given unto virtuous dealings, she deserveth to be celebrated and renowned of all, having shown a virile and generous soul and comported herself with much more valiance than appertaineth unto her like, inasmuch as she first defended her brother against his enemy and valorously slew the latter ;- then, of her own free will, she, as far as in her lay, willed to put herself in the hands of justice, so her brother might not go to prison, things all assuredly worthy of eternal remembrance.

Bandello

to the magnificent Messer Girolamo Cittadino.

What time the Lutheran sect was yet in the bud, many
gentlemen being in company at midday in the house of
our accomplished Signor L. Scipione Attellano and it
being reasoned of various things, there were some who
no little blamed Pope Leo the Tenth, in that he applied
not a remedy thereto in the beginning, when Fra Silvestro
Prierio, Master of the Papal household, showed him certain
points of heresy which Brother Martin Luther had strown
throughout the work which he entitled ["A Tractate] of
Indulgences"; whereas he imprudently replied that Brother
Martin had a very goodly wit and that these were monkish
jealousies; for that, had he then and there provided for
the case, it had been an easy thing to quench the budding
flames which have since made so great a conflagration,
to the irreparable prejudice of all Christendom. Now,
each saying his say, Messer Carlo Dugnano, a man far
advanced in years and of great experience, said, "My
sons, for these heresies, which I understand are presently
sown abroad of the Germans, blame nought but our own
sins, our Lord God willing by this means to chasten
[us,] as He otherwhiles did this our native place of Milan
with those pestilent Arians.[1] Algates, an it were permitted

[1] Referring to the feud between the Arians and St. Ambrose at the
end of the fourth century.

me to speak, I would with all reverence say that it is the
avarice and greed of the priests which have in great part
given foment to these deviltries and will give yet more,
an the Church set not hand to the amendment of the
clergy and eke of all Christians, for that each, in his
degree, hath need of chastening. But we laymen should
not leave the true and goodly way of our forefathers,
to run after the idle inventions of yonder fantastic and
chimerical men, or, rather, monsters, who would fain
know more than behoveth. And belike, if due punishment were bytimes given unto those who err, more than
one ailing spirit would be made whole and yonder folk[1]
would be deprived of occasion to murmur against the
clergy. Wherefore I mean to tell you that which Giovan
Maria Visconti, second Duke of Milan, did in such a
case, not that it behoveth to be imitated (for that in effect
he was a wild beast of a man and of very ill fashions),
but so it may be seen that an extraordinary act of justice
whiles produceth good effects." Dugnano then related
that which I have written down in the following novel
and have published under your learned name, so it may
be to you a pledge of the love which I bear you and
may abide to the world a testimony of our friendship.
Fare you well.

---

[1] *i.e.* the heresiarchs.

GIAN MARIA VISCONTI, SECOND DUKE OF MILAN, LETTETH BURY A PARISH PRIEST ALIVE, FOR THAT HE WOULD NOT BURY A PARISHIONER OF HIS, EXCEPT HE WERE PAID BY THE LATTER'S WIFE.

My grandfather was used, when I was a child, to relate many of the cruelties wreaked by Giovan Maria Visconti, second Duke of Milan of that most noble house, upon his subjects, for that, for every least default, he caused men, women and children be torn piecemeal and eaten of certain hounds, which he entertained solely for such cruelty. But I will not now enter upon particulars, which to relate were an over-long and cruel tragedy; I will only tell you a dire and terrible punishment which he wreaked upon a priest. You must know, then, that the said Duke, whilst riding about Milan, chanced to pass through a street where he heard a great lamentation toward in a little house, together with piteous weeping and smiting of hands and loud shrieks, such as are whiles made of half-frenzied women; whereupon he bade one of his varlets enter the house and enquire the cause of so sore a lamentation. The lackey went and presently returning to the expectant duke, said to him, "My lord, therewithin is a poor woman with sundry children and most bitterly beweepeth her husband, whom she hath before her, dead, for she saith that the parish priest will not bury him, except she pay him, albeit she hath not a farthing to give him." The duke, hearing of this unseemly avarice, said, smiling, to those who rode with him, "Verily, this Master Priest is somewhat over-grasping. Needs must we do a work of charity and let bury this poor dead man and after give alms to his weeping wife." The courtiers replied that this were mighty well done and he accordingly sent to call the parish priest, who, hearing his commandment, came forthright. The duke, seeing him well clad and very fat, judged him to be a priest of the good old times, who went eschewing unease and loved to eat of good and fat capons and drink of the best vernage that was to be found in Milan, and the priest asking him reverently what he commanded him, "We will have you," quoth he, "give burial to the poor man who lieth dead in yonder house and will ourselves requite you according to your desert." The priest replied that he would do it and betaking himself to the church, which was near at hand, donned stole and surplice, he and his clerks and acolytes, and taking up the body, let carry it to the church, chanting the while as most solemnly he might, to approve himself a man of good parts and a right musician, more by token that the duke followed after afoot with all his court.

What while the obsequies were celebrating, the duke caused one of his men bid the gravediggers make as deep a ditch in the cemetery as might be, the which was speedily done, what while he himself abode in the church till the completion of the funeral ceremonies, the which, as you know, what with psalms, evangels and litanies after the Ambrosian form, are much longer than the Roman rite, and Master Priest made them, in his honour, much more solemn than of wont. The body was in due course carried forth the church and that which is usual chanted thereover; then, the gravediggers offering to put the body in the grave, the duke came forward and causing

them halt, bade them take up the rector and bind him
straitly to the dead body and cast him into the sepulchre.
His cruelty was so notorious with great and small that
all feared him as the plague ; wherefore, when the dismayed priests and clerks saw their rector taken, they all,
without awaiting otherwhat, cast cross, sprinkler and holy
water to the ground and made off as fast as their legs
would carry them, themseeming the gravediggers should
take them also and bury them out of hand. Meanwhile,
the hapless rector was by the duke's commandment laid
in the grave, screaming for mercy the while, and was
incontinent covered with earth ; wherefore, the hole being
very deep and the weight of the earth cast upon him
very great, it may be supposed that the poor wretch was
suffocated forthright. When the Duke saw the grave full,
he bade one of his men go to the priest's house and
commanded that all which was found therein of victual
and moveables should be given to the poor widow and
her children ; the which was punctually executed, to the
exceeding terror of all the Milanese clergy, so that for
many a day thereafterward there was no priest let himself be twice required of his parishioners ; and albeit such
a chastisement was in truth over-barbarous and cruel,
it was nevertheless the cause that many priests amended
their licentious way of life. Wherefore, as I said to you,
it were whiles good to use extraordinary remedies. Nay,
I am fain to believe that our forefathers, who founded
the hundred parishes we have in Milan, beside the many
abbeys, churches, monasteries and nunneries which are to
be seen in this city, and enriched them with revenues and
endowments, did it for that friars, priests and other religious persons might live and serve the churches and
minister the sacraments to the poor without payment.

Bandello

to the magnificent Messer Gian Giacomo Gallarate.

The ancient proverb which useth to be said all day long, to wit, that over-familiarity breedeth contempt and is oftentimes cause that the inferior beareth not due reverence to his superior, nay, with rash and presumptuous over-weening falleth whiles into very grievous errors, is generally found to be true; wherefore those who govern others should not make themselves so private and familiar with their subjects as to give them occasion to hold them in little account and presume to do unseemly and ill things; and on like wise servants, when they know themselves loved by their masters, should govern themselves prudently and still wax humbler, presuming as least possible upon the familiarity of their superiors. It was spoken of this matter at the house of the most debonair and learned Signora Cecilia Gallerana, Countess of Bergamo, and various things were said, when Messer Gian Angelo Vismaro, being there in company of many other gentlemen, said, "Mistress mine and you, gentlemen, it skilleth little to debate of the matter in question or to labour [to prove] that overmuch familiarity engendereth contempt for superiors, I having an example before mine eyes, which will give us full assurance thereof;" and here he related that which Captain Biagino[1] Crivello

---

[1] Dim. of Biagio = Blase.

did once upon a time. And for that meseemed the case was mighty strange, I wrote it down, so the remembrance thereof might not be lost, inasmuch as by the good things which are written good example is taken and from ill and lewd actions is derived [this profit] that men abhor them and keep themselves from falling into the like errors. Having, then, written that which Vismaro related, I will have it read of posterity under your name, if withal my toys may avail to last so long; but I write it e'en with that intent,[1] come thereof what may; and not to keep you longer, I will come to the effect. Fare you well.

The Twentieth Story.

CAPTAIN BIAGINO CRIVELLO SLAYETH A PRIEST IN THE MOUNTAINS OF BRIANZA, TO HAVE HIS BENEFICE FOR A KINSMAN OF HIS OWN.

There is none here, my lady countess and you, courteous gentlemen, but knoweth Captain Biagino Crivello, who, having been a very doughty man of his person and having, what while Duke Lodovico Sforza of Milan abode in estate, still borne himself with worship in the wars and held honourable commands, now attendeth to no otherwhat than to live very quietly and daily to visit as many churches as are in Milan, giving himself altogether to the care of his soul's health. He was in exceeding great credit with the said Duke Lodovico and was become so much his familiar and intimate that he seemed, not his subject,

---

[1] *i.e.* for the benefit of posterity.

but his brother. He was endowed with meet substance
and having one only daughter by his dead wife, concerned
himself not to amass possessions, choosing not to take
another wife; nay, all that he gained by his pay, he
being captain-general of all the ducal arbalestriers, he
spent in making good cheer for good fellows, and on
like wise, all that which the duke lavishly gave him he
expended in doing himself honour. Now you know that
the family of the Crivelli is innumerable in Milan and
the neighbouring country and that there are many poor
among them, as often happeneth in great families. There
was, then, a young man of this said family, who, being
well lettered, would fain have turned priest, if he could
have had the means of getting some benefice. It occurred
to his mind that Captain Biagino would be an excellent
means to his end, so but he were willing to aid him,
and accordingly, knowing him to be very debonair and
complaisant, he betook himself to him and told him his
mind. The good captain, hearing this and being a man
who would fain have done good unto all, much more
to those of his kin, freely promised him that he would
bespeak the duke thereof and would do his utmost endeavour to cause him have his intent; wherefore, to make
no delay about the matter, he went that same day to
speak with Messer Giacomo Antiquario, the prince's
secretary and intendant-general of all the ecclesiastical
benefices of the duchy. Antiquario, who was a man of
excellent letters and most upright life and held in exceeding great esteem of all for his chastened fashions, hearing
Biagino's mind and knowing how much the duke loved
him, said to him, "Captain, I know not that there is
any benefice vacant for the nonce, though, an there were,
I should doubtless know it through the office which I

hold. Meseemeth you should speak with the Lord Duke himself and cause him promise you one of the first vacancies; but lose no time, for that His Highness hath already promised many thereof." The captain thanked him courteously and taking his opportunity, bespoke the duke, who, hearing his request, gave him good words in reply, charging him be on the watch to hear if any beneficed priest should die and let him know thereof.

Biagino, having gotten this answer, waited till some priest should go to Paradise, and what while he abode thus, it befell that an archpriest died at Lomellina in the castle-wicks of Count Antonio Crivello. Of this the captain was immediately advertised and went off to demand his benefice of the duke, who, hearing the news and having a mind to bestow that archpresbytery on another, said, "Captain Biagino, pardon us if we complease you not at this present, for that it is not half an hour since we were constrained to promise it to another." The captain believed the case to be as he said and shrugging his shoulders, awaited another occasion. Nor did he abide long ere another priest died and he, seeking to have his benefice, had the same reply from the duke; but he desisted not for that nor lost heart. However, many other benefices falling vacant and the duke still excusing himself for that he had already given them away, Biagino began to perceive that he was making mock of him and said to him, "My lord, by that which I see, you do but bubble me; but, by St. Ambrose his body, you will make me do some extravagance. Give me a benefice and torment me no longer." The duke laughed and told him he would e'en do it; but the thing still went on such wise that, whenassoever some prebend fell vacant and Biagino sought it, the duke said that it was given away, till the captain, waxing angry with these flouts, said in himself, "Cocks' faith, I will e'en make one[1] which shall stick to the hoe !"[2] Now it chanced in those days that, being in the Brianza hill-country in the territory of Merate, he saw a decrepit priest, who had a good fat benefice in those parts; whereupon the captain, without more ado, knocked him on the head and posting off incontinent to the duke, who was at Cusago, a place some three or four miles distant from Milan, demanded the benefice. The duke, according to his usance, answered him that he had already given it a good while agone; whereupon, "Body o' Christ," cried the captain at the top of his voice, "that is impossible, seeing it is not three hours since I knocked him on the head and I have posted it straight hither without drawing rein." The duke abode all aghast at this speech and Biagino, straightway mounting to horse, made for the Adda and took refuge in the Venetian territory; where, making his peace with the dead man's kinsfolk, he had the duke's pardon and to boot a benefice for his kinsman; and all this was caused by the good captain's over-familiarity with his lord.

[1] *i.e.* a vacancy.
[2] *i.e.* which shall ensue to the profit of the maker.

Bandello

to the magnificent doctor of laws Messer Francesco Maria Trobamala.

Azio Bandello, my grandfather, was a man very learned in humane letters and a very famous doctor of the civil law, as you may remember you, for that, he being four-score years old, we still found him, what time we returned from the school of our learned Messer Gerardo Canabo, attended by many clients, who resorted to him for counsel. And for that he was by nature very merry and pleasant and still had some goodly saw, argute and to the purpose of whatsoever was said, he was of all called Messer Azio o' the proverbs. He was wont to say that in the gravest and most momentous parleyings there oftentimes befall certain chances which unexpectedly render a matter, from grave, laughable and whiles, on the contrary, from laughable, grave. That a thing can from grave become laughable we saw, whilst we were yet children, when in Castelnuovo, the Grassi pleading with the Torti anent a homicide and Signor Galeazzo Sanseverino willing that the matter should be argued before himself, to the end that he might make peace between those two noble families, one of our doctors, who was called of all Necessitas, because Necessity knoweth no law, having studied an opinion of Messer Alessandro da Imola, who advised in a like case and put it to

have betided between Titius and Sempronius, after Messer
Antonio Curzio had for some two hours' space spoken
learnedly in favour of the Grassi, Dom Necessitas arose
and having, as is usual, taken leave of Signor Galeazzo,
proceeded to say, "Sir, in this criminal matter which is
toward between Titius on the one part and Sempronius
on the other, the civil law provideth that Sempronius be
[so and so] and that Titius have [this and that];" and
he could nowise avail to come out of Titius and Sempronius, so that, the whole audience bursting into laughter,
the matter, which was criminal and grave, became ridiculous
and was for that day put to silence. Now, I relating this
bourd at Genoa, in the presence of many, Messer Sper-
andio Palmaro, a man of very tenacious memory and great
experience, related a chance happened to a friar in act to
preach, whereby it is plainly to be seen how a little
word can render things of the utmost repute ridiculous;
and I, having written the thing down, according as he
related it, and added it to the number of my novels,
send and give it to you, in common with your brother,
Messer Andrea, who nowadays holdeth a most honourable place among the philosophers and physicians in the
Academy of Ticino, lecturing, disputing and healing, you
being on your side a Scævola, a Paul and an Ulpian
among the doctors of laws. Fare you well.

FRA MICHELE DA CARCANO, PREACHING IN FLORENCE, IS BAFFLED BY A LAD WITH A READY SAYING.

It is not many years since all Italy was in arms and uproar. Duke Galeazzo Sforza had been slain in Milan, amiddleward the church of San Stefano, by Andrea Lampognano and his fellow-conspirators and at his death the whole duchy was turned topsy-turvy, the duchess, his widow, ordering public affairs with Cecco[1] Simonetta on one wise and Lodovico Sforza with Roberto Sanseverino using every endeavour to wrest the governance from Cecco's hands. Ferdinand, King of Naples, kept his son, Alfonso, Duke of Calabria, in the field with a great army against the Florentines, and the Venetians made them ready to expel Ercole da Este from the duchy of Ferrara; whilst the pope and the other princes of Italy were leagued with these and with those. Mahomet, Emperor of the Turks, learning this division among the Italian princes and being still minded to occupy Rhodes and Italy, thought to profit by our dissensions; wherefore he with a sea-armament besieged and took Otranto, a city of the kingdom of Naples, situated on the confines of Calabria and Apulia, between the Ionian and the Ausonian Sea, overagainst the sea-shore

---

[1] Dim. of Francesco.

of La Vellona,[1] with a little interval of sea, which divideth
Italy from Macedonia and which some will have to be
five-and-fifty miles and others threescore. I remember me to
have, whilst navigating it, considered the point and to have
concluded that it might be a little more or a little less.
Certain it is that King Pyrrhus thought to join the one
land to the other by means of cunningly wrought bridges
and Marcus Varro, when prefect of the fleet under Pompey
the Great, had the same thought, what time he purged the
sea of the corsairs ; but both, distracted by other cares, left
so glorious an emprise unaccomplished. The taking of
Otranto by the Turks, being published abroad throughout
Italy, filled all the seigniors and people with dismay, they
seeing the common enemy of Christendom to have set foot
in Italy, where he might hourly be expected to succour his
troops with a new armament. And in truth there was
great fear of the ruin of all Italy, had not God's providence
provided that, ere the Turks could stablish themselves on a
firm footing and extend their dominion in the neighbourhood
of Otranto, Mahomet their emperor died, by reason whereof
Otranto was, no great while after, recovered, its Turkish
garrison being unable to get succour, inasmuch as, Mahomet
dead, Bajazet his eldest son, seeking to make himself master
of the empery and being in Paphlagonia, near the Greater
Sea,[2] was hindered by the troops of Zizimus, his younger
brother, who was presently at Iconium in Lycaonia. Accordingly, Mahomet's sons being thus at daggers drawn,
Achinato,[3] who had occupied Otranto in the former's name,
being hard pressed by Alfonso, [Duke of Calabria,] who had
betaken himself thither with his army, and seeing no hope

[1] i.e. Valona in Albania.
[2] *Mare Maggiore*, i.e. the Black Sea.
[3] i.e. Ahmed.

of succour, avoided the place on honourable terms and was after the occasion of giving the empery to Bajazet.

Now, he being yet in Otranto and all Italy in exceeding great fear of the Turks, the pope let preach a crusade against the infidels for the recoverance of the town; wherefore it was attended to no otherwhat throughout all Italy than to preach and proclaim the holy war against the enemies of the faith; and for that the thing was of the utmost importance, the pope elected many famous preachers of various orders to that office; and amongst the rest was Fra Michele [da] Carcano, a Milanese gentleman and a friar of the order of Saint Francis, to wit, of those that wear the clogs, who was so fat and corpulent that he was of all called, not Fra Michele, but Fra Michelaccio.[1] He was, then, by commission of Pope Sixtus [IV.], sent to Florence to preach the holy war and there began his preachments, exhorting the citizens to take arms in the interest not only of King Ferdinand, but of all Christendom, and bidding them not consider that they were then at war with the said king, who had recalled his people,[2] but do it for the love of the common weal; for that, should the Turks retain possession of the city of Otranto, they would speedily conquer all the kingdom of Naples and would after fall upon Rome and Tuscany. One day, then, all Florence being at the preachment and the father's homily hearkened with the utmost attention, he proceeded to enumerate the various kinds of torments wreaked by the Turks upon

[1] *i.e.* "great coarse Michael."
[2] *i.e.* the army which he had originally despatched against the Florentines, under his eldest son, Alfonso, Duke of Calabria, and which he had now recalled for the recoverance of Otranto.

the Christians and said, "Florentines mine, when the
Turks take a city by storm, you must not think that they
spare either age or sex; nay, they respect none, but put all
to the sword and wreak the greatest cruelties in the world.
Marry, should they e'en take this city by capitulation,
an they let you live, they will want all your possessions
for themselves and all you for slaves and will never desist
till they have made you all renounce holy baptism. They
will take your little children and circumcise them, as do
the Jews; and if you dare to gainsay them, they will
impale you. Your daughters will not be safe in your
arms, for they will take them all to their slaves and
women. Our Lord God keep us from their hands! And
what think you they would do to me, who preach against
them? Woe, woe to me, should I fall into their hands!"
Then, he repeating this once or twice in the fervour of
his speech and saying, "And what would they do to thee,
Fra Michelaccio?" a little boy, who was seated overagainst
the pulpit, rose to his feet and said in a loud voice, "Father,
the Turks would do you no manner of harm, except they
should roast you, capon-fashion, for that you are very fat."
At this merry and argute sally of the lad's, all burst out
laughing and needs must the good friar come down from
the pulpit, inasmuch as all knew that, the fatter good
capons were, the more they pleased him; so that, without preaching more, he departed Florence, misdoubting
him the lad had been lessoned to say that which he said.
And thus an unlooked-for word turned a matter of such
importance into derision.

Bandello

to the magnificent Signor Carlo Attellano.

Amongst the innumerable kinds of follies which vex,
afflict and oftentimes ruin men, body and soul, methinketh
alchymy and sorcery are two of the chiefest, inasmuch
as meseemeth that in these twain the more a man exerciseth
himself and the older he waxeth therein, the more he
laboureth thereat and the more he desireth to practise
them ; the which betideth not of many other kinds of follies,
wherein we see that a thousand occasions (and especially
the approach of age) cause men turn their minds elsewhither
and oftentimes take shame to themselves. The which is
not the case with the alchymist, who, the more he essayeth
himself in the art, the more experiments he maketh and
the more he seeth his endeavours result in smoke, the
more eagerly doth he hearten himself to ensue the emprise,
hoping either to find the quintessence (whereof I for my
part know not if such a thing be) or holding it for certain
to change copper into good gold or at the least into the
finest silver ; nay, the effect not ensuing, he straightway
excuseth the art, declaring the tincture to have been ill
made, the fire to have been of ill charcoal or over-fierce ;
and so, beguiling himself with a thousand other illusions,
he consumeth his substance and his life and is, together
with the Moon,[1] with Mercury[2] and his other idle toys,

[1] The alchymical name of silver.
[2] The alchymical name of quicksilver.

resolved into smoke. Another, by means of the Clavicula
Salomonis [1] (if Solomon indeed wrote it) and of a thousand
other books of conjurations, thinketh to find hidden treasures
in the bowels of the earth, to bring his mistress to his will,
to learn the secrets of princes, to go from Milan to Rome
in a second and to do many other marvellous feats ; and the
more he findeth himself deceived, the more he persevereth
in his incantations, still upheld by the hope of finding
that which he seeketh; nor doth it boot to speak of the
many errors which ensue of this delusion, they being sufficiently manifest. Remember you, Signor Carlo, of the time
when our friend [such an one] made of his chamber a
charnel-house, having more skulls and dead men's bones
there than be at Paris in the Cemetery of the Innocents.
Now, Signor Julius Cæsar Scaliger discoursing these latter
days of these follies, in the presence of the Lady Costanza
Rangona e Fregosa, with Messer Gian Pietro Usperto,
the governor of Signor Ettore Fregoso, a young man very
notable for good letters and excellent usances, the latter,
after the matter had been philosophically debated between
them at length and many goodly and profitable things said,
related, to solace the listeners' minds somewhat, a case
befallen at Bologna, of a scholar who sought to be beloved
by means of enchantments. And for that meseemed it was
worthy to be kept in remembrance, I wrote it down and
have published it under your name, so you may see that
both here and in every other place I am mindful of you.
Fare you well.

[1] A famous treatise on the magical art, attributed to Solomon, but
probably written by Albertus Magnus or some philosopher of his
time.

The Two-and-Twentieth Story.

A STUDENT DIETH OF AFFRIGHT, BEING IN A GRAVE [WHITHER HE HATH BEEN BROUGHT] UNDER COLOUR OF MAKING CERTAIN CONJURATIONS.

Thinking, most illustrious madam, that our debates have in some measure oppressed the minds of all the listeners, I purpose to tell you a story, whereof albeit the end is tearful, nevertheless there occur therein things which savour of the ridiculous and will somewhat solace your dejected spirits; more by token that the case is much to the purpose of that which we have striven, the most learned and ingenious Signor Giulio Cesare and I, to show, to wit, that these conjurations well-nigh always end in ill. You must know, then, that, what time I was in Bologna busied with the study of the laws, as well Cæsarean as pontifical,[1] there were certain students of high consideration, who delighted to spend their leisure in pleasures of all kinds and to live as blitheliest they might and who, between them, hired a house, where, at the hours when there was no study toward, one might still find students of every sort and eke other merry and jocund men. There it was reasoned of pleasant things,

---

[1] *i.e.* civil and canon.

games were played and all gave themselves the best time
in the world, banishing melancholy on every side nor
permitting that any should discourse of sorry or fashious
things, so that it was devised throughout all Bologna of
so gladsome a company. Now it chanced that a student,
who conversed whiles with these, fell in love (as young
men will) with a very fair Bolognese lady and began to
follow her whereassoever she went and to keep her
solicited with letters and messages; but she, for whatever cause, seemed nowise disposed to accept him to
lover; whereat the young man was like to despair and
the frowarder she showed herself, the more he became
enkindled and importuned her the more. The lady,
whether it was that she knew the student to be not the
shrewdest man in the world or that she cared not that
he should send her letters and messages and that others
should know it, accepted all, but gave him no other
reply than that she chose not to occupy herself with
these love-toys.

Now the gallant delighted in tagging rhymes and made
fine sonnets and tercets for that his lady, the which, when
he had commodity, he recited in the house of those students,
of whom I have already told you that they led so merry
a life. Amongst these latter was one, the maddest, merriest
wag in the world, who, hearing the enamoured youth's
compositions, lightly perceived that here was a soft and
saltless soil, wherein he might aptly set his mattock and
keep all the company merry. This his thought he imparted
to other good friends of his and they, having determined
what was to do, committed the charge of the whole to him,
knowing him to be a man who never, an it liked him not,
changed countenance for any laughable thing he saw or
heard, whereas, on the contrary, when he had a mind to

give any one bait,[1] he laughed immoderately at every least
trifle and knew full well to work the vein (as the saying is)
of whomsoever he would.[2] Accordingly, one day, Messer
Giovanni (for so was the enamoured student called) being
in their house, he accosted him, saying, "How long is it
since you composed some fine thing? Prithee, be not so
chary of your goodly rhymes, for that, if indeed I cannot
compose such sonnets as yours, I do marvellously delight
therein and would abide from morning (after I had dined)
till eventide, without eating, to hearken to them, especially
to yours; for that the other day I heard you recite a sonnet,
which pierced my heart through and through; and were I
your lady-love, I warrant you all the Seigniory of Bologna
should not keep me from coming to visit you at home at
midday, to say nothing of anights. But methinketh you
must give yourself a rare time with this mistress of yours,
and much good may it do you; I myself would do the like."
Messer Giovanni, hearing his talk, answered him with a
heavy sigh, saying, "Messer Simone," for such was the
other's name, "you are far and away mistaken; for that I
love the cruellest lady in all the world, of whom I have
never availed to have a kind look, no, nor a least answer,
so that I abide the despairfullest man alive and envy the
dead a thousand times an hour." "That cannot be," rejoined Simone, "but you do well to play secret; keep your
counsel and put no trust in any, for that nowadays a man
knoweth not in whom he may confide, so base are men and
so little trustworthy. Marry, I warrant you you need not
fear lest I should rob you of your loves, seeing I am lodged
on such wise that I would not change my mistress against

---

[1] *i.e.* to hoodwink (*dar pasto a qualch'uno*).
[2] *i.e.* to fool them to the top of their bent (*secondare il filone di
chiunque voleva*).

the empress; nay, were it as you say, I should be for doing
you some signal service in this your case." Messer Giovanni
thereupon proceeded to swear and call the saints to witness
that he was e'en in despair of that his love and that he had
never availed to get a least word of her, much less otherwhat, and that he would give his soul to all the devils to
lie one sole night with her. Messer Simone, hearing this,
fell a-laughing and said, " Marry, since you swear to me
thus solemnly, I must e'en believe you and have the greatest
compassion of you in the world, for that I myself was
otherwhiles at this same pass and know what extreme dolour
it is to love and not be loved. But, if you will hearken to
me and swear to me on the consecrated stone of the high
altar of San Petronio that you will never reveal unto any
that which I shall do for you and that you have courage to
do that which I shall tell you, I promise you to put your
lady by your side, on such wise that she shall never leave
you, save in so far as you shall will it. Nor let this seem
to you an extraordinary thing or an incredible, for that I
have made proof of it for myself and for my friends upwards
of seven times; but it behoveth, above all, to be secret,
lest the thing come some time or other to the ears of the
Inquisitor of Saint Dominick, for that, like as, in the time
of Signor Giovanni Bentivoglio, he who was then inquisitor
let burn Cimera,[1] so would the present one do nowadays
with us, inasmuch as I learned this conjuration, (for it
behoveth to proceed by means of conjurations), which I
purpose to make with you for your benefit, from a person
to whom Cimera herself taught it in her lifetime."

The good simple student, who was really in love, put
that entire and firm faith in Simone's words he would have

---

[1] Apparently a sorceress of the time.

accorded to the likeliest and most certain things which could
have been said; and accordingly, thanking him infinitely
and proffering himself to his bond-slave, he offered to swear,
not only upon an altar, but upon the consecrated wafer
itself, that he would never repeat unto any whatsoever he
should see or hear. Messer Simone, seeing the bird in the
cage, determined to divert himself and his companions and
fool Giovanni to the top of his bent; wherefore, it being
holiday-time, he carried him off, without word said to any,
to San Petronio Church, where, there being none present,
he made him swear that which he would with the solemnest
adjurations in the world. This done, he fell a-walking to
and fro in the church with him and said to him, "I know
none save yourself who could have induced me to do that
which I shall do for you, such is the heartfelt love I bear
you and the compassion I feel for you; for that this past
Lent I promised the friar, to whom I confessed myself, that
I would never more intermeddle with matters of enchant-
ment, he averring to me that I should commit a most
grievous crime; but keep it[1] him who may; [I cannot.]
Now I must tell you that this conjuration cannot be made
except we have certain things which needs must he for
whom it is made take with his own hand from the body
of a dead man. There dieth daily some one in Bologna and
is buried in this or that cemetery; wherefore we will make
shift to disinter him and take that which we need, for that
I will bear you company and we will carry with us two or
three of my comrades, who have aided me in like affairs.
All resteth upon this, that your heart suffice you to do that
which I shall tell you." Messer Giovanni promised to do
all he should bid him, declaring that he was passing stout-

[1] *i.e.* the promise.

hearted and was ready, not only to unearth a dead body, but to do whatsoever other thing. Quoth the other, "It will not behove you draw near the body till I and my fellows shall have uncovered it and cleared all the earth away from it; and when this shall be done, we will make you a signal and you shall go down into the grave and embrace the dead man, kissing him on the mouth and craving him pardon. Then will we give you a pair of pincers, with which you must draw three of his teeth, two from the upper and one from the lower jaw, and put them in your mouth and pull them out thrice in succession; after which you must give them to us, for that we shall still be there present. This done, you must tear off the middle finger-nail of his right hand and the little finger-nail of his left hand. All the other things my comrades have, such as virgin parchment, inscribed with characters in bat's blood, a stone of those which have atop those toads which abide in the earth and many other rare and curious things which need not be here mentioned, the which are all pounded together and buried in a place where the beloved lady must needs pass; and no sooner will she have passed there than she will send that same day to seek you and give you to understand that she is ready to do all you desire."

The good student believed all and declared that which it behoved him do to be a light matter and that, to compass his intent, he would, an it were necessary, carry it into effect by himself. They being, then, agreed upon this, Messer Giovanni began to be all agog with joy, as if the effect had already ensued, and went home, blithe beyond measure, to do his occasions. Messer Simone also went straight home, himseeming each hour was a year till he should have found his comrades and told them the bourd which he had in mind to foist upon the enamoured student.

The others, hearing what had passed, opined that good simple Messer Giovanni had never passed under the ark of Saint Longinus [1] at Mantua and laughed amain over his simplicity. Now they had in their house a serving-man called Chiappino, the wiliest knave in the world, who would have made sauce for the devil himself, bold, presumptuous and tricksy beyond belief. To him, then, the jolly rascals imparted that which they purposed to do and he, who would have slept without fear in a sepulchre, declared himself right ready to do all that was ordained him. Meanwhile, the enamoured student, when he saw his lady, who took no more heed of him than as she had never seen him, said in himself, "Ay, ay, stand upon your dignity, play the cruel, turn your face elsewhither and take no heed of me; for I trust speedily to hold you all naked in mine arms and kiss and nibble that dainty little mouth of yours, vermeil as a ruby;" and so he raved of these things to himself, himseeming he already had his intent; but he knew not, poor wretch, what was in store for him. No great while thereafter it befell that a poor man died and was buried in a certain very lonely cemetery, where no one went day or night. When Messer Simone heard of this, he let Messer Giovanni know it and would have him that same day after vespers withdraw to his chamber and repeat certain orisons, or rather nonsense-verses, which they had written among them, and not depart thence till he should summon him. Meanwhile, they let make, in the cemetery aforesaid, a hole of no great depth, wherein, at the appointed time, Chiappino laid himself, having with him certain fireworks, as you shall hear out of hand. Then, the fourth hour of the night [2] come, Messer Simone, with

[1] See ante, Vol. III. p. 312, note.
[2] *i.e.* the fourth hour after sunset.

two of his comrades, taking spades, hoes and a pair of pincers, went to fetch the enamoured scholar from his chamber and made with him for the cemetery.

The night was dark as a wolf's throat, so that one might scarce be distinguished from other near at hand; but Messer Giovanni ruffled it by the way after the bravest fashion and was like to jump out of his skin for allegresse. When Chiappino heard them enter the cemetery (for, that it being in a retired place, the others made some little noise to advertise him of their coming,) he straightway stretched himself out in the ditch, wrapped in certain ragged clothes which had been provided aforethought, whilst Messer Simone caused the enamoured student kneel down in a corner and leaving one of the crew with him, to say sundry Paternosters, repaired with the rest to the hole aforesaid. There they proceeded to dig and make a noise with the tools they had brought with them and to scatter abroad the earth which had been cast out of the hole, as it were they went about to unearth the dead body; and whenas themseemed time, they called the student and his companion. Messer Giovanni, who had thitherto shown no sign of fear, began to tremble all over; however, heartened by his companion, he made for the hole and Messer Simone said to him, "Come, go boldly in and do your office." Accordingly, the poor student descended all trembling into the ditch; but, as he offered to bend down to embrace the corpse, Chiappino, who had in his mouth I know not what, as it were a nut, full of artificial fire, sent forth a tongue of flame and immediately thereafter another and another and clipped the student fast in his arms; whereupon the latter, who was already more dead than alive, suffocated with extreme fear, died in his arms, what while he played the devil, yelling and howling and spitting fire. The others, hearing Messer Giovanni say nothing and seeing that, when Chiappino opened his arms, he fell to the earth, thought he had swooned for affright and pulling him out of the hole, rubbed him amain; then, carrying him home, they found that he was dead and woeful beyond measure that their jest should have had so strange and parlous an issue, knew not what to do, fearing lest, if the thing got wind, they should be in danger of their lives. However, a little before daybreak, there being none other than they four who knew the thing, they took the poor student and carrying him forth, laid him under a portico, hard by a certain church; where he being found on the morrow, the thing was bruited abroad in Bologna and came to the knowledge of the Seigniory, who caused the body be viewed by the most notable physicians, together with famous surgeons. They, having diligently examined the dead man, concluded with one accord that he had died of some great fright, and he was accordingly buried; but, for that things rarely abide hidden, whenas they are known of more than one or two, the fact got wind, I know not how; wherefore Messer Simone and his comrades departed Bologna, for fear of the law, and repaired to Padua to make an end of their studies, straitly guarding them for the future from the like pranks; and indeed meseemeth such tricks are unmeet to be played upon friends.

Bandello

to the illustrious and reverend Monsignor Sforza
Riario Bishop of Lucca, greeting.

How blameworthy is arrogance in every one may lightly
be apprehended from this, that in all companies the arrogant
are generally shunned and none desireth their commerce;
whereas on the contrary the urbane and the debonair are
ever loved and honoured; and in truth the inordinate
appetite of seeking to precede one's fellows in whatsoever
thing, how great soever the deserts of the person in whom
it obtaineth, will still by persons of sound understanding
be esteemed a vice. Now, pridefulness ill beseeming whatsoever sort of men, as without doubt it doth, meseemeth
it sitteth especially ill upon religious persons, it behoving
those who make profession of humility to set the world
an example of virtuous dealings, and in the contrary case,
matter of scandal is given unto Christians, as a few days
agone befell here in Milan at a solemn general procession,
which was made after the rout of the Venetian host at
G[h]iara d'Adda,[1] when King Louis, twelfth of that name,

---

[1] A battle fought 14th May, 1509, in which the French defeated the
Venetians, and better known as the battle of Aignadel or Agnadella,
a village of the Milanese, situate on the Adda. Ghiara (not Giara,
as in text) d'Adda was the name of the place where the boundary
was marked under the treaty between Louis XII. and the Emperor

returned in triumph to Milan. The Canonical Regulars[1] would fain have had a more honourable place than the monks of St. Benedict, alleging certain arguments of their fashion which are printed, and availing not to obtain the desired place, (for that Messer Sebastiano Giberti, doctor of canon law and vicar of the most illustrious and reverend Cardinal of Ferrara, Archbishop of Milan, wisely refused to allow any innovation to be made,) the said Canonicals took no part in the procession, the which gave occasion to all Milan to murmur. It befell that same day, many gentlemen being in the house of Messer Giacomo Antiquario, a man most eminent for fair fashions, integrity of life and good letters, who had made a very eloquent and learned oration upon the king's triumph, and it being spoken of the question mooted by the Canonicals, that Messer Niccolò dalla Croce, a jurisconsult and a pleasant gentleman, related a brief story, which made us laugh amain and which I, having written it, now send and give to you, so that, whenas whiles you feel yourself weary of your graver studies, you may, intermitting them, recreate yourself somewhat with the reading of this novelling,[2] it being unforbidden unto the gravest and most worshipful of personages to solace themselves bytimes with seemly mirth.[3] We read that the great Scipio Africanus oftentimes, by way of disport, went with his Achates Lælius along the sea-shore, gathering shells and stones such as

Maximilian for the partition of the Venetian territory and as the battle of Agnadella ensured the carrying out of the treaty in question, it is to be presumed that it came to be known by the name of the place where it took visible effect.

[1] A monastic order so called.
[2] *Novelletta.*
[3] Bandello, *Urbanità*, which seems meaningless.

are strewn among the sand. Socrates, also, that most
famous philosopher, was used, after his philosophic studies,
to sport with a little son of his; and thus should we do,
so we may return with a more awakened mind to affairs
of importance. Fare you well.

Ⓣⓗⓔ Ⓣⓗⓡⓔⓔ-ⓐⓝⓓ-Ⓣⓦⓔⓝⓣⓘⓔⓣⓗ Ⓢⓣⓞⓡⓨ.

A READY AND ARGUTE SALLY OF A BUFFOON, MADE, IN THE PRESENCE OF DUKE GALEAZZO SFORZA, AGAINST THE CARMELITE FRIARS.

Our having, gentlemen mine, first heard the very weighty
and learned oration of our most erudite Antiquario, full of
so many goodly histories and bestrewn with so many re-
condite passages,[1] had uplifted our minds on such wise that
we had all abidden well-nigh beside ourselves, had not our
ingenious poet, Messer Lancino Curzio, somewhat awakened
us by recounting the indiscreet contention of the Canonical
Regulars, for that the consideration of their ambition and
arrogance hath e'en made us laugh a little. He hath given
us the digestive[2] and I, without straying from the purpose,
will give you the medicine. You must know, then, that,
in the reign of Galeazzo Sforza, Duke of Milan, there arose
in this city an exceeding grave question of precedence
between the Carmelite friars and the other religious orders,

[1] *Passi*, i.e. quotations.
[2] *Digestivo*, in ancient surgery an *external* remedy, especially an
ointment, as opposed to *medicina*, an *internal* remedy.

for that the former would fain have had the vantage not only of the mendicant orders, but of all the other monks. The others alleged their approved usances, confirmed by divers popes; but the Carmelites avouched that a great wrong had been done them in the past, by reason of the simple humility of their predecessors, and that this ought not to prejudice their rights, they being the most ancient of all the religious orders in the world. The controversy was referred to the Duke's privy council, and he himself, being young, chose to be present at the hearing of the dispute. Accordingly he, one holiday, let assemble the heads of all the religious orders in the Castle of Milan and would have the matter debated in the Green Saloon. It was committed to the excellent Messer Gian Andrea Cagnuola, a most learned and impartial legist, as you all know, to question the parties and cause them produce their arguments; wherefore, turning to the Prior of the Carmelites, he asked him how long his order had been extant. The Carmelite answered that it began under Elias [1] on Mount Carmel. "Then," said Cagnuola, "you existed in the time of the Apostles?" "Ay did we, as well you know," replied the prior; "nay, we alone were friars in those days, forasmuch as Basil, Benedict, Dominick, Francis and all other founders of religious orders were as yet unborn." Whereupon quoth Cagnuola, "And what proof can you allege of this your great antiquity, an it be denied unto you?" Now the duke had a very sprightly and argute buffoon, who, hearing this extravagance of the Carmelite prior's, sprang into the midst and said to Cagnuola, "Dominie doctor, the father saith sooth, for that in the days of the Apostles there were

[1] *i.e.* the prophet Elijah, from whom the Carmelites claimed descent, although the order was not really founded till the twelfth century.

no other friars than the Carmelites, of whom St. Paul writeth, when he saith, ' Periculum in falsis fratribus.'[1] These are of those false brethren."[2] All fell a-laughing at the shrewd saying of the buffoon and the duke, hearing this pleasant trait, commanded that it should be no more spoken of the matter and that the ancient customs should be observed ; the which was approved of all and the Carmelites went away, jeered by the people.

---

[1] As usual, a false quotation. Apparently 2 Cor. xi. 25-6, " I have been . . . . in peril among false brethren " (Vulg., *Fui In* . . . . . *periculis in falsis fratribus*), is meant ; but this passage, of course, does not bear the construction put upon it.

[2] Or " friars " (*frati*).

Bandello

to the illustrious and accomplished seignior Signor Roberto Sanseverino Count of Gaiazzo.

It is continually seen by long experience that in human nature each age hath its diversions and its pleasures, wherein it exerciseth itself, and that which well beseemeth the infantile and childish age and delighteth the beholders were blameable in a youth who should seek to occupy himself withal. On like wise, youth hath its sports and pastimes and a young man may do many things, without deserving chastisement or reprehension, which if one stricken in years should offer to do, he would be deservedly scouted of all. To fall in love and gallant it with women beseemeth unto young men, in so much that, an one see a young man who liveth without love, it will be said that he is not a man and that he savoureth of the salvage and the melancholic. On the contrary, when a man cometh to mature age, it is forbidden him to play the enamoured lover overmuch and [over-amorousness] oftentimes driveth an unlucky old man mad and maketh him the byword of the vulgar. Moreover, it seldom chanceth but some scandal ensue thereof, for that the old man, not having the natural powers which are required in love, becometh suspicious and dieth a thousand deaths a day, fretted by the icy worm of jealousy, which oftentimes causeth him commit a thousand errors; as

happened no great while agone to an unfortunate old man
at Monza, in the days whenas the illustrious Signor Giano
Maria Fregoso, generalissimo of the Venetian army, was
entrenched at Cassano on the Adda. You know that Cesare
Piola came daily to the camp, he being then in sojourn at
his country-seat of Inzago, hard by. He one day related
a heinous folly then late committed by an enamoured old
man, the which was in truth very great and may well serve
to warn whoso heareth it against the like errors; and I,
having written down that which he said and added it to the
number of my novels, have dedicated it to your name. Let
it not mislike you to read it and to remember you that it
cometh from your Bandello, whose family was ever most
devoted to the Sanseverino name. Fare you well.

The Four-and-Twentieth Story.

AN ENAMOURED OLD MAN SLAYETH HIS SON AND HIMSELF FOR JEALOUSY OF A WOMAN.

You being all day long, gentlemen, at blows with the
Spaniards and there being no otherwhat heard here than
alarums and drums and trumpets and the tremendous
noise of the artillery, methinketh it is attended to little
else than to wage war and spy out the enemy's doings,
for that so duty requireth. Nevertheless, it is not forbidden, bytimes, all due provisions made,[1] to take some

---

[1] *Provvigioni fatte*, i.e. precautions taken.

diversion and give some little solace to the wearied limbs. And for that the most excellent Signor Giano Mario Fregoso, your governor-general, hath e'en asked me if I have aught new, it occurreth to my mind to tell you a piteous chance which befell, not a fortnight agone, at Monza. There was in that place one of our Milanese gentlemen, who, having, like many others, departed Milan for the present wars and having great part of his estates near Monza, took up his abode there. He was a widower with two sons, the younger seven and the elder some nineteen years old, and finding himself without a wife, fell in love, albeit he had overpassed threescore years, (without regard to old age, which is much nearer to death than to life,) with a very well-favoured country-wench, the daughter of one of his farmers, whom he had for monies of her father and kept in his house, taking amorous pleasure of her, whenas it pleased him. The elder son lightly became aware of the case; but, albeit his father's lewd life misliked him, natheless he dared not cross him in aught. The wench herself was forwarder than behoved unto her like; wherefore, having already proved with what manner horn men go a-hunting and perceiving that the old man was short-winded and could hunt but seldom, (a thing which nowise pleased her, for that she would fain have abidden without cease in exercise,) she cast her eyes upon the youth, so the son should supply the father's lack. The young man was very handsome and herseemed eke he was better-breathed than his father, who rather invited her to the pleasures of the chase than satisfied her; wherefore, setting her mind daily more and more on him, she became beyond measure enamoured of him. It chanced one day that, the old man being abroad, the wench, impatient of the love which she bore the

youth,[1] whom she then saw before her, and herseeming
she had present commodity to do that which occurred
to her mind, accosted him and in the presence of a serving-
maid, her kinswoman, whom she had brought into the
house and in whom she much trusted, opened her whole
heart to him and instantly besought him to have compassion on her; whilst the maid on like wise exhorted
him to complease her. He, hearing so heinous a demand,
turned to her with an angry air and gave her the foulest
rating was ever given to ribald woman, threatening them
both that, if they ever again bespoke him of such lewd-
ness, he would tell his father all. With that he departed
the house, leaving the two vile women disconsolate.

The lewd and wicked woman ceased not for this rebuff
to importune him and pray and beseech him with tears and
sighs, whenassoever she had commodity thereof, to be
pleased to have compassion of her; but the youth, who was
an honest lad and a well-bred, would lend her no ear and
still threatened to denounce her to his father, yet never did
it, not to afflict the old man, and only studied, as most he
might, not to let himself be found of her alone. She, seeing
herself thus constantly contemned, turned her love into
cruellest hate and having taken counsel with the ribald
serving-wench and agreed with her of that which should be
said to the old man, awaited her opportunity and when the
latter came home one day, abode with the maid in her
chamber, feigning herself all woebegone and having her eyes
big with tears; whereupon, he, entering, found his leman
all amort and the maid as she were weeping-ripe. The
gentleman, who loved the wench more than himself, seeing
her in this plight, asked her lovingly what ailed her; where-

[1] *Impaziente dell'amore*, etc., i.e. unable to conceal it any longer.

upon the wicked and traitorous woman, having forged a long
fable of her fashion, gave him to understand that the young
man his son had sundry whiles required her of love, albeit
she had never consented to him, but had still chidden him,
and that, not half an hour before, finding her alone in her
chamber, he had offered to force her, but that, the maid
coming up, he had taken himself off; all which the villainous
serving-wench confirmed with tears. The old man, hearing
this cunningly-devised fable, abode the woefullest man alive
and kindled into such a choler that he saw well-nigh no
whit of light[1] and assailed with extreme jealousy, felt
himself like to die and said the greatest extravagances in
the world.

What while these things were doing in the chamber, it
chanced that the son aforesaid returned home and mounting
the stair, fell to conversing with another woman of the house
upon a balcony, adjoining the chamber where his father still
hearkened to those two witches, who gave him to understand a thousand lies. The old man, hearing this, clapped
his hand to a sword which he kept at his bedhead and all afire
with ill will against his son and beside himself for choler
and jealousy, issued forth with the naked blade in his hand,
blowing and bellowing like a bull and saying, "Where art
thou, ribald? Body o' God, this is the last time thou shalt
serve me thus, traitor that thou art!" The poor youth,
unknowing what was to do, turned to his father and said,
"Alack, sir, what meaneth this? What is this clamour?"
To which the insensate old man replied furiously, saying,
"Ho, ribald, thou well knowest it, disloyal traitor that thou
art!" To say these words and to aim a great blow at his

---

[1] Cf. the Arabic phrase, "The world grew black in his eyes," of
such frequent occurrence in the Thousand and One Nights.

son's head were all one. The hapless youth, seeing the trenchant sword come whistling down upon his head, would fain have drawn back, to shun the deadly stroke, and forgetting that he was upon the balcony, which had no parapet and was very high, fell headlong down backward and pitched upon a great stone, which stood below, with such force that his head was cloven in sunder and his brains came forth ; wherefore he died incontinent. The barbarous father (or rather enemy), thinking he had jumped down, ran down the stair, sword in hand, crying, "Ribald, thou shalt not escape from my hand to-day ;" but, when he saw his luckless son with his head all shattered and the ground strewn with his brains, that yet throbbed, he was overcome with such vehement dolour that his anger was incontinent quenched and his jealousy took flight. The tenderness of paternal love, reentering his breast, enlightened his blinded eyes and made him see of what a bestial wickedness he had been guilty ; so that, repenting him, when too late, of having lent ear to that malignant and wicked woman, he was all fulfilled with rage and despair ; wherefore, roaring like a ravening lion and calling aloud upon the enemy of mankind, he turned his flashing sword against himself and plunged it into his heart ; then, falling upon his son's yet warm body, he miserably yielded up the ghost and died, weltering in his own and the youth's blood. The ribald wench, who had followed him down, seeing so cruel and unheard a spectacle and stung by her own evil conscience or peradventure misdoubting her (as may well be presumed) of the law, took from her girdle certain keys which she had there and cast them to a woman of the household, who there stood weeping bitterly ; then, betaking herself to a very deep well which was in the courtyard, she threw herself headlong in and was drowned. Such was the end of that

vile and wicked woman, worthy of a more cruel death and
to be torn of dogs limbmeal. The provost of the city
having made strait enquiry into the case and finding that
the ribald serving-wench was an accomplice in all, let put
her ignominiously to death and having cut off her head,
caused hew her into four quarters, the which he hanged to
the gallows without Monza, as whoso passeth there may
plainly see.

Bandello

to the most illustrious lady Eppolita Marchioness of Scaldasole.

Certain unexpected chances oftentimes occur, which bring many into extraordinary perils, especially if a man find himself amongst strangers and understand not their tongue nor know how to make himself apprehended. Now, it being discoursed of these cases at Milan in the house of the most noble and accomplished Signora Ginevra Benti-voglia, wife of the most illustrious Signor Galeazzo Sforza, Lord of Pesaro, and it being told of an Italian soldier, who in Brittany,[1] being ununderstanded nor availing to speak Breton,[1] was wounded and in great peril of his life, Messer Federico Crivello, a very noble and discreet young man, related a strange chance which befell Signor Giro-lamo della Penna, what while he the said Federico was in Poland with the most illustrious Signor Prospero Colonna, and which I having written, our friend Messer Vincenzo Attellano hath prayed me on your part be pleased to impart it to you: wherefore, being beholden to you for a much greater matter, I not only communicate this novel to you, but give and consecrate it unto your illustrious name, so you will e'en vouchsafe urbanely to accept thereof. But

---

[1] Bandello, *Bertagna* and *Bretone.*

what say I? Since you are urbanity itself and the most courteous of the courteous, it beseemeth me not to doubt that you will receive these my trifles most urbanely. Fare you well.

The Five-and-Twentieth Story.

SIGNOR GIROLAMO DELLA PENNA, BEING IN POLAND, CALLETH FOR WAFERS WHEREIN TO TAKE PILLS AND THE NATIVES, NOT UNDERSTANDING HIM, WILL E'EN GIVE HIM THE EUCHARIST.

You must know, worshipful madam and you all, gracious ladies, that these years past Signor Prospero Colonna, a man famous throughout all four parts of the world for his virtue, [his skill in] arms, his liberality and his innumerable other gifts, escorted her ladyship the Queen of Poland, daughter of Duke Gian Galeazzo Sforza of Milan and of the Lady Isabella of Arragon, his wife, from Naples even unto the kingdom of Poland. The said Signor Prospero, as his custom still is, carried with him a great number of gentlemen and servants and amongst the rest myself, who am his creature. Having safely brought the queen thither and presented her to the king and the nuptials (which were of the most pompous and magnificent holden of our days) having been celebrated, the magnanimous Colonnese resolved to return to Italy; but, he being already equipped for the journey, Signor Girolamo della Penna of Perugia, a noble cavalier and an old partisan of the Colonna house, fell grievously sick; the which somewhat delayed the departure.

In Poland also was the most illustrious and reverend Cardinal
of Este, come thither on like wise with a worshipful train
to honour the said nuptials, and he, understanding the
gentleman's illness, went to visit him, carrying with him
his Italian physician, who applied many remedies to the
sick man, so that he began to mend and to be out or
danger; wherefore Signor Prospero, seeing him much
bettered, set out for Italy, whilst Signor Girolamo abode
with his servants, provided with all that behoved unto him,
in the house of a Polack. The cardinal's physician had left
him a certain pill-paste, charging him take one thereof once
a week, an hour before supper. Messer Girolamo accordingly, thinking to ensue the physician's ordinance, bade
one of his servants fetch him a wafer, so he might cover
the pill withal, the lightlier to swallow it. Now you must
know that neither the patient nor any of his servants knew
aught of the Polack language, save such common words
as bread, wine, flesh, oats and the like, which are said
a thousand times a day for the houschold occasions. As
for the patient's regimen, the physician had left the
apothecary the whole in writing. The servant, then,
wanting a wafer for his master, accosted one of those of
the house where they were lodged and plied him with
signs and gestures to such effect that the Polack understood
him, indeed, to want a wafer for his master, but apprehended
the case otherwise than as it was, conceiving, to wit, that
the sick man had grown so much worse that he would fain
take the sacrament;[1] wherefore he answered the Lombard
by signs that he would go fetch that which was required.

---

[1] The word *ostia*, a wafer (whence our "host"), means also the
consecrated wafer, used in the administration of the Eucharist; hence
the Pole's mistake.

Accordingly, he went straight to seek the parish priest and told him how an Italian gentleman, come thither in the queen's company, was grievously sick and would fain take the holy communion that morning; whereupon the priest made all ready and bearing the holy sacrament of the altar in hand, repaired, with the sacring-bell before him and many lighted candles, to the place where the Italian lay, what while the messenger advertised all those of the house that the sick man wished to receive the sacrosanct body of Christ and that the parish priest was on his way to impart it to him. It chanced that all the gentleman's servants were presently abroad, some for one thing and some for another, and those of the household, men and women, hearing that the priest came with the sacrament, went all reverently to meet him and accompanied Our Lord's Body to the sick man's chamber.

Signor Girolamo, seeing this procession enter with lighted tapers, marvelled amain and awaited the issue of such a spectacle; but, when he saw the priest enter, stole and surplice aback and monstrance in hand, he marvelled far more; however, arising as best he might and uncovering his head, he adored the holy sacrament with the utmost reverence. Then, the priest offering to say I know not what and to administer him, he, speaking Italian, said that he was not presently minded to receive the Corpus Domini, as well for that he had not confessed himself of his sins as also because he was not so grievously sick that he should need to take the Viaticum of the Holy Body of Christ; and for that he could speak neither Polack nor Latin, when he said that he was unshriven, he, the better to make them apprehend his meaning, smote himself on the breast twice or thrice in guise of contrition. The priest, seeing this, imagined that he said his "meà culpâ," preparing himself for the reception of the holy sacrament; wherefore, clapping into a discourse of his fashion in Polack and making a thousand signs of the cross, he took the Host in hand, to give it to the sick man; but the latter, making signs the while that he wished not to take it, kept still saying, "Sir, you understand me not; *nolo Corpus Domini.*"[1] Which three Latin words, being understood of the priest, made him think that the sick man was beside himself and wandered in his mind. Signor Girolamo, who had from a lad been still bred in arms and knew but how to read, could speak no Latin and these three words had escaped his lips I know not how; wherefore, unknowing more plainly to express his mind, he marvelled amain at that adventure and could nowise divine the cause thereof. What while they were in this contention, in came the serving-man, who had signed to the Polack that he wanted a wafer and seeing this array, perceived that he had been ill understood; wherefore, coming forward and seeing him who had gone to the church, he signed to him that he had ill apprehended his words; then, taking the pill-paste in hand, he strove to give the priest to understand to what end he sought the wafer and bade him the while return to the church, for that his master had no mind to communicate. The priest, seeing the paste and understanding not what it was, thought that he sought to work some malefice with the sacrament[2] and that master and man were exceeding great ribalds; wherefore, turning to those who accompanied him, he began to say a thousand ills of the sick man and

---

[1] *i.e.* I do not wish (or will not have) the Lord's body.
[2] A piece of the consecrated wafer was supposed to be a powerful ingredient in certain diabolical conjurations.

his servants, declaring that they were wicked folk and sorcerers and that he who lay abed was minded to die like a dog, and added, "Drive them forth the house, lest God cause you perish together with them." The Polacks were already half roused to do the sick man and his servants a mischief, when there came up a native of the country who had sojourned long at Rome and understood our tongue very well. To him the sick man's servant recounted the case of the wafer and he expounded it to the bystanders; whereat the whole thing was resolved into laughter and the priest, laughing himself, returned to the church and sent the sick man a great wafer wherein to take his pills. Signor Girolamo speedily recovered and returned to Italy, where he oftentimes maketh his listeners laugh by recounting the case as it befell, confessing that he had gone in great fear of being cast out into the street like a dog.

Bandello

to the illustrious lady the Lady Ginebra Bentivoglia Marchioness of Pallabicino.

Since I departed your delightsome and fruitful castle-wick of Bargone in the Parmegian [1] and returned to Milan, I have applied to no otherwhat than to despatch that which you deigned to command me, and fortune hath so favoured me that all hath ensued in complete accordance with your desire. I would not withal have you believe that I would fain, like the crow, deck myself with the peacock's feathers and defraud others of their pains. [2] I have, indeed, laboured amain; but, except for the interest of the most debonair Signor Alessandro Bentivoglio, your uncle and my singular good patron, and the counsel of my most discreet and magnificent friend, L. Scipione Attellano, I misdoubt me I should yet be a-beginning; but, praised be God, everything hath been brought to a quiet issue and perpetual silence imposed upon all. And for that in your letters lastly received, after exhorting me to make an end of the business aforesaid, you bid me send you without fail some of my rhymes, I must tell you that I know not what to send you that you have not already seen and read, inasmuch as, since I left you, my muse hath been so sore

---

[1] *Il Parmegiano*, i.e. the territory of Parma.
[2] *i.e.* of the credit due to them therefor.

despited against me that I have not availed to compose
a single line ; and withal I have not altogether lost my
time, having written sundry novels of various chances which
befall from day to day. Accordingly, having written one
of a case newly betided in Milan, I have bethought me to
send it to you, for that it is of the cheats which women
daily put upon their husbands and was related to me by
my most accomplished friend, Messer Martino Agrippa,
who useth to say that the leaves and flowers which Spring
produceth every year are not so many as the tricks which
wives play their husbands ; the which, were they all known
and committed to writing, would make many more volumes
than those of the laws, longsome and wordy as they are.
It remaineth to me to beseech you whiles deign to remember
you how much Bandello desireth to be of service to you.
Fare you well.

The Six-and-Twentieth Story.

A DOCTOR [OF THE LAW] CHANGETH CLOTHES WITH HIS MISTRESS'S HUSBAND AND FORE-GATHERETH WITH HER AT MIDDAY.

No great while agone there was in Milan a young doctor of laws, no less addicted to the service of the ladies than to the study of the Pandects of Justinian, who was enamoured of a young and noble married lady and oftentimes fore-gathered with her on amorous wise. Her husband, albeit noble and rich, was somewhat of an Ambrosian[1] and his wife easily made him believe what she would. He, having certain lawsuits pending with a neighbour of his anent the house-boundaries, entertained a familiar and strait commerce with the doctor, so that the lovers were able without suspect to converse together and take order for their occasions, without the use of messengers; nor was there any in the house who knew of their amours save a waiting-woman of the lady's. It chanced one day that the doctor, mounting

---

[1] *i.e.* a simpleton. The Ambrosians were those strict Catholics who observed the reformed ritual of the Milanese church, introduced by St. Ambrose, Archbishop of Milan in the fourth century. The saint's favourite virtue was chastity and the Ambrosians appear to have been (outwardly at least) Puritanical in their behaviour. The word is constantly used by contemporary writers as a synonym (in an unfavourable sense) for "native of Milan" and generally seems to have implied dunderheadedness, no less than hypocrisy and Pharisaism.

his mule, set out to visit his mistress and by the way he
met her husband a-horseback, going a-pleasuring. The
latter, as soon as he saw him, accosted him and fell to
discoursing with him of his lawsuit; and master doctor,
after he had answered him somewhat concerning the suit,
said to him, "I could not have met any one more to my
purpose than yourself, for that I am minded to go bespeak
a lady-love of mine and went but now thinking where I
could provide me with a cloak, and yours will serve me
excellently well, an you will e'en lend it to me. We will
enter the church of San Nazzaro yonder, where I will change
my gown against your cloak and you can walk about the
church, which is, as you know, dark, and await my return,
which will be within half an hour." "Command me,"
replied the good simple man, "for that I am ready to oblige
you with a greater thing than a cloak." Accordingly, they
dismounted and entered San Nazzaro, which standeth, as
you know, upon the high street [1] of Porta Romana. There
master doctor put off his long damask gown and gave it
to the goodman, of whom he had his sword and Spanish
cloak. When he saw his friend gowned and dragging more
than a span of the skirt on the ground, he said to him,
laughing, "You may walk about the church in all assurance
till I return, for I warrant you no one will know you."
Now the doctor is one of the tallest men in Milan and
the lady's husband is somewhat shorter than myself; wherefore you may conceive how he must have shown in that
long gown. The exchange made, the husband abode
in the church, whilst the doctor, clad short-fashion, called
one of his serving-men to go with him and bade the other
await him with the mule; then, making play with his

[1] Corso.

legs, he repaired to his mistress and told her how he had
exchanged clothes with her husband, whereat she laughed
amain. Then, betaking themselves to a chamber, they
proceeded to enjoy each other on amorous wise and noting
not the flight of the hours, for that pleasure made the time
seem brief to them, they abode some two hours together.
Meanwhile, the lady's husband, seeing the appointed
hour long overpast and the doctor not returned, determined to depart the church and go home to his house,
which was not far distant; wherefore, coming forth, he
said to him who had the doctor's mule, "Do thou tell
thy master, when he returneth, that I have gone home,
where I shall look for him to come take his gown;"
then, mounting his horse, he made off homeward, still
fearing the while to meet some one who knew him in that
habit. Now, by the lady's commandment, the waiting-
woman, her confidant, abode at a window and seeing
her master coming, advertised the lovers thereof; whereupon they, leaving their amorous play, went down and
entering the garden, fell a-walking under a trellis. The
husband, lighting down and seeing his wife in the garden
with the doctor, thought no manner of harm and said,
"I might well have awaited you;" to which the doctor
answered incontinent, "I went to the church and not
finding you there, came hither by the cross-way, without
taking the mule, and found madam in the garden. She
marvelled greatly to see me with this cloak, and when
you entered, I was in act to tell her the cause of this
change of clothes." "Then," rejoined the goodman, "we
missed each other by the way, for that I came along
the Corso;" and thought no more of the matter. Quoth
the lady to him, "Marry, husband mine, I see we have
a diligent advocate, who, whenas he should study, goeth

deluding poor women ; " then, knowing the doctor's need, she sent to fetch confects and wines of price to make a collation, so that master doctor might recruit himself somewhat ; but there was more laughter than confects consumed at that collation, albeit they laughed diversely.[1] Thereafter they sent to fetch the doctor's mule, on which he returned home and many and many a time laughed with the lady over the exchange of clothes. Meseemed for good reasons not well to give the names of the parties and especially of the lady, lest master doctor should lose his diversion and be angered with me, he having sundry whiles bespoken me of this jest ; but, whenas you are back again in Milan, I promise you to cause himself relate it to you, when I am certain he will tell you the names of the husband and the wife, so but you promise him to keep it secret.

[1] *i.e.* the two lovers laughed at the husband's expense, whilst he laughed at otherwhat.

Bandello

to the most affable Signor Gian Angelo Simoneta.

Great prudence, meseemeth, is that of a gentleman, who, abiding with a master whom he knoweth to be capricious and loath to hear himself rebuked of that which he doth out of reason, contriveth so to govern himself that, without incurring his lord's disfavour, he admonisheth him of his error, as useth very often to happen, when the courtier is of alert understanding and with some adroit speech bringeth him to know the default whereinto he hath fallen. This he will follow up with some goodly saw or bytimes by asking the contrary of that which his lord doth unseemly, so that he may use the occasion civilly to admonish him. For there be many who, presuming much more than they can or than behoveth unto them, will without any manner of regard offer to correct[1] their master and will, to show themselves of great authority, rebuke him in the presence of as many as be there ; wherefore the prince, if indeed he avail bytimes to dissemble the anger he feeleth, will not withal fail (as the saying is) to tie it to his finger and after in due time and place avenge himself by putting some insupportable affront upon him who sought to play upon him. Let it remember you of that which Signor Sigismondo

[1] Bandello, *corteggiare* (to court), but this is an evident error for *correggere*.

Malatesta did no great while agone, whenas the Germans
and Spaniards stormed and sacked Rome and plundered
the churches, in that, being presently entered into Rimini,
he stabbed and slew one of his hottest partisans, who had
introduced him into the city in a bundle of hay, for that
he dared to say to him I know not what at table; and yet
that which he said to him was but to admonish him not to
fall again into a certain default, wherein he had, by
unseemly dealing, fallen a little before. It behoveth him,
then, who reasoneth with his masters, maturely to bethink
himself and if there be no other means, to take his opportunity when they are alone and bespeak them, with all
submission, of that which is needful. Now, the worshipful
nuptials of Signor Giovan Paolo Sforza and the Lady
Violante Bentivoglia being celebrated at Ferrara, in the
house of Signor Alessandro Bentivoglio, father of the bride,
and it being discoursed of this matter, Signor Alessandro
Caraffa, who was newly come from France and was on his
return to Naples, told a brief story to this purpose; the
which I straightway wrote down and bethinking me to
whom I should give it, you occurred to me, as a debonair,
pleasant, courteous and most modest courtier. And so I
give it to you in attestation of your gentilesse and eke of
my love for you. Fare you well.

THE HIGH STEWARD OF FRANCE ARGUTELY REBUKETH KING LOUIS XI. OF AN ERROR WHICH HE WAS IN ACT TO COMMIT.

Being these latter days at the French court, I heard many a time discourse of the manners and fashions of King Louis XI. and amongst sundry other not over-laudable parts which those French gentlemen who spoke of him alleged to have been in him, they averred him to have been generally hostile to all the sovereign princes and nobles of France, of whom he put many to death, and to have had in his service none but people of very mean condition, more by token that he exalted many ignoble men to high estate, bestowing on them the greatest and fattest offices. Amongst others whom he raised from the dregs of the people was one called La Balue,[1] who had such power with him that he governed himself in everything according to his deeming and all that he willed was done incontinent; nay, the king made such interest with the pope that he let make him cardinal of Holy Church and gave him more than threescore thousand crowns of benefices[2] in France, albeit he was ill requited it in the long run, for that La Balue played him false. But let us leave this and come to the matter whereof you, gentlemen mine, were debating among yourselves,

[1] Bandello, *Il Balua*.
[2] *i.e.* benefices producing a yearly revenue of that amount.

to wit, on what wise a courtier should govern himself
with his lord, whenas he seeth him do aught unseemly.
You must know, then, that King Louis, desiring to know
the number of men in the city of Paris who bore arms
and of whom he might avail himself, commanded that all
should present themselves armed for review, these on
foot and those on horseback, and of this he gave the
commission to La Balue, who was not then cardinal, but
only Bishop [of Evreux;] which Monsieur de Chabannes,
High Steward of France, hearing, he was sore angered
thereat, knowing this to be no bishop's office. Algates, he
chose not to gainsay the king nor tell him that this that he
did was unseemly; but, going up to him, said to him respectfully, "Sire, I most humbly beseech you be pleased to
do me a favour, which will be to me a cause of exceeding
contentment." "And what," asked the king, "will you
have me do for you?" "I entreat you," replied the High
Steward, "vouchsafe me a commission to go to Monseig-
neur La Balue's bishoprick, to visit and reform his canons."
"How can that be?" said the king. "The commission were neither seemly nor apt unto you, for it sorteth
not that a layman should correct ecclesiastical persons."
"Nay," rejoined the other, "the commission will be at
the least as proper and pertinent unto me as is that
which you have presently committed to the bishop, that
he go review the troops and command men-at-arms."
This sally pleased the king and he revoked the commission aforesaid. Now, had Chabannes said, "Sire, this
sitteth ill; you should not do it; send thither a commissary
of reviews," or other like words, the king, who was capricious, would have belike been angered and would have
persisted in the execution of the commission given to the
bishop.

Bandello

to the magnificent and accomplished Messer Tommaso Paglicaro.

Our friend Messer Giovanni Figino useth oftentimes to make the journey from Ragusa to Milan, he having these many years past kept house at the former place, where he still hath a storehouse of Oriental wares, for that, albeit he is of a very noble and ancient Milanese family and is possessed of honourable wealth, he nevertheless plieth the trade of merchandry with great profit and honour and still, when he cometh, bringeth a thousand goodly toys for gifts to his friends and kinsfolk; nay, to myself, whom certes he loveth no little, he bringeth or sendeth every year a bundle of reeds from the Nile, the which are most perfect for writing. Now, he being the other day come, according to his wont, from the Levant and being present in company with many gentlemen and gentlewomen at the house of the Lady Ippolita Bentivoglia, she asked him to tell some new thing of the affairs of Ragusa; whereupon he, to obey her, answered that he would relate a piteous case newly befallen in that city, he being there and knowing all who figured in the story. Accordingly, silence being made, he proceeded to relate his story, which filled all the company with marvel and pity. When he had finished,

the Lady Ippolita bade me write it and add it to the
number of my novels; the which, it being not over-long,
I did that same day. Then, bethinking me to whom I
should give it, you forthright occurred to me, to whom
I am so greatly indebted, as well for the love which
you have ever borne me as for many kindnesses received
from you, which render me eternally beholden to you.
Do you then deign to take it in that same spirit wherein
I have entitled it to your name. Thereby those who so
lightly entangle themselves in the amorous birdlime may
see how perilous are these flames of love, whenas they
are not orderly governed; and certes it is a parlous thing
that we daily see a thousand scandals befall in matters
amorous for lack of governance and yet we know not
to control our carnal passions. Nay, whereas I said, "we
know not," I should rather say, "we will not," for that,
an we would, none might anywise avail to enforce us.
Let us, then, beseech our Lord God Almighty of His
benignity to grant us a sound mind in a sound body.
Now no more of this, but let us hearken to that which
our Figino goeth about to tell us in this his novel. Our
Lord God prosper your every thought!

TEODORO ZIZIMO OF RAGUSA, BEING SLIGHTED BY HIS MISTRESS, SLAYETH HIMSELF IN DESPAIR.

Since, most excellent lady mine, it pleaseth you command me entertain you and this goodly company with some news of the affairs of Ragusa, albeit I am not practised in story-telling, algates, wishing to obey your commandments in so much as I may, I will briefly tell a strange and piteous case which befell this year in that city; and for that the thing is public and notorious throughout the whole country, I will e'en give the true names of the persons concerned. You must know, then, that in Ragusa were two Greek merchants, who still abode together and seemed to love each other very cordially, doing their business and keeping their accounts in common. The elder of the twain, Demetrio Lissi by name, had not overpast six-and-thirty years of age and the other, who was nigh his thirtieth year, was called Teodoro Zizimo. Demetrio had to wife a very fair damsel, hight Cassandra, who, being accounted the fairest woman of all the country, was, to boot, held most honest, and withal she was most engaging and agreeable and knew better to entertain a company than any other of the place. Now Teodoro, practising all day in Demetrio's house and seeing Cassandra's beauty and her sprightly fashions and goodly

manners, became sore enamoured of her, but, for that he
was very well-bred and discreet and knew how ill it
beseemed to do aught which might tend to his friend's
prejudice or dishonour, he dared not discover his sufferance
to the lady, but burned in secret and wasted miserably day
by day, so that, losing sleep and appetite therefor, he
became lean, haggard and melancholy, as he were a ghost.
Demetrio sundry times asked him the cause of that his
disorder; but he excused himself, saying that he knew not
whence it came. The lady also said to him bytimes,
"Teodoro, how cometh it that thou art grown so melancholy and so disordered, thou who usedst to be the allegresse
of the world?"[1] He, instead of replying to her, sighed
heavily; however, one day, having resolved, ere he died,
to discover his love to her and she asking him how he felt
himself, he answered her, saying, "Cassandra, I should
abide well enough, were I but assured of thy favour, without
which I feel myself manifestly perish." And with this he
told her all his love as best he might, instantly praying her
be pleased to have compassion on him. The lady, hearing
so strange and unlooked-for a thing, sharply reproved him of
that his mad love and told him that this was not the faith
which[2] Demetrio had in him; wherefore she bade him rid
himself of that his humour and bespeak her no more thereof,
for that he would weary himself in vain, she being indisposed
to complease any man in the world of her love, except her
husband. Teodoro, having gotten this response of her,
said, "Marry, with God be it. You will e'en have me
die and I am resolved to die, seeing plainly that the torment

[1] Or, as we should say, "the life of every company."
[2] Sic (*questo non era la fede che*); but the meaning of course is,
"this was not what was due to the faith, etc."

which I suffer in loving and not being loved will in course
of time bring about my death. But it is e'en better to be
rid of dolour at one stroke and make an end of it than to die
a thousand times a day." Cassandra, thinking he said this
as young men do, recked not thereof and bade him apply to
otherwhat, for that these were madmen's ravings; and so,
others coming in, their talk had an end.

Teodoro abode sore disconsolate and well-nigh desperate,
seeing himself unlike to cull any fruit of that his love;
but, unable to desist from loving the lady and whiles
hoping with time to render her pliable to his appetites,
he went deluding himself with false conceits and awaiting another commodity of bespeaking her; whilst she,
albeit she saw him all changed from that which he used
to be, could not withal bend herself to love him, save
as her husband's friend and comrade. One day, Demetrio having ridden without the city, Teodoro, thinking
he would have great commodity of talking with Cassandra, who abode at home with one only waiting-maid,
went to visit her and found her busied with certain
needleworks of hers. Accordingly, he seated himself and
the maid going back and forth on divers household occasions, he fell to beseeching Cassandra to have pity upon
him. The lady let him talk a good while, without
answering him a word, and in the end, half-angered,
she said to him, "Teodoro, an thou persist in these thy
follies, I will retire to my chamber and will nevermore
come whereas thou art; nay, thou wilt cause Demetrio
perceive the little regard thou hast for him. Thou wert
far better leave these fantasies and apply to merchandry,
as thou didst erst. I have told thee and tell thee anew
that I am nowise disposed to complease thee in these
thy dishonest appetites. Bethink thee, then, that this

which I now say to thee is the Evangel[1] and set thy
heart at peace." She said many other things which tended
all to this end, that Teodoro should desist from that emprise and apply to otherwhat. Her every word was a
deadly wound to the poor lover's heart and miserably
transpierced him; wherefore, bethinking him that it was
impossible to him to abide his most cruel sufferings longer,
drunken and blinded as he was with dolour, he took a
poniard which he wore at his side and saying, "See,
then, Cassandra, the end of my troubles, for that this
will put me out of all pain," raised his right hand and
offered to stab himself to the heart. Cassandra, seeing
so extreme a folly, sprang up and seized him by the arm,
to hinder him from smiting himself, but was not so quick
nor so strong but that he gave him a great wound in
the breast, though, being under the right pap and tending towards the arm, it went not overdeep and was not
mortal. The blood, indeed, flowed in great abundance,
but was speedily staunched. The maid ran thither and
said, "Alack, what manner thing is this?" Whereupon
Teodoro, in Cassandra's presence, told her the whole story
of his love, beseeching her to persuade her mistress to
have pity on him. The maid, who was a kind wench,
moved to compassion of the poor wounded man, turned
to her lady and fell to pleading strenuously in favour of
Teodoro, whilst the latter was not wanting unto himself,
but seconded her with his tongue; till, whatever was
the cause thereof, it seemed Cassandra was somewhat
moved and proceeded to comfort her lover, exhorting him
to have a good heart and apply to heal himself and
bidding him tarry no longer, but go get his wound

---

[1] *i.e.* the absolute truth.

dressed. However, he would not depart, except she promised him to have him to servant, and he knew to say so much, with the good maid's help, that Cassandra promised to complease him so soon as he was whole again.

With this promise, he departed and went home, rejoicing; then, forging a certain story of his fashion, how he had been wounded aforenight, he sent for a surgeon, by whom he was diligently tended; and for that the wound was not very deep, he speedily became whole. As soon as he was healed, he returned to his wonted exercise, importuning Cassandra daily to perform that which she had promised him; wherefore she, who, though, moved by compassion and urged by the maid, she had said some kind words to comfort him, had no mind withal to do aught other than honest, abode so chagrined and perplexed that she knew not whither to turn. Ultimately, unknowing what to do, for that Teodoro ceased not to importune her and the maid still exhorted her to complease him, she one day said to him, "Teodoro, thou art e'en resolved not to let me live, such annoy dost thou give me. I am certain that, if I tell this thing to my husband, there will ensue a mortal enmity between him and thee, and I shall nevermore be glad. For God's sake, let me be, I prithee, and give me no more annoy; else thou wilt cause me do somewhat by reason whereof nor thou nor I will evermore be glad; for I am resolved rather to die than to sully my honour." Thereupon Teodoro departed and going straight to the palace,[1] called a notary and made a free and formal donation to Cassandra of all he had; then, going home and there being none to hinder him, he slew himself with

---

[1] *Palazzo*, i.e. the law-courts.

that poniard wherewith he had before wounded himself. The thing after getting wind by means of the maid and Demetrio knowing Cassandra's innocence, he willed her renounce the donation and give the property to a little lad, the son of a brother of Teodoro; the which she very willingly did. For this Demetrio was much commended of all and Cassandra abode in the utmost repute for beauty and chastity.

Bandello

to the Reverend Father Fra Francesco Silvestro of Ferrara, Master-general of the Order of Saint Dominick.

We read, most worshipful father mine, in the Mantuan Chronicles, composed by Platina,[1] that Sordello Visconti of Goito, he who so magnificently defended the city of Mantua against that most monstrous and cruel tyrant Eccelino da Romano, was a man of low stature and of not very noble aspect, but of very good understanding and without peer for bodily strength in his day. Now, the fame of his prowess being very great throughout all Europe, he came to the court of the King of France and doing him reverence, said that he was Sordello Visconti. The king, who had heard many things of Sordello's marvellous feats and had conceived in his mind that he must be a man of great stature, could not believe that a person so small and so ill-shapen could be of any avail; wherefore he received him with no great distinction, nay, well-nigh slighted him;

---

[1] Bartolommeo de' Sacchi, called Platina, (from the Latin name of his native place, Piadena in the Mantuan,) A D. 1421-81.

which Sordello perceiving, he said to him, "Sire, judge
me not till I go into Italy and bring hither witnesses to
testify that I am Sordello, of whom you have heard so much
talk. But if, ere I depart, there is any of these your
barons who doubteth me not to be Sordello, let him come
forward and try his strength against mine on such wise as
shall best please him." Now there was a Frenchman there,
a very tall man of his person and a well-favoured, who was
accounted the doughtiest jouster at the court. He, hearing
Sordello's defiance and making little account of him by his
looks, said that he would break a lance with him and after
try a bout with the sword. Sordello accepted the challenge
and armed himself; and so, in the king's presence, the two
ran and broke their lances gallantly. They then put hands
to their swords; but, at the third venue, Sordello struck the
sword from his adversary's hand and falling upon him, haled
him from his horse; then, carrying him before the king,
as the wolf carrieth the lamb, "Sire," said he, "here is a
witness that I am Sordello; and if any other would fain
testify, let him come forward." The king, perceiving that
men are not to be measured, like cloth, by ells and spans,
was certified of his error and received him very graciously,
entreating him with all favour what while he abode at court,
where Sordello, without going to Italy to fetch witnesses,
wrought many other prowesses, which gave manifest proof
of his valour. Again, in our own times, an ambassador
being sent by the Venetian Seigniors to King Louis XII., it
chanced that, one day, not being very richly clad, he went
to say somewhat to the king; but, when he would have
entered the presence-chamber, the ushers, looking to no
otherwhat than his clothes, twice or thrice shut the door
in his face, what while they admitted those who were
pompously attired. The shrewd ambassador, perceiving

this, returned to his lodging, where he donned a doublet
of murrey ingrain and a surcoat of crimson cut velvet,
with doge-fashion sleeves, and thus richly accoutred, betook himself to court. He knocked at the door and when
the ushers saw him, they freely admitted him and made him,
to boot, a low obeisance, as he passed. Thereupon he
presented himself before the king and after doing him due
honour, doffed his gown and laying it on the ground, made
three great obeisances thereto. All marvelled at this act,
seeing a man of his gravity unclothe himself in the presence
of so great a king and perform those fantastic ceremonies,
and awaited the issue of the matter. The ambassador then
thanked his gown amain for the favour it had done him and
donning it again, said to the king, "Sire, I came to bespeak you of certain letters, which I have received from my
most august seigniory, and came clad in broadcloth, burgher-
fashion, without ceremony; but your ushers twice or thrice
shut the door of your presence-chamber in my face. Accordingly I went to change my clothes, attiring myself as you
see, and by favour of this gown, I have entered. Wherefore
meseemed I should do ill an I honoured it not neither
thanked it for the benefit received." Now you may ask me,
most worshipful father mine, to what end I have told you
these stories; 'faith, it was to come to my novel. It is
commonly said that, whom God made fair, He made not
poor; and the Lombards say to boot, "Clothe a stake in
costly weed; 'twill seem a cardinal indeed." And certes to
be handsome of body and well-clad bringeth greatnesses and
addeth increase to reputation, as, on the contrary, foul
favour and mean habit whiles cause persons of rank and
merit be misprized. The which manifestly appeared the
other day, as Fra Gian Battista Cavriuolo showed us at
length, recounting an adventure which befell Peretto at

Modena; the which, having written it, for that meseemed it was for many reasons worthy of remembrance, I give to you, who are in no danger of falling into Peretto's predicament, inasmuch as nature hath endowed you with a most gracious presence, with affable and engaging fashions and with as good Greek and Latin letters as any of our day; of philosophy and theology I will not speak, you having few peers in these sciences. Fare you well.

The Nine-and-Twentieth Story.

PERETTO OF MANTUA, BEING IN MODENA, IS RALLIED OF THE LADIES FOR A JEW, BY REASON OF HIS MEAN AND ABJECT PERSON.

The season being somewhat irksome, for the extreme heats which prevail, meseemeth not unlawful, after we have accomplished our religious duties, to while away this time of the day with story-telling and other seemly and delectable discourse, knowing that pleasant converse hath no little power to allay mental vexation and eke to solace bodily annoys. You know, then, worshipful father mine, that in the year 1520 the Chapter-general of our congregation was, with great solemnity and to the exceeding satisfaction of all who were present thereat, holden in the pleasant city of Modena, where the people by innumerable tokens showed the great affection they bear our order,

as well by abundantly providing victual for many days for
so many brethren as also by continual frequentation of the
divine offices, of the wholesome preachments and of the
subtle and erudite disputations which were daily holden.
Indeed, we were more than four hundred brethren and
were all excellent well entreated, and so much the more
admirable was the magnificence of the Modenese in that,
knowing our institutes suffered not the eating of flesh-meat,
save in case of infirmity, they lavishly provided us with fish
and other viands conformable to our way of living. In
those days there studied philosophy in the city of Bologna
one Messer Giovan Francesco dal Forno, a native of
Modena and a young man of very goodly and lofty understanding, who, wishing to show his fellow-townsmen that
he had not wasted his time and monies at Bologna, sought
with exceeding great instance to obtain from our superiors
a chair,[1] so he might defend a certain number of his propositions in logic and philosophy, and availed himself to
that end of the right valiant and illustrious Signor Count
Guido Rangone, knowing him to be in such repute with
our brethren that they would not have denied him anything. Count Guido obtained what he asked and Forno
was assigned a day whereon none save he should sustain
or debate theses. Accordingly, having gotten the desired
grace, he sent a man of his to Bologna with letters to
Messer Peretto Pomponaccio,[2] a very famous philosopher
of those days, who had been his master in philosophy,
beseeching him to be pleased without fail to come to

---

[1] i.e. an opportunity of lecturing in their congress.

[2] *Pietro Pomponaccio*, a famous Mantuan philosopher of the 15th-
16th centuries, (A.D. 1462-1525,) called for his dwarfish stature *Peretto*
(Peterkin).

Modena, as well to honour his philosophical exercise as also to serve him as a buckler against such arguments (should any such be objected to him) as he might belike be unable to resolve. Peretto excused himself, alleging that he could not come by reason of certain occupations of his; but Forno, who was loath to debate without his master, mounted to horse and coming to Bologna, bespoke him to such effect that he brought him to Modena. The appointed day come, the young philosopher mounted the pulpit and very featly propounded his conclusions. Those of our friars who argued to the contrary chose not (for that he was in our church) to press their objections overhard, arguing to no other end than to honour him. However, there were many others of various religious orders, as well as laymen, who argued against him as best they knew, to whom he rejoined so aptly and bore himself on such sort that he was supremely commended of all, for that he learnedly sustained his own propositions and adroitly undid the intricate knots of the others' arguments, showing wit and memory in every case.

The disputation ended, Forno was honourably escorted home to his house, where he made a magnificent collation to all those who accompanied him; and Peretto, thinking to return to Bologna on the morrow, said to him, " Messer Gian Francesco, you have, at some inconvenience to myself, brought me to Modena and I have gladly come hither to honour you and to see how you would comport yourself in the battle. All hath gone well and to your exceeding honour and the satisfaction of your friends and kinsfolk; whereof I give you joy. Now, what fine things can you show me in this your city? " It was answered him both by Forno and by others who were there in company that in Modena there were commonly many fair and engaging

ladies to be seen, beside the palace of the Lord Count
Rangone and his brothers, divers goodly sepulchres and
other works [of art], a fine tower and (a thing which all
know and which is often named) limpid and very cool
fountains; and ultimately one said that there was [in such
a quarter] a very fine church of the monks of Saint Benedict,
builded after the modern fashion. "Then let us go there,"
said Peretto; and accordingly he set out, in company of
many, who went with him to honour him, for San Pietro.
Now he was a very little wizened man, with a visnomy
that favoured the Jew more than the Christian, and was
dressed, to boot, after a certain fashion which savoured
more of the Rabbi than of the philosopher; moreover, he
went still shaven and polled and spoke on such wise that
he seemed a German Jew who would fain learn to speak
Italian. After they had taken their fill of viewing the
church, they came forth thereof and fared on along the
street which leadeth straight to the convent of the Carmelite
friars, till they came to the middle thereof, when they were
seen by two very fair and merry ladies, who abode on two
balconies overagainst one another, to breathe the fresh air
and to talk. One of them, seeing Peretto come with so
great a company, said to her fellow, firmly believing that
which she said, "Neighbour, seest thou Abraham the Jew,
how he cometh yonder, well accompanied? Needs must
he have made a banquet to-day or some great entertainment
after the Hebrew fashion, that he hath so many folk with
him." "Ay, certes," replied the other: "he must have
nuptials toward. Look with what gravity he cometh."
Peretto drew near the while and came presently under
the windows where were the two ladies, who firmly believed
him to be Abraham the Jew, so much did he favour him
in aspect and dress; wherefore one of them, who was

somewhat bolder than her fellow, said to him, laughing merrily, "In good faith, Abraham, hadst thou bidden us to yonder nuptials of yours, (or be it banquet that thou hast made,) we had gladly come thither in company of your Jewesses. Ay, we speak to thee, Gaffer Abraham, who farest thus mincingly and proudly with these our Modenese." Peretto, exceeding angered at this speech, raised his head and said to them, "What a devil say you? What a devil is this? Am I belike reputed a Jew of you ladies of Modena? May fire come from heaven and burn you all! Verily you women are such silly, sottish animals and so altogether witless that the sage Plato abode in great doubt if he should place you among reasonable creatures or among beasts. Far wiser, indeed, than we are the Turks, who suffer no credence to be given to women's witness in matters civil or criminal, though all the women of Turkey should testify with one voice." The ladies, hearing this and looking Peretto straitlier in the face, perceived that they had made a mistake and withdrew indoors nor let themselves be seen again. Meanwhile, those who accompanied Peretto could not contain themselves, but burst out into a great fit of laughter at the deceived ladies and their flouted philosopher, which latter, all full of despite and ill-will against the Modenese women, said all the ill of them he knew and might and swore that Modena should never see him again. Now not only was it an easy thing that Peretto should at a little distance appear, to whoso saw him, Abraham and Abraham Peretto; but, moreover, like as Abraham was intent upon the unrighteous acquisition of his neighbour's good with the vortex of his usuries, even so Peretto made a show of believing little in the immortality of the soul, which is the foundation of all the Christian law. Nay, peradventure our Lord God

Almighty permitted that those ladies should prophesy;[1] but, be that as it may, methinketh they who are endowed with a generous and noble aspect are more beholden to nature than those who, for lack of a goodly presence, appear rather monsters than men.

[1] Bandello here uses the word "prophesy" in the old Scriptural sense of " to expound or declare the truth," meaning that the ladies were inspired to declare Peretto's physical and moral resemblance to the Jews.

END OF VOL. V.